just between us

Also by J. H. Trumble

Don't Let Me Go

Where You Are

Just Between Us

Published by Kensington Publishing Corporation

just between us

J.H. Trumble

KENSINGTON BOOKS
www.kensingtonbooks.com

KENSINGTON BOOKS are published by

Kensington Publishing Corp.
119 West 40th Street
New York, NY 10018

ISBN-13: 978-0-7582-7718-3
ISBN-10: 0-7582-7718-0
First Kensington Trade Paperback Printing: October 2013

eISBN-13: 978-0-7582-7719-0
eISBN-10: 0-7582-7719-9
First Kensington Electronic Edition: October 2013

10 9 8 7 6 5 4 3 2

Printed in the United States of America

For all who've been touched by HIV/AIDS

ACKNOWLEDGMENTS

I could never do this without those on the sidelines, quietly cheering me on. My heartfelt thanks go out to Steve Fraser, Peter Senftleben, and everyone at Kensington Publishing, and to my good friend Brent Taylor for making me rethink everything about the story I had to tell. I believe the final result is much better for it.

I also want to thank John Fram and Justin Olson for their openness and frankness in discussing with me their own anxieties about the HIV virus. And Nancy Smith, Aimee Felio, and Antoinette Sherman for slogging through an earlier version and pointing out all my typos and awful redundancies, and Kelley Perez and Elizabeth Reed for their careful proofreading. Your generosity overwhelms me. You are the best!

And as always, thank you to Danny and Anna Trumble for putting up with all the highs and lows of having a parent who writes. I love you more than you could possibly know.

And finally, my fans. Thank you for reaching out to me and sharing your own stories. I heard you, every one of you. I hope you find in these pages whatever it is you need—understanding, empathy, hope, love, or maybe just a good cry.

Chapter 1

CURTIS

Luke Chesser looks miserable and embarrassed as he grinds the toe of his athletic shoe into the superheated concrete not eight feet from me, his clarinet gripped tightly in his right hand. He slaps the instrument against his calf a few times, then glances my way. With my eyes shielded behind dark sunglasses, I feel no compulsion to look away.

It's been a hard couple of weeks for him, but I don't know if what I feel right now is more sympathy or irritation. He's a mess, distracted, directionally challenged. Some days I think it would be easier for Mr. Gorman to change the band's program than to change Luke. He's been persistently dense since day one of marching camp. In fact, he's the reason all two hundred of us are standing here again under the blazing August sun, waiting. He screwed up, and the domino effect took care of the rest.

I squint up at the viewing stand, where Mr. Gorman is conferring with the assistant band director. One day that will be me up there with a microphone clipped to my ear.

It's been almost a year since I loaded up my truck, said good-bye to Dad and Corrine, and headed west on 290 to Austin. I'd spent the entire summer dreaming about walking down Sixth Street on a Friday or a Saturday night with a beer in my hand, staying out all night if I wanted to, flirting with college guys, maybe taking one back to my dorm room or spending a night in his, having sex for the first time, experiencing the freedom that comes with distance.

As it turned out, that freedom wasn't all it was cracked up to be. By the end of spring semester, I couldn't wait to get back.

It wasn't Austin; it was me. Too many guys eager to share their bed for a night. Too much alcohol. Too many pieces of me chipped away and left scattered here and there, everyone taking what they wanted until I could feel myself fracturing under the weight of all that freedom.

A clatter catches my attention, and I look over to see Robert Westfall retrieve his flag from the ground. He's a bari sax player, a freshman when I was drum major. Nice guy, but honestly, I never gave him much thought until I saw him rehearsing with the color guard last week. I hadn't seen that coming. Apparently it's no big secret. I have to say, I admire him for that. Maybe if I'd been more open in high school, I wouldn't have been so boys-gone-wild at UT.

Luke Chesser, though . . . I had him pegged from day one. I can't say why exactly. Just a feeling.

Over the portable PA system, Mr. Gorman calls the band back to set. I lift my sunglasses and wipe the sweat from my brow, then assume a wide stance and fold my arms. The freshmen squirm a little, but snap to attention when I clear my throat.

"Luke," I say in a voice just loud enough to carry across the clarinets. "It's right, left, right, left." One of the girls giggles as the drum majors count off the beat.

"Toes up, toes up," I bark as I shadow the moving section. Anna Newman misses a turn, then scrambles to catch up. "Laura, watch your carriage. Better." I scramble back a few yards so I can get a better overall view of the ripple, then slip in and out of the lines, counting the beats aloud as I go. I duck under the twirling flags of the guard. The program is still new to them, so I anticipate movements, giving a heads-up when I can. I keep my eye on Luke, but he manages to fumble through without any major mistakes this time.

The opener ends with a one, two, three, drop. The kids stand frozen, faces parallel to the concrete.

"Much better," Mr. Gorman says. "All right. Find some shade, take a five-minute water break, and we'll do it again."

I collect my thermos from the curb behind the viewing stand and take a long drink as Adeeb Rangan makes his way across the parking lot to me. His white teeth flash in his impossibly dark face, and I'm amused to see he's wearing a Texas Aggie T-shirt again today.

"What's this?" I ask when he hands me a folded piece of paper.

"The new section T-shirt design."

"Yeah?" Section T-shirts are an annual tradition. My freshman year it was *Reed my lips*. Sophomore year: *Clarinets kick brass*. Junior year: *Shhh... the clarinets are playing*. And senior year: *Fear the clarinets*.

Clarinets just aren't that funny.

Now saxophones, that's a funny instrument.

I unfold the paper. There are two outlines of a T-shirt—a front and a back view. On the front, a formation of graphic faces with hats and plumes, all heads tilted to the right except one, which is tilted to the left. I'm already laughing when I read the caption: *Luke Chesser, you are wrong*. On the back: *Will someone please tell him what to do?*

Those were Mr. Gorman's exact words last week. I felt bad for Luke that morning, but damn, he ought to know right from left by now.

"Does he know about this?" I ask Adeeb.

"He agreed to it."

I scan the edges of the parking lot until I spot Luke again.

"He's worse than the freshmen," Adeeb adds. I smile. "He's gonna drive Gorman crazy, you know."

"Where'd he come from anyway?" I refold the paper and hand it back to him.

"Odessa. But he was only there for the spring semester. He marched with the band at Forest last year."

Woodland Forest is the rival high school a few miles away. They have a good program. A damn good program. Can't blame *them*. They were probably glad to see him go.

"He pees sitting down, you know?"

I look at Adeeb over the top of my sunglasses. "I kind of figured."

He grins at me, juts an elbow in my ribs, and I know what he's thinking. Not gonna happen.

"So when you moving up to Huntsville?" he asks.

"Dorms open a week from tomorrow. You're stuck with me for a few more days."

Across the parking lot, a clarinet girl (Phoebe Verbosky, I think), pours a load of water from her thermos down Luke's back. He whips around and scowls at her. *Come on, Luke. Lighten up.* But he doesn't retaliate. He leaves that to the clowns Jackson Stewart and Spencer Dunn. They're going to be sorry at the next water break when those thermoses are empty. H_2O foreplay will cost you in this Texas heat.

"Those idiots," Adeeb says. "I gotta go break that up before they ruin the pads on those clarinets."

He gives me a light punch on the shoulder. "We're meeting at Cain's after practice. Want to come?"

Adeeb looks up and motions me over to the tables they've claimed near the counter. About eleven of the twenty-seven clarinets are there—Adeeb, Spencer, Jackson, Luke, Phoebe, a few others. "About time," Adeeb calls out as I approach. "I was starting to wonder if maybe you thought you were too good for us now, college boy."

Luke glances over his shoulder. When he sees me, the smile slides right off his face and into his secret sauce.

What did I do?

"Eh, I stayed behind to talk shop with Mr. Gorman." I pull out a chair next to Adeeb and sit, then nod toward Luke. "What's wrong with him?" I mouth.

Adeeb shrugs. "I don't know," he mumbles. "He's got a burr up his ass. He's been in a funk all day."

All day? I think funk is his default.

"He's kind of a drama queen," Adeeb adds and smiles.

Drama queen? I don't think so. Antisocial, morose, depressed. Good thing he's got that all-American boy look about him or he'd be one sad sack. I grab a box of chicken tenders at the counter and settle in to watch the hurricane coverage on the TV affixed to the wall between two banks of windows. Janine is still a ways out in the Gulf, but Galveston is in the cone of probability, so it's news, and you can't turn on the TV this week without getting an update.

"So, who you rooming with this year?" Adeeb asks when the station goes to commercial.

"Don't know."

"That could be bad."

I suppose he's right about that. But I got lucky enough the first time. I roomed with a fellow engineering student. Jared actually *wanted* to be an engineer. I just wanted to play music and party. But he spent most of his time in the library, so we got along okay until I stumbled into the room early one morning and woke him up. He pushed himself up on one elbow and asked in a disgusted voice, "Aren't you afraid you're going to catch some disease?" God, I was pissed.

Abruptly Luke pushes back his chair and gets up.

"Bedtime for Lukey Duke," Adeeb teases in a voice too low for him to hear.

I grin at him as Luke gathers up his trash then hugs the girls good-bye.

"Call me later," Spencer says.

"Yeah, sure." He glances at our end of the table. "See you Monday, Adeeb." Then he turns his back and walks out.

I'm dumbstruck.

Chapter 2

CURTIS

I'm breathing hard as I approach the lake Saturday morning for the last half-mile stretch of my five-mile run.

I intentionally run my circuit so that the lake is on the back-stretch. It's my reward for going the distance. The lake is actually more like a pond. The duck pond we call it sometimes because of the gaggle of ducks that rule over the shoreline. It's tucked between two neighborhoods and bordered on one side by the public side-walk I'm running on.

As the trees recede from the sidewalk, I get my first look at the water, and I'm already thinking about stopping for a bit and enjoying the quiet beauty while I still can. In another week I'll be doing my running in Huntsville, and as far as I know, there are no lakes within running distance of the Sam Houston campus. Suddenly, a duck squawks and takes flight from the western shore, quickly followed by a familiar streak of black and a splash.

I veer off the sidewalk and head down the gentle incline to the shoreline. The Lab, her black nose pointed to the sky, is already in hot pursuit. "Liberty! Come here, girl!" I clap my hands a few times. She ignores me as she gains on the duck and sets off another frantic flight. It's fun to watch, but the dog is too fat for such strenuous exercise, and I damn sure don't want to be playing lifeguard to the beast when her muscles give out. I put my fingers to my lips and whistle, then call again. This time, Libby cranes her neck around, smiles, then switches direction and dog-paddles toward me.

As I wait for her to reach the shore, I'm surprised and amused to see Luke Chesser grab hold of the wrought iron fence that separates the public area from the private backyard where Libby had apparently been nosing around. He grimaces as he wades into the water. If Luke is chasing Libby, then . . . huh.

Libby's paws grip solid ground and she bolts from the lake and comes right to me, twisting and dripping water. "Hey, girl, you catching some ducks today?" I squat on my heels and slap her affectionately on her side. "Keep the leash behind your back," I say to Luke as I see him approach in my peripheral vision.

When he gets close enough, I take the leash and snap it onto her wet collar. The big dog shakes and splatters us both. "You're a pill, aren't you, girl?" She nudges her muzzle into my hand.

"You know Libby?" Luke asks.

"Liberty and I go way back, don't we, sweetheart? I was on dog catcher duty for six long years before I went off to school." I use the neck of my T-shirt to wipe the splashes of water from my sunglasses and squint up at him. "Looks like I've been replaced."

He squats down next to me. Libby rolls over and presents her broad, wet belly to him for a scratching. I take the opportunity to study his face close up for the first time. He's all blond hair, blue eyes, and color spots on his cheeks. He's actually pretty cute when he's not so surly or pissy. "So how'd you end up with this job?" I ask him, dropping back on my butt.

"She's our neighbor."

"Yeah?" Surprise, surprise. "Well, I guess that makes us neighbors then too. We're number eleven."

"Twenty-nine," he says.

I mentally try to place his house on our street. "Ah, you're in the cul-de-sac. Two doors down from Miss Shelley, right?"

He acknowledges that with a nod.

"So how many times have you had to chase this beast down?"

He smiles a little. "A few."

I bet. "She's a little opportunist, this one." I run my hand down her heaving wet side. Damn, I hope I don't have to carry her home again. Last time I had to do that it was heatstroke. She ended up in the doggie emergency room, and that little excursion cost Miss Shelley plenty.

I uncap my water bottle and pour a little into my cupped hand and offer it to Libby. She lifts her nose and holds it there until the water dribbles through my fingers. "I guess she had her fill of water in the lake." I expect some kind of response from Luke—a laugh, a smile, something—but I get nothing. Oh, what the hell. I've had enough of this nonsense.

"You want to tell me what's going on?" I ask.

"What do you mean?"

What do I mean? He knows exactly what I mean. "I've obviously done something to offend you. Cain's?" I reenact for him what didn't happen at the restaurant: "Hey, Curtis, catch you later. Great to see you."

"Offend me?" He huffs. "No, I love being made fun of in front of everybody."

Wow. He just laid it out there. I like that. But, damn, he's sensitive. I think back to practice yesterday. I was giving him a prompt—*right, left, right, left.* If the other kids laughed, well . . . *Aw, hell.* Okay, I was having a little fun with him. But, honestly, he makes it so easy. I fight the urge to smile; that would be the wrong response right now.

"I was just doing my job, Luke. Nothing personal."

"It is not a field tech's job to belittle people. And why me? I don't ever hear you making snide comments to the other kids."

He's got me there. But *snide?* And now I do feel like a jerk.

"Hey," I say, and dip my head until he looks up at me. "Can we reset? I didn't mean it that way. And I apologize if it felt as if I was picking on you. Okay? We good?"

He glares back at me. "Yeah. Sure."

Nope. Not good. Not good at all. I decide to change the subject. Maybe that will get us back to a better place. "So you live on Split Rock, huh? I'm surprised I haven't run into you before."

"Yeah, well, we only moved here a month ago."

"From Odessa, right? Adeeb told me."

"Adeeb was talking about me?" He huffs again.

Touchy. "He told me where you came from. That's all. So you were at Forest last year, huh? That was a pretty short stay in Odessa." He looks at me hard, and I know there's a story there. Okay, I'll bite. "What happened?"

"You really want to know?"

Probably not. I uncap the water bottle again and take a long drink, then get to my feet. Libby scrambles to her feet too. Luke grabs the leash.

"Come on," I tell him. "I'll walk you and Libby home. You can fill me in on the way." I have a feeling I'm going to regret this.

"Where do you want me to start?" he asks, falling into a lazy stride with me.

Oh boy. We shift to the edge of the sidewalk and wait as a bicycle whizzes past us, then resume walking. I glance over at him and note the deep furrow between his brows. He's hardly said a dozen words to me up to now, and even though he looks like he wants to talk, surely this little trip into his past won't take long. I take a deep breath and suggest he start with why they left Odessa.

"Odessa," he says, then scoffs. "My dad got a transfer and since he gets to be the man of the house—"

"What do you mean, your dad gets to be the man of the house?"

"Mom makes more money than him. A lot more. She's a dermatologist. She has a private practice here, but she had to turn it over to her partners when Dad got the transfer."

"You're losing me here."

"She's always let him make all the decisions—about where we live, when we do our homework, who we hang out with—because he can't deal with the fact that she's the one who really supports us. So when he said we're moving, we moved."

"But you moved back?"

He purses his lips and looks away. "Yeah. We moved back."

"So . . ."

He takes up the slack in the leash and wraps it around his hand. "He wanted me back in the closet; I didn't want to go."

Oh. I'm getting the picture now. In fact, that explains a lot more than just his brief residence in West Texas. I wish I'd known. Maybe I could have—

"He hit me," he says suddenly.

He doesn't say why. He doesn't have to. It's a story I've heard too many times. But his admission is like a punch in the gut.

"Mom doesn't know about that," he continues. "It happened just before we moved to Odessa. But then, after we got there, Dad started grilling me about where I'd been and who I was with every time I walked in the door.

"I'm sure Mom wondered what was going on. But whenever she asked, Dad would tell her it was between us men." He laughs a little. "Kind of funny when Dad doesn't consider me a man at all. And then one day Mom asked my little brother Matt if he knew what was going on and he told."

"How did your mom take it?"

"We're back, aren't we?"

"And your dad?"

Libby squats to pee in the dry grass next to the sidewalk.

"He's moving back today," he says quietly. "Any minute in fact."

He looks at me, but I can't do anything but blink back at him for a moment. "Why did you tell me all this?" I ask.

"Because you asked."

Libby finishes up. We follow in silence as she moves on, but after just a few steps, she drops to the ground and lays her head between her paws. Luke tugs on the leash, but the big dog refuses to budge.

Aw, shit. Lazy dog.

"Is she okay?" Luke asks.

Good question. I doubt she's overheated; she's still nice and wet. She didn't seem to stumble before she decided to drop. Not glassy-eyed. Breathing is okay—no heavy panting. Just tired and lazy. "How much weight can you carry?"

"Not that much."

I laugh and look down the path. We're less than a quarter mile from home, but, damn, the dog must weigh ninety-five pounds. And I know this routine all too well. Why walk when you can get a ride? She's much heavier now than she was the last time I carried her. And dragging her, while tempting, is out of the question. But I don't feel like parking myself in this heat until she gives up the game and is ready to move on either.

I slip my phone out of my pocket and call Corrine. She laughs when I explain the situation. "My truck keys are on the counter. And bring a blanket."

"Who's Corrine?" Luke asks when I end the call.

"My twin."

A pause. "Does your dad know?"

"That I have a twin? No. We're keeping that from him until we feel like he can handle it." He smiles and I smile back. I guess he knows a thing or two about me as well. "Yeah, he knows," I tell him.

"I'm sorry I laid all that on you," he says.

"It's okay. I'll send you a bill." I can see from the hurt expression on his face that my little joke has fallen flat. "I didn't mean that, Luke. Look, if it helped for you to unload on me, then I'm glad you did."

He holds my eyes for a moment, then looks away when Corrine pulls up to the curb and turns on the hazard lights.

Corrine's eyes dart between me and Luke. An impish smile plays on her lips. I reach through the open window and grab the blanket from the front seat.

"All right, you big lazy dog." I roll up half the blanket and place it next to her. Luke stoops and supports her head while I roll her onto the blanket, then unroll the rest of the blanket behind her. All that's left is lifting the beast.

"You want to help us out a little here, Corrine?"

"No, thanks. You two big, strong guys don't need me. I'll monitor the tailgate."

I scowl at my sister; she smiles sweetly back at me. "Looks like we're on our own here, Luke."

"I'll take the head; you take the butt."

"The story of my life." Oh, brother. I have no idea why I said that. But Luke smiles at me across the dog, and damn if my heart doesn't thud a little in my chest. "On three, okay?"

We lift Libby and stagger with her to the truck and slide her onto the bed.

"Nice work, gentlemen." Corrine slams the gate, then looks wide-eyed at me, then Luke, then back at me.

"Corrine, this is Luke. Luke, my sister, Corrine."

"Sooo," Corrine says with a grin, "you two . . ."

I give her the look. "Luke's in the band. Clarinet. *Junior.*" I say the latter with just enough emphasis to squash any thoughts of matchmaking she might be entertaining.

She flicks her eyebrows at me; I roll my eyes back at her. "You driving?"

"Hop in."

I slide across the seat to the middle; Luke takes the window.

Corrine has barely eased the truck away from the curb when Luke nods over his shoulder. "Look at that."

Libby is up on her feet again and scrambling up the slick wheel well to heave her front paws over the edge of the truck bed. Once she's there, she points her nose into the wind and drops her long tongue out the side of her mouth. Luke looks back at me and grins.

"We've been played, Luke. Hey, Corrine. You better take it easy on the corners."

"So what's the story?" Corrine asks quietly. We're waiting outside the truck while Luke hands the dog over to Miss Shelley.

"No story."

"He's a cutie patootie."

"Too young."

"You're nineteen," she chortles. "Not exactly an old man, little brother." Corrine is one minute and sixteen seconds older than me, a fact she likes to remind me of frequently. She bumps her hip against mine. "I think you should ask him out."

I yank her ponytail. "I think you should mind your own business." Although, I have to admit, he *is* a "cutie patootie."

"Mission accomplished," Luke says, returning to the truck. "Thanks for the help."

"Anytime. I'll see you Monday at practice."

"Sure."

We're getting back into the truck when an SUV pulls into Luke's driveway and a gray-haired man gets out. I watch through the side mirror as Luke approaches him. They stand there stiffly in the driveway, talking. But I can't help noticing there's no warm hug for Luke like my dad would give me, no handshake, no slap on the shoulder.

Chapter 3

LUKE

I'm not ready for this. I'm not remotely ready for this. But he's here, and I said it was okay. So I really have no one to blame but myself. I will my feet to keep moving forward as I head up the driveway, when everything inside of me is screaming to turn and head the other way. It's not that I'm afraid of him; he only hit me that once. I just really don't want to do this again.

"Luke. How you been?" he asks as he gets out of the SUV. His voice is light, but I suspect this is as awkward for him as it is for me.

"Hey, Dad. How was the drive?"

"Long. I drove all night. You're wet."

I look down at my lake-splattered T-shirt. "I had to get a dog out of the lake."

He doesn't ask what dog. He just nods, then gazes up the street. "Who was that?"

He hasn't even unloaded his suitcases and already it's starting again. I look back as Corrine steers the truck into a driveway seven houses up from ours, on the left. "Just some neighbors."

"Well," he says, slapping his chest. I wait for what comes next, but there's nothing. Finally, after a long awkward pause, he asks, "Is your mom home?"

"She's inside."

He nods.

This is the problem: I don't know how to be around him anymore. My guess is he doesn't know how to be around me either. I'm the reason he and Mom split up. He knows it; I know it.

I've been dreading this moment since our second week in the house when Dad called and begged Mom to take him back. Mom posed it to me this way: "I promise you, Luke, things will be different. You have a right to feel safe and loved in your own home, and to have your feelings respected. But it's your decision. I love your father, but you have to be okay with this before I allow him to set one foot in this house."

It wasn't always this way. I still remember the dad who used to tickle me until I screamed, the one who yelled "That's my boy" when I got an award for collecting aluminum cans in fourth grade. Maybe it's the remembering how things used to be that made me agree. Or maybe I am an optimist like Mom says. Or maybe I just can't stand seeing her in the kitchen every evening with no one to share her day with but a couple of distracted boys.

Dad clears his throat. "You want to give me a hand with these bags?"

"Dad!" Matt makes a run for him, and I take advantage of their decidedly more enthusiastic reunion to escape inside.

"Your dad's here?" Mom asks as I drop the bags at the base of the stairs.

"Yeah. I'm going upstairs. Is that okay?"

She lays her hand on my cheek and nods. "It's going to be okay, Luke. I promise you that."

I smile weakly and head up to my room. I turn on my laptop, then stare out the window as I wait for it to boot up. Another truck, not Curtis's, pulls into the Cameron driveway and into the garage, and suddenly I find myself wondering what he's doing this afternoon. It turns out he's a lot nicer than I gave him credit for. When Spencer first told me he was "g-a-y," I guess I thought he'd eventually reach out to me, take me under his wing, show me the ropes. Instead, he treated me like I was some kind of airhead.

I look back at my computer as Nate Schaper's familiar image appears on my background. He's lying against the headboard on his bed, his guitar in his lap, smiling at someone outside of the frame. I took the photo from his blog, but as carefully as I'd cropped the image, I could never alter the direction of that smile, nor could I forget who was on the receiving end.

And it wasn't me.

That used to hurt. But lately, it's just left me feeling profoundly empty. It's over. I accept that.

I rest my cheek in my hand and look back out the window. Curtis Cameron is my neighbor. How crazy is that?

Dinnertime has been a pretty laid-back affair since we moved into the new house. We're as likely to eat in front of the TV or even in our rooms as we are at the table, but still, we've kind of unofficially laid claim to our own places at the table, so it's a little weird that night when Dad takes the chair at the end. Mom's chair. He could have asked. He could have waited to see where Mom sits. But he didn't do either. He just pulled out the chair and dropped in it.

It's a small thing; I get that. But it sets my teeth on edge.

And then he notes that the lawn needs mowing again. "I assume you're still in charge of yard work?" he asks me.

I glance at Mom. She gives her head a little shake.

"Yeah. I'll get it tomorrow," I tell him.

So this is how it's going to be. We're all just going to roll over and play dead. We're just going to pretend like the last eight months never happened. I don't know who I'm angrier at—my dad for thinking he can just step back in and take control, or my mom for letting him do it. But then Dad brings up the Scout jamboree at Camp Strake next week.

"I thought I'd take Matt up. One last outing before school starts and I have to be back at work."

Matt's face lights up. "Do I get to fly fish this time?"

"Maybe." Dad hesitates, then looks at Mom. "That okay with you?"

Maybe some things have changed. It must be emasculating for him to have to ask her permission.

"Sure," Mom says.

Chapter 4

LUKE

Dad and Matt head out Sunday morning, but by Tuesday it's pretty clear that my paternal reprieve is going to be short lived; we've got a hurricane coming. If the storm stays on its current track, forecasters say it'll likely pass right over us, probably as a Category One or even a tropical storm by the time it makes it this far inland. But with all the trees here, even a tropical storm can do a lot of damage. I was Matt's age when Hurricane Ike hit. I remember the mess it left behind.

Mr. Gorman has already advised us to check the band Web site tomorrow morning for practice information. He doesn't want to make the call prematurely.

"You doing okay?" Curtis asks when Mr. Gorman calls for a water break.

At the edge of the parking lot, Jackson's mom is yoo-hooing and holding up a section T-shirt to let us know they're here. When I agreed to the design, I didn't really think about the impact of twenty-seven kids proclaiming my public shame across their chests every week. "The shirts are here."

"That they are. You know, when Adeeb was a freshman, he used to roll up on the balls of his feet when he marched. On all our performance tapes my junior year, there was always this one plume bobbing up and down. It was all anyone could look at. It used to drive Mr. Gorman crazy. It took him two years to completely beat it out of him."

"Did they put him on a T-shirt?"

He grins. "Nope. That honor belongs to you and you alone." He claps me on the shoulder. "I'm gonna go get my shirt. Want me to grab yours?"

"Yeah, sure. Hey, Curtis," I say as he turns to go. "Thanks."

He winks at me. "Enjoy the notoriety while it lasts."

I'm still thinking about Curtis's pep talk and the way he changed into his new T-shirt right there in the parking lot when Dad and Matt get back Wednesday morning.

"You are not quitting, and I don't want to hear any more about it," Dad snaps at Matt as he unloads two chair bags from the back of the SUV.

I close the kitchen door behind me. He hands Matt the chairs and looks up. "Is your mom home already?"

Don't you see her car parked right in front of yours? I want to ask, but I don't. "She just got back. She saw a few patients this morning, but they rescheduled everybody else."

Matt stalks past me, muttering something that sounds a lot like, "I hate Boy Scouts." I watch him go and wonder what happened to kill all that enthusiasm he left with on Sunday.

Dad slides a gas stove out of the back and stacks the tent on top of it. "Here, take this, and you and your brother store those things in the garage." *No problem, Dad. And you're welcome.*

I follow Matt into the garage. He flings the bags onto the concrete floor. "I'm not going to any more stupid jamborees and he can't make me," he whines just loud enough for Dad to hear him.

"Stop being so dramatic, Matthew," Dad yells back.

Not likely. Matt loves pushing Dad's buttons. He's Dad's favorite—the straight kid, the one who loves fishing and camping and baseball and belching. Matt knows that, and he uses it to settle scores, usually on my behalf. He must have a pretty big one to settle right now if he's dissing Scouts.

"What happened?" I drop the tent next to the chairs as Matt

unbuttons his Scout shirt, wads it up in a ball, and tosses it in a corner of the garage. "He told me—"

"You're home," Mom says. It takes her about an instant to take in Dad's flushed face and the scowl on Matt's. "What's going on? Matt, where's your shirt?"

Matt fixes Dad with a commendably bratty look. "I'm not—"

"Are those bites on your legs?" Mom asks.

Matt looks down. Three or four red, festering sores dot his legs. Not many, but with Matt, it only takes a few.

"Fucking ants."

"Matthew!" Mom stoops to get a better look at the bites.

"I had to use the stupid EpiPen. That thing hurts." He scratches at the bites as if the reminder has suddenly made them itch.

She looks up at Dad as he hauls a cooler into the garage. "Did you take him to the emergency room?"

"It's just a couple of bites. I gave him some Benadryl. He's fine."

Mom cuts him with a look, and Matt and I know it's time to go.

"So what happened?" I ask as we head up the stairs.

"He told me I can't hang out with Samuel Bedford anymore."

Samuel is not just a scouting buddy; he's Matt's new best friend from two streets over. They met riding bikes our first week back. I give Samuel credit for making the move back a little easier on Matt. It's tough having to start all over making new friends twice in one year. Samuel's a nerdy kid, but he's a Scout. It seems to me that Dad would be all over that friendship.

"Why can't you hang out with Samuel?" I ask.

He swipes a wadded up shirt from his bed and smells it. "He says he acts too girly, and he doesn't want me turning out like you."

Nice one, Dad.

"I told him he doesn't have to worry," Matt goes on. "No way is Samuel gay. He's a Scout. And there aren't any gays in Scouts, right?"

"Right."

He pulls on the dirty shirt and grins at me. "I think Samuel likes me."

"Really? Does that freak you out?"

"Nah. He's really good at tying knots. He's gonna teach me some. Hey, maybe I can fix you up with him?"

"He's eleven."

"Ten. But he'll grow up."

I'm not that desperate.

By noon we're getting intermittent showers from the outer bands. I don't have to check the Web site to know that band practice has been cancelled. The last hurricane blew over us in the middle of the night, just as they expect this one to do. We slept through the whole thing. The thing I do remember, besides all the trees down, was the way Mom fussed at us when she found out Matt and I had been tromping through the swollen drainage ditch that ran alongside the perimeter of our neighborhood. It was one of the few times I'd seen Mom and Dad argue about us before we moved to Odessa. Dad said we were just being boys and she was overreacting. Mom said there were all kinds of bacteria in the water. Dad said we were fine. Mom said the fast-moving water was dangerous and that we could easily be swept into a culvert. Dad told her she needed to calm down.

I doubt he'll get away with such cavalier parenting this storm. He's seen Mom's claws.

"That place was a nuthouse," Mom says. She sets two damp H-E-B shopping bags on the counter and hands me an eight-pack of D batteries. "That was it. No C batteries at all."

"I think we have enough. Matt found some in the garage."

"Did you find the portable TV?"

"Got it."

Mom looks at Matt. "Why are you scratching your head?"

He shrugs and rips open a bag of mesquite-flavored kettle chips.

"Don't eat all those," she warns. Then to me, "You want to help me unload the rest of the car?"

"Have you heard anything from Dad?" I ask, handing her one of the lighter bags.

"He had to drive all the way to Huntsville to find a generator.

He'll be home soon." She rubs my back as I lift out the other three bags. "It's kind of weird for you, isn't it?"

I press the trunk closed. "It's okay."

"Look, it's not okay. I can see that. But if it's any consolation, it's kind of weird for your dad too. He's used to calling all the shots, and he doesn't really know how to be a different kind of dad. But he's trying, Luke. Let's be patient with him. Okay?"

She smiles and musses my hair, but as we enter the kitchen she frowns at Matt, who's scratching again at a spot behind his ear. She sighs. "Do you have lice again?" she asks him.

"No. My head just itches."

She picks through Matt's hair and shakes her head. "Great. I've got to run back to the store for some delouser. You are infested, young man."

"Fucking Scouts," he mutters.

"Language, please. And judging from the number of nits in your hair, I'd say you were the one doing the sharing this time." She sighs again and grabs her keys off the counter. "Oh, hey, Luke, I need you and Matt to do me a favor. Would you two run over to Miss Shelley's and hang some plywood over her windows before the rain starts up again."

"I thought we didn't need to cover our windows," Matt says.

"We don't. But Miss Shelley is paranoid. The holes are already predrilled. All you have to do is screw them in. Take your dad's power screwdriver."

"Did you know that lice used to be called cooties?" I ask Matt as we rummage through the tool-storage system. Mom wasn't discriminating when she had the movers pack us in Odessa. They packed everything. I'm not even sure they left Dad a toothbrush. It sure made his moving back easy.

"Are you saying I have cooties?" Matt says.

"Yep."

"Cool." He slides open a large drawer at the bottom. "Found it."

I survey the activity on the street as we head over to Miss Shelley's. Some of our neighbors, mostly people I've never seen before, are scurrying about securing potted plants and patio furniture in their garages, trimming branches, clearing gutters, but many of them are simply standing around talking. No one is boarding their windows.

Curtis's truck is in the Camerons' driveway. It occurs to me that if we hadn't moved here, he'd probably be boarding up Miss Shelley's windows himself.

Miss Shelley points us to a stack of plywood in her garage.

Fortunately, we're covering only the downstairs windows. Even though the rain has stopped for the time being, the wind gusts tear at the plywood as Matt and I struggle to line up each piece on the window frame. I hold the plywood in place while he secures them. He's much better with power tools than I am.

Libby follows us from room to room, tapping on the blinds, barking at us through the glass. Finally, we're done. Matt glances nervously at the sky as he climbs down the ladder for the last time.

"Scared?" I ask him.

"It's just wind and rain, right?"

He's scared.

We finish the other chores Miss Shelley has for us—hauling her patio furniture into the garage, carrying in six cases of bottled water from her trunk, taking down the sunflower flags hanging from her porch. Mom is just getting home as we finish up.

"I'm gonna walk up the street," I tell Matt, handing him the dollar Miss Shelley paid me. "You want to come?"

"Does a bear shit in the house?" He glances up at me anxiously. "You're not going far, are you?"

I'm not planning to go far at all.

Corrine is in the driveway where Curtis's truck had been parked half an hour ago. As I approach, she makes a few marks on the sketch pad in her lap.

"Shouldn't you be battening down the hatches?" I ask.

She looks up and smiles. "Hey, Luke. It's pretty, don't you think?"

Pretty isn't exactly the word I would use. Eerie, foreboding maybe, creepy, the fast-moving clouds low as they bulldoze across the sky. It feels like the entire neighborhood has been captured under some kind of cosmic dome.

"Can I see?" I ask, indicating her drawing.

She drops her feet and offers me the chair they were propped on, then holds out her sketch pad to me.

"You're a damn good artist," I say, studying the details of her drawing.

"I'm working on it. If you're looking for Curtis, he went to get some propane for the grill. He'll be back soon if you want to wait."

"Are your mom and dad doing all the hurricane stuff?" I ask.

"Well, Dad's watching the weather reports. Does that count?" She smiles. "No Mom though. It's just us three."

The information takes me by surprise. I'm still considering how to respond when Corrine says, "Hey, look who's back."

Curtis pulls into the driveway and gets out. "Hey, Luke."

"Did you find propane?" Corrine asks.

"Yep. But I had to wait in line for it. Want to give me a hand?" he asks me.

He hauls a tank from the bed of the truck and hands it to me, then reaches over the side for a second one. We take them to the garage, where a well-used gas grill resides in one corner. Curtis pulls the grill away from the wall then sets down his tank. He takes the other from me, positions it on the hook on one side, and connects the gas line. He looks up at me. "Does your family have a grill?"

Does my family have a grill? I almost laugh. In fact, we do. It's a monstrosity—stainless steel with enclosed tank storage, two drawers, a side burner, and a rotisserie. It's hardly been used. Mom doesn't like cooking outdoors because of the bugs, and Dad doesn't like cooking at all, but he does like owning a nice grill. "Um, yeah, but we don't use it much."

"Well"—he tightens the connection and stands up—"that might change over the next few days. Is your family all ready for the big blow?"

"As ready as can be. I think Matt's a little freaked out."

"What about you?"

"Just another storm."

"Well, let's hope. I tell you what, you got a phone on you?"

I reach into my pocket and hand it over. He thumbs in a number then saves it to my contacts and pushes Call. His own phone rings. He hands mine back, then slides his from his pocket and saves my number to his contacts. "There. Now you have my number and I have yours. You call me if you need anything, okay?"

"Yikes!" Corrine clutches her sketchpad to her chest, scoops up her pencils, and scrambles to her feet and into the garage as fat drops of rain splat on the driveway. Curtis and I exchange an amused look. "Hey, is that your dad?" Corrine asks, pointing with her pencils to the street. I look as the passenger window slides down. Dad ducks down and peers through the open window. He hesitates, and I know he's trying to assess the threat level, who's with who. I feel Curtis look at me, but all I can do is glare at my dad.

Finally, he speaks. "I need you to help me unload this generator. Now."

"You need some extra help?" Curtis asks as he drives off.

I watch Dad pull past our driveway, then back in as the garage door goes up.

"Luke?"

"No. Thanks, but we got it."

"Don't let your dad run that generator in the garage, okay?"

Like I have any say over what my dad does and doesn't do.

I jog home in the rain, and in steely silence we unload the generator. Then I leave him to his new toy.

"Hold still," Mom says to Matt as I enter the kitchen.

"It stinks," Matt whines.

"If you don't quit squirming, I'm going to squirt this water right up your nose. You're wet," she says to me. "Is that your dad I hear in the garage?"

"He's fiddling with the generator."

"I can't breathe," Matt blubbers through the spray. "Why don't you squirt some water up that scoutmaster's nose?"

Mom turns off the faucet. I hand her the towel on the counter. She snatches it and roughly applies it to Matt's head, then looks at me and heaves a sigh of disgust. I raise my eyebrows. "I called the scoutmaster to let him know," she says, "and he had the gall to tell me that Matt didn't get it from any of the other Scouts. 'They're *clean* kids,' he said." She pulls a stool out from the bar and tells Matt to sit, then viciously proceeds to de-nit him with a little blue comb. "What an idiot," she mutters. "I called him so he can alert the other parents, not to blame anyone."

I smile to myself. Mom's anger always flares at what she calls *the willful and persistent ignorance of some people.*

The fact is, Matt picks up lice like other kids pick up colds. Mom says it's because of his shaggy hair and the fact that he never sits up straight, thus putting his hair in contact with multiple surfaces every day. That, and lice like clean hair. I figure Matt's hair must be pretty damn clean, then. We've been through this half a dozen times already.

"Are you done yet?" Matt complains, pulling his head away.

"Sit still. If I don't get every single one of these nits out, they'll be right back in a week, and I do not have time to deal with the school nurse's paranoia. And if you *don't* sit still and let me do this, I'm going to shave your head."

That stops him.

I'm watching her work her way through his hair, scraping the nits she finds down each hair shaft and then removing them with her fingers, when Miss Shelley knocks at the kitchen door.

"Helloooo," she calls out. She lets herself in before I can get the door and immediately takes in the little scene in front of her. "Matt has lice?"

"Yes, Matt has lice," Mom says tightly.

"Ow, ow, ow."

"You need to use gasoline," Miss Shelley says. "That's what my mom used on me."

The horror on Mom's face is trumped only by the horror on Matt's.

I stifle a laugh. "Yeah, try gasoline, Mom."

She shoots me a look. "What do you need, Miss Shelley?"

What she needs, as it turns out, is more cheap labor to haul a dozen plastic tubs filled with her most precious possessions up to the second floor (in case her house takes on three feet of water in a non-flood zone, I guess).

* * *

By the time I've done the deed, Matt is nit free and together we spend the rest of the day on petty chores at home. Mom keeps the washing machine going until she's washed everything in the house that could possibly need washing in the next week or so. She also has me drag down the mattress from my bed and situate it at the base of the stairs. The stairs are in the center of the house, far enough away from windows to provide some measure of safety just in case.

Matt plans to stay up all night and watch the storm, but I suspect he's more anxious than curious. Even so, and despite the increasingly heavy rain outside, he's out by eleven. I watch TV, alternating between late night shows on Comedy Central, a *True Blood* marathon on HBO, and hurricane coverage. Around midnight, the storm comes on shore at Galveston and I get my first text from Curtis: Hold on to your hat.

Aw, it's not so bad. You staying up?

Wouldn't miss it! How's Matt?

Wimped out an hour ago.

That's probably for the best.

Around two AM, the winds suddenly pick up. There's a hard thump against the house. Then another. At four the cable goes out; moments later, the power. And that's when things get really unnerving. I fiddle with the antenna on the small, battery-operated TV but get nothing but static. I keep the set on long enough to locate and turn on our lanterns, then shut it off.

Surprised the power lasted this long. Everything okay? Curtis texts.

How much longer is this going to last? We're getting beaten up here.

A little while. Holy crap. I think we just had a tree hit the house.

Damage?

Don't know yet.

"Is Matt asleep?" Mom asks quietly, coming into the room. I can barely hear her over the racket. She's in her robe and holding her own small lantern.

I look at the lump under the quilt. "He didn't even make it to midnight."

She grins, then flinches as the house takes another hit. "It's just a branch. I'm sure it sounds a lot worse than it is. The radio says the storm's already been downgraded. It's just a tropical storm now. Who are you texting?"

"Curtis Cameron. He's a band tech. He lives up the street."

"Well, why don't you try to get some sleep? We're going to have a lot of cleanup once this blows over."

I wish I could, but by the time the rain slacks up some, the winds die down, and the thumping ends, it's almost eight and Matt's up. He peeks cautiously out the blinds on the back door. "There's nothing but leaves out here," he says.

Mom opens the door slightly and a rain-heavy branch pops into the house, splattering us all with water. She jumps back in surprise. "We have a tree down," she says. Together we force the branch back out, and she secures the door.

Chapter 5

CURTIS

"I hate losing that maple," Dad says as we step out onto the back porch. We pull our hoods on and walk out into the yard so we can get a look at where the trunk made contact with the roof. "I sure don't like the idea of cutting branches in the rain, but I don't think we have much choice." He sighs. "Well, let me get a tarp and the chain saw. You want to grab the ladder?"

We know already that the tree has punched a hole. There's a growing damp spot in the ceiling in my room. But with very little attic in that area, we haven't been able to get up there to rig some kind of patch. And neither of us wants to wait until the ceiling comes down to address the problem.

The extension ladder is mounted sideways on brackets in the garage. I lift it and ease it past Dad's truck. It's a tight fit with two vehicles in the garage. My truck is parked in Miss Shelley's garage. And good thing, because there's a big sycamore lying across the driveway.

Down the street the Chesser house is quiet. From here, it looks undamaged. But everywhere else I look, trees are down, fences are down. Branches and leaves litter the street, and the storm drain situated right at the dogleg is struggling to take in all the water. It's going to be a long day.

Corrine hands me a lidded tumbler of coffee. "You're not going to climb on the roof in this rain, are you?"

I take a sip. "Sure am. Thanks."

"Isn't that kind of dangerous?"

"So is having a ceiling fall in on your head. I'll be careful."

"Have you checked on him yet?" she asks, nodding toward Luke's house.

"What's with all this matchmaking?"

"Matchmaking? Me?" Corrine grins brightly.

My phone rings in my pocket. "We exchanged a few texts last night," I say as I slip it out. I'm expecting to see Luke's name on the screen, but the call is from Ryan. *How sweet*, I think sarcastically. *He's checking on me.* I let it go to voice mail.

"Is that him?" she asks, trying to get a look.

I wipe the rain from my phone and shove it back in my pocket. "Nope."

"Damn. So what did you two text about?"

" 'Is your family okay?' 'Yes.' 'How about yours?' 'Fine.' "

"Ooh. Small talk. That's sexy."

I laugh, take another sip of coffee, and hand the tumbler back to her. Okay, it was a little sexy, all that quiet talk in the dark, even if we were just talking about the storm.

Dad comes out of the garage and sets the chain saw and a gas can on the driveway. I lug the ladder around back and extend it until it rests securely against the shingles two stories up. I get a text as I'm testing the ladder. I'm amused to feel my heart thump a little in my chest. Luke. But it's not Luke; it's Ryan again: *Answer your fucking phone.*

Nice way to greet your ex-playmate, asshole. I delete his text. It'll be a cold day in hell before I read another or answer a call from him.

Ryan Cummins. Just seeing his name on my phone makes my skin crawl. Corrine always says I'm too picky when it comes to guys. The problem is, I was never picky enough.

I never told her about the guys I dated in Austin. Maybe that's because "dated" is a little too romantic for the breathtakingly brief relationships I had. But with Ryan, I thought we were going somewhere. He's a percussionist, from Amarillo. We saw each other for about five incredibly intense weeks, always alone, always in my room when Jared was out. Ryan was deep in the closet. I respected that. Before I met him, I'd spent months "exploring" my sexual identity in a way I couldn't (or wouldn't) in high school, and I was starting to feel a little like I'd lost my center. I was already thinking about leaving Austin.

It's funny, but Ryan was everything Corrine thinks I am, everything I was when I started at UT—innocent, inexperienced. But he was eager to learn, and he was eager to learn from me.

And then he quit coming over, quit answering my calls, quit responding to my texts. He avoided me in the band hall, which wasn't unusual. But then I heard he was dating a piccolo player. A girl. I respected his need to be in the closet; I did not respect his playing games with me and with another human being because he was a fucking coward.

I don't know what his problem is now, and I don't care.

"All right, here you go," Dad says, handing me the chain saw. "It's hot, so you don't need to pull out the choke." He grips the ladder, and I climb, even as I feel the phone buzz in my pocket again. I shake off the anger that's gripping me all over again. *Go play with your little piccolo player, Ryan, and leave me alone.*

I step carefully onto the shingles and survey the tangle of branches pressed against the roof. I pick out a couple to start with, stick the butt of the chain saw between my legs, and pull the cord.

Chapter 6

LUKE

The branch that presses against our back door is attached to a tree that yesterday stood in our back neighbor's yard. It's fallen harmlessly against the house, the weight of the tree bowing the trunk and branches just below where it rests on the gutter.

Dad plugs in a little electric chain saw he picked up in Huntsville. "You boys need to stay out of the way," he says, flipping the switch on.

Gladly.

He applies the blade to a section of bowed trunk. When the blade cuts most of the way through, the remaining wood ruptures, the tension on the trunk releases, and the branches rebound, swiping Matt across the face.

"Ouch." Matt grabs at his cheek.

"Goddammit, Luke! I told you to keep your brother a safe distance." Dad stoops under the branch and grabs Matt's chin roughly and examines his face. "You're fine." Then he turns on me again. "Just take your brother inside and let me finish this."

It's a small scrape. Not even worth a Band-Aid. But blaming me for that?

"He should have cut off the branches first," Matt mutters.

He should have stayed in Odessa.

At the front door, Mom is pulling on a poncho. "Boys, I'm going to check on Miss Shelley."

"Okay if I walk the neighborhood?" I ask.

"Me too," Matt says.

"Doesn't your dad need you out back?" I hold her eyes until she gets the message. "Um, okay," she says. "Do you have your EpiPen, Matt?"

"Yeah," he says in a way that I know means he's lying.

"Show it to me," she says.

He scoffs. "I'm wearing rubber boots and I'm only going up the street."

"I don't care," she says. "You carry that with you always, even if you're just in the front yard. Luke, he goes nowhere without that EpiPen, got it?"

"Fine," he says, and stomps back up the stairs.

I keep to the center of the street, but Matt slogs through the rushing water along the edges. The skinny pines seem to have taken the biggest hit; they're scattered everywhere like pickup sticks— leaning on houses, blocking driveways and the street, balancing on the remains of fences.

Curtis's house is one of those with a tree across the driveway— not a pine, but a big sycamore that stood at the edge of their lot. A gaping hole in the ground at the base of the roots is filled with water. The buzz of a chain saw rips the morning air from some- where around the back of his house.

"Let's go see what's going on," I say to Matt.

"Who lives here?"

"One of the band techs."

As we enter the backyard, a slender middle-aged man is looking up at the roof. "Careful with that, Curt. That gets really slippery when it's wet. Get the smaller branches first."

The buzzing ramps up again, then drops to a chug, and Curtis tosses a branch over the side. "Oh, hey," he says when he sees me. "Dad, that's Luke. He lives down the street."

"That was a night, wasn't it?" his dad says as the chain saw kicks in again. He reaches out to shake my hand. "Everything okay at your house?"

Another branch drops.

"A neighbor's tree took down our fence. Everything else seems okay though."

"Curtis can help you with that tree."

"Thanks, but I think my dad's got it."

"I'm Matt. Can I climb up there?"

"I think Curtis has got that covered." He smiles at me over Matt's head, then checks on Curtis. "How does it look?"

"We definitely have a hole. Not too bad though."

"Are you ready for the tarp?"

"Not yet. Let me get a few more branches out of the way."

More branches fall, then Curtis calls down, "Should we try to push the trunk away from the house now?"

"I don't think so, Curt. It's going to have to be cut, but I don't want you doing that. It's too dangerous. Let's get a tarp on the roof, and I'll call a tree service. It's not going anywhere. Then we'll get the one on the driveway."

He retrieves a blue tarp from the ground. "You want to hold the ladder for me, Luke?"

"I can take it up," I offer. Matt nudges me in the ribs.

Curtis's dad holds the ladder while I cautiously make my way up the slippery rungs. It didn't look nearly as high from the ground as it does from the ladder, and I remind myself with each step not to look down. When I'm almost to the top, I focus my attention on Curtis, who is stooped at the edge, safety glasses pushed up on his head, waiting for me. He reaches his hand out and I hold the tarp up to him.

"Thanks, man. You want to come up and help?"

When I hesitate, he winks and tells me he can handle it himself. I'm not ashamed to admit I'm relieved.

It doesn't take him long to finish the job. He lowers the chain saw to his dad via an orange nylon rope, then I hold the ladder as he descends.

"So you're the infamous Luke Chesser's little brother?" Curtis says to Matt when he gets to the ground. A week ago that might have pissed me off. But coming from Curtis now, it sounds kind of, I don't know, affectionate?

"Luke is infamous?" Matt asks. "For what?" But then he gets it. "Oh yeah, that. Hey, can you teach me how to use a chain saw?"

"Don't teach him how to use a chain saw. Please," I say. "Mom would kill me."

Curtis laughs and pushes back the hood of his poncho. "Sorry, kiddo. I definitely don't want your mom mad at me. But you can help me with that tree out front."

"Mom wouldn't care if I used a chain saw," Matt insists as we head to the front yard.

"He's delusional," I tell Curtis.

Matt marches on, but Mr. Cameron holds Curtis back. "Be careful around Matt with that chain saw, okay?"

That turns out not to be an issue. Libby's out again, stomping through the water, bounding from one house to the next to greet anyone who'll pay attention to her. There is no need for her to run to the lake today since it looks like the lake has come to her. "I'm gonna go catch her," Matt says.

We watch Matt go. "Cute kid," Curtis says.

I scoff. "He's a mess."

Curtis grins. "So, how about you?"

I'm not sure what he means. When I hesitate, he adds, "I promise not to let you cut off any fingers."

Click. The chain saw. Wow. If I had a bucket list, learning to operate a chain saw certainly wouldn't be on it. I don't even want to watch someone else operate one, but I find myself agreeing anyway.

He gives me a quick lesson on safe chain saw use, demonstrating as he goes. "You want to always hold a chain saw with both hands and work at full throttle. Cut with the center of the blade, never the tip. And never use the blade in a direct line with any part of your body lest a kickback slice you open." He grins at me. "Kidding. But, seriously, don't do that."

"I'm going to die."

He laughs. "You're not going to die. I won't let that happen. Trust me, okay?"

It's not that I don't trust him; I don't trust me.

He sighs when I don't take the chain saw. "Okay, I'll cut, you watch." He seats the safety glasses on the bridge of his nose again and demos by cutting a few branches, then points to one that's only about four inches in diameter and well positioned for me to practice on. He hands me the safety glasses—I put them on and wipe my hands on my shorts—then the chugging chain saw. "Hold it with both hands."

I rev up the chain saw, and he takes a step back. Great. I'm going to die alone. I tick off all the safety precautions in my head, hold my breath, and actually cut through the branch.

"Nothing to it." He slaps me on the back and points out another branch. Soon I advance to larger pieces of trunk. Curtis shows me how to cut a notch on the underside before sawing most of the way through the top. When the blade is almost through each section of trunk, I stop and remove the saw, and Curtis kicks the pieces apart.

"We're a pretty good team, huh?" Curtis says when we've cleared the driveway.

I look around at the sections of trunk stacked neatly at the curb. I think he's right. I set the chain saw on the driveway and wipe my stinging hands on my thighs.

"Let me see." Curtis takes my hands and inspects them. "Luke Chesser, you are blistered." He shakes his head. "I should have gotten you some gloves. Come on, let's take care of these."

"Nice work," Corrine says as we enter the kitchen.

"Got some Bactine and some athletic tape?" Curtis asks.

"Did you hurt yourself?" Curtis holds up my hand. "Ouch."

Even without power, the wide kitchen window lets in plenty of light for Corrine to find the first aid supplies in a kitchen cabinet. Curtis holds my hand over the sink and carefully washes the two blisters at the base of my fingers, then douses them liberally with the antiseptic and pats them dry. In the meantime, Corrine has cut two foot-long pieces of tape. She sticks them to the counter, then rips one halfway down its length.

Curtis laces the ripped piece over my ring finger and smooths both sides against my skin all the way to my wrist. I watch his face as he wraps the other piece of tape around my wrist to secure the ends. "You've done this before?"

He smiles. "A few times. But it's usually Corrine doing the first aid."

"More times than I can count." She laughs.

"All done." He releases my hand, and something inside me resets for good.

With my hand securely bandaged and heavy gloves on, we move on to the neighbors' houses, doing what we can to help clear trees from driveways and fences. By early afternoon the rain has stopped completely and the sun is out. We shed our ponchos and leave them on Curtis's driveway.

A tree has taken down a section of Miss Shelley's fence as well, which explains how Libby got loose again. We saw Matt trudging home with her a few hours ago, the hood of his poncho knotted around her collar to form a leash.

My arms are rubber, and Curtis takes over the cutting. Once he's freed the fence from the tree, we prop up the section and brace it with pieces of the trunk that Curtis cut for that purpose.

When the fence feels secure, I collapse on another section of tree trunk and lean back against the weathered cedar boards. "Oh my God. I am so tired." I close my eyes. The trunk shifts a little and the fence gives as Curtis sits down next to me.

"You need to work on those muscles," he says, and I can hear the smile in his voice.

I'm too tired to get indignant.

"How's the hand?"

I pull off my gloves and flex my fingers. "Surprisingly . . . good. A little stiff." I roll my head a few times to stretch my neck and shoulder muscles, then squint at him. His eyes are closed, and I get to study his face for the first time. The thing that strikes me most, aside from the fact that he's damn nice to look at, is the scar—a thin white line that cuts across his forehead, almost the entire width, and I wonder for a moment if he cut himself with a chain saw, but the orientation is all wrong.

"How did you get the scar?" I ask.

"Ah, the scar," he says and rubs it with the heel of his hand as if the reminder suddenly made it itch. "Sometimes I think I should grow my hair longer and cover it up. It still torments my dad."

"I like your hair," I say, and then instantly regret it when it comes out sounding like a lame pickup line. He smiles. "Why does it torment your dad?"

"My dad raised us. My mom died when we were pretty little, so he's been it. He took us to Africa on a business trip when we were about five. He did that a lot. I guess he didn't like being away from us. We usually had a nanny who went with us. Anyway, he took us to some bazaar or something one day and they had these big rusty ceiling fans whirring overhead. We were tired and cranky, I imagine. The nanny carried Corrine, but Dad decided to put me on his shoulders. And then he walked me right into one of those ceiling fans. The blade sliced open my forehead and knocked my brain back against my skull. I don't remember any of it, and Dad doesn't talk about it, but I've heard stories. Apparently, there was a lot of blood, and we're not talking the best hospitals in the world. I think there were a few days there when they didn't know whether I'd make it or not. But I did. We never went back to Africa again, though, and I think Dad still beats himself up over it."

"He seems like a great dad."

Curtis watches a squirrel scamper across a section of fence. "He's the best." After a moment, he looks over at me like he's almost sorry he admitted that, like he feels guilty for acknowledging the great relationship he has with his own dad when mine is so shitty. "How have things been going with your dad?"

I smile at how spot-on my assessment was. I close my eyes. "I don't know. In some ways I wish things could be the way they were before I came out. There's so much tension in the house now. I'm not a high-tension kind of person, you know."

He laughs. "I'm getting there."

For a long while after that we're quiet. The neighborhood sounds different without the hum of air conditioning units and the usual traffic from the thoroughfare bordering our neighborhood. The air has a flat quality to it, and the sound of voices and the occasional buzz of other chain saws seem closer than they probably are. My body feels heavy, as if a huge weight is pressing me down onto the log.

Suddenly, Curtis slaps my knee. The log shifts again as he gets up.

"Come on," he says, reaching out a hand. "I'll buy you a drink."

I can't move, but a drink sounds like heaven. I groan and squint up at him with one eye. He grins, takes my outstretched hand, and pulls me to my feet. I wince at the soreness in my hand, my arms, my shoulders, my back. It didn't take much downtime for pretty much every muscle in my body to seize up.

"Your dad's got the generator going," Curtis notes as we head up Miss Shelley's driveway.

It's chugging along unattended on the driveway. And like everyone else's on the street, our windows are all wide open. But the house is quiet. I consider stopping by and checking in with Mom, but I've got my phone. She'll call if she needs me. And anyway, I'm pretty sure Matt's told her what I'm doing if she hasn't already seen it herself.

"That's hard work, isn't it?" Mr. Cameron hauls a couple more chairs out of the garage and pops them open as Curtis stores the chain saw back in the garage.

I drop heavily into one of the chairs. "I doubt I'll be able to lift my arms tomorrow."

"You're probably right. Are you boys hungry?"

Corrine is smiling at me a little too broadly. She jumps up with an *oh* and opens a cooler next to her chair.

"Whatcha got in there?" Curtis jostles her out of the way and retrieves a couple bottles of water and two plastic-wrapped hoagie rolls. He tosses one of each to me.

"Tuna, you Neanderthal."

"Mmm." Curtis unwraps his and bites off a quarter of the sandwich.

I'm starved, but lifting the sandwich feels like lifting a full-grown bluefin tuna. I take a small bite, then set it on my lap. My mind drifts. It's pleasant sitting outside, not worrying about school or performances or taking out the trash or avoiding Dad. I slide down deeper into my chair and lean my head on the aluminum bar and half listen to their talk—the prospect that we could be without power for days, the fact that food in the freezer is already thawing, the suggestion that we'll all be eating like kings until those freezers are empty.

The hurricane has zapped much of the heat out of the air and the breeze holds on. I don't realize I've fallen asleep until Curtis jiggles my knee.

"Luke, I think that's your dad calling you." He points toward my house, and I glance groggily over my shoulder. Dad is standing in the driveway, his hands on his hips, scanning the neighborhood.

The sandwich is gone, and I assume either Corrine put it away or Curtis ate it. Either way is okay with me because I'm too weary to eat. And I have no strength to push myself out of the chair.

"Come on, Paul Bunyan," Curtis says, offering his hand again.

"I'm grilling chicken tonight, Luke. We'd love to have you."

I'd reach out and shake Mr. Cameron's hand, but I can't lift my arm. "I'd like that, sir. Thank you."

"Where have you been?" Dad barks as I trudge up the driveway.

"Just talking to some neighbors."

"That girl I saw you with yesterday?"

I know what he's thinking—he's won. But I'm too tired to challenge him. "Yeah, that girl."

And with that one word, his entire demeanor morphs from accusatory to smug. I mentally roll my eyes.

"Why are you holding your arm like that?"

My right arm is definitely the sorer of the two, and it's only then that I realize I'm cradling it with my other. "I helped Corrine's brother cut up some downed trees."

"Corrine, huh?"

Not Corrine. Corrine's brother.

As it turns out, I've been summoned to help him and Matt to brace up the fence in the backyard. When we're done, I take a couple of ibuprofen, stretch out on the couch in front of the open window, and fall asleep again.

The generator gives off just enough power to run the refrigerator, a couple of fans, and a small window unit Dad installed in their bedroom. So even though the worst of the summer heat has been blown out, the house is still stuffy, and I wake up sweaty and sore.

The sun has gone down and the house is quiet except for the racket from the generator. With a flashlight, I find the ibuprofen again.

Outside it looks like most of the neighbors have gone to bed, but a few are clustered on driveways here and there chatting, some with lanterns, some in the dark. I don't see my family so I assume they're in bed as well. I wander back down to Curtis's house.

Corrine is reading by the light of a battery-operated LED lantern she's hung from a branch, but Curtis is stretched out on his stomach on a chaise cushion thrown on the ground.

"You're not the only one laid low by the chain saw." She laughs quietly.

I pull up a chair close to hers and sit. "Is he asleep?"

"Dead to the world. You missed dinner, but I saved you some. Hungry?"

"Starved. I've been asleep myself since I got home."

"In that case, let me get you a plate."

"I can get it." I step over Curtis, open the grill, and help myself to some chicken and corn on the cob. My muscles are still fatigued, but the ibuprofen and the rest have helped.

Corrine gets me a soda and some potato salad from the cooler. "We're going to need more ice tomorrow. I just hope we can find some. The power's out everywhere. I heard that H-E-B . . ."

As she talks about what's open and what isn't, I study Curtis, the calves that bulge out from his otherwise slender legs, the way his back rises and falls as he breathes, the thin white scar across his forehead, barely visible in the dim light. He groans, turns his head away, his breathing settling again into a regular pattern.

I like watching him. If anyone had asked two weeks ago if I could have imagined Curtis and me together, I would have laughed. And yet, the possibility looms in my mind. He's so different from Nate. There's no anger, no drama. Just a calm, quiet confidence that I find appealing.

I wish I didn't do that—measure every guy I meet against Nate Schaper. But I can't help it. Despite everything, I still think about him. I would have done anything for him, but I wasn't the one he wanted, and I never had been.

Curtis groans again and shifts on the cushion. I smile.

I realize that Corrine is no longer talking. I glance at her. She's cradling her head in her hand and watching me, a curious expression on her face.

I pick up a wing and take a bite. Down the street a woman cackles.

"So what do you think of my baby brother?"

"Baby brother? Aren't you twins?"

"I'm exactly one minute and sixteen seconds older." She laughs quietly. "So, is he being nice to you guys? I mean, on the practice field? He can be a beast."

"I heard that," Curtis croaks.

"Hey, baby bro," she says, nudging him with her foot. "It's about time you woke up."

His hand shoots out and grabs her ankle. She shrieks and pokes him in the ribs until he lets go. "God, I feel like I've been beat up," he says, getting to his feet. He twists his torso left, then right. "You got a flashlight?"

Corrine hands him one, and he disappears inside the house. Fifteen minutes later he's back out in fresh clothes, his hair still wet from a shower, and wearing wire-framed glasses. He tosses the chaise cushion into the garage and pulls up a chair close to us. Even from a few feet away I can smell how clean he is, and I'm suddenly self-conscious about my own dirty state.

"I'm done," Corrine says abruptly, getting up. "Catch you boys in the morning."

Curtis turns off the lantern and we slump back in our chairs to look at the stars. With the power out all over the region, the sky seems to have exploded with pinpoints of light. Curtis points out Ursa Major, Ursa Minor, Andromeda. I nod my head each time he says, "Do you see it?" But honestly, I can't locate any of them. They look like a bunch of random white dots to me.

"So she thinks I'm a beast, huh?" he says when he runs out of constellations.

I chuckle. A shadowy figure carrying a flashlight emerges from Miss Shelley's house, heads toward mine, stops, then comes toward us.

"There's something I'm curious about," Curtis says. "Why didn't you have the talk with your mom first? She seems pretty understanding. Maybe she could have broken it to your dad a little more gently, and things might have worked out, you know, a little better at least."

"That's a long story. I needed to tell, and he was the only parental unit at home that night."

"That doesn't really explain anything, you know."

I know. But I don't want to tell him the rest.

The flashlight beam sweeps over the driveway, then lights on Curtis's face. He squints.

"Curtis?" Miss Shelley calls out.

"Race you to the door," Curtis says in a barely there voice.

I laugh.

He sighs dramatically and calls out to her: "Is everything okay, Miss Shelley?"

"I can't find Libby. I'm sure she's in the house, she's got to be. Will you come look?"

"Sure." He gropes around for the flashlight, then grabs my arm. "Come on. You're coming with me."

A single lantern illuminates the living room, but where the light doesn't reach, the house is as black as the plush lining of my instrument case. We split up. Curtis searches the downstairs with Miss Shelley right on his heels, jabbering about Libby's freedom run earlier, and how she wasn't sure the trunks we used to brace the fence were going to hold, and how her weak knees make it hard for her to climb the stairs.

I take Miss Shelley's flashlight and search the upstairs, inside closets, under beds, behind doors, all the while fighting the creepy sensation that someone or something is going to loom out of the darkness at me any second. I shine the flashlight into the hall bathroom. Nothing.

I'm about to declare the upstairs clear when from the bathtub, a faint whimper. I pull aside the shower curtain and find the big dog cowering in a tub full of water. "Hey, girl," I say softly, rubbing the trembling dog's head. "Stay right there."

"She's up here," I call down from the landing. Curtis is at the bottom of the stairs in an instant and bounds up to join me. "She's in the bathtub."

"Oh, for Heaven's sake," Miss Shelley says.

"Why is she in the bathtub?" Curtis asks, grabbing my shoulder to slip past me.

"I don't know. She looks scared."

When we enter the smaller section of the bathroom, the dog cowers against the side of the tub, her head down, her body trembling. She whimpers again.

"What are you doing in the water, you crazy dog?" Curtis runs a hand gently across her head and down her back. With the other hand, he pulls the plug, and the water begins draining. "Luke, get me some towels. She's cold."

I find some in a linen closet and pass them over. Libby keeps her eyes averted and hugs the side of the tub more firmly. "I think she's afraid of the flashlight beams."

Curtis glances back at me. "A flashlight phobia? Seriously?"

I shrug.

"All right. Let's kill the flashlights."

In the dark, I feel my way to the tub, stumble over Curtis's legs, then settle on my knees next to him. We rub the big dog down until she's as dry as we can get her. Curtis talks to her the entire time and eventually she begins to relax. The pathetic whimpering has stopped, and she's panting now. A good sign. We try to lift her out, but she resists, so we settle for drying out the tub and making her a bed with some quilts I find in the closet.

"She'll come down in the morning," Curtis assures Miss Shelley when we've gotten Libby settled. "We'll stop by tomorrow and block the stairs so she can't escape there again and make her a hidey hole somewhere downstairs."

"I can't believe my big dog is afraid of a little flashlight. She wasn't even nervous about the storm when it came through."

Curtis shrugs.

"You're good with her," I tell Curtis when we step off the front porch.

"Who? Libby? Or Miss Shelley?"

"Both."

"Hmm. How am I with you?"

His question throws me. I'm afraid to assume too much; the last time I did that, it came back to bite me in the butt. "Well, you haven't made a snide remark to me all day, except maybe for that muscles comment. So I'd say fair to middling."

"Fair to middling, huh?" He looks around at the quiet street for a moment and smiles. "You know, there're still some trees in the neighborhood. Maybe we could do this again tomorrow."

"You underestimate the pain in my muscles right now."

"You're right." He laughs. "Go home. Go to bed. I'll see you tomorrow. No chain saw, I promise."

I watch him head back up the street. As dark as it is, I feel like the sun just came out for the first time in many months.

Chapter 7

LUKE

The heat is back Friday morning, and even with the generator-powered fans, it's too hot to stay inside. There's more cleanup to do anyway, and the fence is down again. Lowe's is selling lumber from their front lot, so Dad was able to pick up some pieces of cedar and four-by-fours. He's been letting Matt wield the nail gun, and I can tell Mom is not happy about it. But as the last of the boards go up, she visibly relaxes.

I hook the retractable clothesline onto the mount and stretch it across to another pine and secure it.

"I hate those things," Mom mutters as she clips a damp towel onto the line.

So do I. I'm just happy my assistance wasn't requested.

Matt gives the extension cord a hard yank and the plug pulls free from the outlet. "Hey, Mom. Can I pitch a tent in the front yard and sleep in it tonight?"

Dad kicks a jutting board back into place. "Sure," he answers before Mom can.

"Can Samuel sleep over too?"

"No," Dad snaps.

"Sure," Mom says at the same time. Her hand freezes on the

clothespin mid-clip and she glares at him. "Why can't he ask Samuel over?"

I toss a poncho over the line and wait to see how long it takes Dad to back down.

He grumbles something incoherent, then says, "*Fine.*"

Not long.

I'm helping Matt assemble the poles fifteen minutes later when Curtis pulls up in front of the house and rolls down the passenger window. "I'm off in search of ice. Does your family need anything?"

I doubt it. But I sure do. "Can I go with you?"

He grins, then reaches across the cab and pops the door handle. "Sure. Come on."

"Yeah, go with your boyfriend," Matt says, nudging me in the ribs.

Boyfriend. I kind of like the sound of that.

The roads are still littered with trees and other debris and the surprisingly heavy traffic is slow moving as cars navigate one bottleneck after the other. We pass several community association crews doing the same kind of work we spent all day doing yesterday. "How are the muscles today?" Curtis asks. He glances over at me as we wait for traffic to move on.

"I sure wouldn't want to be one of those guys today."

"Yeah, me either."

The parking lot at the H-E-B Market is almost full, and a line snakes out of the front door and around the side of the building, something I've never seen before. Curtis pulls into a spot and we take our place at the end of the line and watch as shoppers leave the store with bags of ice and not much else.

The line moves quickly. The store is operating on emergency generators, and just inside the propped-open doors, employees are loading bags of ice from pallets into shoppers' carts as they pass by. A freestanding whiteboard reads: *Limit: 4 bags per customer.*

Once inside the dimly lit store, we see the shelves have been picked almost clean, as if a horde of locusts has moved through and eaten everything in its path. Curtis holds up his list. "Somebody's going to be pretty disappointed."

We wander up and down the aisles with our bags of ice in search of the handful of things Corrine wants.

Batteries. Aside from a few off-brand nine-volts, there's nothing. We have better luck with spaghetti sauce. There's no Ragu or Newman's Own, no Classico, no Barilla, no Prego. But on the bottom shelf there are a few jars of Sister Celeste. Curtis laughs, shrugs, and puts the last remaining jars in the cart.

And that's it. There's no milk, no bread, no lettuce.

"They still have Cracker Jacks," I note, pointing to a near-empty shelf.

He reaches way back and snags the remaining three-pack. "Looks like it's spaghetti and Cracker Jacks for dinner. You are coming tonight, right?"

"Are you kidding? I wouldn't miss spaghetti and Cracker Jacks." Mostly I don't want to miss *Curtis* eating spaghetti and Cracker Jacks. I take the boxes from him and toss them in the basket with Sister Celeste and the dripping bags of ice.

We round the corner, and that's when I see him, waiting to check out a few lanes down. I can't believe it. It's been—what?—almost eight months since I last saw him. Yet suddenly it feels like it was yesterday.

Curtis bumps into me with the cart and apologizes. "You okay?" he asks when I don't react.

"I'm fine," I mumble. I pull the cart numbly into the first line under a big sign hanging from the ceiling: *Express Lane. 15 items or less.* Nate hates those signs. "It's fifteen items or fewer," he once told me. "If you can count it, you use fewer, not less." I never understood what the big deal was, but he was a stickler for word usage.

He's alone, but even from several lanes away I can see that he still wears Adam's earring. I didn't expect that to hurt so much. He slips his phone from his pocket and puts it to his ear, then laughs. I don't have to hear the conversation to know who he's talking to. The look on his face says it all, the way he dips his chin when he talks so no one can hear what he's saying, the way his smile extends to his eyes.

"Is that somebody you know?" Curtis asks, and I realize I've been staring.

"No." I quickly shift my eyes to the cashier, who's waiting with a bored expression on her face. I pull the cart forward and wait while Curtis checks out. When I look again, Nate is disappearing through the open doors.

As we pack the bags of ice into the coolers in the bed of Curtis's truck, I scan the parking lot, but there's no sign of Nate or his car, and I kick myself for letting the opportunity get away.

Curtis vaults over the edge of the truck bed and folds his arms. "Did something happen back there?"

"No." My eyes meet his, and I know that if he presses, I'll tell him everything, about the guy who broke my heart, about the things I'm starting to feel for him. But he doesn't press.

Chapter 8

CURTIS

"Did you two lovebirds have a fight?" Corrine whispers.

"Lovebirds?" I grin at Corrine, then glance over my shoulder at Luke, who's emptying the bags of ice into the cooler. "No. I don't know what's going on." But I have my suspicions.

I've never met Nate Schaper, but we all know who he is. He was the guy from the other school who was so brutally assaulted my senior year. It scared the hell out of Dad. I don't think I could've done it, but after he recovered, he agreed to testify before Congress on hate crime legislation and for weeks his face was all over the evening news.

I'm not surprised that Luke knows Nate, but I'd bet money there's more to it than that.

"Well, go make nice with him," Corrine says. "He's too cute to get away."

That he is.

"So who's sleeping in the tent tonight?" I ask Luke when we're back outside. Anything to get him smiling again.

"Matt and his buddy Samuel."

"Can I check it out?"

"If you really want to."

"I really want to."

Matt abandons his bucket of water balloons and proudly shows us in. It's been a long time since I slept in a tent. I stretch out on the floor, lace my fingers behind my head, and close my eyes. "Not bad." It's not particularly comfortable, but I could surely fall asleep if everyone left me alone for a few minutes. Then again, if I had Luke alone in the tent with me, sleep might have to wait. I chuckle to myself. *Down boy.* Damn. He's still in high school. *Get a grip, Curtis.*

"Hey, guys," Matt says, coming through the door flap. "Can Komodo dragons kill you with their spit?" His face is bright with curiosity. I really like this kid. I exchange a grin with Luke, causing Matt to narrow his eyes. "What's so funny?"

"Why are you asking about Komodo dragons?" Luke asks.

"Because Mason says they can kill you with their spit, and I don't believe him."

"Who's Mason? That kid you were filling water balloons with?"

"Yeah. He lives up the street."

"Actually"—I prop myself up on my elbows—"I think that's kinda true." They both turn to look at me. "Komodo dragons? Spit? But it's because of all the bacteria in their mouths. I mean, I think they have some venom too, but it's really the bacteria that makes their bite so deadly. That doesn't really hold true, though, for those living in captivity."

"Oh, man," Matt says. "I can't wait to tell Mason. He thinks he knows everything. Hey, it'll be kinda crowded, but you and Luke can sleep in here tonight too."

"Tempting," I say, exchanging another amused glance with Luke, "but I'm sure you don't want a bunch of old-timers around spoiling all your fun."

"How old are you anyway?"

"Nineteen. How old are you?"

"Eleven. Luke's seventeen," he adds quickly, then gives his brother an elbow.

That little matchmaker. Well, that makes two of them now.

"All right," Luke says. "It's getting claustrophobic in here." He makes his way out, "accidentally" stepping on Matt's fingers in the process and making him yowl.

I hide a laugh behind a cough.

"Shall we go deal with that dumb dog now?" I ask as I straighten and stretch. We promised Miss Shelley, but mostly I'm looking for an excuse to hang out with Luke a little longer, find out what makes him tick.

And I plan to start with Nate Schaper. I admit it—when I saw Luke looking at him in H-E-B, I didn't like it. Not one bit.

We start with blocking Miss Shelley's stairs, using an interesting selection of large plastic storage tubs, then we make a bed for Libby in the downstairs guest bathroom.

I try to find an opening to ask about Nate, but the timing isn't right.

"You're coming for spaghetti this evening, right?" I ask once we're outside again. "Corrine will have a fit if we don't dispose of that entire bag of thawing meatballs. You gotta eat what you catch in H-E-B, you know."

"Yeah. Of course."

My ringtone goes off. "How did you know about Komodo dragons?" he asks as I slip the phone out of my pocket.

"I read. You should try it sometime."

"Ha, ha."

I don't recognize the number, but I'm feeling pretty charitable at the moment. I press Answer Call and put the phone to my ear as I head back up the street.

There's no hesitation, no greeting, just the irritating snap of Ryan's voice. "You blocked my number, asshole. I've been trying to reach you for days."

Great. I consider ending the call, but I'm sick of him polluting my phone, and I want him gone from my life for good. "I blocked your number because I have nothing to say to you."

"I left you voice mails. Have you even—"

"No, I haven't listened to them. And I don't plan to listen to them." I glance back at Luke; he's watching me go.

"You *fucking* ass," he shouts at me through the phone. "Why didn't you tell me?"

"Tell you what?"

"Do you think I would have slept with you if I'd known?"

"Known what? What are you talking about?"

"I *fucking* hate you."

Well, I don't much like you either, pal. And I'm not interested in his drama either. I'm about to end the call anyway (in fact I'm pulling the phone away from my ear) when I hear the word "tested."

I put the phone back to my ear. "What?"

"I got tested . . . two weeks ago. I'm fucking positive."

I stop in the middle of the road and my heart kicks up a wild beat. "Look, I'm sorry, man, but—"

"You're sorry all right. Why didn't you tell me you were infected?"

"You didn't get it from me," I snap back.

"Well, I didn't get it from the *goddamned* water." His voice breaks. "You were the only one. And you did this to me. How am I supposed to tell my parents? They don't even know I'm gay." A sob escapes from his throat, and I feel bad for him. But there's no way he contracted the virus from me. I'm not stupid.

"I should have stayed away from you. I knew what they were saying about you. You disgusting piece of shit."

Who the hell does he think he is? There's no telling where he's been dipping his dick. Dad's standing in the driveway talking with Mr. Solis from across the street. He looks my way and waves.

"You've ruined my fucking life, Curtis. I wanted you to know that."

He ends the call before I get a chance to defend myself. What a dick.

I stop a moment to say hello to Mr. Solis, then grab a couple of beers from the cooler and take them up to my room. It's hot, but with all the windows open in the house, there's a cross breeze. I lie across my bed and stare at the ceiling and try to calm down.

I'm not about to let Ryan Cummins hijack my life. He screwed up, and I feel bad for him. But that has nothing to do with me.

I force my mind back to Luke. I look out the window and smile to myself. I cannot believe I'm thinking about dating a high school kid, a junior at that. But I can see myself with him. I take a sip of beer and imagine him sitting in the stands when I perform with the

BearKat band. I imagine me sitting in the stands when he performs. I imagine meeting him after a game, sitting in the truck outside of Sonic, eating chicken tenders dipped in gravy.

But what about Nate Schaper? Where does he fit in? And Luke's dad? Would he make things difficult?

These are the things I want to ask him tonight. Maybe we'll take a long walk after dinner and really get to know each other.

I take another sip of beer and allow my mind to conjure up images of how that might end.

Luke doesn't come for dinner. I try not to let my disappointment show, but I can't help an occasional glance at the cul-de-sac. On the driveway next door to his, a group of neighbors have gathered around a smoking grill. It's that way up and down the street, carnivorous feasts, a by-product of all that meat thawing in freezers. I can't tell for sure if Luke is among them. I keep watching for him to break from the crowd and head up the street, but he doesn't.

"So, what *did* you say to piss him off?" Corrine asks.

"I didn't piss him off."

"You didn't piss off who?" Dad asks. "Luke?"

Corrine flicks her eyebrows and Dad suddenly gets it. "Ah. I like him, Curt. You should invite him down for dinner soon."

"Maybe I will." In fact, I did, and he stood me up.

I offer the last box of Cracker Jacks to Dad, but he declines.

When it gets dark, Dad calls it a day. I grab a couple more beers and, at the last second, the Cracker Jacks, and Corrine and I head up the street to visit some old friends.

At the corner, a group has gathered on the Bernards' driveway. Corrine and I join them. I'm sure a few of the adults note the bottles in my hand. Ms. Wettersten for sure, who in her syrupy and slightly disapproving voice asks if I'm twenty-one already.

Corrine moves through the crowd, but I join a group of kids in a corner of the driveway. Most of them, like me, will be heading off to college again in the next week. They trade stories about all our teenage drama—getting busted with pot or porn, wrecking our parents' cars, throwing parties that got out of hand.

"Hey, Curtis," Will Spears says. "Remember that time we started that fire with that magnifying glass?"

I force a laugh and shake some popcorn into my mouth.

"What happened?" Thomas Weingold asks. Thomas—Tommy—is a junior like Luke. I wonder if they'll have any classes together, if they'll buddy up eventually for some neighborhood mischief.

"We charred an entire section of our fence before my mom could put out the fire with the water hose." Will laughs. "I thought she was going to kill us both."

We were ten. Not much younger than Matt.

Maybe I misjudged Luke's interest. He had an invitation. He even had my phone number. But he just didn't show. And then, without warning, Ryan's words hit me again: *I knew what they were saying about you.*

"You're here!" I hear Corrine squeal.

I look up and see Luke, and panic grips me.

Chapter 9

LUKE

Corrine grabs my hand. "Curtis said you were coming for dinner. We missed you."

"Sorry. Family stuff," I mumble.

The truth is, I couldn't bring myself to go. Seeing Nate again hit me hard. I think I always knew in the back of my mind that he and Adam would patch things up, but I guess I still held out hope that one day it would be us again.

Who was I kidding? He was glad to see me go. He cared about me, he worried about me, but he was glad to see me go. I was a complication. I pushed him to be with me that last time; he didn't want to. It was a token, a consolation prize, a way to once and for all end our relationship, and it almost cost him Adam. I think it's pretty clear now they got past that.

I find Curtis. He's stretched out on a lounge chair in a circle of kids, most of them older, a few younger. Our eyes meet for a moment, then he turns back to the conversation, even though it's pretty obvious he's not participating.

There's another guy. How else do you explain that phone call, his reaction, the way he stumbled, the clenched fist, the look on his face when he glanced back at me with the phone gripped in his hand? And now this less-than-enthusiastic reception.

I should have stayed home. I almost did, but the urge to see him was greater than my need to protect myself from another rejection. I'd leave now, but Corrine is already steering me toward that group.

She introduces me around. There are no chairs left, and I stand awkwardly until Curtis pulls his feet in. I sit on the edge of the lounge chair, as the other kids return to their stories.

"I was just about to polish off your Cracker Jacks," he says, passing the box to me. There's a hint of something in his voice, and I can't help thinking he's mad at me. For what? For showing up? For not showing up? For his other boyfriend troubles?

I tip the box up and shake what's left of the popcorn into my mouth, then retrieve the candy-cane-striped surprise packet from the bottom. I fold the edge along the perforation, back and forth, and then carefully tear it from the packet. It's some kind of historical "Who am I" guessing game. I remove the center page and follow the directions, folding it first one way and then the other so that the picture of the young man transforms into an older George Washington and then an even older George Washington again.

I look up to find Curtis watching me. He holds my eyes until I hand him the game. When he reaches for it, I pull it back. "Are you mad at me?"

He scoffs and glances over at his friends, but they're laughing about something and completely oblivious to us. He snatches the game from me and plays with it for a long while. Young, old, young, older. It's a stupid game, and I'm wondering at his fixation with it when he abruptly pushes himself up and gets unsteadily to his feet.

"I'm going home." He grabs a beer bottle from the driveway next to him. A second, empty bottle falls over and rolls under the chair.

"I'll go with you."

The others wave us off, but Corrine catches my eye and mouths, "What's going on?"

I shrug.

Curtis moves with long, quick strides, and I have to jog a little to catch up, but once he's out of the light and in the darkness of the street he slows down and walks with one hand shoved deep in his pocket. He tips the bottle back and takes a long drink.

"You drink," I say.

"No, I don't," he responds. "I'm drinking, yes. But I definitely don't drink. Drinking. Drink. There's a difference."

I don't see the difference. "Look, I'm sorry about dinner. I didn't feel much like eating. And my parents—"

"I'm not mad at you," he says, cutting me off. Then he laughs, loudly, as if his being mad at me is the funniest thing he's ever heard, and then he throws his arms out and spins around in the street. "I'm not fucking mad at you!"

I stop and watch him. After a few unsteady spins he slings an arm around my neck, throwing me off balance, and takes another pull on the bottle. He laughs again, a maniacal, crazy kind of laugh. "How can anybody be mad at you, Lukey? I've been fielding questions about you for the last hour."

That's a lie. I barely registered on anyone's radar at the party.

He leans into me and we both stumble a little. I grab him around the waist to steady us both, but he flinches and takes his arm back. And suddenly the laughter drains out of him. The bottle slips from his hand and clanks to the concrete. I pick it up.

It's hard to make out his face in the dark, but I can hear his breathing, ragged, heavy. "What's wrong?" I ask him.

There's a long pause, and then, "Can I kiss you?"

Is that what this is all about? He's been wanting to kiss me? Did he think I'd say no?

I step close to him, so close our mouths are almost touching. "I'd like that."

He threads his fingers through my hair, lets them trail down over my cheek and across my mouth, then folds them into a fist. I kiss his knuckles, but he doesn't kiss me.

"I have to go," he says quietly.

"Don't go. Please. Whatever it is, maybe I can help."

"I'm just tired, Luke." He turns and stumbles, then gets his footing and disappears into the dark.

* * *

I sleep in the tent with Matt and Samuel. The moon is high in the sky now, and with the flap tied back, I can make out Curtis's house through the netting. I fall asleep wondering what happened, and hoping that whatever it was, it happens again.

Chapter 10

CURTIS

I feel my way along the wall to the staircase, then make the climb to the second floor. I can hardly breathe. I couldn't kiss him. I wanted to, but then all I could think was, what if Ryan was right? The questions cycle through my brain like cards in the spokes of a fast-moving bicycle wheel.

If I were sick, I would know it, wouldn't I?

Am I?

Did I give it to him?

Did he give it to me?

If it's true, wouldn't there have been more phone calls?

Was I careful enough?

Sober enough to know?

I'm still awake, wrestling with questions that have no answers, when the light in the bathroom suddenly comes on. I check the time on my phone. Three twenty AM. I get up, close the windows, and turn on the air conditioner so the house will cool down for Dad and Corrine.

Outside I stretch out on the bed of my truck and stare up at the stars and try to remember everything I know about HIV. Dad used to tell us knowledge is power, but my thoughts are such a jumble I can't fix on anything. And there's so much I don't know, so much I never dreamed I'd need to know because I'm not that guy. I don't care what Ryan thinks he heard.

Frustrated, I get up and walk. The sidewalk that stretches from our neighborhood to the lake is still strewn with debris, and in the dark I stumble. My heart thuds in my chest, and I force myself to breathe deeply to calm my nerves.

Sick people feel sick, I tell myself. And I don't feel sick. I feel strong, healthy.

The moon emerges from the clouds and reflects off the swollen lake. I walk to the shore and gaze across its quiet, smooth surface, then close my eyes and let the calm seep into me.

I've never had an HIV test. Just the thought of it scares the hell out of me. Ryan's wrong. It wasn't me. It's not me. It can't be me. But if getting an HIV test is what it takes to put this behind me, then I'll get one. And I will never, *never* put myself in this position again.

And then . . . I'm going to kiss Luke Chesser.

The walk has been good for me. I'm feeling better, more hopeful when I finally make my way back to the neighborhood. I walk to the cul-de-sac and sit on the curb in front of the cluster mailboxes across from his front yard. "I *am* going to kiss you, Luke Chesser," I say softly. The thought makes me smile. In fact, I plan on kissing him a lot. And he never has to know about this scare.

No one has to know.

It's almost dawn when I get home. Corrine is in the kitchen, starting a pot of coffee. She starts when I come in the door. "I thought you were still in bed. Where've you been?"

"Just walking." I grab a cup out of the cabinet and prop myself on the counter in front of the dripping coffeemaker.

"Ah. Walking, huh?"

"Yes. Walking. Alone."

"Oh, damn. I thought maybe you and Luke were playing kissy face under the stars somewhere."

I wish we had been. "Nope. Just walking . . . all by my lonesome." I look over my shoulder and grin back at her. "I think he likes me."

"Eh."

I wad up a paper towel and throw it at her.

"When did the power come back on?" she asks.

"Around three, I think."

"Have you been up all night?"

I shrug.

She digs through the cooler for an open can of evaporated milk, pours some into each of our cups, then props herself in front of the coffeemaker next to me. "Thank God for electricity." She pouts. "So does this mean you're going to move into your dorm today?"

"What's today?"

"Saturday."

"You're kidding." I've completely lost track of the days. The residence halls open at ten. I haven't even packed. "Wow. That depends. You want to help me with laundry?"

Unlike my twin, I don't own tons of clothes. We get it all done in two loads, with a third for clean towels. By one I'm packed up and ready to go.

"You want me to follow you and help you get settled?" Dad asks.

"Nah. I'm good." I look down the street at Luke's house. I've thought about walking down to say good-bye, but I don't want to risk his dad answering the door. I don't want to make things worse for Luke. I'll call him. And at Wednesday practice, I'll see him again. Everything's going to be okay, I tell myself. Amazing even.

When I look back at Dad, he's scratching his head with an amused look on his face.

Chapter 11

CURTIS

The drive to Huntsville takes about forty-five minutes. Traffic is light, but the parking lot I'm assigned to is already half-full when I pull in. I shoulder my duffel bag, collect my keys, and get about the business of settling in.

"How's the room?" Dad asks when I call.

"Small and moldy smelling."

He laughs. "Good thing you don't have allergies. Crank that window unit up high. It'll help."

I'm way ahead of him on that. The dorm is the oldest on campus. I chose it for two reasons—it's close to the band hall and it's cheap. I still feel guilty about wasting my dad's money on my less-than-stellar performance in Austin.

"Is your roommate there yet?"

"Not yet."

We talk for a few more minutes as I empty the duffel bag onto my bed and find a few drawers to stuff everything in. When I hang up, I haul the rest of my things in, including a small refrigerator. I plug it in and stock it with some bottles of water and soda carefully arranged so that the Heineken bottles in back are more or less hidden.

I did a lot of drinking at UT. Fake IDs were easy to come by, and clubbing on the weekends and drinking was just part of what we did.

I'm done with that scene, and all that came with it, but I still like to have one or two beers on hand for when I want to kick back and relax.

I plug in a lamp, put away my toothbrush and razor and shaving cream, and I'm done.

I'm thinking about walking down to the band hall, maybe practicing a bit, when Luke calls. I lie back on my bed. I wonder if he can hear the smile in my voice when I say, "Hey, Luke."

"Power's back on."

"I know. I was up when it came back on at three this morning."

"Three? Really? Why were you awake?"

"The light came on in my bathroom and woke me. How was the tent?"

"Crowded. Stuffy."

"I bet."

There's a pause, then he says, "About last night . . ."

He hesitates, and so do I. I feel like the emergency brake is on, and I don't dare release it until I'm off this steep hill. Don't get his hopes up; don't get mine up. Not yet. Soon, but not yet.

I clear my throat. "Um, did I act badly? If I did, I apologize. Too much work, too much heat, too much beer. I don't even remember climbing into bed last night. Please don't hold anything I said against me."

I silently will him to know that I meant it when I asked if I could kiss him. I want him to hold on to that a little while longer until I *can* kiss him. Until I *do* kiss him.

"No. I just wanted to make sure you're okay."

I bask in that. "I'm good. I'm up in Huntsville. I got here about an hour ago."

"Oh."

He's disappointed. I like that. "I wanted to stop by and say good-bye before I left, but, well . . . Anyway, I'll be there for band practice on Wednesday."

He's quiet, and I imagine this is good news for him. He *better* be smiling on the other end.

We talk about band, about school starting for him on Monday and for me on Wednesday, and when I reluctantly let him go a while later, all thought of going to the band hall is gone. All I want to do is lie on my bed and think about him.

I stare at his name in my contacts for a long time. Outside my room, there's conversation and laughter as others move in and get acquainted or perhaps reacquainted. In the back of my mind, I know I have to get tested before I can really move forward with Luke, before I can really explore if there's something real going on between us.

And I will.

But right now, I just want to enjoy a mental rerun of the past few days—the way he tromped through the water barefoot when that dog played him; the way he shrank back when I handed him the chain saw; the way his cheeks flamed when Matt told me how old he is; the way he stepped in close to me when I asked if I could kiss him.

I hear a key in the door. I start and squint into the bright sunlight coming through the blinds as I try to orient myself. A skinny black guy with a buzz cut and an armful of clothes on hangers backs through the door. He turns and pushes it closed with his foot, then takes in the room.

"Great," he mutters as he kicks aside a beer bottle. It rolls into the other one with a clank.

"Sorry." I collect the bottles and drop them in the trash.

He glances at me, then opens the closet door and begins hooking the hangers on the rod.

"I don't usually drink."

"Whatever," he says.

When he heads back to his car, I straighten my bed, then take the bottles out to the dumpster. *Great first impression, Curtis.*

When my roommate enters again, he's got a floor lamp in one hand, a music stand in the other, and a padded tuba case as big as he is strapped to his back. I thank the gods for one small favor.

"Here, let me help you," I offer, taking the lamp and stand from him. I set them up next to his desk. He mumbles a thanks as he un-

straps the case, then places it on the floor next to his bed. I extend
my hand. "I'm Curtis Cameron. Clarinet."

"You're not going to be a slob, are you?"

"No. I swear. What's your name?"

He hesitates, then shakes my hand. "Jaleel Smith."

"Jaleel? J-A-L . . .

"E-E-L. You want me to write it in chalk for you on the wall?"

"No. That's okay. Freshman?"

He eyes me with irritation. "Senior."

"Sorry." I chide myself for making that assumption. I am not
making a good first impression.

"First year?" he asks, positioning his lamp.

"Yeah. I transferred from UT. Sophomore."

He squats next to his desk and threads the cord behind the back
legs. "Any good?" he asks, inserting the prongs into the outlet.

All-state clarinet two years in a row. "Pretty good, I think."

"Music major?"

"Yeah."

"Marching band?"

"Absolutely."

He stops what he's doing and eyes me again. "You know how
you know when a clarinet player is at your house?"

Like I haven't heard this one a million times.

"He doesn't know where to enter or what key to use. We've got
more clarinets than we know what to do with. Can you play a trombone?"

"Um, I had a couple of weeks on it last year."

"We need a trombone. Borrow an instrument and start practicing. And don't leave your shit lying around. I can't stand living in a
pigsty, and I'm not cleaning up after you."

I think I'm going to like Jaleel.

Luke calls me again that evening.

"So, you nervous about your first day at a new school?" I ask
him.

"A little," he admits. "I've got Jackson and Spencer in a few
classes."

Oh boy. Those two are trouble, but in a good way, I guess. I'm glad he's got friends he can connect with during the day.

"Can I ask you a question?" he says.

"Shoot."

"Is there another guy?"

Another guy? Besides him? The question takes me by surprise, but it makes me smile too. "Why would you ask that?"

"That phone call."

"What—" Oh, hell. Ryan. He saw that. Is that why he didn't come for spaghetti last night? Jaleel is sitting at his desk, polishing the bell of his tuba. "Hold on."

I let myself out of the room. There's still a lot of activity around the dorm, so I head up toward the fountain in the center of the campus where it's quieter, where I can talk without worrying about who's listening.

"No other guy, Luke. That was just someone I marched with in the Longhorn band." But since he brought it up . . . "Can I ask you a question? How do you know Nate Schaper?"

There's a hesitation. "How do *you* know Nate?"

"I don't. I just know who he is from all the news reports. But I got the impression in H-E-B you *do* know him. You want to tell me about it?"

He doesn't. I hear it again in his second hesitation. "I dated him. For a little while. But that's all over now."

I'm not so sure about that. "When was the last time you talked to him?"

"December twenty-fourth, last year."

The fact that he knows the exact date irks me. "Who broke up with who?"

"I really don't want to talk about that."

I bet you don't. I'm surprised at my own reaction. But the last thing I need is to get involved in a rebound relationship, or to be a salve for someone else's broken heart. I'm not interested in playing games either. I had my fill of that in Austin.

We turn to safe subjects—band, school—but the budding intimacy in our conversation is gone.

* * *

Classes start on Wednesday, so I have a few days to learn my way around, collect my schedule, buy textbooks. The band hall is open on Sunday this weekend so all the returning band members can check in. Mr. Martinez, the band director, is happy to have me march a trombone. He loans me one, then spends half an hour with me in a practice room reviewing slide positions and practicing scales. I work for another couple of hours on basic tunes the band plays—"The Star Spangled Banner," "The Horse," the fight song.

I have a new appreciation for brass players, trombone players in particular. My lips feel numb and swollen, and my arms tremble every time I lift the instrument now.

Mr. Martinez sticks his head back in the practice room. "How's it going?"

"It's good. A little slow, but I'm getting there."

"Well, don't kill yourself. As long as you look like you're playing, that's good enough for me."

But it isn't good enough for me. If I'm going to march with a trombone, I'm damn well going to play it, too.

Monday, Jaleel and I walk across campus for lunch at Schlotsky's. Our path takes us past the university health center. I note the hours and consider stopping by on our way back and making an appointment—or maybe they can test me right on the spot—but I have other things on my plate right now. The test is a formality anyway, peace of mind. It can wait a few more days.

After lunch, we head to the band hall. Our first marching practice is this afternoon. We're on a Monday, Tuesday, Thursday schedule, with games on either Fridays or Saturdays. The rehearsals aren't nearly as grueling as those in a high school band. High school bands are about competition; college bands are about entertainment.

On Wednesday I make my first three classes at eight, nine, and ten, meet my professors, collect my syllabi, then I spend some time practicing in the band hall before I head out. I want to have enough time to stop by the house, say hi to Corrine and to Dad if he's home early, pick up some things I left behind.

I'm excited about seeing Luke, but I have to admit, my enthusiasm has been slightly tamped down by one Nate Schaper. I still can't get over the way Luke looked at him in H-E-B. I admit, I want him to look at me that way.

Oh, hell. He does look at me that way. *Let it go, Curtis.*

"Quit hogging the practice room, clarinet," Jaleel says to me through a crack in the door.

"Hey, Jaleel. Listen to this." I play the fight song for him. He winces, then screws up his face like something smells bad.

"Man, that sounds like shit."

"I think it sounds pretty good for only four days of practice."

"I think you better start putting in longer days."

I laugh. Any more practice and my lips will explode. "Hey, I'm getting ready to head out. You've got the room to yourself until about eight."

"Aw. You cut me, Cameron. I ain't no slam-bam willy. This boy needs time to love the ladies."

Yeah, right. Although, I have to admit, he does seem to have quite a fan club among the band girls.

Things are working out pretty well with Jaleel. He's neat, low profile, funny, and not nearly the jerk he tried to make himself out to be that first day. That's a good thing, because the dorm room is cramped. There's one built-in desk with two drawers separating the knee holes. Jaleel likes to work at the desk; it's too close quarters for me, so I work on my bed. I'd be regretting going cheap if it weren't for him.

I get home around one, do a little laundry, take a brief nap in my own bed, chat some with Corrine.

"Sooo . . . are you excited about seeing him today?" she asks.

I shrug like it's no big deal.

She grins at me across the bar. "You're so full of it."

The field techs meet with Mr. Gorman in his office at three to go over the performance and what we're working on today. The loss of those three days of band camp to the hurricane has put them behind schedule, but Mr. Gorman is confident that if we push the kids, they'll catch up.

Through the window that looks out over the band hall, I see Luke assembling his clarinet. He's got a cheese stick stuck in his mouth like a cigar. He's cute in his Nike athletic shorts and section T-shirt. I'm surprised to see him wearing the shirt, but proud that he's embraced the good-natured ribbing he's been getting. I can't wait to see him in his full uniform Friday night. We don't have our own first game for another week. It may be a while before I can watch him perform again.

"Curtis, you've got all the woodwinds today," Mr. Gorman says.

"No problem."

"All right, let's get to it."

I want to walk out to the parking lot with Luke, but Adeeb snags me as soon as I leave the office. "Hey, college boy. What's this I hear about you playing a trombone this year?"

I catch Luke's eye and give him a smile. "You heard right."

"Just don't go turning all macho brass on us, okay?"

"It'll never happen."

It's a good rehearsal, all things considered. Afterward, Adeeb calls the clarinets in for a brief meeting in the band hall. I lean against the instrument lockers. Luke smiles here and there, and I know he knows where my eyes and my thoughts are focused.

"Any questions about the game this weekend?"

As always, the freshmen have a lot of questions . . . about where to be, when to be there, what to wear, game-day meals. As a new student, I'm sure Luke has plenty of questions of his own. I plan to personally answer them in private.

"Got your cell phones?" Adeeb says. "I'm going to give you my number. I expect you to text if you have any questions. I don't want any screwups on game day. Got it?" He rattles off his number a few times for the new kids.

"Hey, Curtis," Jackson says. "Can we have your number too? Just in case?"

I see him nudge Luke, who assumes a bored, disinterested expression.

Luke's already got my number, Jackson.

Damn, the world is rife with matchmakers.

He has to get home for dinner, and I have to get back up to school, but at least I get to walk with him out to the parking lot.

"Can we get together this weekend?" he asks.

"Hmm. Let me think on that?"

He looks at me like, *Really? You have to think about it?*

I laugh. But there's something we need to discuss before we take this next step. "Listen, um, can we keep this just between us for now?"

The smile slides from his face. "Why?"

Because I don't know how this is going to turn out. "It's kind of a conflict of interest. I don't want to appear to be playing favorites or anything. Just for a little while, okay?"

"Sure. Whatever."

Whatever? Damn, he's prickly. I glance around to make sure no one's in hearing range. "How about after the game Friday night? I'll buy you a burger at Sonic."

"Sonic, huh? You overestimate your powers of invisibility. That place is crawling with band kids after the game."

"You can tell everybody that you're trying out for drum major in the spring, and I'm helping you."

"But I'm not trying out for drum major."

Some girls skirt past us. "Bye, Luke. Love the shirt!" He smiles and waves them off.

"Maybe you should," I tell him. "I could be your personal coach."

"Tempting, but I'd be laughed out of the band hall."

He has no idea how appealing he is, how regal he looks on that field. "You underestimate your powers of improvement. Come on. You should really think about it. You've got all the raw material."

"Yeah, right."

We're standing at his car now. Luke digs the toe of his athletic shoe into the concrete. It's an awkward moment; neither of us knows yet how to say good-bye.

"You know, the answer is still yes," he says.

"The answer to...?"—*Can I kiss you?*—"Oh." My face reddens. I glance around again. A group of band moms are cackling over something a few feet away. Two spaces down some kids are directing a euphonium player, clearly a new driver, in backing his parents' Suburban out of the tight parking space.

I turn back to Luke and shrug my apology. "Let's save it for Sonic, okay?"

Chapter 12

CURTIS

"All right. Let's go. Let's go." It feels good, right, to be standing in the aisle Friday night and slapping hands with the kids as they file out for their first halftime performance. I favor Luke with a wink as he passes by me (which earns me an air kiss), but beyond that, I am a model of band-tech decorum.

When the stands are empty, a couple of the other techs and I follow Mr. Gorman to a spot below the press box. When the buzzer sounds, the players rush off the field and the kids take their places to a drum tap. They stand frozen as the announcer introduces them.

"Come on, Luke. Don't screw this up," Mr. Gorman mutters.

I scan the front line, but before I can locate him a sudden urge to cough sets me hacking into my shoulder.

"Catching a cold?"

"Nope. My throat's a little scratchy. Too much trombone." I hold my breath as the drum majors count out the beat. And then in one beautiful, synchronized move, every woodwind tilts his or her head to the right.

"Yes!" Mr. Gorman says.

*   *   *

"Did you see that?" Luke's face is bright as he vaults into my truck after the game. He rode over on the bus, but he's leaving with me.

I laugh. "I saw. Nicely done."

"Did we look good?"

"I'd say you looked damn good."

My neck is stiff. I roll my head as he unzips his jacket and tosses it onto the bench seat in the back. Then his shoes. Then his over-alls—bibs they call them. Then his T-shirt. The truck is illuminated by the sodium vapor lights towering over the stadium parking lot. When he's down to his regulation black compression underwear, size snug, he retrieves a pair of cargo shorts, an American Eagle T-shirt, and flip-flops from his duffel bag and pulls them on.

"All right, I'm ready."

Damn. So am I now.

I park the truck in the farthest space at Sonic, facing a wooded area that runs along one side of the parking lot. It's not too busy yet, since a lot of the kids are riding the bus back to the band hall first for their cars. Instead of burgers, we order chicken tenders with gravy.

"Was that your mom I saw sitting with your dad?" I ask, opening my box. The smell of chicken and french fries and grease is mildly nauseating.

"The one with the camera surgically attached to her eyeball?"

"That's the one."

He smiles. "She hates football, but she never misses one of my home game performances."

"Your dad was there too. That's good, huh?"

He dunks a chicken tender in his gravy. "Mom makes him go. In case you didn't notice, he spent the entire game on his BlackBerry. Can we not talk about my dad?"

"What do you want to talk about?" Stupid question. I'm off my game here. In truth, I feel a little spacey. I cough. Great. I'm getting my first back-to-school cold and I've been in class three days.

"You're getting a cold," Luke says.

"It would appear so."

"I got swine flu last December. A little cold doesn't scare me."

I chuckle, but everything about this feels wrong to me. And I don't know why. Luke takes a few more bites, then gathers up the trash off the seat and stuffs it back into the bag and sets it aside on the floor. The entire cab smells of fast food, and I'm regretting making this our first date. It should have been something more organic, something more romantic.

He scoots across the seat until he's right next to me and smiles shyly. "Ask me again," he says quietly.

I smile back, but then another cough forces me to turn away.

"If you're trying to get out of kissing me, it's not going to work."

I gaze into his blue eyes, amused. Trying to get out of kissing him? Not a chance. And then he says, "I've got a strong immune system," and my skin goes cold. The smile slides from my face.

"Did I say something wrong?"

I force myself to smile an assurance, but it comes off pretty half-assed. "No. I think you're right, though. I've picked up a cold and I'm not feeling so great right now. Would you mind if I dropped you off at your car and went home?"

"Sure." He slides back over to his side of the cab and buckles his seat belt. He stares out the side window as we make the drive back to the band hall.

Chapter 13

CURTIS

"Oh my God, Curtis. Dad! *Dad!*"

My eyes flutter, but the effort needed to open them seems too great. I shiver and roll my head. The pillow feels tacky beneath my cheek.

"Curt, you okay, buddy?"

"He threw up in the bed."

A wet washcloth on my face, a thermometer between my dry lips. Someone holds my head and the pillow slides away. Another slides in its place. The thermometer beeps and I shiver again. "One-oh-five. Jesus Christ, Curtis."

"Corrine, get him some Tylenol."

I feel Dad sit next to me on the bed, his hand on my neck, my forehead. "That's some fever." He presses two pills into my mouth, then lifts my shoulders and holds a glass of water to my lips. "Come on," he coaxes me. "You need to swallow these. We've got to get the fever down."

I struggle to prop myself on one elbow, then take the glass from him and sip. The water tastes alkaline, sweet, not right. I swish it around in my mouth and swallow. Another sip. Another.

"Take it easy." He takes the glass from me. "You need the fluids, but let's get it into you a little at a time."

I drop back to the mattress. There are more wet rags, cold ones. I shiver again and grasp about for the quilt before I realize it's already tucked around me.

"Do we need to take him to the emergency room?" Corrine asks.

"No," I murmur. "No emergency room. It's just a cold."

"That's a damn high fever for a cold, Curt. I think you may have the flu."

"I had a flu shot."

"Well, we'll give it an hour. But if that fever doesn't come down, we're taking you to the ER."

No ER. I close my eyes and give in to the fog.

"You awake?"

I open my eyes to see Corrine hanging on to my bedroom door. My back hurts. In fact, everything hurts. My voice sounds rusty when I speak. "How long was I asleep?"

"Hmm, maybe a couple of hours. You look much better."

I feel like hell. I notice that my sheets are clean, but I have no memory of being rolled around so they could be changed. My mouth, ugh. I push myself up against the headboard. A hard shiver rattles me as I reach for the water bottle next to the bed.

"You up for some company?"

"Do I look like I'm up for company?"

She mouths a *Sorry* at me as Luke steps through the door behind her. "I'll, uh, let you two chat."

Luke watches her go, then turns back to me. "You really were sick," he says.

I smile weakly and take a shaky sip. "Yeah, and it's kicking my ass."

He looks relieved, maybe a little embarrassed, which is completely unnecessary. I probably would have reacted the same way. "I'm sorry about last night," I offer.

"It's okay. I'm sorry about the way I reacted. I thought . . ."

"You don't have to explain." I stick the thermometer in my mouth, then pull the quilt up around my shoulders. I'm definitely sick, but I don't feel the panic I felt last night. It's just a cold. I've had dozens of them during my lifetime. The thermometer beeps. "One-oh-one point five."

"You still have a fever."

"That I do, but nothing like it was this morning."

"Can I do anything?"

"You can get out of here so I can take a shower. I'm sure I look like crap."

"No you don't."

What a sweet thing to say. He's still standing in my doorway looking fresh, rosy cheeked, and damn adorable. If he were closer, I'd reach out and take his hand. And then I realize I haven't even held his hand yet. I plan to correct that very soon. But no Sonic. The very thought makes my stomach turn over again.

"Can I have a rain check on last night?" I ask him. "But no fast food."

He grins impishly at me. I take that as a yes.

The fever and the body aches linger on into Sunday.

"I think you should stay home, at least until the fever breaks," Dad says.

"I'm fine, Dad. Really. I promise"—I cough into my hand a few times—"if the fever goes on more than a couple more days, I'll make an appointment at the university health center."

I'm sitting across from him at the dining room table in my boxers, a blanket thrown over my shoulder. Corrine hands me a bowl of chicken soup she made herself with all organic ingredients. I don't have much of an appetite, but I force myself to take a bite. It makes her happy, and it's the least I can do after she cleaned up my vomitus yesterday morning.

Dad sighs and props his chin on his fist. "You'll keep taking Tylenol on a schedule? I don't want that fever spiking again."

"I promise. Round the clock."

"I still think you should stay in bed a few more days."

I smile weakly at him. I appreciate him more than he knows, but he worries. And I'm fine. It won't be the first time I've masked a fever with Tylenol and gone to school anyway. No way I'm letting a fever keep me from a practice or a performance. And I'm not about to let it put me behind in my classes either. It's only the second week. If I miss classes this early on, I'll feel behind the beat all semester.

I drag myself through classes Monday and Tuesday. By Wednesday morning, there's no denying I'm run down. I'm achy, tired. The fever is in its fourth day, and I promised Dad.

I make an appointment at the health center for late morning. Maybe I can get a vitamin shot or at least some assurance that this fever has just about run its course.

The health center is located on the far side of campus from my dorm room, but it's a short walk from my ten o'clock class.

A heavyset woman with graying hair pinned in an old-fashioned bun calls me back and directs me to a treatment room. She smiles as she closes the door behind us and asks me to step on the scale. "We're seeing a lot of flu right now. Happens every fall." She notes my weight—162.

I step off the scale and take a seat on the treatment table as she pulls a cuff from the wall. My hands tremble. Doctors' offices always do that to me. Maybe that's natural, or maybe it's a throwback from my head injury when I was a kid.

"Just relax," the nurse says as she wraps the blood pressure cuff around my arm. She places a stethoscope on the inside of my elbow and pumps up the cuff. "You're warm. How long have you been running a fever?"

"About four days."

"One twenty-two over eighty-four," she says, releasing the air. "A little high, but understandable." She wraps up the cuff and places it back in the plastic holder on the wall, then takes my temperature. "Are you taking anything for the fever?"

"Tylenol."

"When did you last take it?"

"A couple of hours ago."

She notes everything on the computer, then pats my leg and tells me the doctor will be in shortly.

I check the time on my phone: 11:32. Luke is probably having lunch right now. I wonder who he's sitting with. Jackson? Spencer? Phoebe? I make a mental note to ask him.

And then I try to picture our second first date. I wonder if he dances. I imagine holding him close in some dance hall, whispering in his ear, nuzzling his ear, kissing his ear. Breathing in the great peppermint smell that always wafts from his skin.

Soon, Luke.

I scan the pamphlets tucked in an acrylic display case hanging on the wall—*Alcohol and Substance Abuse, Depression and Suicide, Eating Disorders, Stress, Prescription Medication, STDs. . . .* I look at my phone again and think about texting Dad to let him know I'm okay.

A firm, quick knock on the door. "Curtis," the doctor says, stepping in. He reaches for my hand. "I'm Dr. Nguyen. So I understand you've been running a fever," he says, checking the nurse's notes. "Let's have a look."

He feels the glands around my neck, then checks my throat, my eyes, my ears. "Cameron. Hmm. I went to UT with a Cameron. Derrick. We called him DC. Any relation?"

"That's my dad."

"No kidding? Small world, huh? How's he doing? I haven't seen him in years. Is he designing skyscrapers?"

"Mostly bridges and roads."

"Yeah? And what about your mom? How's she doing?"

"She died when I was a baby."

He studies my face. "I'm sorry. I didn't know." He presses a stethoscope to my back and chest. "Chills? Body aches?"

I nod.

"Well, I'd say you've got the flu. Your chest sounds a little rattley, so I'm going to go ahead and start you on some antibiotics just in case you're working on a secondary infection here—we've been seeing some cases of pneumonia already—but I suspect this flu's about run its course. You should be feeling much better in a few days in any case."

"No blood test?" I ask.

He scoots his stool over to the computer. "Any reason why you think you need one?" He taps out some notes on the keyboard.

I take a deep breath to steady myself. "I thought maybe you could test for HIV while I'm here. It's just, I've never had one, and I thought it would be a good idea."

"Sure. No problem. We generally do that with a mouth swab though. We can have results in about twenty minutes."

"Okay. Great."

"I wish all our students would get tested. It should be part of everyone's routine health screening." He stands and reaches for my hand again. "Let me get the nurse back in here. Be sure and tell your dad hello for me."

"I will."

He's not planning to come back in again. I take that as a good sign. Routine test. Routine results.

I hadn't actually considered asking for an HIV test until I did. But I'm relieved to get this out of the way. Twenty minutes. I expected to have to wait weeks. I breathe a little easier knowing that in twenty minutes, I can take off that emergency brake and move on with my life. Because I've got some making up to do to a cute blond high school kid next weekend.

"All right," the nurse says, coming through the door with a small package from which she removes a plastic stick with a pad on one end. "This will only take a second."

I open my mouth so she can swab my outer gums on top and on bottom.

"That's it." She drops the swab in a vial with some liquid and gives me a reassuring smile. "Can I bring you some magazines to read while you wait?"

"No, I'm fine. Thanks."

I check the time again: 11:50. If I text now, I might catch him before he heads back to class. Still running a fever, but antibiotics ordered. I intend to collect on that rain check soon. I miss you.

I stare at that last sentence for a moment. It's funny . . . telling him I miss him seems like more of a declaration than a kiss or a rain check. But I know he'll like that. And it's true. I'm smiling to myself when I press Send.

In a moment, he texts back. Spencer just asked what I'm smiling about. ☺ I miss you too. After game Friday?

Can't. Have my own game. Drum major coaching on Saturday?

Drum major coaching—riiight. Ha ha. I appear to have some deficits. Be prepared for some intense one-on-one instruction.

One-on-one instruction, huh? The flirt.

I'm still sitting on the treatment table, smiling down at the screen, when there's a knock, and Dr. Nguyen steps back into the room. Despite the fever, my skin goes cold. He takes the stool and swivels to face me, then clasps his hands in his lap and studies them for a moment.

My eyes blur. *Please. No. Tell me I've got pneumonia. Tell me I've got herpes. Anything. Just—just not this.*

He lifts his eyes to mine. "The HIV test came back positive, Curtis."

I feel all the breath go out of me, like my lungs have suddenly collapsed. I note that my shoelaces are getting dirty. I need to throw them in the wash next weekend when I get home.

"We're going to do a follow-up test, a blood test this time. It'll take about two weeks to—"

"So it's not for certain then."

"The oral swab is more than ninety-nine percent accurate, Curtis. We'll do a follow-up test to confirm, but the odds that the results are wrong are very, very slim."

"But there's a chance."

"Curtis, look, this is hard, I know. But I want you to focus on what you can do."

More than 99 percent is not 100 percent. That means the test gets it wrong sometimes.

Dr. Nguyen grips my shoulder. "You're young, you're strong. You can fight this. HIV is not the death sentence it once was. There are drugs, very effective drugs, to manage this disease. You've got a long life ahead of you, Curtis."

"But you still don't know for absolutely certain."

He studies me, takes in a deep breath, and lets it out. "For your safety and the safety of others, I think we need to assume you've contracted the virus."

"Is that why I'm sick now?" My voice sounds angry, combative.

He releases my shoulder. "You have the flu, Curtis. That's all. It *could* be your immune system is compromised and making it harder for your body to fight it off, or it could be the flu virus is just running its course. I'm sure you're going to be feeling better in a few days."

There's hope; I cling to it.

"We're going to know one way or the other in a few weeks. Until then, you need to take some precautions. You can infect someone else if you engage in risky behaviors."

I can't accept this. He's wrong. The test is wrong.

He pulls a pamphlet from the wall and hands it to me. *HIV: Facts and Information.* "The facts, some dos and don'ts. I want you to read this carefully." Then he pulls another pamphlet, the one titled *STDs: The Facts.* Maybe he wants to scare me into keeping my dick safely inside my pants. There's no need; I'm plenty scared enough.

"Listen. If you'd like to talk to someone, there's a great group—"

"No."

"It might help."

I shake my head and he sighs. "I'll give you a call when the results are in, and we'll take it from there. Okay? Talk to your dad. He'd want to know. You're going to need his support."

Why would I scare my dad to death over something that's not for certain?

Missed you at practice. Mr. G says you're still sick.

A little run down. But getting better.

So this weekend?

IDK, Luke. Let me see how I'm feeling.

I cough a few times into my elbow, then shake an antibiotic and a couple of Tylenol into my hand and swallow the pills with a swig of water.

"Why don't you take a couple of days off until you're over this thing?" Jaleel asks. "You've probably already infected half the brass section with all that hacking. You're playing like shit anyway."

"I'm fine," I snap.

"Well, I'm going to bed." Jaleel pulls his T-shirt over his head, wads it up, and tosses it into a canvas hamper. "You want me to leave the TV on?"

"No. I've got some research to do."

He flips off the TV and the lamp by his bed and slips under the sheet. I set my computer aside and turn the air conditioner to high, then settle back on my bed.

The article was published eight months ago. It's an analysis of several comparative studies of what they call the positive predictive value of the oral swab versus the traditional blood test for HIV. In other words, how many people who tested positive were correctly diagnosed? In high prevalence settings, that percentage tested at 98.65 accuracy for the oral test (about what Dr. Nguyen told me), and in low prevalence settings, 88.55. I don't know if I was in a high or low prevalence setting. Surely a college campus in Texas is low prevalence. That would mean that out of every one hundred people who were swabbed, eleven received a false positive.

Eleven.

Jaleel is curled up facing the wall. He stretches his legs out, then rolls onto his stomach. I wait to see if he's going to turn toward me. When he doesn't, I take the pamphlets from my philosophy book, where I tucked them as I was leaving the clinic.

I can't bring myself to look at the one on HIV. Instead, I open the one on STDs. Inside is a chart of diseases, the symptoms, how you get them, how you treat them, the outcome if not treated. I scan down the first column—herpes, genital warts, chlamydia, gonorrhea. It's like someone's given them the nastiest sounding names they can think of. The whole thing makes my flesh crawl.

Luke hasn't responded to my last text. I told him I'd be there Saturday, and then I took it back. I guess I can't really blame him for being miffed.

Thursday morning the fever breaks. I get up with a renewed sense that everything is going to be okay, that I am one of the 11 percent.

My first stop is Starbucks for a nice hot coffee; my second is the pet store. I've got a semester-long biology project I need to get

started on. I pick up two ten-gallon aquariums and a few other supplies. My third stop is a bait shop.

"What the hell are those?" Jaleel asks when I get back to the
room. He wrinkles his nose and peers into the bait bucket.

"Water dogs. Six of them."

"You know, the days of swallowing live goldfish are looong
gone. And ain't nobody gonna swallow one of these things."

I laugh a little. "They're not for any kind of initiation. Say hi to
our new roommates."

He lifts an eyebrow at me.

"I have to test a couple of theories on what triggers their meta-
morphosis to this." I scoop up the lone tiger salamander from a
small travel aquarium.

Jaleel looks at it a moment, then peers back at the water dogs.
"Show 'em a mirror. That ought to do it."

Good one.

There are different theories about what triggers the change
from water dog to salamander. One says iodine, another says low
water level. But the general consensus is they change when they
want to change. If I'm lucky, one or two will transform before the
semester ends.

"You look better," Jaleel says.

"I feel better."

In fact, I feel so good that I make it to my first game Friday
night, sleep in Saturday morning, then head home early afternoon
with my new roommates. I'm hoping the trip to and from won't
traumatize them. I could fake my daily notes on their appearance
for a few days—it's unlikely the water dogs will metamorphose anytime soon—but I love watching them, and I want to show them to
Luke.

I stop by Smoothie King near the freeway and pick up a Blue-
berry Heaven. I feel great. Not only is the fever gone, but the cough
as well. I am a little tired, though. I figure the extra calories, pro-
tein, and antioxidants will do me some good. When I get back in
the truck, I text Luke: Get your Nikes on. We're running.

You're coming home?

I'm coming home.

Nikes. Um, why?

Because you need more air?

Surrounded, you know. How about a movie instead?

How about we build up your lungs first? Drum majors have good lungs. Trust the maestro.

I thought that drum major thing was just a ruse.

☺

I listen to some Hedley on the drive back, sip at my smoothie, and think about Luke. One day we are going to make beautiful music together. I believe that. With my whole heart, I believe that.

Chapter 14

LUKE

I honestly thought he was kidding. I focus on matching my stride to his, but after three laps I'm lagging behind, winded, a sharp pain in my side.

He turns and jogs backwards. "Breathe. Not with your chest. Focus on inflating your belly with slow deep breaths."

"I'm"—*gasp*—"breathing. Geez. Remind me again"—*gasp*—"why I'm doing this?"

"Aw, quit whining." He laughs. But I notice he's struggling too. He slows his pace, and when I drop to a walk, he does too. "You are frustratingly adorable, but you're a long way from drum major."

"Adorable, huh?"

"Emphasis on frustrating."

I roll my eyes and Curtis grins back at me. "You need to play better," he says, "and that means more air, and that means increasing your lung capacity, and that means running and training your lungs to breathe properly."

I'd settle for catching my breath right now. "What do you want to see at the movies tonight?"

"I want to see you sitting next to me."

I can't help smiling at that. With him walking backwards, I

quickly close the distance between us. I use the collar of my shirt to wipe the sweat from my brow. "How about we forget about all this running and go make out in your truck?"

"Aw. That would be a dereliction of my duties."

"I won't tell."

"Your performance will." He grabs a fistful of my T-shirt and gives it a tug. "Come on, let's sprint this one."

Shit. I struggle to catch up with him, but he's already too far ahead, and I'm too out of breath. I veer off onto the field and collapse on the grass and close my eyes. I'll just wait here until he runs out of steam.

The sun is hot, but there's a nice breeze and I feel like I'm floating. And then I feel his shadow over me an instant before he nudges me in the ribs with the toe of his shoe.

"Come on, Goldilocks. Get up."

I squint up at him. "Can't we work on my salute or something?"

"Nope. That comes after you make drum major anyway. Come on. You have to be well-rounded. That means everything—your conducting, your marching, and your playing—have to be top notch. And that means you have to get in shape."

He holds out his hand. I want to grab it, yank him down on top of me, but I ignore it and close my eyes again. Maybe if I just lie here, he'll lie down beside me.

He bounces his toe against my side.

"Leave me alone."

"I don't want to leave you alone."

I squint up at him again. "Blow me."

"Tsk tsk. Now stop flirting with me and get up. We have work to do if we're going to turn you into a snappy drum major."

"You do know I'm only doing this to have an excuse to spend time with you."

"Then you better make it look good."

I reach for his hand and let him pull me to my feet. But when he tries to pull away, I hold on. He relaxes his hand and we lace our fingers together. I take his other hand too and step in close to kiss him.

"PDAs are so pedestrian," he says with a fake scowl.

"No they're not." I kiss him again. "Besides, look around you. Not much P here."

His mouth widens in a smile, and I take advantage of the moment to try to kiss him more deeply, but he sidesteps and tugs at the shoulder of my T-shirt. "Let's save it for tonight, okay? Come on. A few more laps and I'll let you off the hook for the day."

I plant my hands on my hips and stare at the laces in my shoes. "Why do you always pull away when I kiss you?" I look up again and his smile falters.

"I just want to take things slow, okay?"

"How slow is slow? Am I going to be middle-aged before I can stick my tongue in your mouth?"

His smile returns slowly, but his eyes dance with amusement. "Well, that's a lot of time to work with, isn't it? You want to stick your tongue in my mouth, then you're going to have to earn it. Come on. Let's go. And this time, focus on your breathing."

We're catching a late movie, so I'm stuck having dinner with the family. I wouldn't mind so much, but no one seems to be speaking this evening.

I eye Matt across the table. "What's going on?" I mouth.

He puts two fingers to his lips and mimes smoking.

Oh. That again. Mom's been trying to kick the habit for years. Actually, it's not much of a habit. She'll smoke a pack or two when she's stressed, and that'll be it for a long while. But Dad hates it. And he always acts like her smoking is a personal insult to him, like every time she sucks on a cigarette, she's blowing the devil himself. I've never actually seen Mom smoke, but I've smelled it on her.

I glance at Dad scowling into his mashed potatoes, then at Mom, who's forking a pea around her plate.

I check the clock on the microwave.

"You want to know why you should never shower with a Pokémon?" Matt asks. He grins at me, then looks around the table, but Mom and Dad keep their eyes on their plates.

So I ask, "Why?"

"Because he might try to Pikachu. Get it? Peek-at-you." Matt pretends to catapult a piece of lettuce at me with his fork.

"Dare you," I mouth, then clear my throat. Might as well get this over with. "I'm going to a movie with a friend tonight."

That gets Dad's attention. "With that girl? Karen?"

Really? "It's Corrine. And no. I'm going with her brother, Curtis."

Mom looks up at me with sudden interest, but Dad glares, his jaw twitching. "Is this some kind of date?" he growls.

I hesitate, then look at Mom for support. "Um. Maybe."

"Isn't he that young man you were cutting down trees with?" she asks.

Dad doesn't give me a chance to answer. "You're not going out with an older boy."

"I already told him I would."

"Well, now you can tell him you're not."

I glare back at him. Then I turn back to Mom. "He's one of the field techs. He's helping me get ready for drum major auditions."

"You're trying out for drum major?" she asks.

I shrug. "I think so."

"That's great. I'd like to meet him first, though."

Dad flings his napkin on the table. "He's not dating an older boy. Who knows what kind of diseases he'll catch."

Wrong thing to say. I can practically see the neurons of indignation fire in Mom's brain. "I don't think we can make those decisions for Luke anymore, John," she says tightly. "And we can talk about this later."

That shuts him down cold.

"Hey, I heard about this new Texas-style survivor show that's going to be on TV," Matt says suddenly. He glances around, but Mom and Dad are glaring at each other. "So, all the contestants have to start in Dallas, and then they have to drive all over Texas, to San Antonio, Houston, Lubbock, everywhere and then back to Dallas. But the deal is, they have to drive a pink Volvo with bumper stickers that read 'I love the Dixie Chicks,' 'Boycott Beef,' 'I Voted for Obama,' 'George Strait sucks,' 'I'm here to confiscate your guns,' and 'I'm gay.' If anybody makes it back to Dallas, he wins."

I snort tea out my nose.

"Go to your room," Dad barks at him.

"It was a joke," Mom snaps.

Matt gets up anyway and slinks off, but grins at me as he rounds the corner to the stairwell. I hear the front door open and close. Dad's fists clench on the table. "I'm fed up with the disrespectful behavior in this house."

Then move out.

A sudden, weary calm settles over Mom. "Luke, if you're done, would you go check on your brother?"

I don't have to be asked twice. I have a feeling Dad will wish he'd left the table, too, before long.

I find Matt sitting on the trunk of my car, barefoot. "You should have shoes on."

"It's almost fall," he says, as if that explains everything. He pulls a bent cigarette and a lighter from his pocket.

"Where'd you get those?"

"Mom's bedside table." He lights the cigarette and attempts to draw in a deep breath, but the second the smoke hits his lungs he starts coughing and slides off the trunk. "Damn." *Cough.* "These things are"—*cough cough*—"awful." He puts the cigarette to his lips and tries again. Same thing, more dramatic.

"Mom's gonna smell the smoke on you."

"No, she won't." *Cough.* "She's immune to the smell 'cause she's smoking, and Dad doesn't ever hug me anymore, so I'm good. Besides, I've got gum." He slides a pack out of his pocket and hands it to me. I punch a square out of the foil packet, stick it in my mouth, and hand the pack back to him.

"I don't know why she wants to smoke this crap. I feel like I'm gonna throw up."

"Just don't throw up on my car."

He fakes gagging on my trunk, then stubs out the cigarette on the ground and tosses it out in the yard. From his pocket, he produces a little bar of soap, the kind they leave in hotel bathrooms.

"You thought of everything."

"I'm a Scout. Always prepared."

He heads around the side of the house to the water spigot, and I look up the street. Curtis's truck is in the driveway. Soon, I'm going to be sitting in that truck with him. Maybe I'll take his keys; he's not getting away from me this time.

"A cockroach!" Matt hunkers down under the lamplight. The bug is spasming on the concrete, its legs too short and inflexible to find purchase. Ick. "Hey, give me your shoe."

Not in a million years. "I'm going in to take a shower."

"Be sure to pack some condoms."

"Ha, ha."

I sit on my bed and reread his text: Hey, you mind if we skip the movie tonight? Guess I haven't fully recovered. Need sleep.

"Shouldn't you get going?" Mom asks from my doorway.

I hold my phone up. "Curtis cancelled."

"Oh. Everything okay?"

"Yeah. He just got over the flu. I ran with him earlier today. I guess it knocked him back a little." Either that, or I've scared him off. Or maybe he's really not that into me.

"Well, the flu will definitely do that to you. It may take him a couple of weeks to get his full strength back. Sorry about the date, though." She sits on the edge of the bed. "Sooo, tell me about him."

I shrug.

"Well, I want to meet him."

"Is Dad going to be a problem?"

She sighs. "No. Absolutely not. He'll come around, Luke. That thing at the table was a knee-jerk response. We talked about it. It's not going to be a problem. Okay?"

Chapter 15

CURTIS

"I thought you had a date tonight," Corrine says, coming into the kitchen.

I look over my shoulder. She's wearing a fluffy robe and her wet hair is twisted over one shoulder. "Too tired. That flu really kicked my butt."

"What are you making?" She takes the printed recipe from the counter.

"Do we have any tofu?"

"Of course we have tofu. A smoothie, huh? Yum. Wheat germ, cinnamon, flaxseed . . . We don't have any carrot juice."

"I'm using extra V8." I slice the last bit of mango off the seed and drop it into the blender with the Greek yogurt. Fortunately, my sister is a health food junkie, so while many of the ingredients read like a new-age sticks-and-berries spice rack, we actually have most of what the recipe calls for.

"So what's with the smoothie? I don't see Heineken on the list anywhere."

I give her a smirk. "I just want to get back in shape as quickly as possible."

"Hmm. Might that blond cutie have something to do with that?"

"Maybe."

"Better throw in an extra kiwi then. He looks pretty virile to me."

"Very funny."

Corrine pulls a bar of tofu from the refrigerator and measures out three ounces into the blender. I seat the lid and press Purée.

"Where's Dad?" I ask over the whirring.

"Going over some plans in his office. So was Luke disappointed you cancelled?"

"Probably."

She leans her elbows on the counter and grins up at me. "Devastated, I bet."

I hope not. I am tired, but the truth is, I'm also a little afraid of him. Or at least I'm afraid of me with him. I keep reminding myself that there are eleven false positives in every one hundred HIV oral swabs. And you don't get HIV from kissing anyway. But I don't want to start something I can't finish.

No, I'll keep him at arm's length until I get the go ahead, then watch out, Luke. I may even have to forget about that going slow part.

"You're smiling," Corrine says.

I think about running with Luke Sunday morning, but it's pouring rain. I wouldn't mind seeing him soaking wet, but I figure I better not push my luck. Maybe I'll run this evening when I get back to school.

I was hoping you could watch me breathe, he texts.

<<Grin>> Too wet. Shopping with Corrine, then heading back to Sam. Keep running!

Can I see you before you go?

"You *have* to have pomegranate juice," Corrine says, choosing a thirty-two-ounce bottle marked Pure and Organic. We've already selected a blender for my room, and now we're shopping for assorted health food crap I can take back with me.

Corrine is in her element, flitting up and down aisles, looking at labels. She has tremendous faith in the benefits of eating healthy, organic foods. I'm serious about taking back control of my body, but I can't quite muster up her level of enthusiasm.

"Sounds delicious," I say absently, still trying to decide how to answer Luke's question.

She rolls her eyes at me. "It's tart. But that's what the honey is for." She places the bottle in the basket. "Speaking of honey . . ." She tries to get a look at my screen. I turn it so the little snoop can have a good look.

"Well, what are you waiting for? Say yes."

I text back: Be home soon. Come on over. I have someone I want you to meet.

He doesn't seem too thrilled about the third-party involvement until I introduce him to my new roommates a little while later. I fold a pair of jeans and watch with amusement as he peers into the water-filled aquarium near the window. "What the . . ."

I grin at his reaction. "Those are water dogs."

"Those are the creepiest things I've ever seen."

They are pretty creepy—shark gray, with four tiny legs and three hairy-looking appendages on each side of their heads. The biggest is about eight inches long. I set the jeans on a stack and snap the lid off a plastic container and extract a long, filthy earthworm.

Luke takes a step back. "Nasty."

I lower the earthworm over the water. A water dog snaps it up suddenly, and Luke starts. I actually find that kind of cute.

"What's with the Medusa headgear?" he asks.

"Those are gills."

"Gills? Those things are definitely not fish."

"Nope. They're larvae. They evolve."

"Into what?"

"Into this." I remove a rock from the dry tank and lift out the hefty, slick, yellow-spotted salamander. "Hello, Sebastian," I say, stroking its head.

"That is so gross."

"Sebastian's not gross, are you, sweetheart? He's a tiger salamander. Here, you want to hold him?"

I thrust it at Luke; he backs away. "No. Yuck. I don't like bugs."

"He's not a bug. He's an amphibian. Come on, pet his head. He likes that."

"No. Get that thing away from me."

"Well, well, well, I finally found something that repels Luke. If I'd known that, I would have introduced Sebastian to you yesterday." No, I wouldn't have. I don't want to repel Luke; I just want to cool his jets for a little while longer.

"Ha ha," he says, clearly not offended. "Why are you growing salamanders, anyway?"

I place Sebastian on my shoulder and the creature immediately lunges for my ear. I gently pry his mouth off my earlobe. "Biology project. I have to document their transformation." I place the salamander back in the tank and dry my hands on my shorts.

"Aren't you going to wash your hands?"

"Nope."

I return to my laundry. Luke lingers for a while over the tank, then turns to wandering the perimeter of my room, poking around in my bookshelf, looking at the photos of Dad, Corrine, and me on a family vacation. I pick up a pair of cargo shorts and shake them out. A mechanical pencil and the STD brochure—folded and damaged from its trip through both the washer and dryer—fall to the bed. I glance up at Luke. He picks up my instrument case and sets it on the bed. I slip the brochure under the pile of laundry.

"What's this?" he asks, releasing the latches.

"I'm marching a trombone this year."

"You play clarinet."

"Not this year. The band needed a trombone, and, anyway, music majors have to pick up different instruments."

He takes the bell piece out of the case and then the slide and works at putting it together. He clearly has no idea what a finished trombone looks like up close.

"You're gonna damage that."

"No, I'm not."

"The slide needs to be at a ninety-degree angle to the main instrument. No, ninety degrees."

"Based on what?"

Oh, brother. I can't help smiling. "Here, give it to me." I take the instrument, assemble it, release the slide lock, then hand it back.

He lifts the instrument to his lips and blows, pushing the slide out and bringing it back in, the long note going low and back to high again. He's got good lips for a brass instrument. "How do you play notes on this thing?"

"There're six positions on the pipe. The more you lengthen the pipe, the lower the note. The positions are the equivalent of valve positions on a brass instrument."

He looks at the slide for some markings, but there are none. "And you're just supposed to know where the positions are?"

"Pretty much. Position one, all the way in; six, all the way out; three, the brace even with the bell; four, the edge of the slide even with the bell; and the other two positions are about halfway between one and three, and four and six." He tries to follow along. "Here, let me show you." I get behind him and move to place his hands in proper position, but he cringes.

"You have salamander hands."

The better to keep you behaving. I wipe my hands down the front of his shirt, which is kind of nice. He looks down in disgust, but when I reach back up to place his hands in proper position, he says, "I think you missed some."

"Blow," I whisper in his ear.

He twists his head to look at me over his shoulder, then engages my mouth, and I let him.

"You know, my sister could come in any minute," I say when he pauses for a breath.

"Let's lock the door."

"Let's not."

I take the trombone from him. "Come on. You can help me with my laundry. I need to get on the road soon."

"Can I ask you a question?" he says, picking through my laundry, looking for my underwear, no doubt. He finds a pair and holds it up with an amused expression of his own, then folds it and sets it on my stack. His face grows serious again. "Do I taste bad?"

I laugh. And then I laugh harder. Oh, Luke. "No. You don't taste bad."

"Then what is it? You always hold back when I kiss you, like you don't really want to."

I try to think of some plausible excuse, but really, I have none, not without disclosing something I have no intention of disclosing. Oh, hell. There's no danger in kissing. And I'm certain I'm one of the eleven percenters anyway.

I drop the towel I'm holding and give him a little *come here* gesture with my finger.

"What?" he says.

"Come here. Come on." I'm tingling with anticipation, because I'm going to kiss this kid. I mean, really kiss him. He smiles back at me and slowly makes his way around the corner of the bed.

"Closer."

When he's inches from me, I take his face in my hands, and this time when I kiss him, I don't hold back. He presses into me and I get a little preview of our future together. Damn, he turns me on. I pull away so I can kiss him from a different angle. "You taste amazing," I whisper to him.

A sharp knock on the door saves us from ourselves. Corrine sticks her head in. "Oh." She grins. "I've got your stuff packed in a small cooler, Curtey. Um . . . I guess I'll just leave it in the kitchen for you. Take your time." She backs out and closes the door behind her.

We smile at each other. "I've got to get going."

He nods. I keep one eye on him as I fold up the last of my laundry.

"What's this?" He picks up the washed and dried pamphlet and unfolds it before I can take it from him.

"Just trash I left in my pocket." I pluck it from his hands and toss it in the basket next to my desk. He watches me as I stuff everything in my duffel bag. I don't know what he's thinking, and I'm not about to ask.

"Okay. That's it!" I zip up the bag and toss it aside. "You want to help me get Sebastian and company to the truck?"

Chapter 16

CURTIS

I keep up the fresh smoothies for about a week before I finally concede that a dorm room does not provide an ideal environment for such complicated preparation. Fortunately, there are simpler ways to boost one's immune system, including this concoction I found online. I tracked it down at a health food store ten minutes away.

"That is some nasty-looking shit." Jaleel wrinkles his nose.

"It's not so bad. You want to try some?"

He mimics vomiting.

The green color is a little off-putting, and, frankly, so is the taste. Actually, it's pretty awful, but I didn't buy it for its flavor. One scoop in some bottled water and I'm good to go.

I choke it down as I stuff my feet into my running shoes and tighten the laces. Jaleel rolls back over and pulls the blanket over his head.

It's still dark outside, but there are plenty of lights around campus to mark my path. There's a lot of moisture in the air, and I see flickers of lightning off in the distance. The rhythmic slap of my athletic shoes against concrete helps me focus on every muscle, every tendon, every breath as I take inventory of my body.

All systems go. I'm back up to five miles, but I admit, it's tough.

I really wanted to go home again this weekend, see Luke, but I had a mid-afternoon game Saturday, and tons of reading to do Sunday.

And I'm anxious; it's been almost two weeks since my blood test. The call could come any day now, the one that either sets me free or seals my fate forever. I've tried not to think about it. I remind myself, if I was sick, I would know. But the nagging worry is there, distracting me during lectures, shattering my focus when I'm studying.

Luke has kept my spirits up with his texts and phone calls. Apparently I communicated something to him with that kiss. He's loose, and funny, and charming, and eager to do it again.

So am I.

The call comes Wednesday as I'm hustling from one building to the next between classes.

"Curtis, it's Kathy in the Student Health Center." She sounds bright, happy. No one with bad news to deliver would sound that chipper. I heave a sigh of relief. "We have the results of your test. Dr. Nguyen would like you to come in to discuss them."

"Can't you give me the results over the phone?"

"I'm sorry. We're not allowed to do that. I've got an opening at eleven thirty."

Annoying bureaucracy. All it would take is one word—negative.

I tell her I'll be there. I check the time on my phone: 8:57. I jog the rest of the way to my class. Two and a half hours to freedom.

"You look much better today," Dr. Nguyen says, shaking my hand. He runs through the usual battery of observations—my glands, my throat, my chest. "Did you finish your course of antibiotics?"

"Every one." I smile.

"Good. Your lungs sound clear." He drapes the stethoscope around his neck again. "How's your dad doing?" He seems upbeat. A good sign. Nevertheless, my heart is hammering in my chest, and I want him to get on with it.

"Great."

He smiles and slaps me lightly on the shoulder, and then his entire demeanor changes.

I go cold.

He breathes in, breathes out, holds my eyes for a moment. He glances over his shoulder at two chairs lining the wall. He pulls one out for me. "Why don't you hop down and have a seat."

My legs tremble. I get to my feet and move to the chair. He sits opposite me, presses his hands together, then presses them against his mouth.

Just say it.

He folds his hands and places them deliberately in his lap. Only then does he look up at me again. "We got the results from your blood test. The test is called an enzyme-linked immunosorbent assay test. You may have heard it referred to as the ELISA antibody test. It detects the presence of HIV antibodies in your bloodstream. It's highly accurate, Curtis."

He pauses. I clutch at the last thread of hope even as I feel it slip through my fingers.

"It confirmed the results of the swab."

I can't breathe.

He pauses to let the news sink in, but I'm reeling, unbalanced.

"You can fight this, Curtis. I won't kid you; it won't be easy. But researchers have made tremendous strides over the past thirty years in treating HIV. There is much to be hopeful about. The most important thing right now, though, is to get you into a treatment program. Studies show that HIV patients who begin antiretroviral drug treatment early have much better outcomes. I can treat you here in our office, but—"

I look away.

"—I'd like to refer you to an HIV clinic. We have one right here in town, a very good one. It's all completely confidential, and the location is discreet. They have resources we don't have—drug counselors, support groups. I think they can serve you much better than we can." He takes another pamphlet from the rack and holds it out to me. "Their phone number is on the back."

I turn the pamphlet over and stare, unfocused, at the address stamp.

"I can make the appointment for you, if you'd prefer."

I shake my head.

"Have you talked to your dad yet?"

I shake my head again.

"Would you like me to talk to him?"

"No," I whisper.

He looks down at my tightly clenched fist. "Curtis..." He stops, takes a deep breath and lets it out, then leans forward, his elbows on his knees. He claps his hands together a couple of times softly. "This is not a death sentence, Curtis. Do you hear me? You've got a tough road ahead. But you *can* fight this. You owe it to yourself and to your family to fight this. You have many, many good years ahead of you if you take care of yourself. I want you to remember that. You do what you have to do, and you go out there and live your life."

My legs jiggle. I will them to stop.

"I'm always here if you want to talk."

He waits for a response, but I have none to give. He stands and grips my shoulder. "You're welcome to stay right here, take whatever time you need. I'll take care of things at the desk so you won't have to check out."

Quietly, he lets himself out.

I focus on the small things. Stand. Shoulder backpack. Open door. Walk, one foot in front of the other. Look left, right. Cross the street. Cross again.

Hold it together, Curtis.

The dorm is just ahead. Find keys. Open door. Close door. Lock.

Numb, I crawl into bed.

"I thought you'd be headed south by now," Jaleel says when he returns to the room that afternoon.

I close my eyes and will him to go away.

"Hey." He shakes my foot. "Wake up. You sick again, man? Cause if you're sick—"

"I'm not sick."

"He lives!"

Leave me alone.

"Hey." He shakes my foot again. "Come on, man. You never

sleep in the afternoon. You wanna go get some lunch?" A pause. "Hey. Curtis. Yo. You sure you're not sick again, man?"

"I said I'm not fucking sick!" I throw my blanket off and stumble to the bathroom.

"Well, whatever it is, you don't have to take it out on me," Jaleel mutters.

I sit on the toilet, my face cradled in my palms, until I hear him leave again, then return to the room, grab my keys and my wallet, and head out to the 7-Eleven a few blocks away.

The clerk doesn't even blink when I present my fake ID.

Sam Houston State Park is a couple of miles south of the university. I pull my truck under a stand of pines in a secluded area and cut the engine. It takes three bottles of beer before my hands stop shaking enough to send a text.

Mr. G. Can't make it today. School is kicking my butt this semester.

I press Send, then let the phone drop in my lap. I polish off the rest of the six-pack, then curl up on the seat and cry.

I wake up in the dark, disoriented. My cell phone is lying on the seat in front of my face. I take it and force myself to sit up. My stomach turns over. The door creaks loudly in the quiet forest as I open it. I stumble out and throw up in the brush. Then I step over the vomit to urinate. As I relieve myself, I peer into the night. I can't help feeling like I'm looking at my future—infinite blackness, solitude.

I zip up and as my eyes adjust to the dark, I find the trail to the lake.

No moonlight reflects off the surface. Just an inky blackness as far as I can see. I kick off my shoes and wade into the water. It's cold, and the mud at the bottom squishes between my toes. I slip my hand in my pocket and run my thumb across the smooth screen of my phone.

Did I do this to you, Ryan? Did you do this to me?

Does it even matter?

We've both been given a death sentence. Who else would want me now? Who else would want you?

I skim my fingers across the surface of the water.

Maybe we can make a go of it again. Maybe we can watch each other waste away, grow emaciated, sick. One of us can watch the other die, then die alone.

The thought makes me laugh, and then I feel my eyes swim again. I blink to clear them.

Before I know what I'm doing, I have my phone in my hand and a number on the screen. I press Call.

A sleepy voice answers. "Curtis?"

I feel a lump form in my throat.

"Curtis? Are you okay? Where are you? What's wrong?" His voice is stronger now, and I can almost see him sitting up in bed, his blond hair tousled. "Curtis! Talk to me. What's going on? You're scaring me."

I clear my throat but the words stick. I clear it again. "Oh, hey." I say in a voice weaker than I'd hoped. "I just called to see what you're up to."

There's a pause. "It's three in the morning."

I check the time on my screen: 3:42. *Shit.*

"Sorry. I was . . . pulling an all-nighter. I didn't realize the time. I'll just—"

"No, don't hang up. Are you okay? You weren't at practice today. I texted you."

"I'm fine. Just—just, you know, busy. Look, I've gotta go. I'm sorry I woke you."

"I can come up there," he says quickly. "Whatever it is, we can talk it out."

Tires crunch across the gravel a dozen or so yards back as headlights skim across the lake.

"No. I'm fine, really. I'll talk to you soon. I gotta go." I end the call before he can respond.

I can just make out the park ranger's truck behind the headlights, idling at the edge of the tree line. A door opens, closes, and the beam of a flashlight blinds me.

I step back onto the shore, keeping my hands open and out from my sides.

"It's a little late for a swim."

I squint into the light. "I was just taking a walk."

He approaches slowly, sweeping his flashlight across the shoreline. "Are you staying at a campsite here in the park?" he asks.

"Uh, no. I'm in my truck."

"You have a camper on the back?"

"No, sir."

"Do you have some ID on you?"

I reach into my back pocket for my wallet.

"College student?"

"Yes, sir," I say, fishing for my driver's license. "Sophomore."

He drops the light long enough to glance at my ID, then shines the beam in my eyes again. "Have you had anything to drink, Mr. Cameron?"

"No."

"Is anyone here in the park with you?"

"No. I came alone. I needed to get away for a while."

"Girl troubles?"

"Yeah." Sure.

"What are you studying?"

"Music education. I plan to be a band director."

He hmphs like he's not impressed. "Well, Mr. Cameron, we prefer that our guests not wander around the park in the middle of the night. It makes the other guests nervous. I think it's time you head back to campus. Would you like a ride back to your vehicle?"

"No, sir. I can find my way."

"Do you have a flashlight?"

"No. I'm okay."

He studies me a moment longer, then drops the flashlight beam to the ground. "All right, then. Why don't you get moving."

I tug on my shoes and head back up the road. He trails me in his truck, lighting my way.

I drive around for the next couple of hours. Luke calls, texts, but I don't respond, and by six he seems to have given up. I shouldn't have called him.

I have some damage control to do with Jaleel. I start with a hot cappuccino from Starbucks, the smell of which makes me want to throw up again, but I hand it over with an apologetic smile.

"Better?" he asks, taking it and sitting up in bed. His skinny legs drop over the side and he takes a sip.

"Yeah. Sorry. I was just in a foul mood."

"No shit. So what happened?"

"Nothing. Personal stuff."

"Is there a lady involved?"

I hold his eyes for a moment, then shake my head. "No."

He nods like he doesn't believe me. "Well"—he takes another sip—"if you ever want to talk, you know where to find me." He gets up and stretches. "I fed the water monsters for you last night."

"Thanks."

He shakes his head. "Nasty."

I smile a little. "You're a good roommate, Jaleel."

On Saturday, Dad calls. "Curt, I just got an Explanation of Benefits from the insurance company. Did you have an HIV test?"

I swallow hard and glance at Jaleel. He's playing some game on his computer. I get up and take the call outside. "It's a routine thing they do at the health center."

"Curtis"—he pauses—"There are two tests here."

I try to laugh, sound natural, normal. "They were doing a study, comparing the results of oral swabs to blood tests. I agreed to be a guinea pig. No big deal."

Another pause. "Is everything okay?"

"Everything's great. How's Corrine doing?"

He laughs. "She's plotting out a garden. God help us."

I laugh back.

A few minutes after I hang up, Luke calls. I don't answer.

Chapter 17

CURTIS

The days, the weeks that follow are a blur.

I finally make the call, then wait over an hour at the clinic to give my history and a shocking amount of blood for a duplicate ELISA test to confirm the results again. Then another test, something called a Western blot. I ask; the doctor tells me that the odds of a false positive in this two-step testing protocol is something like one in 250,000 in a low-risk population. I'm not considered a member of that population.

Then more blood tests and more bad news.

My CD4+ T cell count (a type of white blood cell that fights infection) is 598. It should be over 1,000. My viral load—the number of HIV RNA copies per milliliter of plasma—is over three hundred.

I can't even begin to comprehend what all that means.

The doctor shows me a generalized chart of the relationship between T cell counts and viral loads over the course of untreated HIV infection. All I can focus on is the red line that represents viral load. It rises sharply at about year eight, peaking at year ten or so.

At the end of that red line, there's an arrow, and a caption: *death*.

For the second time, I cry.

A Risk Reduction Specialist conducts a Partner Elicitation Session. I give her names, phone numbers where I have them, whatever bits of information I can remember. No one can tell me when I contracted the virus, so everyone has to be contacted. I don't know who to be angry at and who to feel guilty about. I don't know if Ryan gave it to me, or if I gave it to him, or if there's any relationship at all between his infection and mine. Nothing's quite real, but it's all terrifying just the same.

It occurs to me that I never got a call from the health department. Did Ryan lie about how he contracted HIV? Did he try to argue that he had to have come in contact with infected blood, maybe through a cut on his hand when he tried to mop up someone's bloody nose? Or did he diagnose himself with a home test?

They're going to contact the others. What will they think when they get the call? How many lives have I ruined? How many more angry phone calls will I get?

I should be the angry one. I am angry. Someone did this to me.

Another counselor, a Ms. Sanchez, discusses my drug therapy with me. The good news, if there is such a thing anymore, is that there are highly effective combination antiretroviral drugs today—one pill, once a day, not the multi-pill cocktails of a decade or so ago. But it's shockingly expensive: more than $2,000 a month. There are state programs, but as long as I'm covered under my dad's insurance, I'm not eligible.

"It's time to have a hard talk with your dad," Ms. Sanchez tells me. "Decide what's the best course. Depending on his insurance plan, it may be best if he drops you from his coverage so that you can qualify for a state plan. There's some red tape involved, and it may take some months before you can get started on the drugs. But you're okay right now. You have the time. Think about it. Take a little time to get your head together, then have the talk, okay?"

I nod.

"Has anyone talked to you about joining a support group yet?"

I shake my head.

"There's a group that meets right here on Wednesday evenings. Seven o'clock. I think you'll find it very helpful in coping with your diagnosis. You don't have to call ahead. Just show up."

I pay with cash and ask that they not file with my dad's insurance company.

Chapter 18

CURTIS

Time. She said I have time.

But how much, and at what cost?

Jaleel's got a date tonight, so I prop myself against the headboard and settle my computer on my lap. It takes some searching, but I finally find a chart similar to the one they showed me at the clinic. I use a straightedge to mark the intersection of my T cell count and viral load. The best I can tell, I was infected about a year ago.

I'm stunned; I hadn't even started seeing Ryan.

The doctor believes the virus has already gone through the acute stage—what the chart labels a "wide dissemination of virus seeding of lymphoid organs." I only have a vague sense of what that means—and is now in a period of clinical latency. According to the chart, it will be another three years or so before my viral load overtakes my T cell count, and another three after that before I develop something called "constitutional symptoms."

I have to remind myself that this is the course of the infection *without* treatment.

I should have told Dad when he called. I don't know why I didn't. I think about picking up the phone now, or just getting in my truck and driving home, but what am I going to tell them?

I didn't get this disease because someone sneezed on me or because I held on to a banister when I climbed the stairs, then rubbed my eyes.

I invited this disease in.

And the worst part is . . . I can't even pin a person to it.

And I can't look at the chart anymore.

I pull up the Starlight Photography Web site. Starlight is the company that shoots the professional photos at all the high school events. There are hundreds of images, organized by event. I click on the Bands of America competition from last weekend and scroll through them. Clarinets are featured in this year's program, so there are quite a few of Luke. I save each of them to my desktop. My favorite—a close-up, photo #483—captured him playing, his lips pursed around his mouthpiece, his ruddy cheeks puffed out, his eyes looking off toward Mindy.

Have I ever noticed how blue his eyes are?

I smile to myself. I've noticed.

I don't know why I called him that night from the park. I think I just needed to hear his voice. It's been weeks now. Surely Corrine has verified that I'm not dead. So there's no real excuse why I've slammed the door in his face. He must hate me. I wouldn't blame him.

I hate me sometimes.

I save the close-up to my desktop and continue browsing through the pages. Photos of the color guard are scattered here and there. Robert Westfall is in quite a few of them. He's nice looking— short-cropped blond hair, sideburns that extend to his earlobes, nicely filled out. He's a junior. Beyond that, I don't know much about him. Still, he'd be a nice match for Luke. The thought pangs me in an unexpected way.

It's almost one AM when Jaleel lets himself back in the room. "You still up?"

"Yep. How was your date?" I ask as he empties his pockets.

He grins back at me. "Her roommate's sleeping at her boyfriend's apartment tonight."

Hmm. No need to say more.

"What are you working on?" he asks.

"Nada mucho. Just looking around."

He eyes me. "Why don't you let me fix you up with a sister? You sittin' in this room alone every night. You need some action, man. A little mm-mm-mm."

"I don't know about a sister. But I might be interested in a brother," I deadpan.

He looks at me as if he's really seeing me for the first time and I shrug.

"All this time I been thinkin' you sittin' there reading your little books, and you been checkin' out my junk?" he says with mock indignation. "My *man*hood? Baby, you don't wanna piece of this." He flexes his knees, laces his fingers behind his head, and thrusts his pelvis at me a few times. "I may be small, but I'm packin' some serious shit here."

I smile and turn my laptop around so he can see the screen.

"Ah, so this is the little whitey you been jerkin' off to at night."

"His name is Luke Chesser. He's in high school. A junior."

"High school? So, are you two . . ."

"Naw. Too young."

"So why you got a photo of him on your computer screen?"

I shrug. "He's nice to look at."

"If you say so." He starts to pull his T-shirt over his head, then stops and assumes a defensive stance, hands up, palms out as if to warn me. "Now, I'm a gonna strip down to my skivvies. You can control yourself, right?"

"I'm pretty sure I can control myself."

" 'Cause I got some dangerous stuff here."

Yeah, me too.

"You know," I tell him, folding my arms, leaning back against my pillows, and giving him a good once-over, "now that you mention it . . ."

"Oh-ho-ho-ho-ho. You wish, white boy." He lifts his T-shirt over his head, wads it up, and flings it at me.

I pull the shirt from my keyboard and toss it back to his bed.

When he comes out of the bathroom, he sits at his desk and boots up his computer.

I need to tell him. He has a right to know. We share a space. We share a bathroom. It's unfair not to give him a heads-up so he can protect himself. I think of it as a practice run.

"Hey, Jaleel, man, can I talk to you for a minute?"

"Sure." He swivels his chair around. "What's up?"

I take a deep breath. I've thought about how I would say this, how I could make it less frightening, less pitiful. But there's no putting lipstick on this pig. "I had an HIV test about a month ago." He waits. I'm hitting him with a lot tonight. But I can't back down now. "It was positive."

"Okay." Then after a moment, "That sucks. You all right?"

"Yeah. I thought you should know."

He shrugs. "Anything I can do?"

"No, but thanks."

He turns back to his computer.

That wasn't so bad. I watch him hunch over his keyboard, thrum his fingers lightly on the keys, then scratch at the back of his head. I have a sudden urge to get up and hug him.

He lets out a long sigh, then spins around again, stretches out his legs, and folds his arms. "Is that why you disappeared a couple weeks ago?"

"That was the day they confirmed my diagnosis. There was no more telling myself that it couldn't be true."

"Have you told your family?"

"Not yet."

He tips his chin at my computer. "Does he know?"

I shake my head. "No."

"Are you going to tell him?"

"He's just a guy."

"You're not fooling me, Cameron." No, I can see that I'm not. "How many photos of him you got on that computer?"

I crook a smile, then let it go. "A few."

He leans forward and props his forearms on his thighs. "This is pretty serious, isn't it?"

Tears prick at my eyes; I blink them back and nod.

"How did you get it?"

I prickle and lock my eyes on his. "You really want me to answer that? You want a blow-by-blow, names, locations, positions—"

"Come on, man. I'm not judging you. It was just a question." He lets out a heavy breath. "Shit," he swears softly. "I'm sorry. I shouldn't have asked. It's none of my business, and it's irrelevant anyway."

I look away a moment and regain my composure.

"So, what's the prognosis?"

"A lifetime of heavy-duty drugs, blood draws, secrets."

"Secrets, huh?" He rubs his hand across his face, scans the room. His eyes light on the blender and his brow pinches. "Is that why you were drinking that crap?"

I smile a little.

He smiles back. "Something that foul has got to have some serious immune-boosting properties. So why've you quit drinking it lately, what's up?"

I shrug. "It seems pointless, you know."

"What I know is that my man Magic has had HIV for years, and he's doing pretty well last time I checked. Drink the shit, okay? And whatever else you have to do. I don't want to have to break in a new roommate. Got it?"

I do smile now. He has no idea what he just did for me. My eyes swim.

"And if you cry, I'm gonna smack you from here to forever. And while you're at it, maybe you should go ahead and tell little whitey there. If he can't take it, fuck him."

I huff. "That's exactly what I'll never do with him." It's out before I can stop myself.

"Aw, man, come on, don't talk like that. There's more than one way to love your man, you know what I mean?" He waggles his eyebrows at me, and for the second time I want to throw my arms around him.

"You're a good friend, Jaleel."

"And don't you forget it." He stands, grabs my shoulders, and gives me a little shake. "Go to bed."

I grab his wrists. "Thank you."

"Don't mention it." Then he surprises me by pulling me in for an embrace. "It's gonna be okay, man."

He shuts down his computer and climbs into bed.

It's gonna be okay. Maybe he's right. I pull out my cell phone.

Notes from the Maestro: run, breathe. I'll see you soon. BTW, you looked great at BOA. Photos. Cute.

Cuter in person. Don't understand you. Nothing for weeks.

A lot going on here. We'll talk soon. Okay?

I'd rather talk now.

I know he would. But I can't do this over the phone. I need to see his face, his reaction. I need to know I can trust him, and I need to know he won't be disgusted by me.

I can drive to Huntsville next weekend. Sunday, he texts again before I can respond.

No. I'll drive down. Want to see Dad and Corrine too.

Promise?

Promise.

On Monday, Jaleel moves out.

I watch him pack up his things and pretend it's no big deal.

He shakes his head as he slowly wraps his computer cord neatly around the power supply. He secures the cord with a Velcro strap, then places his fists on his hips and studies his shoes. "I wouldn't have told my momma if I'd known she was gonna react this way. You know that, don't you?" He lifts his eyes to mine.

"It's okay, man. You don't have to explain."

"No, I think I do. You're a great roommate, Curtis. A good friend. And there's no way in hell I'd be moving out if my parents weren't paying the bill. My momma's—"

"She loves you. She's worried about you. I get that. It's a scary thing."

"Oh, come on. I'm about as likely to get AIDS from you as I am to suddenly wake up white one morning. And they know that. I don't know. I guess it's because I'm their only kid and—"

"It's okay, Jaleel. If I were your parents, I'd probably feel the same way."

He looks at me as he stuffs his computer in a bag. "It's not right."

"Where are you moving to?" I ask, changing the subject.

"Sam Houston Village. Somebody dropped out and they've got

an empty bed. It's more expensive, but at least there's central air and . . . *shit.* I fucked up, man. It wasn't mine to tell. I thought, you know, they'd be supportive. I didn't think they'd go all parental on me."

"Did your mom tell the school why she was moving you?"

"I don't know," he says softly.

I swallow the lump in my throat. I realize now, in a way I hadn't before, how quickly my diagnosis can undo me, how easily that information can spread and destroy my life, maybe more so than the disease itself. I push the thought away.

"So," I say, smiling so he'll get that hangdog look off his face, "who's your new roommate?"

"Some dude. Dan something. He's a criminal justice major." He chuckles. "Me, roomin' with a future prison guard. Kinda scary, isn't it? It's like tossing a chicken in a cage with a pit bull. I'm countin' on you to leave a light on for me, just in case. Okay?"

"You're welcome here any time."

"And you're my witness, man," he says, shouldering his computer case. "I didn't steal this computer."

I smile a little. We exchange a moment of what I think is quiet respect for each other. "It won't be so bad," I tell him.

"I mean it, man. Leave a light on."

"Do you have everything?" A stylish black woman stands in the doorway. She glances at me, then back at Jaleel. "We need to go. Your dad's got the car running."

"I'm coming." Jaleel looks back at me, uncomfortable now with his mom standing there. "I'm sorry, man. Are you gonna be okay?"

I force a smile. "I'm gonna be fine. Go. Hope your new prison guard makes his bed."

He laughs a little. "Still friends, right?"

"Yeah. Of course." I get up and shake his outreached hand.

"Okay, well . . ." He looks back at his mom until she steps out of the room. "You call me if you need anything."

I swallow hard again. There's something I have to know before he leaves. "Have you . . . ?"

"No, man. I haven't told anyone else."

I nod and look away. He gathers me up in a back-slapping hug. "I'll see you in the band hall, okay?"

The room is quiet with Jaleel gone. Soul-sucking quiet.

I don't go home the next weekend. I tell Dad and Corrine that I'm swamped with schoolwork. But the truth is, I can't face them. Sometimes I feel like I'll never go home again.

By the end of October, I'm emotionally shriveled, hungry for meaningful human contact. And then Mr. Gorman calls. I jump at his plea to travel with the band the next weekend.

Chapter 19

CURTIS

Dad is looking over blueprints at the kitchen table when I walk in the door Friday night.

"Curt?" He pushes away from the table and grabs me up in a big hug.

"Hey, Curtey," Corrine calls from under a quilt on the couch.

"This is a nice surprise. You should have let us know you were coming. We'd have"—he clears his throat—"saved some dinner for you."

"Eh, I'm good. I ate before the game. What'd you guys have?"

Dad glances at Corrine. "Um, stuffed baked eggplant."

"Sounds yum—"

Dad makes a face and gives his head an infinitesimal shake.

"Mmm," I finish with a grin.

"Are you staying all weekend?" Corrine asks.

"I'm just home to sleep. I'm going to Dallas with the high school band tomorrow."

"Oh, that's right," Dad says. "October. The big end-of-season competition. What time are they leaving?"

"Oh-dark thirty, as usual. I need to be up at three."

"Then you better get to bed." He hugs me again. "We've missed you. You doing okay?"

"Yeah. Hey, I'll be back Sunday morning early. Maybe we could do something on the grill Sunday afternoon? Hang out?" *Talk?* I need to talk. I need my family.

"Sounds good to me. Between you and me," he says quietly, "I'm starving to death."

"I heard that," Corrine calls from the living room.

Three AM comes way too early. When I arrive, the parking lot behind the band hall is already buzzing with activity as kids in pajama pants and hoodies unload pillows and blankets, duffel bags and instruments from their vehicles.

I stick my head into Mr. Gorman's office. "Good morning."

"Good morning! You look bright and chipper. Ready to go?" he asks.

"Ready as I'll ever be. What bus you want me on?"

"The clarinets are on three. You want to take that one?"

I hesitate. "Um, sure."

There's an undercurrent of panic in the band hall as kids race the clock. Across the room, I see Luke step out of the uniform room with Spencer. Both have their garment bags slung over their shoulders. I notice that Luke's hair is still damp from an early morning shower, his cheeks pink from the nippy morning air. I wonder if he knows I'm here.

I step outside, away from the pandemonium. Under the sodium vapor lights, a group of parents and band kids are systematically loading props and larger instruments into the equipment truck—an impressive eighteen-wheeler with the band's logo painted on the side. It's a well-organized team endeavor, perfected over the many weeks of games and competitions.

"Here, let me do that," I say to one of the moms. I take her place on the side of one of the xylophones and help guide it up the ramp.

When all the equipment is secure and the doors have been slammed shut, I walk back through the band hall and check for stragglers.

"I think we're good here," Mr. Gorman says, striding out of his office with his clipboard. "Let's hit the road."

Five Greyhound buses are idling in the side parking lot, loaded and ready to roll.

"Currr-tis," voices ring out as I board bus number three.

About midway back, Luke's head snaps forward. I catch his eyes for a moment. There's surprise, a flash of anger. I look past him and wave off the other kids. I won't be able to avoid him the entire trip; I just hope I can avoid him long enough to work out some plausible excuse.

I settle into a seat behind the chaperones and grab a few more hours sleep.

We're outside Dallas when activity on the bus wakes me. One of the parents is passing back bottles of water. Another hands me a shopping bag stocked with bananas, apples, granola bars. I hand it back, then get up and make my way to the bathroom at the back of the bus.

Luke is still asleep. One earbud has fallen from his ear and rests in the folds of the blanket he's tucked around his shoulders. I slip past him and take my place in the short line.

"Hey, man," Adeeb says. "About time you showed up again."

The bus lurches as the driver accelerates. I grab the back of Adeeb's seat for support. "Busy. Mr. Gorman says the program looks good."

"Better than good. I think we've got a real shot this time."

As he talks, my eyes wander back up the aisle. Luke stirs and presses the earbud back in his ear. I find myself wondering what he's listening to. We've never talked about music before. In fact, there's so much we haven't talked about. So much I still want to know about him. So much I'll never know.

He's cracking open a bottle of water when I come out of the bathroom. I walk past him without stopping.

The kids are groggy and stiff as they tumble out of the buses. They have half an hour to stretch, perk up, and get in uniform. Before they have time to get nervous, they're warmed up and on the field.

I watch from high in the stands alongside Mr. Gorman and the other directors. "Come on, guys," he says softly as the drum majors count down the beat. "Just like we did it in rehearsal."

I find Luke in the front line of clarinets. Again, I'm struck by how regal he looks in his uniform. I make a mental note to mention this to Mr. Gorman later. I do think Luke would make an amazing drum major. Mr. Gorman needs to start seeing him that way too if Luke has a chance in hell of making it.

Who am I kidding? Without my help he has no chance of making it. He doesn't want it enough. Maybe he doesn't want it at all. Especially now.

Mr. Gorman punctuates each movement on the field with his comments. "You got it, you got it. Nice."

"Don't screw this up."

"Beautiful."

"Come on, guys. Keep it up. Focus. Focus. Come on."

I follow Luke as he moves smartly through the performance. Every movement, flawless.

"It's okay. Good recovery, Blake," Mr. Gorman says.

I scan the field, and home in on the euphonium players, but everything looks good. And then . . . a tear in the program. The brass players inexplicably drop behind the beat.

"Holy crap, guys," Mr. Gorman growls. "Pick it up, pick it up. Watch Mindy."

I hold my breath as the band closes formation and brass gets in sync. It was a noticeable flaw, but the rest of the performance was exquisite. Still, finals are no longer a sure thing, and that's a shame. All that work . . .

"Almost there," Mr. Gorman says softly. "Slow, slow. Measured steps." The band hits the final note and freezes. "*Yes!*" Mr. Gorman turns and grips my shoulders. "Let's hope the judges were too dazzled to ding us too badly."

But the kids know the tear could be a fatal flaw. Outside the stadium, I take a bottle of water from one of the moms and work my way through the glum faces, looking for Adeeb. I don't see Luke until someone pushes him and he stumbles backward into me.

"You looked good out there," I tell him.

"Thanks," he says in a way that suggests he doesn't give a rat's ass what I think, then turns his back to me.

The kids spend the afternoon watching other bands perform, napping on the buses.

It's dinner time when Mr. Gorman lifts the megaphone to his mouth: "You're marching in the finals, guys." He pretends to wipe sweat from his brow as the kids whoop and high-five each other. "Please be back at the buses and in uniform by eight. We perform at nine thirty. And please do not wander off," Gorman says. "I expect you to be somewhere between the buses and the stadium at all times. Is that clear, band?"

Half an hour later, I'm standing on a small rise with Mr. Gorman when suddenly he shakes his head. I follow his eyes. In a stand of trees twenty feet away, a couple of kids are engaged in some pretty serious making out.

"Leave room for Jesus," Mr. Gorman booms. The two spring apart. As they walk past us, red faced, Gorman clears his throat loudly. They part ways on the sidewalk, and then I see Luke huddled there with Spencer and Jackson. He turns away quickly.

"Let's go, let's go, let's go!"

There's been an error in the marching assignments and ours has been moved up by half an hour. The kids hustle to get back into their uniforms.

"Let's go, people!" Mr. Gorman calls through the megaphone. He runs his hands anxiously through his hair.

I step up into bus three. "Make sure you have your gloves and your hats." I hug the pole as kids hurry past me. "Come on, come on. Get your instruments and get moving."

Luke is on his knees halfway down the aisle frantically searching under the seats. "Luke. Let's go."

Nothing.

"Luke!"

"I can't find my fucking skull cap."

Christ. I move up the aisle, quickly scanning the seats and the floor space between them, dodging kids at the same time. "Why didn't you put it in your hatbox?" I find the hatbox with his name on it and check to make sure it isn't in there. Then I rifle through his duffel bag. Nothing. "You're just going to have to go without it."

"I can't go without it."

"You have no choice. Let's go."

"I've got it," he says. He gets to his feet and slips past me without so much as a look and jogs down the aisle.

He's the last to get off. Instrument cases are strewn haphazardly on the concrete outside the cargo doors as the kids head to the warm-up area. I toe the lids closed as Luke picks through them to find his own. He opens the case, snaps together his clarinet, then promptly drops it, mouthpiece down, onto the concrete.

"*Shhhit.*" He picks it up and inspects the mouthpiece.

"Let me see." I pull off the cracked reed and inspect the mouthpiece beneath it. "You chipped off a piece."

"I can't play it like that. God*damm*it. Mr. Gorman is gonna kill me." He puts his hands on his hips and utters a frustrated growl.

"Well, it ain't good, that's for sure. Do you have a spare mouthpiece?"

The look on his face is answer enough. I look up at the only other two kids still gathering up their stuff. "Go, guys. Tell Mr. Gorman Luke will be there in a minute." I hand him back his clarinet. "You can use my mouthpiece."

My own case is tucked in a corner of the cargo bin. I take it with me out of habit more than anything else. I pull it out and remove the mouthpiece, the reed still attached.

I pause—a moment of irrational fear.

"Here," I say, unwrapping a new reed. I stick it in his mouth to soften while I remove my reed and wipe down the mouthpiece. I look up at him as I tighten the ligature around the new reed. "You okay?"

He fixes me with angry eyes. "No. I'm not okay."

"It happens." I hand the clarinet back to him, knowing full well that he wasn't referring to his instrument. "Try that." He takes the clarinet, but he doesn't play it. He wants to talk about what's going on. I can see it in his face. I drop my eyes and inspect his uniform instead. "You're a mess. Turn around and let me zip you."

"I'm fine," he snaps.

"Luke . . ."

"You know, if you didn't want to be with me . . . *great. What-ever.* But you could've at least had the decency to tell me. Tell me to leave you alone. Tell me to go to hell. *Some*thing."

I watch the last of the kids disappear around the corner of a building. When he gets tired of waiting for me to respond, he drops his eyes, then turns and heads off after them.

It's three AM when the buses pull back into the school parking lot. We're all bleary-eyed and foggy-brained as we unload under the sodium vapor lights. I want nothing more than to get everything stowed as quickly as possible, get home, and crawl into bed.

I'm heading out to my truck a few minutes later when I see Luke working to remove the lug nuts on what must be a flat tire. Jackson and Spencer are huddled around him.

"You got it?" I look in the window to make sure he's got his parking brake on.

Luke applies pressure to the lug wrench, and the tire spins. "Can somebody hold this?"

"You're gonna have to let the car down and loosen the lug nuts first or it's just going to spin," I tell him.

He growls in frustration. He swipes a forearm across his eyes. He's tired. It's cold out, but he unzips his jacket and tosses it to the side. "Jackson, just hold the damn tire."

I let them try until I can't take the pain anymore. He glares at me when I flip the switch on the jack to L and lower the car. The lug nuts are tight, but with the tire securely on the ground, he's able to loosen them with a good stomp or two on the lug wrench.

"So, um, we're going to head out," Jackson says as I jack the car back up.

Luke looks up at them like they're a couple of Benedict Arnolds, but I see Spencer flick his eyebrows as he gathers up all his gear. Luke sneers back at him.

"Call me tomorrow," Jackson tells him.

"Come on," I tell Luke. "Let's get this tire on and get you home."

I let him do the work. He removes the flat, and I stow it in his trunk as he secures the new tire, but the jack throws him. I show him the switch that determines whether the jack is raising or lowering the car. He flips it to L and lowers the car. And damn it, the spare is flat also.

"Mother*fuck*er," he mutters, kicking the tire.

The parking lot is almost empty. The street between the lot and the band hall where parents earlier lined up to pick up kids has cleared out as well. The band directors are locking up. I know Mr. Gorman will make a swing through the parking lot before he leaves to make sure no stragglers are left behind.

"Well, your car is going nowhere tonight. Come on. Grab your stuff. I'll give you a ride home and tomorrow your dad can bring you back and you can get your tires fixed."

"Mr. Gorman'll take me home."

"Luke, he lives on the other side of the freeway, and you're seven doors down from me. I'm taking you home."

He doesn't budge.

I check the time on my phone—3:42—and huff. I just want to get home. I pick up his jacket, get his duffel bag from the trunk. He stands there, his arms tightly wrapped around himself. I hold out his jacket. He doesn't take it.

Dammit, Luke. My brain is so sluggish I can hardly think, and even if I could, a parking lot at almost four in the morning is neither the right time nor the right place to talk about what's going on. But I can't stand to see him this hurt and angry anymore. He deserves some kind of explanation, however vague. I squeeze my eyes shut and try to find my center.

"Luke, this isn't about you. This has nothing to do with you."

When I open my eyes, he's looking at me. He knows I'm not talking about the flat or the drive home. "Then what is it?" he asks.

Mr. Gorman's headlights sweep across us as he turns down the aisle. He pulls up next to Luke's car and rolls down his window. "Is that the spare?" he asks.

"Yeah," Luke answers.

"Hop on in. I'll give you a ride home."

"I'll take him," I say, shouldering his duffel bag. Luke shoots me an angry look; I ignore it. "We live on the same street."

"Well, let's move it, then, fellas. Be careful driving home."

The streets are quiet, and for the first few minutes, so is Luke. The traffic light ahead turns yellow, then red. And even though there isn't another car in sight, I feel compelled to stop.

I feel his eyes on me too. I don't know what to say to him, but I've opened the door, and it's clear he plans to walk through it.

"I haven't heard a word from you in weeks," he says abruptly. "You don't take my calls. You don't respond to my texts." He huffs. "If you've got something going on with some other guy, you could at least have the guts to tell me."

So that's what he thinks. I wish it were that simple. And maybe it would be easier on both of us if I told him yes. But something in me won't let me do it.

I sigh wearily. "Luke, there's no other guy."

"Why don't I believe you?"

"I don't know," I snap. "Why don't you?"

"You know, I thought I knew you, just a little. I thought there was something going on between us. I thought you were this really great guy that I could connect with."

I shake my head as he goes through this litany.

"And as it turns out, you've been playing me. I feel like the slide on your damn trombone. You pull me in, then push me away. You completely ignore me, then out of the blue you call me in the middle of the night. What was that, Curtis? Some kind of booty call? Were you too drunk to remember I was too far away to just hop in the sack with you? Who else did you call that night?"

"Shut up, Luke." The light turns green. I press hard on the accelerator. I can't wait to get this little prick out of my truck.

"No. Come on. I want to know who else you called that night. Did you have a good time? Where'd you wake up?"

I bristle at the insinuation. "You don't know anything about me." I take the corner into our neighborhood too fast and Luke braces himself against the door.

"You're right about that. You're not the person I thought you were."

"Maybe I'm not."

That wounds him. I can see it in his face. He wants me to defend myself. To tell him he's wrong. To declare myself. But that's not going to happen. Because in some ways, he's right.

"I hate you."

"I hate myself," I mutter.

"No you don't. You enjoy this game."

I wheel around the cul-de-sac and slam on the brake in front of his house and turn on him. "You think I enjoy this? You think I want to pull away from you? You think I like seeing you hurt? You think I like knowing there's nothing—*nothing* I can do about it?" The words are out before I can rein them in.

"That's a pretty dramatic performance for a playboy," he says coldly.

I lose what little composure I have left. "I am not a *fucking* playboy." Luke recoils at the anger in my voice and I don't give a shit. "I'm just a guy, Luke. A guy who made a mistake. You never made a mistake? You never did something you regret? I'm just a guy who didn't use a *fucking* condom." My eyes swim, but my blood is roiling.

Confusion pinches his features. "What are you saying?"

"Do I have to spell it out for you? *Goddammit*, you are so *fucking* dense sometimes." I don't want to say what comes next, but my fury has built up momentum and I'm helpless to rein it in. "I have HIV, Luke. You want to know why I pull away from you? Because I'm afraid for you. I'm afraid for you to be near me. You think you don't know me. You're fucking *straight* you don't know me." My voice cracks. "I'm sick, and I'm not going to get well. And I'm not going to drag you to the grave with me."

His face twitches as he struggles to absorb what I'm telling him. He looks out the window at his house. Someone has left a light on for him.

Say something.

Finally he turns back to me. "How many?"

"What?" I ask, confused.

"How many guys did you have to bend over for to win that lottery?"

I feel a coldness seep through me, a hate so fierce I can hardly contain it. "Get out of my fucking truck. Get out. *Get out!*"

He slams the door. I squeal my tires as I round the cul-de-sac and head back to Huntsville.

That sanctimonious little shit. Does he think this is some kind of prize?

How many guys did you have to bend over for?

I play his words over and over and over again in my head. I have never hated anyone in my entire life. But right now that's what I feel—hate. White hot hate, for him, for Ryan, for Jaleel's mother, for this *fucking* disease.

As I merge onto the freeway, I'm blinking furiously to clear my eyes.

My rage sustains me for most of the drive back to Huntsville, but by the time I reach the huge statue of Sam Houston on the side of the freeway, my rage is spent and I'm fighting an overwhelming exhaustion. A light rain begins to fall. All around me the landscape is dark, bleak.

I turn on my wipers. They scrape rhythmically across my windshield as I struggle to focus on the wet road ahead.

Too many people know—Jaleel, his parents, maybe university officials now, Luke. Who knows who he'll tell?

The sign for my exit looms ahead. I slide my truck into the right lane and squeeze my eyes shut for a moment. So tired. I struggle to open them again and start when I realize I'm on the shoulder. I steer back into my lane, then exit without further incident and turn down Avenue J toward my dorm.

I have to text Dad when I get in. He doesn't wait up for me anymore, but he does rise early, and if I'm not there, he'll worry. I don't want him to worry. I don't ever want him to—

The truck hits a bump, and my eyes spring open. I slam on the brakes; they lock and the truck goes into a skid, then slams head-on into a utility pole in a head-snapping impact.

In an instant, all goes quiet except for the light patter of rain on the windshield.

The door squeaks open. "Hey, buddy. Are you okay?" A man in a plaid robe, his gray hair greasy and sticking out in every direction, leans in.

It takes a moment for me to make sense of his question and form a response. "Yeah. I-I think so."

"You scared me to death. I was heading out to pick up the newspaper. A few seconds later and you might have hit me. Where were you heading?"

I try to think. "Um . . . shit . . . my dorm." I look across the steering wheel, past the wipers, past the utility pole that rises like a grotesque ornament from the hood of my truck, down the street, and try to orient myself. "It's just a couple more blocks."

"Well, it doesn't look like too much damage. See if you can put it in reverse and back out."

I realize then that the engine is still running, my foot still planted firmly on the brake. I shift into reverse and ease the truck back. The man walks to the front for a closer look. I note then that he's holding an umbrella.

My chest hurts when I try to draw in a deep breath.

"Just cosmetic, I think," he calls back. "But you need to get this checked out tomorrow." He returns to the open door and hesitates. "You sure you're okay?"

I nod.

"It probably wouldn't hurt for you to get checked out by a doctor, too. You think you can make it to your dorm?"

"Yeah. Thanks."

"No problem. Be careful out there."

I make my way slowly back to the dorm, focusing tightly on keeping my breaths shallow and fighting an irrational fear that tries to convince me I'm not getting enough air.

When I let myself in, Jaleel sits up on the spare bed.

"What the hell?" He tosses aside the blanket he was sleeping under and crosses the room to me. "What happened?" He grabs me around the shoulders and guides me to my bed.

I try to lie down, but the movement sends exquisite pain ripping through my chest. "It's nothing," I pant. "I guess I fell asleep and hit a utility pole."

"Holy shit. Who brought you home?"

"I drove."

"Come on, let me see." He unzips my hoodie, then pulls my T-shirt up over my head. I look down. There's a red mark in the center of my chest, a little swelling maybe, but the skin isn't broken. Jaleel presses his fingers into what's likely just a bruise. The pain is marginal.

"Does it hurt?"

"Only when I try to take a deep breath."

"Did your airbag deploy?"

"No. I guess it wasn't that bad. I had my brake on. My tires skidded on the wet grass."

"Wearing your seat belt?"

"Yeah."

"I'm no doctor, but I'd say you fractured your sternum, buddy. That happened to my grandma once. That seat belt locks on impact and *bam*, blunt-force trauma to the chest. You probably need to go have it x-rayed."

Fuck. I don't need this. "What did they do for her, your grandma?"

"They gave her some ibuprofen and told her to take it easy for six weeks. Not much you can do. You can't put a cast on it; you gotta breathe. But you gotta make sure there's not any other damage. Come on. Let's get you settled and I'll get you something."

He stacks up the pillows on my bed, then insists I not try to help as he eases me down on them, but I can't help contracting my abdominal muscles, sending another wave of pain through my chest. I try to relax as he heads for the bathroom. I hear him rummage around in the medicine cabinet. "What are you doing here anyway?"

"Sleeping."

"You know what I mean."

He comes back into the room with a couple of pills. "Well, I was kinda hoping I could move back in, unofficially, of course."

"Roommate trouble?"

He huffs. "Just sick of hearing how great affirmative action is for guys like me. Ignorant motherfucker. You got some water in the fridge?"

"Can you get me a beer?"

"Well, you probably earned one." He grabs a bottle from the refrigerator, twists off the lid, and hands it to me. I swallow the pills.

"So'd you break a window?" I ask.

He smiles. "Oh, you'd love that, wouldn't you? Nope, I had a spare key. My momma made it so she could get in if I were lying on the floor dying or something. I didn't turn it in when I moved out."

I smile back weakly. "I'm glad you're here."

"Yeah. Me too. So what were you doing out on the road this early in the morning? Boyfriend troubles?"

"I told him."

Jaleel's face grows serious. "And?"

"And, it wasn't good."

He runs his palm over his head, then takes a drink from my bottle without hesitation. Does he even realize what he just did?

"Fuck him," he says with disgust.

"Hey, Jaleel, I need sleep. You gonna hang around?"

"Well, I'm sure as hell not going back to that redneck motherfucker. So if it's okay with you?"

I nod and fight back tears again.

"Get some sleep, buddy. I'll take you down to the health center this afternoon for those X-rays. You're not going to be playing the trombone for a few weeks, that's for sure, but hell, marching season's almost over anyway. Garcia'll get over it."

Jaleel wraps himself in his blanket and settles back on the bare mattress. I slip my cell phone from my pocket and hold it up to my face.

Arrived late. Drove straight back. Rain check on that cookout? Your birthday next weekend, right? I love you, Dad.

I press Send and stare up at the ceiling and listen to the water dogs slap around in the tank. I wonder if Jaleel fed them last night. I make a mental note to ask when he wakes up. I try not to think about breathing because thinking about it makes me feel like I can't get enough air, and the anxiety of that thought kicks up my heart rate.

Relax, I tell myself. *Relax, think about nice things.*

How many guys did you have to bend over for to win that lottery?

His words come back to me suddenly. I finally fall asleep thinking that he's not who I thought he was either.

Chapter 20

LUKE

I can't separate my anger toward Curtis from my anger toward Dad Sunday morning. It's a hard knot of resentment lodged in my chest as I jack the car up again. Posers, the both of them.

"How'd you get home this morning?" Dad asks as I lift the spare off the wheel.

"A friend brought me."

"A friend. What friend?"

I look up at him as I drop the tire to the concrete. "Curtis, Dad. Curtis brought me home."

He glares down at me, the muscles in his jaw working. I roll the tire to the back of his SUV and heave it into the back on top of the other flat.

"Did he drive you straight home?"

I slam the gate with more force than necessary. "Yeah, Dad. *Straight* home."

"Don't use that tone with me."

I swear under my breath and head for the passenger door. "Can we go, please?"

"That's the guy that stood you up, right? I would've thought you'd have learned your lesson by now."

What lesson, Dad? That all gays are worthless pieces of shit? Is that what I am?

I stare out the side window. He wouldn't dare talk to me this way if Mom were here, but he can't help himself when she's not. It's a flimsy truce they've established. She says this is hard for him. She says he's trying. I don't see it.

The drive to Discount Tires is made in stony silence. I haven't slept, and I'm so tired now I can hardly keep my eyes open.

I take a seat next to Dad in the waiting room and thumb through the pages of a *Sports Illustrated*. I don't know anything about sports, and I couldn't care less, but the guy at the counter said it would be about an hour before the tires were ready. It's either *Sports Illustrated*, *Money* magazine, *Car and Driver*, or stare off into space and risk conversation with my dad, who's sitting stiffly in the plastic chair next to me. I choose to feign interest in an article about college football.

What I'd really like to do, though, is curl up on the filthy floor and sleep, forget about Curtis and his little bombshell.

HIV. Fuck. I'd considered that there was another guy, that maybe he'd met someone at Sam. I'd never considered this.

He isn't who I thought he was. But who was that? Did I really think at nineteen he was completely inexperienced? Did I think that he'd never been involved with another guy before? Was it one guy? More than one?

I'm afraid for you. I'm afraid for you to be near me.

Well, at least I give him some points for that. At least he's not out there spreading the joy. How long has he known?

And then I remember the phone call. That afternoon after we got back from H-E-B. He'd stood in the street talking, his fist clenched. Talking to who? The health department? One of his old fuck buddies?

Suddenly a lot of things are making sense now. Spinning in the street with a beer bottle clutched in his hand that night. Always holding back.

I mentally add up the weeks. He's known for some, what, ten weeks? And he never said a word to me? What does that say about where we were headed as a couple?

I feel the weight of my cell phone in my pocket. Despite everything, I want to text and make sure he made it back to school okay. At the same time, I hope he curls up in a hole somewhere and dies. I'm surprised at my own anger. This should be a time for compassion, but I don't feel it. Maybe Dad was right. Maybe I should have given more credence to his standing me up than I did.

The smell of rubber in the waiting room is overwhelming, and that, coupled with the lack of sleep, leaves me nauseated. I get up and stretch my legs. "I'm gonna go to the bathroom." Dad barely glances up as I head to the counter. The guy points to a short hallway at the far end of the store.

I lock the door behind me, then sit on the toilet and take out my phone and stare at his name in my contacts.

What a waste. So much potential and he threw it all away for a dick up his ass. Who knows what else he's got.

Dad waits until I get the tire back on my car, then heads to Lowe's. It's a relief to see him drive away. I can't deal with him another second. I can't deal with anyone right now.

But as I come around the dogleg, there's Libby, bounding up the street. She veers into the Camerons' driveway, where Corrine is washing her car. Reluctantly, I pull to the curb. If I can catch the dog now, I'll spare myself a trip to the lake.

"Hey, stranger," Corrine says brightly when I get out.

"Hey, Corrine." I walk around the car and open the back door so I can shoo the dog in.

Libby pauses to consider the open door, then noses Corrine's leg and flops down on the wet concrete, her tail wagging furiously. Corrine drops the soapy rag in a bucket and stoops to pet her.

"You dumb dog," she says, laughing.

I casually make my way over so as not to spook Libby, then stoop down and wrap my fingers securely around her collar.

"If you're looking for Curtis, he drove straight back to school this morning."

"Yeah, I know."

"You knew? Well, good, then maybe you can explain it to me.

He texted Dad, but no explanation why. And when I called him, he didn't answer. We had plans today. That's not Curtis, you know."

That's exactly Curtis, I think.

"I don't know, Corrine," I say with an unfair sharpness. "I don't know where Curtis is or what he does. He doesn't check in with me."

"Ouch. Did you two, um, have a lovers' quarrel or something?"

I tug at Libby's collar and try to get her on her feet, but all I manage to do is drag her a few inches across the concrete. She's making it clear she's not going anywhere yet. I yank hard at her collar. "Get up, dog."

"Hey, hey, hey!" Corrine says, prying my fingers off Libby's collar. "What's going on?"

"I'm trying to get this damn dog home."

"Looks to me more like you'd like to kick her home . . . or somebody else."

I huff and stand up. I don't give a crap where Libby goes or what she does either. If Miss Shelley wants her dog out of the lake, she can drag her out herself. Some people have no business owning dogs in the first place. I turn and stalk back to my car.

"Come on, Libby," Corrine says behind me. She jogs to my car door. Libby follows and bounds onto the backseat. She settles, smiling, her tongue lolling to the side, looking like she's ready to be chauffeured home. "Good girl." Corrine closes the door behind her, then leans against it and folds her arms across her chest.

"All right. Let's hear it."

"There's nothing to hear, Corrine."

"Come on. Talk to me. What's going on between you two? Curtis is acting all squirrely. He rarely comes home anymore. You're acting squirrely. So what gives?"

It hits me—she doesn't know. She's as in the dark as I was.

"Dad and I've been thinking that maybe you two were having some secret rendezvous up in Huntsville and that's why he hasn't been coming home. Am I right?" The breeze blows a strand of hair across her face. She sweeps it back, then gathers her hair into a ponytail and twists it over her shoulder. "No rendezvous?"

"Not with me."

That makes her laugh. "Then the mystery continues." She sighs. "You know, he's different around you."

"How so?"

"I don't know. He's never been interested in anyone before, and, well, it's kind of nice to see him all fan-girly."

Fan-girly? Curtis? How do you grow up so close to someone and know so little about him? *Never been interested in anyone before*. Curtis's problem is he was a little too interested in everyone, apparently.

"Hey," she says, giving my sleeve a tug. "He's coming home next weekend for Dad's birthday. I'm making carrot cake. You'll come, right? Whatever it is, you two can work it out."

Chapter 21

LUKE

There's no working this out.

And it's no surprise when Curtis doesn't show again for Wednesday's rehearsal or Friday night's game. I wouldn't show my face either if I were him. It's an away game, so it's late when I get in. I climb into bed with no intention of getting out again until at least Sunday. And with Dad out of town and Mom working this weekend, I might just pull it off.

I'm tired, tired of everything—school, band, Dad, Curtis. I just want to sleep and think about nothing for a long while.

"Hey, you got a hat I can borrow?"

I groan and reach for my phone. 8:30. I squint over at my closet, where Matt is rummaging through my things. He rises up on his toes and grabs at something on the high shelf. A fly fishing rod is propped against the door.

"Does this mean we're having fish for dinner?" I ask groggily.

"*Pft.* I'm not actually fishing. Dad's making me practice casting. But I still hate the Scouts."

No he doesn't. I push the quilt aside and get up. "What do you want?"

"You got one of those fishing caps, the kind they put pins in?"

"Do I look like someone who would own a fishing cap?"

"If it had a big pink feather in it." He grins at me.

"Ha, ha." From the top shelf, I grab a dusty baseball cap with the band's name embroidered across the front and pop it open, then settle it on his head. He straightens his glasses.

"Hey, you want to go with me? I'm going to the duck pond. Maybe we can fatten up the ducks some while we're there."

"I'm not going anywhere with anybody in camouflage."

Matt laughs and wriggles out of the multi-pocketed vest and tosses it on my bed.

I glance out the window. It's sunny, the sky a deep blue, but the heater hasn't kicked on, so I know it isn't cold out. I can't help checking out the Camerons' driveway. Curtis's truck isn't there. I'd bet money that he'll disappoint his family again this weekend. I wonder how long he thinks he can keep this up, this pristine image of himself, this façade of wholesomeness.

"I'm gonna grab some bread," Matt says. "I'll meet you downstairs."

I haven't spent a lot of time with Matt lately. I vow to change that. Sometimes I think he's the only person in my life I can really count on to be there for me, no matter what.

Except for the occasional jogger, the hike and bike paths are quiet this morning. It's cool out, but, as I expected, still warm enough for shorts.

I pinch off pieces of bread and drop them as we make our way to the edge of the lake. The ducks gather around us, squawking and jockeying for position. When the bread runs out, so do the ducks, and I settle in to watch Matt cast.

"Do you see that turtle right there?" I follow his finger until I see the small brown head just above the water some ways out. "I'm going to put my line in riiight there."

I watch as he whips the rod back and forth and then releases the line. It zips out in a wide arc and lands some distance off the mark, but I'm impressed. Matt, not so much. He mutters an obscenity and reels the line back in.

My mind wanders as he repeatedly casts and reels in. I pick up a stick and absentmindedly trace Curtis's name in the dirt. I don't want to focus on him, but he keeps rising to the surface of my mind like a bloated body.

Goddammit, you are so fucking dense sometimes.

You want to know why I pull away from you? Because I'm afraid for you. I'm afraid for you to be near me.

You think you don't know me. You're fucking straight you don't know me. I'm sick, and I'm not going to get well. And I'm not going to drag you to the grave with me.

My eyes blur.

An ant crawls over the edge and drops into the C. I blink to clear my eyes, then flick the ant out with the stick. Nobody and nothing messes with my Curtis. *My Curtis.* He could have been my Curtis. Luke and Curtis, Curtis and Luke.

Two more ants make their way into the R.

"Fucking ants!"

My head snaps up. Matt's stomping and slapping at ants swarming over his ankles. I scramble to my feet. "Where's your EpiPen?" I rub my hands up and down his legs, but the ants keep appearing out of nowhere. I realize he's standing in an ant bed so flat he hadn't noticed it. I push him away, then yank his shoes and socks off and brush at his feet, but already he's been stung at least a dozen times.

"Where's your fucking *EpiPen*?"

"I don't have it." His voice sounds rusty, and I'm shocked at how quickly he's reacting to the venom.

"*How can you not have your EpiPen!*" I scream at him.

"It's in my vest. Besides, it's winter," he gasps. "There aren't supposed to be ants out here in winter."

There's no winter in Texas, at least not enough winter to send the ants underground. And it's only November anyway.

What did Mom tell me about anaphylaxis reactions and emergency responses? What what what? I struggle to remember, but I'm rattled by the wheezing in each breath Matt draws in. *Calm down, Luke. You have to calm down. Think.*

I fumble in my pocket for my phone and dial 911. As I relay what's happening to the emergency operator, I get Matt down on the sidewalk and force him to tilt his head back to open his airways.

Welts are already rising on his arms, and his face is pale as he struggles to draw in air. I can see the panic in his eyes. I have to be calm for him.

"Just breathe, Matt," I say as evenly as I can.

I give our location, then press End and call Mom. After four agonizing rings, her voice mail picks up. *"Dammit,"* I scream at the phone.

Matt slumps over suddenly. In an instant, everything Mom has told me becomes crystal clear. His blood pressure has dropped, and fainting is his body's final attempt to keep his blood pressure up. He isn't getting enough air.

I stretch him out on his back, tilt his head up, and force air into his mouth, but his lungs don't expand.

"Don't you dare die on me, Matt."

I fling my phone aside and with numb fingers find Matt's in his pocket. Curtis won't recognize Matt's number; I pray to God he'll pick up. I don't know why I call him. I just need someone to tell me what to do.

I try again to force air into Matt's mouth, but it's useless.

Curtis picks up just as I hear the sirens in the distance.

"Curtis, it's Matt. He's not breathing. Ants—"

"Where are you?" he barks, cutting me off.

"The duck pond."

"I'm almost there. Have you called nine-one-one?"

"Yeah, but he's not—"

"It's okay, Luke. I'm making a U-turn right now. I'll be there in—"

"They're here."

The emergency vehicle jumps the curb and the EMTs rush to Matt's side. I fall back on my butt and scoot out of their way.

They move fast. A woman jabs Matt with an EpiPen as the man quickly checks his pulse. He presses a bag to Matt's face and squeezes. "He's not moving air." He tips his head back and flashes a penlight in his mouth as the woman relays information across the cell phone tucked against her shoulder.

Curtis's truck pulls up behind their vehicle.

"Can you get a tube in?" the woman asks.

"I don't know."

"Try a number five," she says, handing him a tube.

"What's his name?" the woman asks me.

"Matt. He didn't have his EpiPen. Is he going to be okay?" I ask as Curtis stoops down beside me.

"We're going to do everything we can," she says to me, then speaks into her cell phone again.

Curtis wraps an arm around me and I lean into him as the woman inserts a needle into Matt's arm and starts an IV drip. "Any other allergies?" she asks.

"I don't think so."

The only color on Matt's face is in his lips, which have turned an alarming shade of blue. He looks like he just stepped out of makeup for some horror flick, and I feel my stomach turn.

The man shakes his head slightly. "No good," he says, abandoning the tube.

"Trache him." And then loudly to Matt, "Hang in there, Matt. We're gonna get you some air."

Curtis pulls me to him as the woman attaches white discs to Matt's chest and the man preps his throat. When he presses the scalpel to Matt's skin, I turn away. Curtis holds my head to his chest as it really hits me that this is the day, the moment I lose my brother.

A small group of people have gathered on the sidewalk, and I find myself wondering what it feels like to be one of them, to be sympathetic, but grateful this isn't happening to someone they love.

"All right, there you go, buddy."

I look back and wipe my eyes. Miraculously, Matt's chest rises and falls as it should, and color floods back into his welt-covered face. The EMTs lift him onto a gurney. The man pats his arm. "We're going for a little ride, Matt."

"Come on, Luke," Curtis says, helping me to my feet. "We'll follow them to the hospital."

"What's his last name?" the man asks before closing the doors.

"Chesser," Curtis answers for me. The EMT jots the name down on a piece of masking tape adhered to his pants leg.

"Dr. Chesser's son?"

Curtis nods.

"All right. Let's roll."

Curtis flips on his hazard lights and stays right with the fast-moving ambulance, taking advantage of the openings created by the siren before they can close again. On an open straightaway, he glances over at me. "Strap in, Luke."

I pull the seat belt across and snap it into place. Somewhere in the back of my mind I note that Curtis isn't wearing his.

In the ER, Matt is wheeled away and we're herded to a counter in the waiting room. Curtis takes over, answering questions and filling out forms himself, gently pressing me for information he doesn't have.

But all I can think about is how long Matt went without breathing. What's the magic number? Three minutes? Five? Ten? At some point the brain starts to die. How long? Why can't I remember how long?

I'm staring numbly down the hallway when the glass door behind us opens and Mom rushes in. I meet her halfway. She grabs me by the arms. "Where's Matt?"

"I don't know. Back there somewhere."

"Stay here." She rushes down the hallway, taking full advantage of her status as an MD to access those areas mere mortals can't.

Curtis finds us seats in the waiting room, then buys me a bottle of water from the vending machine. He cracks the lid and insists I drink.

I stare at the bottle in my hands. "I should have made sure he had his EpiPen."

"It's not your fault," Curtis says.

"I'm my brother's keeper."

"You were there. You called nine-one-one. You saved his life."

"I don't know, Curtis. He wasn't breathing for a long time."

"It wasn't as long as you think. The EMTs worked amazingly fast."

I want to believe that. But even moving fast takes time. What if it wasn't enough? I rest my elbows on my knees and press my forehead into the water bottle and pray like I've never prayed before. Curtis rubs the back of my neck.

We sit that way for a long time, maybe hours, until Mom stoops down in front of me. I search her eyes, terrified of what she's going to say.

"He's in ICU now. He's still intubated through his trachea, and will be until the swelling goes down. It'll probably be another couple of hours before they remove the tube and let him wake up."

"Was there any damage to his brain?"

"We don't know yet." She looks over to Curtis. "I'm Luke's mom."

"Mom, this is Curtis."

She glances at me, then turns back to Curtis. "Thank you for being there."

"Can I see him?" I ask.

She nods. "But just for a minute."

A monitor beeps rhythmically next to him. Tubes snake out of his throat and arm. Something inside me rips open. But seeing his chest rise and fall, then rise and fall again, fills me with such relief that I realize I hadn't been completely convinced that he was still alive. I press the back of my hand to his cheek and feel his warm skin.

Curtis said this isn't my fault, but it is. I teased Matt about his vest. I'm the reason he took it off.

Mom lets me cry for a few minutes before she hands me a tissue, then gives me a reassuring hug.

The two EMTs who responded to my 911 call step into the room. "How's he doing?" the woman asks.

"Bridget, Mark." Mom gives them each a tight hug. "He's doing okay. Thank you. We were very lucky to get you two."

"No problem, Dr. Chesser," the woman, Bridget, says. "I'm just glad we got there in time. Your son here did a good job getting him help." Mom musses my hair. "We'll try to stop in again a little later if we can."

"Why were we lucky to get them?" I ask after they leave.

"Because there are only a handful of teams that can perform a tracheotomy in the field. If they hadn't, I don't think Matt would have made it. Hey, why don't you go back to the waiting room? I'll let you know when he wakes up."

I make my way back, but Curtis isn't there, and I think he's left me, gone home. But a few minutes later he's back, carrying two white bags and a drink holder with three Styrofoam cups—soup and iced tea. I take one of the bags and a tea in to Mom.

"Mom tells me to give you a hug," I tell him when I sit down again. But I don't deliver it. He hands me one of the smaller Styrofoam cups, but my hands are trembling and I find it hard to hold on to it. Curtis takes the cup back and removes the lid himself, then scoops up some noodles on a spoon and holds it to my mouth. I press my lips together and shake my head.

"Have you eaten anything today?"

"I'm not hungry."

"You need to eat something. You'll feel better."

I notice then that his hands are trembling slightly too. I take the bite before he drops it in my lap. I force the noodles down, but when he offers another bite, I refuse. He takes a few bites himself, then lids the cup and sticks it back in the bag on the floor. When he sits up, I notice he does so with his forearm pressed to his chest.

For the next several hours, we sit there. A dozen times I start to say something to him, to apologize for what I said, to ask how he is, but the timing seems all wrong. I lean back in my chair and close my eyes for a moment, then start awake.

"It's okay if you sleep," Curtis says softly. "I'll wake you when there's news."

I shake my head and sit up again. "I don't want to sleep."

But the next thing I know, Mom's hand is on my arm. I force my eyes to open.

"He's awake," she says, smiling.

"You think there's some kind of merit badge I can get for this shit?" Matt asks sleepily when I come through the door.

I laugh a little, but when I see the small white bandage where the tube had been removed from his throat, I break into tears again.

"Seriously, Luke, that is so gay."

He wants me to give him the blow-by-blow on everything that happened after he passed out and seems proud that he's been the cause of so much drama. But even with all his joking, when he blinks, his eyes stay shut a fraction of a second longer than normal until he seems to struggle to open them again.

"That's enough for now," Mom says quietly.

She walks me out to the waiting room as Matt drifts off to la-la land. "Your dad can't get a flight out until tomorrow morning," she says. "I really don't want you staying alone tonight. I'll call Jackson's mom. Curtis, could you drop Luke there? They're just a few streets over."

"I'm fine by myself," I tell her.

"I'm sure you are, but I'd feel better if you weren't."

"He can stay with us," Curtis offers. When Mom hesitates, he adds, "My dad and sister are home."

She checks to see if this is okay with me, and I nod.

I hadn't noticed the damage to his truck before, but as we approach it head-on in the brightly lit parking lot I'm surprised that I hadn't. The entire grill is smashed in, the bumper hanging almost to the concrete.

I stop. "What happened?"

"It's nothing. My truck skidded on some wet road. Come on. Let's get you home." He takes my arm and guides me to the door.

Chapter 22

LUKE

It's dark when Curtis pulls the truck into his driveway and cuts the engine. Neither of us makes a move to get out. We stare at the lighted windows.

I have no intention of staying here, not after he's worked so hard to put distance between us, not after what I said to him. But I do need to say something now, before I go.

"Thank you for being there."

"You don't—"

"No. I do. You didn't have to come. I don't know that I could have gotten through the day without you. It meant a lot to me. I wanted you to know."

He nods. "Then, you're welcome."

There's so much more I want to say, about how ashamed I am for what I said, about how much I've missed him, about how I want to be there for him the way he was there for me, but I feel a swell of emotion building in the back of my throat, and it acts like a dam, holding all the words back. I swallow hard, get out, and head down the street to my house.

"Luke. *Luke*. Wait up." He falls in step beside me. "Where are you going? You're staying with us tonight."

"I'm a big boy, Curtis. You don't have to babysit me. I think I can spend a night alone in my own house. I just want to sleep in my own bed."

"Then I'm staying with *you.*" I stop and look at him. He shrugs. "Look, I know you don't much like me right now, and I don't blame you. I don't much like myself. But I promised—"

"It's not that."

He takes a deep breath and lets it out slowly. "I promised your mom I wouldn't let you stay alone. If you don't want me staying, I can call Spencer or Jackson for you. But I'm not going to break my promise to your mom."

I'm too tired to argue.

We make the short walk to my house. On the way, he calls home to explain why his truck is in the driveway and he's not. I can tell from the conversation that he called from the hospital and explained what was going on.

"What about your dad's birthday?" I ask when he ends the call.

"How do you know about that?"

"Corrine told me."

He sucks in an audible breath. "Did you—"

I know what he's asking. "No," I answer before he can get the words out. I wouldn't do that. It's not mine to tell.

He exhales. "Dad's birthday is tomorrow. It's okay."

Once in the house he insists I eat something despite my protests. He rummages around in the pantry and pulls out a box of macaroni and cheese and a can of chili. He pauses after a couple of turns with the can opener and presses the inside of his wrist to his chest.

"What's wrong?" I ask.

He holds out the can opener. "You think you could do this?"

"Sure."

I get up and open the can.

"And this." He hands me the box of macaroni.

"You're hurt."

"A little shoulder harness injury. It stopped, I didn't."

I really look at him. "The accident. Are you okay?"

"I'm okay. See." He holds his arms out and makes a 360 turn. "A utility pole stopped my skid."

"Curtis, shit."

"I'm *fine*. The shoulder harness locked and I fractured my sternum. I already had X-rays. It's a small hairline fracture. No big deal. But can openers and such are going to be my nemesis for a couple more weeks. I'm fine, really," he says, taking the open box from me.

I fill the pot with water and place it on the stove. He takes over from there.

"When did it happen?"

He adjusts the flame under the second pot and empties the chili. "Last Sunday morning."

The drive back to Huntsville. I did this. "Curtis . . ."

He looks over his shoulder at me and kind of smiles. "I fell asleep, Luke. That's all."

"You could have been killed."

"I wasn't."

I watch him as he stirs the chili. When the macaroni is done, I drain it and measure out a quarter cup of milk. He mixes in the butter and the powdered cheese. Then I add the chili.

We sit at the table and eat right from the pot. In truth, though, we're just picking at it.

"How are things going with your dad?" he asks, threading a couple of pieces of macaroni onto his fork.

I shrug.

"Not so great?"

"Not so great."

He takes a deep breath and winces. "So what were you and Matt doing at the lake today?"

"He wanted to practice casting, add another badge to his weighted-down sash."

Curtis smiles. "He's really into that stuff, huh?"

"Like you wouldn't believe."

"What about you?"

Why are we making all this small talk? I look through the wide window to the darkness beyond and shrug. "I tried. It just gave my dad more reasons to hate me."

"Do you really believe he hates you?"

"I don't know," I say quietly.

"Hey," he says. I look back at him. His eyes are soft, a beautiful shade of green that matches the shirt he's wearing. "Don't give up on him, okay?"

Who are we talking about, Curtis?

I take a bite of the macaroni and chili, then instantly regret it. I force it down.

"I told Mr. Gorman you were thinking about auditioning for drum major."

I roll my eyes. I'm so tired, drained. "I'm sure he loved that idea."

"Actually, he kind of did. He thinks you should go for it."

"He does not."

"Baffling, I know." He grins. "Come on. You'd make a really good drum major. I meant it when I said you should consider it."

"I wouldn't even know how to prepare."

"Well, that's something I can still help you with."

"You don't have to do that."

He sighs. "Luke, I want to do that. I need to do that." He presses his lips together. "I understand if you don't want to, you know, be around me. But I need to do something. Do you understand that?"

I think maybe I do. *Talk to me, Curtis.*

He presses his forearm to his chest again and takes a deep breath and changes the subject. "Your mom seems really nice."

"She is. Do you miss your own mom?"

"I never knew her. Corrine and I were still in prenatal ICU when she died. She had a blood clot, probably in her leg. The clot broke free, passed through her heart, and lodged in her lungs. She was home alone. She collapsed and died before anyone knew."

"And your dad never remarried?"

"Nope."

"Why?"

"I don't know. He seems happy enough with his work and me and Corrine and the house, and he just never seems to need more."

But you do. I feel it.

"You look tired," he says, and I realize I've been resting my chin in my palm for some time. "Why don't you head upstairs, take a shower. I'll clean up."

"Your chest."

"I'm okay. The heavy lifting's done."

I'm more emotionally exhausted than physically. I take my time in the shower, thinking, trying to imagine what he must be feeling, trying to sort through my own feelings. Mostly what I feel is shame, for what I said to him, for the conclusions I jumped to. He has every reason to hate me, but he's here, and he's been here all day, waiting with me, feeding me, giving me hope, just being present when I needed him. And all this time dealing with a secret too big for anyone to carry alone.

Suddenly I want to scoop him up in my arms and never let him go. But I don't think he'll let me do that.

When I get out of the shower, I find him sitting at my desk.

"You've got a photo of Nate Schaper on your computer," he says as I watch him from the doorway.

There's a bite in his tone and it knocks me off balance. It's not just a photo; it's the background on my computer screen. I fish a pair of flannel boxers from my drawer and pull them on. Nate's photo has become so much like furniture in the room that I haven't even thought about it in months.

"I just haven't bothered to change it," I tell him. But I plan to, right now. I reach across him for the mouse, then click through a few screens until the photo background is replaced by a standard Windows background image, a skeletal white branch with five transparent leaves on a black background.

He stares at the screen for a moment longer—*What are you thinking, Curtis?*—then stands and stretches. I notice that he doesn't look at me. "Why don't you go to bed," he says. "I'm gonna grab a quick shower first. Can I . . ." He reaches into my drawer for something to wear.

"Help yourself."

He chooses a pair of flannel pants and a white T-shirt, then stands there fingering the material. "Do you have a spare room I can sleep in?"

Look at me, Curtis. I'm not afraid of you.

"There's one on the other side of the bathroom. Mom hasn't gotten around to decorating it or anything yet, but I know she's made up the bed."

"Ibuprofen?"

"Top drawer on the left of the sink. Mom keeps extra tooth-brushes in the cabinet below."

He finally looks up at me, smiles weakly. "Go on to bed."

I lie in the dark and listen to the spray of the shower. So close, yet so far away.

If Matt were here, he'd tell me to go get him. I smile to myself, but then find a lump forming in my throat again. Matt's absence is almost palpable. I take my phone off the bedside table and text Mom in the dark.

How's Matt?

Sleeping. And you need to do the same. Goodnight, sweetheart.

After a while I hear the shower cut off and Curtis's footsteps in the hall.

I'm sure I drifted off, but I'm awake again. The house is quiet. I get up and make my way into Matt's room and lie down on his un-made bed and stare at the darkness. I've never spent a night in this house—or the one in Odessa, or the one I grew up in—without ei-ther Mom or Dad or Matt. It's a strangely empty feeling.

I turn on the lamp next to his bed and survey his messy room. Just the way he likes it. Piles of clothes on the floor, dishes with dried bread crusts and hardened spaghetti on his desk, empty beef jerky sleeves everywhere, video game discs. But it's easy to tell what he really cares about—a slingshot he got for Christmas, a pair of binoculars, the scouting sash with all his badges on it. Each of these is hanging neatly from a pegged rack on one wall.

He's the kid my dad always wanted.

"He's coming home," Curtis says from the doorway. I roll my head to look at him. He's leaning against the door facing, his arms folded. My plaid flannels and white T-shirt look good on him.

"I know. Can't sleep either?"

"I saw the light go on. What are you doing in here?"

I press my lips together. "Just thinking. You know, when I was in the ICU, before Matt woke up, the EMTs who brought him came to check on him. Mom told me we were lucky that we'd gotten the team we did because not all teams are trained to cut holes in people's throats. I keep thinking, what if we'd gotten a different team? Matt would be dead now."

"But you did get that team, Luke. And your brother is going to be fine."

"What about you?"

He drops his eyes and runs his fingers through his short hair.

"Why didn't you tell me?" I ask.

"I think the answer to that is pretty obvious, don't you?"

"I didn't mean what I said."

"Yeah. You did mean it, Luke. And you were right." He shrugs, but there is a profound sadness in his eyes. "I played the lottery, and I won the jackpot."

"I wasn't right. I just—" I look away. I just what? I suck in a deep breath and turn back to him. "I just wanted to be the only one."

"I wish you had been," he says softly. "You wanted a fairy tale prince, someone to sweep you off your feet, give you a happy ever after. But I'm not that guy, am I?"

You could be.

"Can I ask you something?" he says. "Would I have been your only one?"

I don't answer.

He scoffs. "Nate Schaper. I kind of figured."

"It wasn't like that. We never . . ."

"You never what? Fucked?" He laughs derisively. "Because that would be disgusting, right?"

What? "No."

He looks up at the ceiling and blinks a few times. "Look, you were right. You don't need a babysitter. I'm just gonna change and go home."

"Don't go," I say quickly as he turns. "I don't want you to go."

He grips the door frame, his back to me. "Luke—"

"Stay with me."

He shakes his head. "I don't think that's a good idea."

"Please?"

He turns and looks at me again with shimmering eyes. His voice is choked when he speaks. "Don't make me want something I can't have, Luke."

I shift over in the bed to make room for him and hold out my hand. "Please."

"I can't—"

"You can. It's okay," I whisper. "Lie here with me."

At first he does nothing, then slowly he crosses the room. He presses his forearm to his chest and settles on his side next to me.

I brush my thumb across the scar on his forehead; he closes his eyes. "Let me be there for you," I say quietly.

His breathing quickens; his face pinches. He gives his head a quick shake.

"Let me be there for you, Curtis. I want to be there. I want to be part of this. I'm not afraid of you." I brush my mouth against his jaw, his ear. "I love you. Don't you know that?"

He sniffs and wipes his face against the pillowcase. "Don't love me, Luke. I'm not worth it."

"Don't say that. Don't ever say that." I find his hand and slip it beneath the waistband of my boxers.

He resists, but once his hand touches me, his fingers unfold and his hand slides down my erection. His breath quickens. The pain in his face breaks my heart.

"It's okay," I whisper again. "You won't hurt me." I reach for him.

"Don't." But his hips are already pressing into my hand.

"I'm not afraid of you."

"You should be," he chokes out.

"We'll be careful. I promise you that, okay?"

He starts to protest, but I press my mouth against his, and he gives in to me with heartbreaking fierceness. He won't allow me to touch him, though. That's okay; it's not too difficult to come up with a work-around.

Later he falls asleep in my arms, and for the first time in a really long time, I feel at peace.

"What the hell?"

I start and my heart kicks up a wild beat at the suddenness and the volume of Dad's voice. The overhead light is on, and Dad is standing in Matt's bedroom doorway. Curtis is lying across me. He stirs, looking first at me and then at Dad. I have an instant to note that it's still dark outside before Dad barks, "Get out."

"Dad . . ."

"I want him out of this house."

Curtis starts to get up, winces, then slips an arm between us and presses it against his chest. I don't know who to look at. "Are you okay?" I ask Curtis.

"Get the *fuck* out of my house!" Dad screams.

I'm trapped under Curtis's weight as he struggles to lift himself off me. I brace my hands against his shoulders to take some of the weight out of his effort.

Dad takes a step into the room, red-faced and breathing fire, and for a moment I fear he's going to physically throw Curtis out himself.

"I'll be down in a minute," I say as calmly as I can.

He glares at the two of us; I glare back. Then he mutters something I can't make out, and leaves. It isn't until we hear his heavy tread reach the bottom of the stairs that either of us draws a breath.

With my help, Curtis manages to sit up. He's breathing heavily.

"You need some more ibuprofen."

He glances at the empty doorway. "This is my fault. God, I'm so sorry, Luke."

"Don't be. He has to face this. He and my mom already broke up once over his homophobia. Since he's come back he's been trying to act like he's okay with it, but he's never actually had to look it in the eye, you know. This was bound to happen eventually." Who am I kidding; it was already happening in so many small ways.

"It's not just homophobia, Luke. He found you in bed with me. In his house. In your little brother's bed."

"Trust me. If you had been a girl, he'd be going out to get us donuts right now."

He smiles over his shoulder at me, then winces. Sleeping draped over my chest, apparently, wasn't the best position for someone with a sternum fracture.

We dress in my room. "I hate to leave you," he says quietly. "Your dad looks really angry."

"I can handle my dad." He looks dubious, but I'm not worried about Dad. I'm worried about Curtis.

We head down the stairs together. I show Curtis to the front door. I can hear the coffeemaker gurgling in the kitchen.

"Are you sure you're gonna be okay?" Curtis asks quietly.

I nod. "I'll call you later."

"Okay." He backs out and I close the door behind him.

I don't want a confrontation with Dad, but there's no getting around it. When I enter the kitchen, he's standing at the counter, stiffly pouring a cup of coffee. He looks up, then slams his cup down on the counter, sloshing coffee onto the countertop. He's clearly ready to do battle. Well, I am too.

"I'm seventeen. This is none of your business," I say.

"What happens in *my* house *is* my business."

"It's my house too. You weren't even supposed to be home until later this morning."

"I rented a car so I could be by my son's side as soon as possible. I stopped by to pick up a few things for him, and I find you fucking some guy in his bed."

"Curtis slept here. That's all he did."

"You expect me to believe that?" He laughs with derision.

"I don't care what you believe. It was Mom's idea. She didn't want me staying alone."

"Oh, this was all your mom's idea. Right. And I suppose she

okayed you two sharing your brother's bed while he lies in a hospital."

"Curtis was there, too. At the hospital. He was there when they cut the hole in Matt's throat. He was the one who sat with me in the waiting room for hours until we knew Matt was going to be okay. Ask her."

"He was draped over you like toilet paper over a pile of shit."

His words should shock me, but they don't. He wouldn't dare talk to me like this if Mom were here, though. I stride over to the coffeemaker with all the confidence of one who's protected by an impenetrable shield.

I don't realize his words were a warning sign until it's too late.

I reach past him for a cup hanging on a rack next to the coffeemaker. He grips my wrist and twists it painfully. "You even smell like him," he spits at me.

I don't even think before I react. "Yeah, you're right. We did it all night long. I took it in the ass, just the way he likes it."

The smack comes hard and fast, and I stumble against the island and put my hand to my stinging cheek. Dad's fists hang from his tensed arms.

"You get up there and wash him off of you before I take you to see your brother or God help me, I will break every bone in your body."

I stand under the steaming water, furious at myself both for letting him get to me and then for obediently doing what he said.

He doesn't look at me, not once, as we head to the hospital. He knows I won't tell Mom. But if he bothered to look at my face, he'd know how unnecessary that is anyway.

Matt's been moved to a regular room on the fourth floor. We locate it in stony silence.

"What happened to your face?" Mom gasps when we enter. When I don't answer, she looks to my dad and then back at me. "Who hit you?" she demands.

Dad can't hide his lingering anger, and she knows. She pushes past him to the hallway; he follows. The door closes behind them, but we can hear every word of her barely constrained fury. "I want you out of the house by the time I get home," she tells him. "You can get a hotel room or sleep in a ditch for all I care. You will *never* lay a hand on one of my sons ever again. Do you understand me?"

Matt seems shaken by the exchange, but recovers quickly when Dad reenters the room. It's not like this is the first time he's witnessed a parental expulsion. Mom allows Dad two minutes to see Matt, then holds the door open until he walks through it.

I nod when she asks if I'm okay. She doesn't ask what happened. My guess is she knows enough to piece it all together. "Is Curtis okay?"

"Yeah," I say, grateful that she asked.

"He has no right to do that to you," she says. "I love your father, but I will not tolerate violence in my home, not against you, and not against anyone else. He has to know that."

I nod, and the guilt I feel at provoking Dad eases a bit.

"Did you bring any food?" Matt asks.

Are you okay?

Instead of returning Curtis's text, I call and fill him in. Within an hour he appears at Matt's door with hoagie sandwiches for Mom and me, a chocolate shake for Matt, and a box of BeanBoozled jelly beans. "For when you're all better," he tells Matt.

His eyes linger a moment on my cheek. They flash with anger. He turns to Matt again and holds out a handful of dice. "How about a game of Farkle?"

He tells us the rules are simple. Then he proceeds to lay them out, and they're anything but simple. He grins at the confused looks on our faces. "Let's play. You'll get it."

I wouldn't have bet good money on that, but we do get the hang of it by the end of the first round, which Matt wins handily. He insists we play again.

The rounds became more enthusiastic and competitive as the afternoon wears on. We're still playing when the doctor finally signs the release orders, and Matt is set free.

While Curtis brings Mom's car around, we wheel Matt out in a wheelchair. As we wait at the curb, Mom squeezes my hand. "About last night," she says quietly over Matt's head. "Are you and Curtis—"

"No," I say before she can finish. That's not exactly the truth, but it's enough truth, and she says, "Okay."

Curtis helps Mom into the car, and I get Matt buckled into the front seat and close the door.

I look at Curtis over the roof of the car. "Should I . . ."

"Go with your family," he says. "If you want, stop by later for cake. I know on good authority that Dad and Corrine would really like to see you if you're up for it."

"Your Dad's birthday. I forgot. Oh, man, I feel bad for keeping you here all afternoon."

"It's all good. I wanted to be here."

Chapter 23

CURTIS

It felt good to focus on someone else for a change; it feels good to focus on Dad now, but it seems wrong that he grilled the steaks himself. It's his birthday. But he insisted, and I don't think I've ever seen him happier. I can't imagine spoiling this day for him.

"Currr-tis," Corrine calls back to me in the family room. "You have company." She pulls the front door open wider and Luke steps in.

Dad sets his knife and fork on his plate and jumps up to shake his hand.

"Happy birthday, sir."

"Thank you, Luke. Come on in."

I spear a piece of steak with my fork and watch Luke take in our little family scene. I'm amused at the flustered look on his face when he realizes he's interrupting dinner.

"I'm sorry. I didn't know you were—"

"Nonsense," Corrine says. "Let me get you a plate."

"No, I—I already had dinner."

"I make a pretty mean steak," Dad says. "We've got extra. Sit down." Without waiting for an answer, he heads to the kitchen.

Corrine flicks her eyebrows at me, then picks up her plate from the coffee table and scurries to an armchair, leaving the spot on the couch next to me empty. I gesture for him to have a seat.

He sits next to me, then reaches over, takes the fork from my hand, and eats the steak. And he doesn't just take it in his teeth. He sticks the entire fork in his mouth—a small, but deliberate statement. It doesn't change anything though.

He glances at Corrine, who seems to be fascinated by Cialis's effect on erectile dysfunction in a TV ad. Then he looks back at me and clears his throat, smiles, like we share some big secret. And I guess we do. More than one.

Suddenly I'm wary. I've done something I swore I wouldn't do. I've let him get close to me. God help me, I don't want to hurt him again. And if he's thinking what I think he's thinking, this can't end well.

"You've had a rough couple of days," Dad says, setting a plate down in front of him. "Dig in, kiddo. Steak and baked potato with all the trimmings. I'm sure you'll find someplace to put it. How's your brother doing?"

"Good. I'm just glad Curtis was there."

Corrine gives me a knowing look from across the room.

"Well, we're lucky he didn't end up in the ER himself. From the looks of that truck—"

"Dad, really, it was no big deal."

"Your truck tells a different story, Curt. And by the way, I'm not letting you take that mangled mess back to Huntsville in the morning. You can drive my truck until I get it repaired. I'll pick up a rental for a few days."

"You're staying tonight?" Luke asks.

"Dad won't let me drive back after dark." I give Dad an affectionate smile and cut another piece of steak. "Besides, we need to work out a plan for you if you're going to audition in the spring."

"Audition for what?" Dad asks.

"Luke's trying out for drum major."

"I think that's great. You couldn't ask for any better teacher than Curtis, Luke. He's legend at the high school."

I can't help rolling my eyes at that. Dad shoots me a proud look. "He's got a bright future ahead of him."

"I won't be building any bridges."

"Nope. You'll be building something more important—strong hearts and minds."

My nose burns. I feel Luke's eyes on me.

"Come on, you two. Eat up."

We watch CNN and eat. Luke exhibits an amazing appetite, and he looks a little too happy. He has to know last night was a mistake. And if he doesn't, I have to tell him.

When we're done, Dad collects all our plates; Corrine joins him in the kitchen.

"So we're working out a plan tonight, huh?" Luke says quietly, his eyes dancing.

"That's my plan. And you can get that smug look off your face. That's all we're doing—planning." I sound mean, but what choice do I have?

He looks away at the TV for a moment and chews on his lower lip. Then he twists his head sharply back to me.

"Why do you always do that? Try to push me away?"

"Because I can read you like a book. You think that last night changes everything. You think we're going to be a couple now and everything's going to be just peachy."

"What's so wrong with that?"

"But nothing has changed, Luke," I say, talking over him. I lower my voice again. "I'm a walking contagion. Don't you—"

"Blood and semen, Curtis," he hisses at me. "Blood and semen. That's the only way you can infect me. I'm not stupid. I know how HIV is transmitted. I know—"

"Jesus, Luke. Keep your voice down." My heart rate picks up and I glance toward the kitchen.

"Why haven't you told them?"

"How do you know I haven't?"

"Because Corrine—"

All the air leaves my lungs in one big whoosh. "Oh, fuck, you—"

"No. Geez, Curtis. I wouldn't do that. I just knew from the questions she asked me that she didn't know."

I close my eyes and try to slow my heart.

"Why haven't you told them?"

"That's none of your—"

"Ha-ppy birth-day to you," Corrine sings as she brings in a chocolate-iced cake she made herself from scratch. The flames trail behind the forty-six candles like a wind-whipped Arizona wildfire. Dad's behind her, pretend coughing and waving his way through the smoke. He laughs as he drops into a chair for the rest of his birthday song, and I can't help thinking he'll still be a fairly young man when I'm dead.

Corrine retrieves a gift from underneath an end table and places it on his lap.

"Aw, you guys are too much," he says.

He blows out the candles. Corrine cuts the cake as Dad slides the framed sketch from the wrapping. She worked on it in secret for months—a sketch of Mom hugely pregnant with the two of us, her belly draped in a long, flowing gown. Dad is standing behind her, his hands intertwined with hers across her belly. It's from a photo Dad keeps in his bedside table, one of the few family photos we have. We're all there, Mom, Dad, Corrine, me. Corrine finished it a few weeks ago, and I had it framed.

Dad props the sketch on his knees and quietly studies every detail of it, his eyes sliding smoothly across the glass. I swallow past the lump in my throat as I feel Luke's steadying hand on my back.

"I don't know what to say," Dad says quietly. "You've captured her beautifully."

Corrine dabs a finger at the corners of her eyes.

Dad takes a deep breath and stands. "Um, if you'll excuse me a minute, I want to go hang this." He grips my shoulder as he slips past me, embraces Corrine for a long moment, then slips out of the room.

"I'm just, um, going to put the cake back in the refrigerator for now," Corrine says.

I nod. We both know we aren't going to see Dad again for a while. After all these years, he still mourns Mom's loss, his loss. And I think now, he probably always will. It's hard to watch, but it's a beautiful thing too, a love so strong that it can hold two people in its grip long after they've parted.

I grab Luke's shirtsleeve and give it a tug. "Come on."

He follows me up to my room. I open my closet and pull out a couple of jackets and toss one to him.

"Where are we going?" he asks.

"Somewhere we can talk."

Downstairs I call out to Corrine that we're going out for a while. When she doesn't respond, I stick my head in the kitchen. She's standing over the lopsided cake, crying. She swipes furiously at her eyes when I say her name again.

"Hey," I say, putting my arms around her. "It's just a cake."

She laughs through her tears and sniffs. "I hate seeing him like this. I shouldn't have done the sketch."

"No. You should have. He loves it. There's nothing wrong with being sad about losing someone you love. He'll be okay. He just wants to spend some time alone thinking about her."

She nods, but another sob escapes her and I hold her closer. I look over my shoulder at Luke waiting in the doorway. "We were gonna run out for a while, but I'll stay if you want."

"No, you two go," she says, pushing me away. She smiles over at Luke. "You take care of him, okay? He seems a little trouble prone these days."

"I will," Luke says.

"Are you sure the truck's safe to drive?" Luke asks when I click the Unlock button on my keypad.

"We're not going far."

I pull up against the curb and put the truck in park. We walk past where the EMTs saved Matt's life and down to the water's edge. With the sun down, it's chilly out. I hold my chest and ease myself down to the ground. Luke sits next to me. I gaze out across the water, at the moonlight reflecting off the surface, at the tiny ripples that hint of life just below the surface—turtles, maybe fish.

"Why are we here?" Luke asks.

"To get some things straight."

He knows where this is going. I can almost feel his defenses go up. But I can't worry about that; there are things I need to say, and I'm damn well going to say them.

"I'm not your fairy-tale prince, Luke. I'm not anybody's fairy-tale prince."

"Oh, brother. Just because—"

"Stop. Just stop. It wasn't just a couple of times, Luke. Are you hearing me? And it wasn't just a couple of guys. Do you know that I don't even know some of their last names? You were right."

"Curtis—"

"I never dated anyone in high school. And it wasn't because I didn't want to. It was because I liked the way everyone looked up to me. Drum major, boy next door, wholesome, untainted." I scoff. "But I was bound and determined to make up for lost time when I got to Austin. You know, you're not the only one who knows how HIV is contracted. I knew too. But knowing isn't enough. You can pack your pockets with all the condoms in the world. But when you're in the heat of the moment, you're naked and your dick is screaming for release—"

"I don't need to hear this."

"—you don't think. You just go with the moment. You're not worrying about the consequences."

"Oh, come on, Curtis. It's not like you were trolling around in a bathhouse in San Francisco."

He's not listening to me. If there's one thing I took away from last night, it's that I can't trust myself with him. I wanted him. And I was so close to taking him.

And I know something else—I can't trust him to put on the brakes.

"Last night," I say, turning to him. "That can never happen again." That's not what he wants to hear. I can see it in the way he looks away, the way his arms tighten across his chest. "We're not going to be a couple, Luke." I shrug. "Not ever. You have to understand that if we're even going to be friends. You have to understand that friends are all we're ever going to be."

"Do I have any say in the matter?"

I wait until he turns back to face me. "You can say no. I'll drive you home and . . . well, that will be that."

"You know I can't do that."

I hoped he couldn't.

He sighs next to me. "Okay. You win," he says softly.

We watch the moonlight on the water. I point out a turtle's head slicing a small wake through the water's surface.

"Why haven't you told them?" Luke asks when the turtle ducks beneath the surface again.

"You saw my dad tonight. It would kill him."

"He'd want to know, Curtis. Have they started you on drugs yet?"

I shake my head and run through the whole insurance issue. "So I can't qualify for state programs as long as I'm insured under his plan, and I can't use the insurance or even cancel it without Dad knowing."

"Curtis . . ."

"Look, I'm not going to die tomorrow. I've got time."

"But you're leaving yourself open to all kinds of viruses and bad stuff."

I smirk. "It doesn't get much worse than this."

"Oh, yes, it does," he responds. "A lot worse."

"I don't need you to lecture me on this, Luke. I got this, okay?"

"But—"

"Okay?" I say, more forcefully.

Chapter 24

LUKE

It's not okay.

It's not even remotely okay. But I play along; he's given me no choice.

He leaves me Sunday night with a list of things to work on. Top of the list—running. Great. He wants me at three miles by the first of the year. Frankly, I couldn't care less about being drum major, but if it gives him something to focus his energies on, then I'll play along with that too.

I hit the pavement Monday as soon as I get home. And Tuesday. And Wednesday.

"What's with all the running?" Mom asks when I drag myself inside Thursday evening.

I grab a bottle of water from the refrigerator and twist off the cap. "Curtis says I have to run if I'm trying out for drum major."

"So, what, the audition includes a sprint or something?"

"No. Apparently, I have to increase my lung capacity if I want to play better. And I have to play better if I want to make drum major."

"Curtis, huh." She drops some bite-sized pieces of fish into a paper bag and smiles. "So, are you two a thing now?"

I shrug. "He's helping me get ready for auditions."

She crunches the lid of the bag closed and gives it a good shake. "Did Matt catch those?"

"The fish?" She laughs. "No. Tilapia. I picked it up at H-E-B. If I had my way, he wouldn't be going fishing again for a looong time." She sighs. "Your dad wants to take him next weekend."

"Are you okay with that?"

"He's his dad. I have to be. But the doctor and the mom in me worry. I can't turn it off."

I watch as she lays the breaded pieces in a sizzling hot pan of olive oil. "Can I ask you a medical question, Mom?"

"Sure."

"What's the prognosis for people who contract HIV today?"

She freezes and her face goes white. Then she looks at me and I see real fear in her eyes. "Luke—"

"Mom, it's just a research question for school. I just, uh—well—I'm not sure if the articles I'm reading are the most up-to-date. And they're hard to follow."

She exhales audibly, then gives me an embarrassed smile. "Well, that's not my field, but I believe if it's caught and treated early and the patient takes his meds religiously, he could conceivably have a near-normal lifespan."

"How early is early?"

"Well, before he, or she, of course, becomes symptomatic. They're seeing some amazing outcomes with the new antiretroviral drug combinations. No cure yet, but the treatment results are very encouraging. I thought you were taking physics this year?"

"It's for my English class. We're writing papers on social issues."

"Well, that's a big one. There's still a lot of stigma and irrational fear surrounding HIV."

"Do you know anyone who has it?"

With tongs, she lifts a piece of fish to check the doneness. "Me, personally? No." She glances back over her shoulder at me, a worried expression on her face. "Do you?"

I shake my head.

"So when is Curtis coming home again? I'd like to invite him to dinner."

"This weekend, I think."

"How about Saturday, then?"

How far today?

Almost two miles. About killed me.

Ha ha. Keep at it.

Mom wants you to come for dinner and a movie Saturday. You don't have to.

I want to. I like your mom.

How's your sternum?

Mending.

Are you feeling okay?

Luke, I'm fine.

The last game of the season.

It's always one of those bittersweet times. We're exhausted and tired of losing all our evenings to rehearsals and Friday nights to performances, of juggling schoolwork and family obligations. The seniors are freaking out over college admission applications and SAT and ACT tests. And yet, we all know we're going to miss this come next Friday.

The best part—it's alumni night. I don't know any of the alums except for the handful that served as techs this year, but there's been a lot of hugging and jousting since we got into the stands, and it's kind of infectious. I wish Curtis had come down tonight instead of waiting until morning.

I'm thinking how much he would have enjoyed this when I see him coming up the steps in a Sam Houston BearKat hoodie and jeans, his clarinet in his hand. He slips into the row with the drum majors. There are shouts of "Curtis!" "Hey, Curtis," from the kids. He waves as he makes his way down the aisle. Mr. Gorman gives him a big fist bump, then pulls him in for a hug. They talk a moment, then Curtis nods and pulls a pair of white gloves from his pocket and slips them on.

Mr. Gorman holds up a ringed notebook—"The Horse." I put my mouthpiece in my mouth as Curtis steps up onto the seats. He scans the row of clarinets until he finds me and winks. I smile back at him. Then he counts down the beat with the other drum majors.

As I play the familiar song, I watch him. It's the first time I've seen him conduct. He looks so at home up there, so alive, so happy, and I'm reminded of what his dad said—he's legend here. I can see why; he directs with confidence and a sense of passion and fun that I don't see in the more mechanical movements of the other drum majors.

Spencer nudges me when the song ends. "You two should really get together."

Curtis waves off the drum majors, collects his clarinet, and climbs his way up three benches, through the flutes and bass clarinets and the first row of clarinets. Every kid he squeezes past seems to feel the need to pat him on the arm or slap him on the butt as he goes. He steps over hat boxes and thermoses as he scoots down the aisle toward me.

I look at Spencer and grin.

"Uh-uh," he says, surprised.

I flick my eyebrows at him and shift over to give Curtis room to squeeze in between us.

"Nice," I say to him. "I've never seen you do that."

"Can I play here with you guys for a while?"

My nose burns. "Yeah, you can play here with us."

"Let's do it, then." He nods toward the drum majors, who are watching the football players gathering in the inflated football helmet at the end of the field. When the players begin to move out, the drum majors count down and we launch into the fight song.

I can hear him playing next to me, strong, clear. He bumps me with his hip when he catches me watching him, but he's grinning when he does it. I like this Curtis. This is who he really is. This is the Curtis I want to see more of.

When the song's over he leans into me. "You know, I can't hear you when you play. Why is that?"

"Because you're playing so loud?"

"I play loud, because I know how to breathe. *You*, however, still need to learn how to breathe."

"I do, huh?"

"Yes, you do. And we're going to work on that, starting tomorrow."

"Yes, sir. Whatever you say, sir." I salute with my clarinet. "Doesn't that hurt? All that breathing?"

He slaps his chest lightly. "I took my meds before I came. I feel good."

"You know, I never returned your mouthpiece."

"I know."

"I'm sorry."

"Don't be," he says.

I can't help feeling like we're talking about more than instrument parts here.

Adeeb is in the row behind us. He dips his head down between ours. "You two want to get a room?"

"Maybe we will," Curtis laughs back at him, but when he turns back to me, the laugh dies in his throat. He looks down at the field. "I'm sorry."

"Don't be. It was a joke. I got that."

He palms the back of his head. "Listen, I'm gonna head up to the trombones, see if I can borrow an instrument, play with them for a while."

"You don't have to go."

He smiles weakly. "I'll catch up with you later."

But he doesn't. Even after our halftime performance.

I unzip my jacket and fold it up on the seat and take a drink from my thermos. The temperature has dropped considerably since we got in the stands, but I'm warm from the performance and the nip in the air feels good on my bare arms. I crane my neck, and when a few kids shift just right, I can see him near the top of the stands, chatting up the trombones.

"Is he coming back?" Spencer asks, looking back with me.

"I don't know."

"Just friends, huh?"

"Just friends."

I'm hoping that he'll come by the band hall after the game, but he doesn't. And when I get home, all lights are out at his house. I sit in my car in the dark driveway and text him.

You didn't have to leave.

Get some sleep. I'll see you tomorrow.

I half expect Curtis to ditch our plans and head back up to Huntsville early the next morning, but around ten, I get a text.

Run. I'd go with but too sore. Hanging with family but I'll be at your house around four.

Promptly at four o'clock, he's standing on my doorstep, looking freshly showered and decidedly sheepish.

"You overdid it last night, huh?" I ask him.

"A bit."

"You sure you're up to this?"

"You're doing all the heavy lifting. I'm just here for the show."

"Hope you didn't pay much for your ticket."

"Curtis!" Mom says, coming around the corner. "I thought that was your voice." She makes a beeline for him and wraps him in a big hug. I grin at the surprised look on his face. That's what you get when you stand up for one of Mom's kids—undying devotion. "You're staying for dinner, right?" she asks when she releases him.

"Yes, ma'am."

"Great. Luke says you're into healthy, organic food. All I can say is, I tried."

Curtis glances at me, a touch of annoyance in his eyes that doesn't reach his voice. "I'm sure it'll be great."

"We'll see. What are you boys working on today?"

"Um, breathing," I say.

"Breathing. Okay! Matt will be home soon. Dinner in about an hour and a half. Okay?"

"Great." I motion with my head to the stairs. Curtis follows me up. The instant he closes the bedroom door behind him he rounds on me.

"Healthy, organic food? What the hell was that?"

"Oh, come on. You need to eat well, keep your immune system strong."

He huffs and looks off at the lamp or something on my desk, then he squeezes his eyes shut a moment and clenches his jaw. "I don't need a nanny. And I damn sure don't need a dietitian."

"Okay, I'm sorry. I was trying to help."

"Well, don't. Get your clarinet."

His flash of anger has thrown me. "Look, we don't have to do this."

"We're doing this. Just get your damn clarinet."

"No. I want to talk about this."

"This? What this? My HIV? Is that the *this* you want to talk about? Well, I don't want to talk about it."

"Mom said that the prognosis for HIV patients is really good for those who catch it early and get started on their meds."

He looks at me, his mouth hanging open, but he says nothing.

I hesitate a moment. "Curtis, she says that you—I mean, not you, people—can have a near normal lifespan if they take care of themselves. But you're not taking care of yourself."

He huffs and starts this crazy kind of laugh. "You told your mom?"

"No. I—I asked some questions. That's all. She's a doctor."

"You talked to your mom about my *fucking* HIV?"

"I told her it was for a research paper."

"You are a piece of work, you know that?"

The comment stings. "Can't I care about you? This is the defining thing in your life, and you won't even talk to me about it."

"That's it. Right there. *Right* there, Luke." He jabs his finger at me. "This is *not* the defining thing in my life." He's shouting.

I glance at the door.

"HIV is *not* what defines me. You get that? It is not what defines me. I am not my disease. I am a human being. A guy." His eyes shimmer and he drops his voice to a whisper. "Just a guy. That's all

I am and all I ever wanted to be." He looks around wildly, like he's trapped and doesn't know how to get out.

"Curtis," I say softly.

"You just don't get it, do you?" He sniffs. "I don't want to talk about my fucking disease. I don't want to talk about it, I don't want to think about it. I don't—I don't want this."

"I know."

"Do you, Luke? Do you know? Because I sure as hell don't know anything anymore."

"You don't have to know anything right now," I say gently. His bottom lip is trembling, his motions twitchy.

"I just want to be me again. You know. I don't want this."

I take him in my arms and hold him to me.

"I don't want this, Luke," he whispers into my neck. "But I can't make it go away. Nobody can make it go away."

"It's okay." I stroke my fingers through his hair, down his neck. "It's okay."

His breath hitches. "It's not okay. It's never going to be okay. Never."

"Shhh. Just hold onto me."

He clings to me like I'm the only thing keeping him on his feet, and maybe I am. And I will stand right here and hold on to him as long as he needs me. His tears on my neck soak into the collar of my shirt. I kiss his temple, the tears at the corner of his eye, his cheek. He turns his head to me and finds my mouth with his, hesitates.

"You can't hurt me by kissing me, Curtis." His eyes are those of a frightened animal. "It's okay," I whisper. "You can't hurt me." He bites down on his bottom lip, then allows me to press my mouth to his. It's not a deep kiss. I sense he won't allow that, but I marvel at how intimate it is, brushing our lips together, breathing into each other's mouths. I feel his muscles begin to relax. "I love you," I murmur.

He stills, then pulls away.

I let him go. He sits on my bed and opens the latches on my

clarinet case. He pauses to wipe his face on the neck of his T-shirt, then snaps the instrument together.

"We don't have to do this, Curtis."

He lets out a heavy breath, then holds out the clarinet to me. "I came here to teach you to breathe, and I intend to do just that. Please, Luke," he says when I hesitate, "I need to do this."

I take the clarinet.

"I'm gonna run to the bathroom. You warm up, okay?"

"Sure."

I run automatically through a few scales. I'm still shocked. I had no idea how fragile he was, how quickly and easily he could spin out of control. And I know this now too—I can't help him. He won't let me help him.

I can only be there for him. I make a vow to myself and to him: I will be there.

When he comes back a few minutes later, his face washed, he's the all-business Curtis. It's like the previous ten minutes or so never happened. It's all about my breathing technique now—keeping my shoulders still, using my diaphragm, letting it do all the work, blowing like I really want the air to reach the bell of the clarinet. He's focused and he pushes me again and again to practice proper form.

I can hear the difference in my sound, the strength, the clarity of each note.

We feel Matt pounding up the stairs moments before he opens the door.

"Hey, Luke," he says. He's puffing hard like he just ran home from the lake, his face pink from the cold air, his eyes bright. "Mom says Curtis is—oh, hey, Curtis. Mom says you're staying for dinner."

"I'm staying."

"Oh, good," he pants. "Cause I've been saving those BeanBoozleds you gave me until you came over. We can have 'em for dessert. Okay?"

Curtis bites back a grin. "Sure."

"Okay. Good."

Curtis and I share an amused look as Matt scoots out of the room for a shower. "They're just jelly beans," Curtis says.

"Oh, no. They're much more than jelly beans," I tell him. "One, you gave them to him, and as far as he's concerned, you're some kind of naturalist god." He laughs. "And two, BeanBoozleds are an experience that must be shared. Have you tried them?"

"Nope. I just thought they looked like something Matt would like. Am I going to regret this?"

"It doesn't say 'Caution' on the box for nothing."

I break down the barrel of my clarinet and set it back in the case.

"So where's he been?"

"Matt? Dad took him casting."

"Really?"

"I guess he thought Matt needed to get back on the horse, so to speak."

"Why didn't you go?"

"You really have to ask? Besides, I wasn't invited."

I feel Curtis watching me as I latch the case closed. It's no big deal. Spending the day with my dad and a rod and reel is not my idea of a good time. "Come on," I say, standing. "Let's go pick out a movie to watch with dinner."

"No family conversation around the table?"

"Not when Dad's gone."

In the family room I scroll through the On Demand listings. Curtis wanders along the shelves looking at books, photos, odds and ends of our lives, a stack of dusty CDs.

"Your parents like country music," he says, thumbing through a stack of jewel cases. He pulls one out and holds it up to me. I glance over. George Strait's *It Just Comes Natural*. "Can I play it?"

"Yeah. The CD player's in that cabinet." I nod to the doors at his knees. I keep scrolling as he removes the CD and feeds it into the player. "You like action, comedy, documentary . . ."

"Anything. Choose something Matt will like."

"Something Matt will like," I mutter. That would be slasher movies. And Mom's not going for that at all. I choose *Diary of a Wimpy Kid*. I'm clicking my way through the screens when I hear a vaguely familiar guitar intro come through the speakers and Curtis ask, "Do you know how to two-step?"

I glance over my shoulder and he gives me a little *Come here* gesture.

"Kidding, right?"

"Not kidding. Come on. I'll teach you." When I hesitate, he sweetens the offer. "You get to hold on to me."

"I can't say no to that."

"Clasp my hand," he tells me. "Now place the other one on my shoulder." He puts it there for me. "Okay, your right foot first. It's two quick steps, then two slow steps—one-two, one . . . two, right-left, right . . . left. You feel it?"

I watch my feet until I get the rhythm. When I look up, he's watching me. I smile; he smiles back. "You're doing good," he says.

I try to remember the name of the song, but it escapes me until the chorus, and then I remember—"Wrapped." It's a song about getting over someone until you see them again and then you find yourself wrapped around their finger once more. My smile softens as I hold his eyes and contemplate his song choice. "I like this song," I tell him.

"So do I," he says softly. His hand tightens on mine. "Come on, dance closer to me and I'll teach you to spin."

He holds me against his chest. "Just relax and follow me. We're going to spin clockwise. You'll step back with your right foot, then forward with your left. We're not doing geometry here, so just let it flow naturally."

We spin. I feel like I'm all left feet, but it gets a little easier with each step. He presses his cheek to mine. "There you go."

"Can I cut in?" Mom says from the archway.

We spring apart. She's leaning against the facing. How long has she been there?

"Sure." I drop onto the sofa and Mom steps into my place. She moves easily with Curtis, and soon they're spinning in the small space. I prop my cheek on my fist and watch. I love seeing him like this, relaxed, confident, happy. Just the way I saw him when he directed the band. And I know it's true—I love him.

And I'm not letting him go.

He twirls Mom under his arm and glances at me. I smile my appreciation, and he winks back.

Mom doesn't eat with us. I suspect dancing with Curtis brought back too many memories of better times. She was smiling when she handed us our plates, but I could see the sadness in her eyes.

The salmon is dry and tasteless; the brown rice, overwhelming; and the asparagus, asparagus. But Curtis eats every bite as Matt sorts through the BeanBoozleds. He's made a separate pile for each color—black, gold, yellow, blue, brown, orange, green, white, red, and a darker yellow.

"Okay," he says, all serious-like to Curtis, "you want to try skunk spray or licorice, or rotten egg or buttered popcorn."

"What do you want, Luke?" Curtis asks me.

"No, no, no. You bought the BeanBoozleds. The honor is all yours!"

"Okay. I'll take skunk spray or licorice." Matt holds out two black jelly beans and Curtis chooses one and pops it in his mouth. He screws up his face. Matt laughs and sticks the other in his mouth and chews. He's smiling for the first few chews and then he's running for the kitchen trash can, spitting and gagging.

Curtis laughs. "Licorice. Yum."

"You tricked him."

"All's fair . . ."

Matt comes back in, wiping his mouth. "Ew, nasty. Bleh."

"What's next?" Curtis asks.

Matt wipes his mouth on his sleeve again. "Okay, let's do rotten egg or buttered popcorn. I choose first this time." He takes one of the light yellow jelly beans and carefully places it on his tongue. When it passes the first test, he bites down. "Ugh, rotten egg." He soldiers on, chewing away while Curtis enjoys his buttered popcorn.

I can't help laughing at the two of them. I've played this game. Curtis can't beat the odds forever. Sure enough, he chooses barf in the next round and Matt gets peach, then they both get centipede and booger before Curtis lucks out with coconut to Matt's baby wipes. I lose track of who gets dog food, moldy cheese, toothpaste, and pencil shavings.

Curtis could quit at any time—I did—but he doesn't, and it's clear he's made a friend for life with Matt.

"He worships you, you know?" I tell Curtis on the front porch some time later.

Chapter 25

LUKE

The months slip by. The rest of November, December, January. Dad shows up every other weekend and takes Matt fishing or camping or out for ice cream or a burger. I avoid him, and he avoids me.

But Curtis is home every weekend now. We work on my breathing technique, practice conducting, run, hang out.

We don't talk about his HIV.

He hasn't told his family. I'm sure of that. And he hasn't started treatment yet. I'm worried about him, scared for him, but I'm careful to avoid setting him off. He seems healthy and happy for now, but I know it can't last. In any case, my hands are tied.

It's the second Saturday in February. We've got my house to ourselves, but there's no talk of taking advantage of that. We're going to watch a movie, a nice, safe movie.

"How about *Napoleon Dynamite*?" Curtis suggests. He grins at the disgusted look on my face and sighs. "All right." He scrolls back up to the M's. "*Marley & Me*. It better be good."

"Dog beats doofus any day."

"We'll see about that." He props his feet up on the coffee table. I tuck a throw pillow under my head and stretch my legs across his lap. He raises his eyebrows. "Really?"

"I'm getting comfortable."

He rolls his eyes and presses his thumbs into the arch of my foot.

Perhaps I'm too comfortable. It was a long week. Then last night we stayed up late playing Farkle with his dad and Corrine. And up again early this morning for a full five-mile run. I can do that now, but I'm beat. I struggle to keep my eyes open.

The last thing I remember about the movie is Marley bunching up his haunches to empty himself in the surf at a dog beach. A dog barks. No, not *a* dog. Dogs. Lots of dogs. Inexplicably, I'm looking out my bedroom window. They seem friendly enough, their tails wagging as they frolic about with some kittens.

Farther out there's a fence, the kind you see around horse pens—white, not too tall, with a flat rail running along the top. A mama cat walks along the rail, a yellow-striped kitten clinging to her back like a circus performer on a trick pony. The scene strikes me as harmonious, happy. I go downstairs for a closer look.

Before I can go more than two or three steps into the yard, a big stocky dog—maybe a pit bull—opens its wide jaws, picks up one of the kittens by the head, and begins to swing it like a pendulum. With one more big swing, the dog heaves the kitten over the fence where other dogs are now waiting.

With relief I watch the kitten land on its feet, unharmed. And then one of the other dogs snatches it up. It happens so fast I have no time to react. I feel the kitten's skull crunch in my bones.

Then the stocky dog picks up a second kitten.

No. Nooo! I'm screaming, but no sound comes out. I'm vaguely aware of Curtis at the end of the couch. I try to call out to him—*Curtis!*—but I can't get his attention. *Curtis!* I try to run to the kitten, but my feet won't move. In one swift move, the dog tosses the kitten over the fence where it, too, is quickly eaten. The big dog is going for a third kitten when I feel Curtis shaking my leg.

"Hey, Luke. You're moaning. Wake up. The movie's over."

I groan and roll over onto my stomach.

He shakes my leg again. "Lu-uke," he singsongs. "Wakey, wakey. I gotta go home."

"I had a bad dream," I mumble into the cushions.

"What about?" he asks. He smacks me twice on the butt, then kneads my calf.

I keep my eyes closed, trying to hang on to the dream and wanting to let go at the same time, knowing it was just a dream but still living it somehow. As best I can remember, I tell him, every detail, then I sit up groggily and lean my face into my hands.

"That is the saddest thing I ever heard," Curtis says with mock seriousness.

"Quit it," I say, backhanding him in the stomach. "It was awful."

"It sounds awful."

"All those little kitties. They had no idea. None. They thought the dogs wanted to play with them, and the entire time the dogs just saw them as kibble."

Curtis doesn't say anything. I take my hands from my face. He's chewing on his bottom lip and trying not to laugh.

"Quit teasing me. It was sad, I'm telling you."

"Very sad," he agrees.

And then I actually feel like I might cry. It was a stupid dream. Stupid, dumb, not real. Still, I feel my emotions rise up and start to spill over.

"Come here," Curtis says, pulling me to him.

I go, gladly, drawing my knees up and making a ball out of myself and nestling into him. He wraps his arms around me and pets me like a dog. I'm sure he thinks that's quite funny. I don't care.

I like having him here.

We're inseparable when he's home now. But those invisible boundaries are still firmly in place. No repeat of that night in my room. I was cautious around him at first, uncertain as to exactly where the lines were drawn. It's funny, though—once I demonstrated my willingness to play by his rules—no intimate contact, no talk of his HIV—he drew so close to me that it's almost like we are a couple. I know that others are starting to see us that way too.

"Do you ever remember your dreams?" I ask him.

"Sometimes."

"What do you dream about?"

"Stuff." He chuckles and rubs my head with his fist.

I know instinctively, or maybe from experience, that my next question will cross the line, but I can't help myself. "Do you ever dream about me?"

He gets still and quiet.

After a few awkward moments I sit up and take a drink. The ice has long since melted and the soda's settled on the bottom. I swirl the glass before I take a second sip. I'm grasping for something to say that will take us into safer waters when Curtis gets up abruptly and slaps me on the knee.

"I gotta go." He picks up our glasses.

I follow him into the kitchen, where the not-so-subtle smell of vinegar catches his attention.

"What have we here?" he says, peering into the glass bowl on the counter where Matt has sunk two chicken leg bones in the pungent stuff.

"Something Matt read about in *Boys' Life*. He's trying to turn the bones into pretzels."

Curtis pokes his fingers in the vinegar and flexes the bones slightly.

"The vinegar is supposed to—"

"Break down the calcium in the bones," Curtis finishes.

"I find the fact that you know that kind of stuff mildly disturbing. You know, maybe you should be hanging out with my little brother."

Without looking up from the bowl, Curtis tweaks my side with his wet, smelly fingers. "Nah. You'll do."

"Cool, huh?" Matt says, holding up a bone pretzel several days later when the decalcification process, or whatever you call it, is complete. *Pretzel* isn't quite the right word. The bone is too short to be shaped into anything more than a tenuous knot.

"What's this?" I pick up a vinegar-splashed valentine from the counter, the kind that comes boxed as a class set plus one for the teacher. On the front are the characters from *Ed, Edd n Eddy* and the words *You electrify me*. On the back, printed in scrawled block letters, *Samuel*.

I grin at Matt. "Samuel gave you a Valentine's card?"

"Um, no. He told me to give it to you."

I drop the card. Creepy.

"Oh, hey," Matt says, putting down the pretzel bone. He fishes for something in his pocket. "I'm supposed to give this to you." He hands me a small red plush dog, in upright position, its stubby arms splayed out to the sides. Its coat is nubby, like you see on old teddy bears. Secured to its chest is a satiny red heart stamped with one word: *Woof.*

Matt says it's from Curtis, but I knew that the moment I saw it.

It was Sunday, the day after the stupid dog dream. We were poking around the Hallmark store looking for valentines for Corrine and my mom.

"You should give this one to Corrine," I told him, opening a card that sang "I'm just a hunk, a hunk of burning love." I grinned.

"That's sick," he said, taking the card from me.

We amused ourselves with tinny renditions of "Cupid," "Love Me Tender," "I Think I Love You," and Curtis's favorite, "Bad to the Bone."

"I think maybe we should stick with something a little less incestuous," Curtis suggested with a wink as he returned all the cards to their slots.

"How about a singing bear?"

"How about flowers and a plain card?"

I continued my search for something sweet that didn't scream "creepy brother." I slipped another one from the rack. "How about this one?"

I looked up, but Curtis wasn't there. I found him one aisle over in front of a display of stuffed animals. On the shelf next to a litter of red kittens with red hearts stamped with "Meow" was a litter of little dogs.

Curtis picked up one of the dogs. "Grrr," he growled, assaulting the kitties. "I'm going to eat you."

"Noooo," he made the kitties cry back. "Don't crush our skulls, you mean dog."

"Very funny," I said.

Later, I went back and bought one of the dogs for him.

Apparently he'd done the same for me.

"Hey, Matt." I pull out my cell phone and hand it to him. "Take a picture for me."

Chapter 26

CURTIS

The photo is cute—Luke pressing pursed lips into the dog's belly. I hold it out for Jaleel to see.

"Um, isn't that the same red dog sittin' on your pillow right now?"

"Yeah. I found it in my duffel bag when I got back yesterday."

"I think you two got a couple of twelve-year-old girls living inside you."

I force myself to smile a little over my shoulder at him.

"So, today's the big day, huh?" he says.

I slide my phone back in my pocket and snap the lids on the two travel aquariums. Only four of the water dogs have evolved. The other two seem firmly stuck in the larvae stage. I thought it would be fun to release them with Luke next weekend, if for no other reason than to watch him squirm, but I changed my mind half an hour ago.

"Yep. Today's the day. You want to come with me?"

"Nope."

Good. Because I don't feel much like company today.

I had another blood draw a couple of weeks ago. I didn't tell Luke about it. I haven't told Jaleel either.

The results came back this morning. My T cell count is dropping like a rock. It's down, and my viral load is up. I was feeding the salamanders when Dr. Nguyen himself called. I didn't go to the

HIV clinic to have my blood drawn; that felt too much like giving in. I wanted to prove to myself that I was stable, that I could continue skirting along, maybe indefinitely.

But Dr. Nguyen had been alarmed; I could hear it in his voice. He pressed me to take responsibility for my health.

I ended the call and dropped another worm in the tank. I felt trapped, like I was in that tank, able to see the world around me, but unable to engage it. And I suddenly wanted to let the creatures go. Right then, right that minute.

I head out to a wooded area not far from campus. I feel like I can't breathe. I press the window down button, but nothing happens. I try the other windows. Nothing. Dammit. I've blown a fuse.

And I feel like I'm about to blow another one. Sometimes I think the universe has stacked the deck against me. I can't catch a break.

I'm hyperventilating and driving too fast. I slow down and pull onto the shoulder.

I let myself cry, for what I've lost, for what I'll never have again, for the road I'll have to travel if I'm going to live, for the crappy life I'll regret every minute I do live.

I can't do it; it's too much.

And for the first time, I consider the alternative—the freedom of having a choice.

I get out and lift the aquariums from the bed of the truck and trek through the woods until I find a small pond. There are dozens of them out here. I scoop out the two water dogs and release them into the water, then I gather up the salamanders, one by one, and place them gently at the edge of a fallen branch. And one by one they burrow under the branch and the leaves until I can't see them anymore.

Luke's in love with me. And I'm in love with him. But I can't have him. I will never have him. And it's time I set him free, too.

I stay for a while and watch for the salamanders, but they don't come back.

They're not coming back.

Neither am I.

Chapter 27

LUKE

On Friday, Curtis pulls into our driveway right behind me, reaches over, and opens the passenger door. Mom is tying balloons to the gas light in the front yard. She waves to him.

"You're home early." I lean against the door, ready for some light banter, but the look on his face stops me. "What's wrong?"

"Nothing's wrong. Hop in."

"Sure." I close the door behind me, then push the button to roll down the window, but it doesn't go down. "What's wrong with this window?"

"A short. None of them are working."

I open the door again and tell Mom I'll be back. She waves me off.

"So, where are we going?"

He presses on the accelerator and we whip around the cul-de-sac. "Shopping."

"For . . ."

He looks irritated. "Matt's birthday. What else? Today, right?"

"I don't recall mentioning that. How did you know?"

"He texted me." He glances over as he pulls to a stop at the corner. "Apparently subtlety is not in the Chesser genes." I smirk; he smiles back, just a little. "It's okay. Twelve is a big one."

Something's happened. I can feel it in the silence as we make the short drive. He's spiraling again. Slowly right now, but I fear it's going to pick up speed, and there will be nothing I can do to stop it.

We stroll through the mall, stopping at the pet store so Curtis can halfheartedly tease me about the kittens in the window, then at Spencer Gifts so he can halfheartedly tease me about all the sex toys I've never heard of.

But we're not shopping; we're wandering. Aimlessly. There's something going on in his head, something dark.

We stop at Pretzel Time. I stand back and watch him order. I notice the slump of his shoulders, the way his hand shakes when he holds out a ten-dollar bill. He looks tired, defeated. He hands me a pretzel and an Icee. "Come on."

We sit quietly on a bench in the center of the main aisle. I watch him watch shoppers move past us until I can't stand it anymore. "Do you want to talk?" I ask.

He kind of laughs—a laugh with no humor behind it—and points with his pretzel at the passing crowd. "Pick one."

"Pick one what?"

"A guy. I want you to show me what kind of guy you like."

So that's it. We're not here just to pick out a gift for Matt; we're here to pick out a guy for me. I cringe at the thought. "You already know what kind of guy I like."

"Come on," he says, dully. "What about that one?" He's pointing at some biker-looking dude with his pants so low he has to walk with one finger hooked in a belt loop to keep them from dropping to his ankles. His hair is black and greasy. A studded collar circles his neck.

"You obviously have a low opinion of me."

He doesn't laugh. He doesn't smile. "What about that one?"

This time he points out a super skinny guy with his baseball hat cocked at an odd angle. He looks like a super nerd trying desperately to be cool and failing miserably. I stare back at Curtis. He can't be serious. But if he wants to play this game, then I'll play. And he'll see how silly this is.

Coming up behind nerd guy is a real contender, if there is such a thing. He wears his hair short, his shirt snug, and his jeans just low enough to be sexy without being grungy. "How about that one," I say, pointing him out.

Curtis smirks. "Shallow, pretty boy. All swagger, no substance. Probably doesn't even know the difference between a pianissimo and a fortissimo."

The guy pauses in front of Abercrombie & Fitch and then goes in.

"Figures," Curtis says.

"Here." I hand him my pretzel and Icee. "I'm gonna check him out."

Serve you right for starting this, I think as I make my way into the store. I poke around for a bit, making no effort at all to single out Shallow Pretty Boy, until the loud music and missing Curtis drive me out again.

I find my half-eaten pretzel and Icee on the bench, but Curtis is gone. I pick them up, wipe the condensation from the bench with my cuff, and toss them in the trash.

I find him at a kiosk not too far away. He doesn't look at me when I lean on the glass counter next to him.

He holds up a chain from which dangles a stainless steel dog tag encased in a black rubber edging. The metal is smooth, not yet embossed with its owner's name and vital information. "Do you think Matt will like it?"

"He'll love it."

He fills out the information and hands it to the attendant, who goes to work punching out the letters and numbers. We watch, and when I dare, I look at Curtis. His eyes are fixed on the embosser.

"Did you get his number?" he asks.

"Nope, but I think I got yours."

He takes my hand below the counter and crushes my knuckles until I yell, "Ow."

"Aw, cool! Thanks, Curtis!" Matt slips the chain over his head and looks again at his name embossed on the metal.

"You want to go with me to Adeeb's section party tomorrow?" I ask Curtis when Matt goes to check out his image in the bathroom mirror. The party is no big deal. Just a bunch of clarinets hanging out. Adeeb's making burgers on the grill. I don't care if I go or not. I just think it would be good for Curtis to hang out with old friends. I feel certain he'll say no, but then he surprises me.

"Sure. Why not?"

His truck is already there when I arrive Sunday afternoon. I'd hoped we could come together, but he told me he had errands to run on the way. If he was back to avoiding me again, why did he come to the party? Sometimes I just don't get the way his brain works.

I peek in the window when I pass his truck. Whatever errands he had didn't involve any kind of cargo. The seat, the floorboards, the bed—all empty. I zip up my hoodie and head up to the Rangans' front porch. A petite woman in a colorful sari shows me in and points to the back patio.

"Hey, Lukey Duke's here," Adeeb calls out when he sees me.

I wave to some friends and cross the yard to the bricked area in the corner where he's flattening burgers on the grill with a long spatula. Curtis is stretched out in a chair next to him, a paper plate balanced on his thigh.

"Hope you're hungry," Adeeb says. He fixes me a burger, then toes open a cooler next to the table.

I grab a soda and settle into a chair next to Curtis. He picks up a red Solo cup from the bricks and takes a sip. "What are you drinking?" I ask.

"Vodka." His burger sits on the paper plate; he's only taken one, maybe two, bites.

I lift my eyes to Adeeb, and he shrugs.

Curtis stares off at a game of volleyball that's starting up in the yard. He takes another sip of his drink.

"Why don't you let me get you a soda or something," I say quietly. I reach for his drink.

He jerks it away from me, then stands and dumps his plate in a trash bag next to the table. "I'm going inside for a bit, man," he says to Adeeb.

Adeeb looks over his shoulder at me and shrugs. "Last call for burgers," he shouts out to the kids.

I take my burger and move to a seat next to Spencer. He's sitting with a bunch of the girls, watching the game. He nods toward the volleyball net in the center of the yard, where Jackson's got trombone Anna balanced precariously on his shoulders. She's squealing and clutching at the net.

"I thought this was a clarinet party."

"She came with him. She'll be lucky if she leaves alive, though."

I take a bite of my burger and watch them. One of the kids has his phone out and is videotaping the whole thing. It'll be all over YouTube by midnight. I'd bet money on it.

I look toward the house. I want to follow him, make sure he's okay, but I know he'd resent that. If he wanted me to come, he would have asked.

The time stretches out as the sun begins to sink below the horizon.

"What happened to Curtis?" Spencer asks.

"Huh? Oh. I don't know. I think he might have gone home."

"Trouble in paradise?"

I turn and study my friend. I wish I could spill my guts, tell him everything. This is too much to carry around alone, too much responsibility, too much of a burden. Not that Curtis is a burden; he'll never be a burden to me. But this knowing that he's sick and that he's not getting the help he needs. Am I doing the right thing by keeping his secrets? He'd be angry if I told his dad. No, he'd be furious. But he'd get the help he needs. And then he'd get better.

And maybe, just maybe he'd forgive me.

But even as I rehearse in my head what I'd say to his dad, I know I won't do it. Curtis is a grown man. He has the right to make his own decisions. No matter how stupid.

I look at the house again. Still no Curtis. He's gone, and so is my reason for being here. I wait another half hour, then I get up. "I'm going home, man. I'll catch you later."

I'm checking the time on my phone when I run into Curtis coming out of the house.

"Where you going?" he says loudly, throwing an arm around my shoulder and sloshing me with his drink. He reeks of vodka.

"I thought you'd gone home."

"No no no no no. We're gonna play volleyball. Right, Adeeb?" he shouts over his shoulder. He hustles me out the door, still hanging on to me. "Come on guys, let's start a game. I call Luke."

We team up—Adeeb, Samira, Curtis, and me against Jackson, Anna, and a couple of other kids.

I haven't played volleyball since eighth-grade PE. What I know about the game is pretty much this: If the ball comes at you, hit it.

I contribute mightily to the other team's score until Curtis sidles up behind me and says in a low voice, "You hit it like this." And then he slides his hands up my arms to my wrists and cocks back my hands. "You have to get up under the ball," he whispers. He's pressed to my back, his mouth right against my ear. Someone wolf whistles and he staggers back to his position.

He's hammered, but at least he's having a good time. He deserves it, so what the hell.

With all the extra coaching I'm getting, my technique improves in the second game. When it's my turn to serve, Curtis holds up his hands in a time-out sign and stumbles over to me, completely oblivious to the grins and snickering from the kids.

"Toss the ball in front of your serving shoulder," he says huskily from close behind me. "Keep your elbow high and back. That's it. God, you are so fucking sexy." He doesn't even bother keeping his voice low. "Hit the middle of the ball with the middle of your hand, then follow through on your arm swing."

"Okay, I got it," I say, shrugging him off. Honestly, this is embarrassing.

"Do you, Luke?" he asks. "Do you really get it?"

I get it. More than he realizes.

"Come on," Adeeb yells. "Let's play."

Curtis smacks me on the butt and stumbles away.

By the time we get to our third game, it's almost too dark to see, even with the porch lights on.

"Come on, one more game," Curtis insists. He takes another couple of swigs from his drink and sets his cup near the net, then assumes the position. A couple of plays in, he collides with Samira and goes down flat on his back, laughing like an idiot.

"All right, game over," Adeeb says. "Come on, man, I'm taking you home." He offers his hand to Curtis.

"No," Curtis says, his eyes still closed but his mouth stretched in a wide grin. "Luke can take me home. You'll take me home, won't you, Luke?"

Adeeb shakes his head. "Your call, man," he says to me.

"Will you help me get him to my car?"

Between the two of us, we manage to get Curtis through the house and into the front seat. It's not that he's so drunk he can't walk; he's just so drunk he can't be trusted not to stagger up the middle of the street and get himself run over. His head lolls back against the head rest. I get into the driver's seat, then reach across him for the seat belt.

He nuzzles my neck. "Do you love me, Luke?"

Adeeb snorts and tells me not to take advantage of him, then closes the passenger door.

Curtis smiles and rolls his head toward me as I lock the seat belt into place. "Do you, Luke?" he says. "Do you love me?"

"You know I love you, Curtis." I turn the key in the ignition.

"You say that now," he says giddily, "but just wait until the real freak show starts."

"There's not gonna be a freak show. Come on. I'm gonna get you home so you can sleep it off."

For some reason, that makes him laugh. "Are you gonna put me to bed? Maybe you can sleep over with me. Sleep in my jammies tonight. I don't sleep in jammies. Did you know that? You're so cute when you do that."

"Do what?"

"Roll your eyes."

So I roll them again.

Corrine and his dad look up in alarm as I help a giggling Curtis through the front door. "Dad, Corrine," he gushes. "How are you guys? Sooo good to see you."

"What happened?" his dad asks, jumping to his feet.

"We were just playing some bolleyvall," Curtis says, slumping against me.

Corrine clamps a hand to her mouth; her eyes dance with merriment.

You're not helping, Curtis.

"He's fine." I struggle to get a better grip on him. "He had a little too much to drink at the party. I'm just going to get him to his room, if that's okay."

"Curt, what were you thinking?" his dad says. "Haven't we been through this before? If you can't be responsible..."

I doubt Curtis is hearing a word his dad says, seeing as how he smiles maniacally through the entire lecture and keeps repeating, "Okay, Dad," and gripping me even tighter around the neck. Then, with his dad still talking, he dismisses him with, "Luke is going to take me to bed now."

I blush furiously. "I'm gonna get him upstairs."

His dad shakes his head as I usher Curtis up the stairs. The second we cross the threshold to his room, he's all over me. His hands, his mouth. He's making it damn hard to behave honorably, but I at least make a lame attempt at it, noting the obvious. "You're drunk."

"Yes, I am," he says, backing me into the closed door and pressing against me. "And you're wearing way too many clothes."

Faster than I thought any drunk could, he has both my hoodie and my shirt off and he's grappling with the button on my shorts. Not that I'm complaining, but I know him, and he'd never do this sober. "Come on, Curtis. Cut it out."

"I don't want to cut it out, Luke," he says, kissing along my jaw, his fingers finally freeing the button from the buttonhole. "But I do want to get it out." And he does.

I drop my head back against the door as his fist grips me. All rationality leaves along with most of the air in my lungs. And then we're on his bed, and his mouth is everywhere. And I'm sure as hell not stopping him. Not this time.

I draw him to me and return his passion. His shirt goes easily enough, but when I try to unbutton his shorts, he pushes my hand down and shows me how he wants to be touched—through the thick twill of his cargo shorts.

Uh-uh. I'm not afraid of him. He got his way last time. Before he can stop me again, I free my hand and slip the button on his shorts.

"Don't," he whispers.

"I love you," I whisper back to him. I slide my hand down the length of him and he moans and gives in to me. It strikes me as I pull him firmly against me, that this is who we can be. This is who we are. And I'm sick to death of pretending otherwise.

"I'm gonna be sick."

"Hold on." I sprint naked to his bathroom and grab the small trash can next to the toilet. I barely get it tucked under his chin before he's puking his guts out. When he finally falls back on the bed, I tie the trash bag closed and set it aside. His eyes are closed and he's panting. I kiss his damp forehead.

His face screws up like I'm torturing him. "You have to take a shower, Luke. Now. Please."

"It's okay. It's just semen on skin, Curtis. You didn't hurt me. I promise you that."

"No, no. Please. You have to scrub. Get it off of you. Please, get it off of you. *Get it off get it off.*" His voice is small, desperate. Tears roll down the sides of his face.

"Okay," I say softly. "I'll shower. You just lie here. Try to relax. Everything's going to be okay."

I shower for no other reason than to calm him, but I make it quick. I dress in the bathroom, then dampen a washcloth to clean him up with. But when I come back into the room, he's asleep. I wipe him down, then pull the quilt up over him and kiss him lightly on the lips.

I sit with him for a while, studying his beautiful face, the scar on his forehead, the slightly chapped lips. I wish I had a magic wand that I could wave and make all the bad things go away. Finally, I turn off the light and close the door behind me.

"Everything okay?" Mr. Cameron asks as I come down the stairs.

I want to scream at him. *No, everything is not okay. Don't you see your son falling apart in front of you? Are you that blind? Help him.*

But I don't. I made a promise to Curtis. God help us both.

"Yes, sir. He's fine. He fell asleep while we were talking."

"Thanks for getting him home, Luke."

"Yeah. Anytime."

Chapter 28

CURTIS

Corrine slides a mug across the bar to me. I wrap my fingers tightly around it and stare into the coffee.

"Curtis . . ." Dad pauses. He expects me to look at him, but I can't. He sighs. "I'm worried about you, okay? You know I've never minded you having a drink or two. You're a grown man. But son, you had your truck yesterday. I hate to think that if Luke hadn't brought you home, you might have tried to drive home yourself."

Luke.

Corrine stands quietly off to the side. I feel her eyes on me.

I've disappointed them. I've disappointed myself.

"I know that you told me you fell asleep when you hit that utility pole, but I need to ask you . . ."

Semen on skin. He thinks it's nothing. It's not nothing. My semen is teeming with the virus.

"Were you drinking that morning?"

It only needs a break in the skin—a small cut, a scrape, a nicked cuticle.

"Curtis, are you listening to me?"

I lift my eyes to my dad. "I wasn't drinking."

He hesitates, then nods. "Okay." He grips my shoulder and smiles. "You look like you don't feel so great."

He has no idea.

"No chance you'd want to go with us to the art show on the waterway this morning?"

I shake my head.

He laughs lightly and wraps his arms around me from behind. "We'll only be gone a couple of hours. Take some Tylenol and lay off the coffee. There's Gatorade in the pantry. And eat something, okay? And it wouldn't hurt to get a few more hours of sleep." He kisses me on the cheek. "I love you, Curt."

"I love you too, Dad." *More than you know.*

I'm still at the bar when I hear his truck back out of the driveway and head up the street. I get up, my head pounding, nausea biting at the back of my throat, and get my truck keys. I get in, start the engine, then open the garage door and pull into the empty space. I close the door behind me and lie across the bench seat.

It takes a moment for the swimming in my head to stop. The rumble of the truck is soothing, and I think I could lie here forever.

How long will it take? My eyes feel heavy. Just a little while. I'll fall asleep, and then I'll fall forever asleep. It'll be so easy.

It'll be hard on them. I know that. But they'll cope. They'll remember me the way I am now. Maybe they'll never know about the virus killing me from the inside out. The gay plague. They won't have to be ashamed of me.

And Luke. Luke, Luke, Luke. He's resilient. He'll be okay. He'll grow up, marry some great guy, raise a bunch of orphans. I allow myself a small smile. He'll be a great dad. He'll probably even learn to love camping and fishing. I try to picture him with a rod and reel in his hand, but what I see is Luke with that chain saw, tentative and plain scared at first, then bold and confident, cutting through those branches like he'd been doing it all his life.

I'll never be able to hurt him again.

I breathe in deeply and close my eyes. The rumble of the truck is oddly comforting. I want to sleep.

The minutes tick by.

I check the time on my phone: 9:34. Dad and Corrine haven't been gone that long. They're probably just getting started, making their way up the wide sidewalk along the waterway where the art exhibits are set up. Corrine has a few pieces in one of the exhibits. I can feel her excitement. We're like that, feeling each other's emotions. At least we used to.

What will she feel when my heart stops beating?

The thought makes my nose burn. Tears spring to my eyes. I love them so much.

I push myself up, turn off the ignition, and raise the garage door.

The sun is too bright, but my head only pounds when I move it too quickly. I try not to move it too quickly. I reseat my sunglasses. At least they hide my bloodshot eyes.

The sidewalk is crowded with art lovers. I pull out my cell phone.

Where are you?

You're here? Squeeee! Behind the Pavilion. Booth 65.

I'm at fifty-two. I continue up the sidewalk until I see them ahead, Corrine on her tiptoes scanning the crowd for me. I wave. She elbows her way upstream and meets me halfway with a big hug.

"Oh my God, you're not going to believe it. They've already sold one of my pastels!" She's breathless and bright eyed as she grabs my hand and tugs me toward the booth.

Dad gives me a warm smile and grabs me around the waist. "I think they've created a monster," he whispers in my ear.

He's proud. I'm proud. I have so much here. There has to be another way.

A woman picks up Corrine's other pastel and studies it. "How much?" she asks the attendant.

"Two fifty."

The woman sets the pastel back on the stand and continues on.

"Will you take three hundred for it?" my dad asks.

"Dad," Corrine says.

"I already lost the other one. It's only a matter of time before I lose this one, too, if I don't grab it now."

"Three hundred? Seriously?"

Dad winks at the attendant. "I'd pay more if I had that much cash on me."

I smile at Corrine. I can't believe Dad's carrying *that* much cash on him. Then again, that's Dad. Always prepared. He and Matt would get along great.

Corrine rolls her eyes at us both. "Come on." She tugs at his sleeve. "I'll make you a million pastels if you want. Let's leave this one for someone else. Let's go look around."

Dad stands his ground. He counts out six fifty-dollar bills and hands them to the attendant. "Hold it for me. If someone else really wants it, they're going to have to beat my offer."

"You're incorrigible," Corrine says, taking his arm.

We wander a ways down the sidewalk. Dad stops at a pretzel vendor's cart and orders three. He glances at me, then adds three orange juices. He passes back the pretzels and juice. The pretzel is warm, a little sweet, salty. I realize how much I would have missed moments like this.

"Two salted pretzels, one nacho cheese, please," someone says next to me.

I look up to see Robert Westfall, the band guard, standing at the cart with a pony-tailed older woman—his mom, I imagine. Dad takes a step over to give them more room as he pockets his change.

This is the first good look I've had at Robert. He's wearing an LSU T-shirt and jeans, the hems of which are seriously mangled. He's more solidly built than Luke, his blond hair shorter, short in fact. I note the way it kicks up a little in front. He smiles at the attendant and says thanks as he takes the pretzels. He hands one to the woman and they wander off into the crowd.

"Let's sit and eat," Dad says.

I look back down the sidewalk, but Robert and his mom are gone. I feel my phone buzz in my pocket.

You okay?

I'm fine.

Back in Huntsville?

Nope. At art festival with family. Heading back soon. See you next weekend.

"Is that Luke?" Corrine asks. "You should have brought him."

"He couldn't come this morning."
Is that a promise?
I'll be back. It's spring break. Keep practicing.

"Whew, that was close," Jaleel says, pulling the door closed behind him. "I sure wish my momma would call before she just shows up at my door."

I'm lying on my bed scrolling through my contacts. I crane my neck to look at him. "I can't believe she hasn't figured out yet you're not living there."

"That's because I'm a master of subterfuge, and don't you forget it." Jaleel kicks off his shoes and stretches out on his bed. He laughs. "She told me how proud she is that I'm making my bed every day." He looks over at me and grins.

Jaleel's bed in his other room stays made. He's been sleeping wrapped in a blanket on the bare mattress in my room for months now. I told him a few weeks ago that I didn't know why he didn't run to Target and get another set of sheets, but he told me he has to keep all receipts. His mom scrutinizes every dollar he spends.

"So, how was your weekend?" he asks.

"It was okay."

"Did you see whitey?"

"Yeah, I saw him."

After a moment, he sits up again and clasps his hands between his knees. And he just sits there.

"What?"

"I did some research."

"About?" I ask warily.

"So, here's the deal. Guys who take their drugs, their viral loads drop to undetectable. It's almost like they don't even have the virus anymore. Undetectable, man. Short of a cure, you can't beat that."

"But I'm not taking the drugs."

"Oh, that's right. You're not taking the drugs." He looks away for a moment, and I brace myself for a lecture.

Don't go there, Jaleel. I don't want to fight with you too.

When he turns back to me, I feel the hairs on the back of my neck stand on end.

"Do you have any idea how arrogant that is?"

I huff. "You don't know anything about me."

"Yeah, good try, Cameron. I know plenty about you. You think you're too good to get this disease."

"I don't—"

"Yeah, you do. If it were cancer or MS or—"

"It's not the same, and you know it. I didn't just *get* HIV. I acquired it."

"You think only bad people get HIV? You think just because you let some guys stick their dicks up your ass—"

"Shut up."

"Man, look around you. Kids are having sex all over this campus. And I'd bet you good money more than half of them ain't usin' gloves. Hell, my freshman year that's all the guys could think about—gettin' their first sex. You ain't that special. And I'll tell you somethin' else."

"Oh, please do."

"You the biggest homophobe I know."

I roll my eyes and turn away.

"I mean it, man. You hidin' like you embarrassed for people to know you have sex with guys. At least my momma's honest about her fear. But you, man, you act like this is all about everybody else. But it ain't. It's you. You the one who's afraid of what everyone will think of you. Curtis Cameron. Big ol' drum major, ruttin' in the gutter. It's a virus, man. It's not me that don't get it. It's you. HIV don't care if you gay or straight. But when you go actin' like you ashamed, you make it that much harder for the next guy. Stand up for yourself. Fight. And to hell with everybody else. What if it were your little friend there?"

"Leave Luke out of this."

"Is that what you doin'? Leavin' him out of this? If it were him instead of you, man, you'd never let him hide behind his pride. You fuckin' this up, man."

"Can you just go?"

"No, I ain't goin'. You gotta face this, Curtis. You gotta face it head on. Man up. There are enough homophobes in this world already."

I stare at my phone. Eventually, he sighs and wraps himself in his blanket. When he turns to the wall I light up my phone and text Adeeb.

Hey, man. What do you know about Robert Westfall?

Why? You interested?

Funny. Just wondering. Is he okay?

He's all right.

Playing on my team, right?

You have to ask? Really?

Dating anyone?

Ha, ha. You want me to put in a good word for you?

Just answer the damn question.

Don't think so. I won't tell Lukey Duke you asked. ☺

I'm asking for Lukey Duke for your information.

Aaaaaaah. The plot thickens.

You got a phone number?

That one's got issues.

Oh, great. What kind of issues?

Sick dad.

And . . .

And nothing. I'll get the number.

Thanks, man.

A few minutes later he texts back the number. I add it to my contacts.

I am not a homophobe.

Chapter 29

LUKE

I expected Curtis to pull away again after last Saturday night's melt-down, but he seems okay. Not great, but he responded to my texts all week. So that's progress. Still, I didn't know if he'd actually show up this weekend until he pulled into the driveway half an hour ago.

I watch him through the Camerons' back window as I peel the shell from a boiled egg and rinse away the bits under the faucet. He's on the back porch with his dad, loading a cooler with sodas and beer and ice for the block party.

"You want to know what Dad told me the other night?" Corrine asks.

"What did he tell you?"

"He says, 'Corrine, I hope you like cold weather, because we're going to have to move to New England one day so those two can be married.'"

She mimics her dad's voice perfectly. I smile and hand her my egg. I take another from the bowl and crack it against the edge of the counter.

"Don't think we don't know that you're the reason Curtis has been home every weekend for the past few months," she says, bumping my hip with hers. "He seems so much happier since he met you, more playful, less serious."

He's a good actor, I think, or they just haven't been paying attention.

I've been trying to take Curtis's pulse since he got in. He seems relaxed, but guarded; friendly, but distracted. We haven't talked about last Sunday; it's almost as if it never happened. Almost.

Since our house is positioned right in the middle of the cul-de-sac, our driveway has become ground zero for the party. I sit back in my lawn chair, eat a couple of Corrine's deviled eggs, and watch Curtis dodge water balloons in the street. He lobs one gently back at the Solis kid, a third grader. He lets the next balloon hit him square in the chest. The kid squeals when Curtis clutches at his wet shirt with mock shock.

"I've had enough," he protests. He turns to go. The kid launches another balloon. Curtis arches his back as the water splatters him. "Aw, man. In the back. Cheap shot."

"Curtis seems to be having a great time," Mom says, dropping into the chair next to me.

I can smell the cigarette smoke on her. It's subtle, mixed with the smoke from the grill. She's smiling, but there's a tinge of sadness in her eyes. I look back at Curtis. He's gathered up another armful of balloons and this time, the Solis kid gets wet.

Mom absently dabs a paper napkin against the palm of her right hand.

"Let me see," I say, taking her hand. I turn it palm up. There're two blisters, broken and oozing at the base of her middle and ring fingers. Ouch. "Did you get these sweeping the driveway this afternoon?"

"Well," she says with a small smile, "I might have raked the yard too."

"Why didn't you ask me to do that?"

"It's nothing," she says, taking her hand back. "It gave me something to do. Your dad and I used to love throwing outdoor parties . . . when you were younger. Do you remember that?"

I shake my head no. I don't remember.

She drops her eyes and sighs, then smiles back at me again. "I guess I'm out of practice. And sweeping and raking was his job anyway."

She misses him.

"I've got a killer headache, and since it looks like there are plenty of adults out here to keep the order, I'm going to go in for a while." She pats my knee and gets up.

"You need to put something on those blisters," I tell her.

"Hey, who's the doctor here?" She musses my hair and heads to the house.

I scan the crowd of neighbors. The adults, mostly couples, are standing or sitting in small groups, talking, laughing, eating, snapping photos of the kids and other happy couples. I watch Mom walk up the driveway to the front door alone.

"Want a drink?" Curtis asks, handing me a skewer of shrimp.

I stretch my foot out to stop a runaway ball, and kick it back. "I'll get one in a minute."

He takes the chair Mom vacated. "Where'd your mom go?"

"Inside."

"Ever the hostess."

"I don't think so. Not today."

Something in my voice gets his attention. I feel him study my profile. "What's going on with your dad?" he asks.

"Nada mucho." I sigh and look back at him. "Where's your dad? I expected him to be at the grill, feeding the multitudes."

"He doesn't like parties."

"Why?"

He shrugs. "Probably the same reason your mom's not here."

I have an image of an older Curtis, writing music or marching programs alone in a room, absorbed in his work, but disconnected from the world.

"Can we talk about last weekend?" I ask.

He scrapes his teeth across his lower lip. At the edge of the driveway, Matt's climbing the ladder to the dunking booth. Samuel stands ready with an orange ball poised in his cocked arm. Matt seats himself on the bench, then holds his arms high in the air. Samuel throws and misses. He throws again, misses. "Lame-o," Matt shouts. "Come on. You're throwing like a little girl."

Curtis smiles at Matt's taunts.

"Go get him wet," I tell him.

"I can't dunk your little brother."

Maybe. Maybe not. But he seems relieved to have the conversation go somewhere else.

"Oh, please. He lives for this stuff."

Curtis grins. He hands me his skewer and wipes his hands on his shorts.

"That's right, bring the big dog in," Matt says as Curtis approaches the tank. I see Matt grip the bench.

Curtis takes the ball and winds up for a throw, then pauses and drops his arms. "I can't do it," he says. Matt eases his grip, then Curtis fires the ball and Matt goes down in a big splash.

Samuel presses his face to the Plexiglas window as Matt comes up sputtering and laughing. "Oh, you got wet," Samuel teases.

I hear Corrine's "Woo-hoo" from out in the street.

Curtis laughs. "And that's how it's done," he says, returning to the seat next to me. He dusts his hands like it's all in a day's work.

I wish he could always be this way.

The sun is beginning to drop behind the horizon. Mr. Solis drags a fire pit to the center of the driveway and begins loading it with dry firewood.

"Need some help?" Curtis asks.

"I think I got it. Just sit back and enjoy."

I wish Mom would come back to the party. There are other singles around. Like Miss Shelley, for instance. And it's not like she and Dad ever clung to each other. More like they orbited each other, like there was a gravitational pull between them that kept them in balance. And now that's gone, and Mom seems a little lost.

She was more than happy to let the party happen on our driveway. But now there's a party, and she's not here.

I study Curtis's face as a flame flickers then flares in the pit. He surprises me by reaching over and gripping my hand on the arm of the chair. I wrap my fingers around his and grip back.

"Let me have your phone," he says quietly.

"Why?"

"Just let me have it."

I hand it to him. He retrieves his own from his pocket and copies a number into my contacts, then adds a name, and hands it back.

Robert Westfall? The color guard?

"What's all this about?" I ask.

"I want you to call him."

"Why would I call Robert? I don't even know him."

He's quiet for a long moment. Samuel's on the bench now and Matt, soaking wet, is winding up for a throw. He nails the bull's-eye on the first try. Samuel goes down. Curtis flashes a quick smile, but then it's gone again.

"I think you should get to know him," he says.

This time I laugh. I think I know where this is going. He's got to be kidding. Me and Robert Westfall? "Funny."

But Curtis isn't laughing. "I hear he's a good guy and—"

"He's not even gay, Curtis."

"He twirls a flag and dances with girls," he snaps. "He's gay. Besides . . . I asked around."

He's serious. He's *fucking* serious. He actually wants me to hook up with another guy. "If this is because of last weekend—"

"That should have never happened, Luke. It was stupid, and reckless, and—"

"It was beautiful."

"And that's part of the problem. You have no sense of self-preservation. I can't handle that kind of responsibility, okay? I've got enough to worry about. And being around you all the time, I just can't—I can't do it anymore. I need you to do this for me."

"Do what? Ask out a guy I don't even know, a guy I have no interest in whatsoever?"

"Yeah," he whispers.

"You're cracked."

"Maybe I am. But I'm not taking you down with me."

I scoff. "Quit being the martyr, Curtis. Just stop with all the games, all the drama. You want to be with me, and I want to be with you. We'll work it out. We'll figure out—"

"I don't want to work it out," he snaps again. "That's what I'm trying to tell you, if you'd listen for a change."

I'm stunned into silence.

Curtis huffs, an angry note. "You've got this whole fairy-tale fantasy about the two of us in your head. Like we're going to ride off into the sunset together, get married, raise a bunch of little Colombian babies together."

Now I scoff. Not because he's wrong, but because he's more right than he knows.

"It's not going to happen, Luke. I need you to do this. I need you to let me go so I can let you go."

And I'm angry now. "You're just gonna throw me away. Hand me over to some guy like I'm a—a spare mouthpiece you don't need."

"Oh, come on. Now who's being dramatic? You fall in love with guys like a kid falls in love with a new puppy."

For the second time, I'm stunned into silence. Is this how he thinks of me? Some fickle little kid with a crush? I thought I knew nothing about him, but it turns out he knows nothing about me.

"You want me to call Robert?" I thumb my screen and light up my phone. "Fine. I'll call Robert. I'll call him right now."

Curtis eyes me with a mixture of anger and what I think is hurt. But he asked for this. I find Robert's number and press the Call button. "Maybe he's free right now," I say with as much sarcasm as I can muster.

Robert won't know my phone number; hell, he doesn't even know me. A part of me hopes he won't pick up, but another part of me wants to push this all the way, to make Curtis feel the sting of rejection the way I feel it. To make him see how utterly stupid and flawed his plan is.

But Robert does pick up.

He seems wary, confused when I tell him my name. It takes him a few seconds to place me. I don't even bother with making nice on the phone.

"Hey, you want to meet me for pizza this evening? Little Caesars?" I choose the restaurant because it's close. I could walk if I wanted to, but more to the point, I have no interest in investing more than a mile or two in this sham.

He hesitates, then says, "Okay, sure. What time?"

"How about now?"

"Um, okay. Give me, um, twenty minutes."

"Great. I'll see you there."

I end the call and shove the phone back in my pocket.

"Now?" Curtis says.

I give him the finger and get up. "I have a date. I need a quick shower. Maybe I'll see you around."

Chapter 30

LUKE

I take a sip of my soda and look around at the Friday-night crowd. Every stool at the counter is occupied. Same with the smattering of tables in the center and the five booths along one wall. Robert and I are sitting at one of those booths, the same booth, I suddenly realize, where I sat with Nate more than a year ago.

How very different that date had been. There'd been so much to talk about, so many questions I wanted to ask him, questions he answered, elaborated on. I know now how broken he was over his breakup with Adam, but he didn't let it show. Well, he didn't let it show too much. We traded favorite things, most embarrassing moments, and then he kissed me standing outside in the parking lot. Okay, maybe I kissed him first, but he kissed me back. My very first kiss.

I would give anything if I could have given that honor to Curtis. I'm pretty sure I won't be kissing Robert tonight.

That all seems so long ago, another life. I remember, too, that Nate had ordered pizza. Food seems like too much of a commitment with Robert. I didn't order any. He's said nothing about it.

I can feel him watching me now, no doubt wondering what the hell we're doing here. And I feel guilty. We shouldn't have dragged him into this. It's our problem, mine and Curtis's. Something we have to work out together. But here I am with Robert.

He clears his throat, and I turn my attention back to him. "So, um, I hear you're auditioning for drum major."

"Yeah. Maybe."

He nods.

This is awkward. When Robert isn't twirling a bed sheet, he plays bari sax. We're in wind ensemble together. The bari saxes sit a couple rows back from the clarinets. We'd never even spoken to each other until I called him this evening.

He rolls his straw between his thumb and middle finger.

This is going to be a long evening. I can see he's thinking the same thing.

"Can I ask you something?" Robert says. "Are we on a date?"

"That depends," I say, a little uncomfortably.

"On what?"

"I guess it depends on whether or not you want to be on a date."

"I thought you and Curtis were a thing."

"Me and Curtis." I chuckle lightly, but there's no humor there. I blow air through my lips. "I don't know what we are."

He props his elbow on the table and rests his cheek on his fist. "So . . . I'm a little confused here."

Yeah, you and me both.

"Look, shit, I owe you an apology. I shouldn't have dragged you into this. It's all so stupid. Curtis kind of made me ask you out."

"Wow."

"He says we—me and him—can't be a couple."

"Because . . ."

Because he wants me. Oh, that makes sense.

"I don't know," I tell him. "The age difference, I guess." I shrug off my lie. "He thought if I dated someone else then maybe it would keep us from becoming, you know."

"So, the two of you are using me as some kind of human no-fly zone?"

"Basically."

He shakes his head. "Man, I know how to pick 'em."

I smile. "I hope you won't hold it against me."

"Nah, but you are going to owe me."

"Can I owe you a little more?"

He raises his eyebrows, then gestures for me to go on.

"Think we can stretch out this *date* for a while? I don't want to get home too early, you know. He wanted this, so I want to give it to him."

"Hmm. Do you mind if I say I'm feeling a little *used* here?"

"No. You're right." I reach for my wallet and start to get up. "Listen, I'm sorry about—"

Robert leans back in his seat. "I'm not saying no. Just, um, I've never been on a date before. This is not exactly the way I pictured it happening. It kinda sucks." He hesitates, then laughs and sighs.

I smile in return and settle back down.

"Friends?" I ask.

"Sure. But can we eat? I'm starved."

Over pizza, we decide to kill a couple more hours at a movie. I let him choose. As he searches the Cinemark listings on his phone, I scan the sidewalk in front of the restaurant and the parking lot beyond.

Why are we doing this, Curtis?

"Are you expecting a drive-by?" Robert asks.

"Huh?" I turn back to him.

"You've been staring out the window. Are you expecting Curtis to drive by?"

I shrug. Expecting? No. Hoping? Yes.

Robert chooses some sci-fi flick. I can't focus on the movie; I'm wondering where Curtis went. I was in the house five minutes. Just long enough to check on Mom, tell her I was going out for a while, then change into jeans. I didn't even bother with a shower. When I came back out, his truck was gone.

Maybe he went back to Huntsville for the rest of break. Maybe he ran an errand. I don't know, and the not knowing is killing me.

Robert leans into me. "Deep thoughts?"

I shake my head and take a handful of popcorn.

"Just call him," he whispers.

He has no idea how badly I want to do that. But Curtis named the game, and I'm going to play it.

I glance over at Robert. I like him. I've even enjoyed his company this evening. But Curtis should be the one sitting next to me. Maybe he's drinking. Maybe he'll be drunk when I get home and he'll try to relieve me of my clothes again. Maybe I'll let him.

"So, what was your favorite part of the movie?" Robert asks as we leave the theater.

It's cool out. I zip up my hoodie. My favorite part? Huh. I glance at him apologetically.

"I didn't think you were watching," he says.

We meander down the sidewalk toward Market Street. "There's something I still don't get," Robert says as we wait for a walk signal. "If he likes you, and you like him, why doesn't he want to be together? He's only three years older. That's nothing. It's not like you're in junior high."

Smart guy. It was a lame excuse, but I can't tell him the truth. I can't betray Curtis. I shrug. "It's complicated."

"Apparently. Look, it's"—he checks the time on his phone as we cross the street—"ten forty. Call him."

"What am I supposed to say?"

"I don't know. But you'll figure something out. Just touch base. It doesn't have to be any deep conversation. Connect with each other. Whatever it is, you two can work it out. But you've got to talk."

I wish it were that easy. But despite our earlier anger at each other, despite the meanness of his words, I need to hear his voice. I need to know he's okay.

Robert sees the decision in my face. "I'll go get us a Starbucks. Give you some privacy, okay?"

Chapter 31

CURTIS

The sign for US 183 North looms ahead. I steer my truck across the sweeping ramp into Austin.

I take my phone from the passenger seat and check the time as I merge onto the highway: 10:02.

I shouldn't be here. I just know I couldn't be there anymore, sitting at home with Dad and Corrine, watching a movie, pretending like we're a normal family, or worse, hanging out with everyone at the block party, while Luke is out there with another guy. I wanted him to go out with Robert; I just never thought it would make me feel so crappy.

How much do I really know about Robert Westfall? Nothing. He seems nice enough, but don't they all? I could have just thrown Luke to a wolf for all I know. The thing is, I thought I'd have to fight a lot harder to make Luke go. And if I'm being honest, I didn't really think he would.

But he did.

So I went too.

I wonder if he's home yet. I left before he did, told Dad a friend had invited me up to Austin for spring break, and threw a few things in a small duffel bag. There was a hint of worry in his face, but I'm nineteen. He told me to drive safely, gave me a hug, waved me off.

I wish he had told me no.

I want a beer, but I don't want to go to a bar. I choose a Mexican restaurant instead, one with its own bar off the main dining room. It's a place I've been to many times. The wait staff is young and seems to turn over frequently.

I fish through my wallet for my alternate ID and slide it into the window in front of my driver's license. In my experience, the harried wait staff rarely gives more than a cursory glance at IDs, as if they're uncertain what they're looking for so they're just going through the motions.

I have no idea where I'm sleeping tonight. I figured I'd make a few phone calls when I got here. Surely someone will let me have a couch or a blanket and a few square feet of floor space. Hell, I can sleep in my truck.

Even this late, the restaurant is busy, loud—a three-man mariachi band serenading patrons; fajitas sizzling on hot, cast-iron pans; a hundred voices talking, laughing.

I step into the bar area, where the conversation is more subtle, and find a stool at the end of the bar. I offer my ID and order a cerveza. The waiter pops the cap and slides it across the bar to me, along with a basket of chips and salsa. I push them away. I should eat something; I've only had a few deviled eggs and half a dozen grilled shrimp today, and that was hours ago. But my stomach feels raw, knotted.

I set my phone on the bar and stare at the black screen. I want to text him. Make sure he's okay. And then I chide myself for that thought. What do I think, that Robert's going to maul him? That flag-twirling boy next door? Luke's more likely to take advantage of him, just to teach me a lesson, than Robert is to lay a hand on him. But Luke wouldn't dare. If nothing else, he has to know the risks out there now.

But, damn, he was angry. I would have been, too, if I'd been him. But it's for his own good. He'll see that in time.

And I'll—I don't know what I'll do. I can't think about that right now. I feel as if I'm on emotional overload. One more piece of crap and I'll shut down, go dark.

I realize my bottle is empty. I ask for another. As I'm reaching for it, I feel a presence on my right side.

"Curtis Cameron."

Leaning against the edge of the bar next to me is some guy I've never seen before with bleached white hair, too-full lips, and a silver hoop in his ear. I resist the urge to lean away.

"Do I know you?"

"I don't know, but you should."

I smirk and take a sip of my beer.

"You shouldn't be drinking alone. Mind if I join you?" He doesn't wait for me to respond. He signals the waiter for a beer. "So," he says, reaching across me for the chips. He snags them with one long finger and drags them to him. "You're back."

"Look," I say, irritated. I fix cold eyes on him. "Do you mind? I don't know you. I just want to—"

"Drake Murdock . . . senior tuba." He holds out a hand to me.

I stare at it a moment and search my memory bank. There was a junior tuba last year—dark hair, same earring. I'm pretty sure I never slept with him. "You bleached your hair," I say, ignoring the hand. He retrieves it.

"I think it looks pretty good on me." He grins broadly, showing off straight, white teeth. "You like it?"

"Drake, look, I didn't come here to socialize."

"Neither did I." The person on the stool on the other side of me gets up. Drake takes his beer and the chips and walks around me to take his place. He leans his forearms against the bar. "I was having dinner with some friends, I saw you sitting in here, thought I'd come say hi."

"Well, your fajitas are getting cold."

"I had a fried avocado with chicken. They're pretty good. You ever try one?"

I roll my eyes at him and will him to disappear.

He snaps his fingers at the waiter. "Can we get a fried avocado with chicken, two forks, please."

"I'm not hungry," I tell him. "And I believe you've already eaten."

"I'm a growing boy. What can I say? And you look like you could use a meal. You waiting on a phone call?" He nods down at my phone.

He's not going to go away. I resign myself to that fact. I ignore his question and ask one of my own. "How was marching season last fall?" I really couldn't give a fuck, but we're not talking about me anymore.

"It was all right. But, honestly, if I never play 'The Eyes of Texas' again, it'll be too soon. And between you and me, I hate fringe and bric-a-brac."

I smile at that. He pops a chip in his mouth and smiles back.

"I'm from Wisconsin, you know."

"No. I didn't know." *Until a few minutes ago, I didn't even know your name, Drake.* "Why are you in Texas?"

"Because Wisconsin–Madison turned me down flat. But, you know, their loss."

"What are you studying?"

"Environmental engineering."

"Aren't you worried about polluting the water with all that peroxide?"

He raises his eyebrows, but he seems amused by my question. "You don't like my hair."

I shrug.

He grins. "Me either. But I interned at an engineering firm last summer and I came back to school feeling a little too corporate." He sighs. "Guess I better get used to corporate, huh?"

"So you planning on designing better solar panels?"

"Water treatment systems." He laughs. "A lot of peroxide and crap out there. So, are you back at UT?"

"No. Just visiting for a few days."

The waiter sets a plate and two forks down in front of us. Drake gestures for me to give it a try.

Oh, what the hell. I fork open the crusted avocado and spear a chunk, along with a piece of chicken. He doesn't pick up his own fork.

"So where are you staying tonight?" he asks.

"Don't know. Didn't come with any plans."

"I've got an empty room in my apartment."

I take a sip of beer and study the hopeful look on his face. There was a time when I would have jumped all over that offer. There was a time when I *could* have jumped all over that offer. That time is long gone. I shake my head. "No, thanks."

"Oh, come on," he says, leaning into me. He takes a chip from the basket, then reaches across me to scoop up some salsa and promptly dribbles it across my lap. "Oopsie," he says in my ear.

Motherfucker. I grab a napkin.

"I can lick that off for you," he says in a low voice.

"No thanks," I say, irritated. I should have known. With the napkin, I pick off the bits of tomato, onions, and pepper, but there's still a salsa stain right on my crotch. I toss the napkin on the counter and head to the men's room.

"Hurry back," Drake calls after me.

What a prick. I use a wet paper towel to get out most of the stain. I didn't bring an extra pair of jeans with me, and I don't want to be smelling like a Mexican restaurant the entire drive home.

And yes, I'm heading home. I'm done here. I don't know why I came. Maybe I am some kind of sick, closeted masochist.

Chapter 32

LUKE

I've been pacing up and down the sidewalk along the bulwark since Robert left, rehearsing what I want to say to Curtis.

But everything I've come up with sounds so melodramatic, so teenage girlish.

I check the time on my phone: 10:55. I've already wasted fifteen minutes. I just want him to come home. I sit on the bulwark and make the call.

"Curtis's phone," a male voice says.

"Who's this?"

"A better question is . . . who is Luke?"

That throws me a moment, but then I realize my name would have displayed on Curtis's screen. "Where's Curtis?"

"He's busy right now. Are you his brother?"

"No, I'm not his brother. I'm his boyfriend."

"Ah. His boyfriend. He didn't tell me he had a boyfriend. But, you know, if he had a boyfriend, then why's he sitting here drinking in a bar alone? Looks to me like he's solo tonight."

Fuck you. "Let me talk to Curtis."

"No. I think that I won't. You see, he's with me tonight. Maybe all night. I'm thinking I might need to remove the battery from his phone. No interruptions that way, you know what I mean?"

"Oh, really? Well, did he tell you he has HIV, asshole?" It's out before I can stop myself.

He goes quiet, then mutters something. I don't catch the words, but the tone comes through loud and clear. I feel movement behind me. I turn to see Robert standing there, a shocked expression on his face. I look at the screen and see the call's been ended.

"Holy shit," Robert says.

I look up at him again. "Please don't share that with anyone. Curtis—"

"I won't. I swear to you." He hands me a coffee and sits on the bulwark next to me.

Chapter 33

CURTIS

I leave the men's room and reach for my cell phone as I head to the door. It's not there. Fuck. I'd hoped to just go, but there's no avoiding returning to the bar for my phone.

Drake is still sitting there talking on his phone. He swivels in his seat as he ends the call and looks at me. It's not a come-on look. He sets the phone back on the bar, and I realize it's mine. He was talking on my fucking phone. I stride over and reach across him for it.

He leans back on his stool. "You didn't tell me you had HIV, man."

I freeze, then grab my phone.

"You just let me sit next to you, share food with you . . ."

We didn't share anything, asshole.

I tuck my phone in my pocket, turn my back on him, and head toward the door.

"Man, I wouldn't touch that with somebody else's dick," he calls out after me.

I'm trembling when I open the Answered Calls folder on my phone. I know who called even before I see his name.

Why would he do this to me?

Who else has he told?

I put the truck in reverse and whip out of the parking space, then slam it into drive.

Outside of Austin I stop at a convenience store for coffee. I won't repeat the mistake I made last time of driving tired. I want to get home in one piece.

I want to be alert when I break his fucking neck.

Chapter 34

LUKE

Robert and I sit quietly on the bulwark and watch little kids play barefoot in the shallow fountain on the green. I twist the cardboard wrapper around and around my cup.

Where is he? And what the hell was he thinking? Was he really planning to go home with some stranger in a bar?

That guy on the phone, he didn't know. I'd bet money on it. The way he reacted when I told him. Curtis had to be drinking, not thinking. There may be a lot I don't understand about Curtis, but I do understand this—he would never forgive himself if he hurt someone else.

He may never forgive me for stopping him.

Maybe the guy left. Maybe Curtis will come back and the guy'll just be gone and Curtis will never know why. Maybe he'll just get in his truck and head home.

There are so many thoughts, so many questions swirling around in my head. I'm scared for him. And maybe that's the only reason I can't focus on how hurt I feel right now.

"Who were you talking to?" Robert asks finally.

"I don't know. I called Curtis's phone and some guy answered." I feel him study me, but I can't look at him.

"I'm sorry," he says quietly. "About everything. I guess it all makes sense now."

I scoff. "I wish it did, but nothing makes sense to me anymore. There's no reason why we can't be together. I'm not a kid."

"Well, actually, you are."

I glare at him. "You're not helping here."

"I'm sorry. But it's a pretty big deal. And you don't know what you're getting yourself into. I mean, Curtis seems like a great guy, but, come on. There are a lot of great guys out there."

Like you? Is that what you're trying to say, Robert?

There's an uncomfortable moment of silence as he realizes what he's implied.

"Anyway," he says, "that's a big risk you'd be taking. They call that a serodiscordant relationship. It's not easy on either partner."

"And you know that because . . ."

He flashes me a quick, embarrassed smile. "I grew up in a family of doctors. It's a family hazard."

Yeah, I know.

He sighs heavily. "The bottom line is, he doesn't want that. And you can't make him. When it comes to you, he may be a lost cause."

I rankle at that comment, but something about it sticks to me. A lost cause. Is that the kind of guy I'm attracted to—lost causes? Nate? Wounded, first by those thugs who'd assaulted him and then by Adam, who'd moved to New York and left him to fend for himself. He needed me, and I was there for him. And now Curtis?

"He's not a lost cause. He's just scared."

"And what about you? Aren't you scared?"

My knee-jerk reaction is to answer no. But what if the worst thing that could happen happens? Am I really willing to take that risk? I imagine myself lying next to him at night, talking quietly about our dreams, constellations, the stupid clarinet, whatever's on our minds.

He's not the boogeyman, and he's not a freak show.

He's a human being. A good, kind, intelligent, proud human being.

"No. I'm not scared," I answer. "I'm in love with him."

"Why?"

The question frustrates me. "I don't know why. How do you quantify something like love?"

"Can I make an observation?" Robert asks. "I think you like being needed."

I look into his clear, blue eyes and see no meanness, no smugness there. "Why is that wrong? Is that any less reason for falling in love with someone than a cute ass, or a love of puppies, or something equally as arbitrary?"

"I don't know. I've never fallen in love."

Maybe not, but one day he's going to make some guy very happy.

He looks at me and smiles quietly. "If Curtis is who you really want, then I hope it all works out for you. Happily discordant forever after."

"You make it sound kind of creepy."

"Nah. Actually, it sounds kind of beautiful to me."

"Thanks."

It's almost eleven, and the last of the kids is crying and struggling as an older man lifts him out of the fountain and hoists him over his shoulder. He rubs his feet vigorously to warm them. I look back at Robert.

"So, who gets your heart racing?"

He smiles impishly at me. "You know that cheerleader, the one who had a boot on his left foot at the start of the season? He fractured it in a fall at cheer camp. We're chemistry partners. He has tons of boyfriends, or so he claims. I'm just waiting for him to realize how shallow they all are and decide to drink from my well."

I laugh. "That is so bad."

He takes a deep breath. "What can I say? I'm a sucker for a boy who can touch his toes in the air. Even if I weren't in the guard, I'd go to football games just to watch him."

That reminds me of when Nate came to a few of my games to watch me perform. It's a memory, a connection, nothing more.

"He's always acting like he's some kind of ghetto queen," Robert continues, "and he likes to pretend he's this ditzy blond."

I laugh because I know exactly what he means. "Nic's in my English class."

"Really? Who does he sit by?"

"Um, a couple of the other cheerleaders. As far as I can tell, he makes pretty good grades."

"He's really not ditzy at all," Robert says, smiling vaguely at nothing in the distance. "In fact, he's really smart. You don't get into AP Chemistry by being dumb. He makes the rest of us look like we're still playing with chemistry sets. And for all his swagger, he's really sweet too. Like this one time I left my lunch at home and I didn't think I had any money in my account, so he gets out his lunch and divides everything exactly in half and lays it out on a sheet of notebook paper. He had all this weird organic kind of stuff. Anyway, I had to hide it under my desk until class was over, and then I had to carry it to the cafeteria on this paper and it had this funny chemical smell by then, but I ate it. Every bite." He grins and glances over at me. "What's Nic like in English?"

"Ghetto queen. Ditzy blond. The kids call him Whore-Hay because of his tan."

Robert laughs in a way that tells me he's in on the joke (Whore-Hay, Jorge). "It's not real, you know. He spray-tans. He's a hot mess, isn't he?"

"Yeah." A hot mess. "Hey, I'm kind of tired."

He nods. "You know, it's not too late. Maybe you'll still get to see him tonight."

"Maybe."

I drop Robert back at Little Caesars and head home to wait.

From my bedroom window, I can just see Corrine's car, sitting alone in the dark driveway.

I find myself thinking about what Robert said. Maybe I do like being needed. If I'm being honest, that's about the only thing Nate and I had going on between us. His heart was splintered, and I held it together for him.

But Nate wasn't mine; Curtis is.

How do I make him see that he does have a future, a future with me?

I call him again.

He doesn't answer.

I text: Where are you?

He doesn't respond.

"Please don't do anything stupid," I whisper to the night.

My cell phone startles me awake. I lift my head from the window-sill. My neck is stiff, my eyes dry and scratchy. Through the window I see his truck parked next to Corrine's car.

"Curtis?" I answer groggily.

"I want to talk to you," he growls at me through the phone. "I want to talk to you right *fucking* now."

"Where are you?"

"In your goddamned driveway."

I'm already on my feet. I turn back to search the ground below. "Are you okay?"

"No," he shouts at me. "I'm not okay." I can hear his voice through both the phone and the window now.

I grab a hoodie from my doorknob. "I'm on my way."

I quietly make my way down the stairs. I can't imagine what happened in that bar after the call ended, but it couldn't have been good. He's angry. I get that. But once he calms down, he'll see that I only did what I had to do—save him from himself.

I flip off the porch light, then let myself out the front door.

Curtis is pacing in the driveway. When he sees me, he stalks over. "You *fucking* jerk!"

I barely get the door pulled closed before he grabs the front of my T-shirt and shoves me up against it. He presses his forearm to my throat.

I don't know if I should be frightened or just grateful that he's in one piece.

"I ought to break your fucking neck."

"Curtis, let me go," I say calmly.

"How could you? You humiliated me."

"Curtis—"

He shuts me up with more pressure against my Adam's apple. "You have no idea what you've done to me." His voice is barely a whisper, but thick with emotion. "It'll be all over Austin by the time the sun rises."

He was in Austin? Why? I brace my hands against his chest and shove him away, then slip away from the door so he can't trap me again.

He advances on me as I back down the sidewalk. "I trusted you. And this is what you do to me."

"Curtis. I didn't do it to hurt you. I did it to save you."

"Save me? *Save* me?" He laughs.

In the dim light of the gas lamp, I can see his face contort in fury. He could grab me again if he reached out. I glance behind me and sidestep around a planter of petunias Mom put there last weekend. He seizes that moment of distraction to shove me. I stumble backward, then fall on my butt on the sidewalk.

What the hell?

I'm pissed now. "Stop it, Curtis." I scramble back to my feet. "Don't pin this on me. You were the one drinking and planning to go home and fuck some guy you met in a bar. I couldn't—"

"*What?* I wasn't going home with anybody. Are you fucking crazy?"

"He said—"

"I don't give a fuck what he said. Is that the kind of person you think I am?"

"No, I—"

"You think I don't know the death sentence I'm carrying around inside me?" He's shouting. "Do you have any *fucking* idea what this virus has already cost me? And now you want to make ab-solutely fucking sure that every ignorant motherfucker out there knows what a walking piece of crap I really am?"

"No," I whisper. He's like a wounded animal, scared, in pain, lashing out. "Curtis," I say softly, reaching to embrace him. "You're not."

He moves to put some distance between us, but I lock my arms around him. I'm not letting him go. I'll be the scaffolding that holds him together, the rebar that gives him strength. I will be those things for him. I want to be those things for him.

"Get away from me," he spits, struggling to break my hold on him.

"No." I tighten my grip.

"Get the *fuck* away from me. I hate you." His voice cracks. "I fucking *hate* you."

"No, you don't," I say quietly.

He can't hold back the tears as he struggles against my hold. "Please let me go so I can *kill* you." He knees me in the groin at the same moment the porch light goes on and the front door opens.

"Luke? Curtis? Stop it, you two."

Panic flashes across Curtis's face. I release him and drop to one knee, gasping for breath. Mom rushes out the door to me. Curtis stumbles backward, trips over the planter, and hits the concrete, his head striking a landscaping rock at the edge of the sidewalk. He cries out and curls up on his side. His arms go up to cradle his head. It happens so fast.

Mom stoops and grips my shoulders, her face all shock and confusion. "What is going on here?"

"I'm okay, I'm okay." But I can see that Curtis is not okay. "Mom—"

"Oh, sweet Jesus." Mom releases me and scurries over to Curtis. He mumbles something and puts up his hand as if to keep her away. It's covered in blood.

"It's okay, Curtis," she says gently. "Let me have a look." She reaches to lower his hand.

I scramble to my feet and grab her wrist.

"Mom, don't."

"Luke, what's wrong with you? He's bleeding."

"Please, please, don't—you can't—" I see the raw little circles of torn flesh on her palm. "Mom, he has HIV."

Mom stares at me in shocked silence. She looks back at Curtis. "Go get me some clean towels, Luke. And some latex gloves. You'll find some under my bathroom sink."

As I turn to go, she lays a comforting hand on Curtis's heaving back. "It's going to be okay, Curtis," she says gently. "I need you to sit up and apply pressure to that wound. Can you do that for me?"

I'm back in one minute flat. Curtis is sitting, but slumped over, his eyes open, but unfocused. Blood seeps from under the hand he has pressed to his head and runs in rivulets down his face.

"You've got to keep your head up, Curtis." Mom reaches out

for the gloves and snaps them on, then takes the towel from me. "Okay, you can let go. I'm going to do this for you, now. It's okay. You're going to need some stitches."

I'm awed at her calmness and the kindness with which she speaks. Curtis is crying quietly, and trying not to, but there's something so defeated in his face.

"Luke, I need you to call his father."

I hesitate. "I—I don't have his number."

"Then run down to his house." When I don't go, she looks up at me again.

"His dad doesn't know."

She closes her eyes a moment, and when she opens them, I see understanding and pity. She turns back to Curtis. "Go get his dad," she says more quietly.

I don't hesitate this time. This is the moment. There's no hiding behind shame anymore.

I sprint up the street and pound on the Camerons' door, and I keep pounding until I see lights go on through the side window. A moment later, Mr. Cameron throws open the door. He's in a flannel robe, barefoot.

He takes in the look on my face. "What's wrong, Luke? What's happened?"

I swallow. "It's Curtis. He's in my driveway."

"In your driveway?" he says, tying his robe. "He's supposed to be in Austin."

"He's not. He's—he's hurt." Behind him, Corrine rushes to the door in a fluffy robe. Mr. Cameron pushes past me and hits the sidewalk at a dead run.

Corrine pauses, her eyes bright with fear.

"He's not okay, Corrine. He needs you guys."

She searches my eyes and nods.

We jog side by side back to my house. When Corrine sees Curtis, she gasps.

He's back on the ground, his knees drawn to his chest, his wound bleeding freely. Mom is blocking Mr. Cameron, her bloody, gloved hands behind her back.

"He's my son!" Mr. Cameron snaps.

"I know, I know," Mom says gently. "But right now, he needs you to be calm and safe."

She's told him.

"Luke, get some more gloves," she tells me at the same time Mr. Cameron says to Corrine, "Go get my truck. And grab me some clothes. Anything."

"I've already called nine-one-one," Mom says.

"I'm taking him. It'll be quicker."

When I get back out, Mr. Cameron is stooped in front of Curtis, rubbing his shoulder. "It's okay, Curt. Everything's going to be okay."

Mom is holding pressure on the wound again. I hand the gloves to Mr. Cameron. He slips them on. Mom wraps another large towel around Curtis. Up the street Corrine is backing the truck out of their driveway. In the distance, sirens.

Mr. Cameron lifts Curtis to a sitting position, then hoists him to his feet. Curtis's knees buckle. His dad holds him tightly against his chest as Corrine pulls in close.

I hurry over and open the back door, then stand back with Corrine as Mr. Cameron eases him into the back seat of the cab. "What happened here, Luke?" she asks.

"Corrine, he's sick. He needs you guys."

"Sick? But ..."

"He has HIV."

"He ... what?"

In the back of the truck, Mom is showing Mr. Cameron how to hold pressure on Curtis's head.

She pierces me with a look. "How long have you known?"

I look down at my feet. Too long.

"Corrine," Mr. Cameron says, "I need you to drive."

"I can drive," I offer.

Corrine glares at me. "I'll drive."

"Did you bring a change of clothes?" her dad asks her. She hesitates, then mutters a curse.

"Luke, you drive. Corrine, run home and change and meet us at the ER."

I climb into the cab. Thankfully it's automatic. Mom takes a step back and nods at me. I check the rearview mirror. Mr. Cameron has his arm around Curtis, one hand pressed over Curtis's on the wound. I put the truck in reverse and get moving.

Curtis hasn't said a word since the fall. He waits on a treatment table, his right arm folded tightly across his chest, his left elbow braced against it. He cradles his head in his open hand. His eyes are closed, but he rocks gently to and fro, breathing shallowly. He reminds me of a turtle without a shell to withdraw into—exposed, vulnerable.

"All right, Curtis, let's have a look." The doctor is young, maybe thirty. He pulls Curtis's hand away from his head, then takes the towel from his dad and gently peels it from his temple. A nurse stands by with sterile swabs that the doctor uses to clean around the wound enough to get a good look. There's a deep gash in the side of his head, just at the edge of the longer scar he got when he was a kid. It's only bleeding a little now.

Corrine steps quietly into the room and takes the chair next to me.

"Yep, you're going to need some stitches here. A close encounter with a planter, huh?"

As the doctor prepares to flush out the wound, Mr. Cameron pulls his keys from his pocket and tosses them to me. "If you want to take my truck, Corrine can take us home when we're done."

"I'd like to stay."

Next to me, Corrine stiffens. Mr. Cameron takes note of that, but says nothing.

Curtis winces as the doctor flushes out the wound.

"I understand you're HIV positive," the doctor says.

When Curtis doesn't respond, the doctor glances at Mr. Cameron, who nods. "Okay, this is lidocaine," the doctor says, taking a syringe from the nurse. "It'll numb the area so we can suture you up, but it's going to hurt a little at first." As the doctor inserts the small needle around the edges of the cut, Curtis bites down on his lower lip.

"What medications are you taking?"

Again he has to look to Mr. Cameron for a response. Mr. Cameron looks to me. "He hasn't started treatment yet," I answer.

"Well, we have some great clinics around here if you'd like a referral."

"Is this something his primary care doctor can handle?" Mr. Cameron asks.

"You might want to check with him . . . or her first, but I don't see why not. But you might want to consider an HIV/AIDS clinic. They offer counseling, other services he might not have access to with a primary care doc."

The doctor whips in half a dozen or so stitches, then ties off the knot and pats Curtis on the knee. "There you go, buddy. I want to get a quick CT scan, and if all checks out, you're free to go." He nods toward the hallway, and Mr. Cameron follows him out.

An attendant wheels in a wheelchair and gets Curtis into it. "This will only take a few minutes," he says.

"We'll be here when you get back, Curtey," Corrine says as they disappear through the door.

When they're gone, she rounds on me. "How long have you known?"

I want to lie, tell her I just found out. But there've been too many lies already. "He told me that night he wrecked his truck."

I watch her run the numbers in her head. "That's been four months. And you didn't say a word?"

"Corrine, don't you think I wanted to? He wouldn't let me. It got to the point where every time I brought it up, he exploded."

She wants to be angry at someone. And that's okay. But it only takes her a moment to see the impossible situation Curtis had put me in. Her eyes shimmer. "But I don't understand. Why wouldn't he tell me? He's my twin brother. We've always told each other everything."

I look down at my feet.

"How did he even get it, Luke? Did he tell you that?"

"Corrine . . . I can't. That's something you have to ask Curtis."

But I can see in her face that she can add two and two and get four. "You?" she asks.

"No. Not me."

Mr. Cameron steps back into the room and closes the door behind him. "Luke, I need to know what you know."

I nod. I try to relay to him as accurately as I can how I found out, Curtis's reluctance to tell them. But the more I talk, the more I realize how little I do know. I've been almost as clueless as they. Curtis has obviously kept so much hidden, even from me.

"Why did he feel like he couldn't tell us?" he asks when I'm done.

"He didn't want to disappoint you, but, well, I suspect there's more to it than that. I think he's ashamed."

Mr. Cameron exhales and drops his head back and blinks at the ceiling.

The doctor wheels Curtis back to the room himself. "All checks out. No concussion. His regular doctor can take those out in about ten to fourteen days. Put a little antibiotic ointment on it each day to prevent infection. It'll help with scarring too." He jots the names of a couple over-the-counter ointments on his prescription pad and hands it to Curtis's dad, then stoops down to look at Curtis. "All right, buddy. Go home, take it easy for a few days, okay? And stay away from planters."

Curtis nods. It's the first response I've seen from him since he fell.

The sun is coming up by the time we get back. Curtis has to be exhausted. He hasn't slept in almost twenty-four hours, and then the trauma of last night. He's walking fine on his own now, but Mr. Cameron keeps a ready hand on his back as they enter the house. Curtis looks around like he doesn't know what to do. His dad gently nudges him toward the sofa, then sits on the coffee table facing him.

"You want to get some sleep?"

Curtis nods.

"I can bring you a pillow and blanket and you can sleep right here."

Curtis's face contorts. His dad reaches out and lays a hand on his cheek.

"I'm sorry," Curtis whispers. "I'm so sorry."

"Oh, Curt." Mr. Cameron shifts to the couch and gathers his son to himself. Tears shimmer in Corrine's eyes.

I quietly let myself out of the house.

Mom's watching from the front porch in a pair of sweatpants and a hoodie as I come up the drive. I suspect she hasn't been back to bed. "Is he okay?"

"I think so."

Mom heaves a sigh of relief. "Thank God. And what about you? You have to be exhausted."

I shrug. "Did Matt sleep through all this?"

"Every minute of it." Her brows pull together and I know what's coming next. "What happened here tonight, Luke?"

It's time for a come-to-Jesus meeting. I take a steadying breath. "Do you have any coffee?"

We sit at the kitchen table, two steaming mugs before us.

"How long have you known?" Mom asks. It's the question everyone wants to know.

"Late October. That night I got the flat tire."

She picks nervously at her cuticles. "How long has he had the virus?"

I shake my head. "Maybe a year, year and a half. He found out right before the school year started."

"Has he started drug therapy yet?"

I shake my head again.

She sighs heavily and presses her fists to her mouth. I know what she's thinking. I skim my hand along the top of the mug and wait for her to say it.

"Do you know his viral load?"

I shake my head.

"His T cell count?"

"No."

"I have to ask you, Luke . . ."

I know you do.

"That night your dad—that night Curtis stayed with you . . ."

"You know how you always told me that you and Dad weren't raising children; you were raising future adults?"

She looks out the window for a long moment and closes her eyes. "Oh, Luke."

"I need to be able to talk to you about this, Mom. Adult to adult."

With her ring finger, she pushes away a tear shimmering at the corner of her eye, then turns back to me. "You can't see him anymore, Luke. You know that, don't you?"

I expected this. She's being a mom. But I need her to be more than that right now. I need her to be that dispassionate champion of rational thinking that I know she is.

"This is Curtis we're talking about, Mom. The same Curtis he's always been. The one who was there for me when Matt almost died. The one who danced with you in our family room. He's not a piece of garbage you toss in the trash just because he's sick."

"I'm not saying—"

"Yes, you are. He's a human being, Mom. He feels damaged enough as it is. And I'm not turning my back on him. I'm gonna be there for him. Today, tomorrow, forever."

She smiles quietly. "You're a compassionate, idealistic young man, Luke. But your idealism isn't going to make this go away. You have to be a little selfish right now."

I scoff. "Maybe I am being selfish."

"I could forbid you."

"No, you couldn't."

I can see in her face that that was just a Hail Mary pass anyway.

"Can't you just be friends? Support him that way?"

"No. I don't want to."

"And what about Curtis? Is that what he wants?"

"He's just scared."

"And he should be. He's already put you at extraordinary risk."

"It was just semen on skin, Mom. No cuts on my hands. No sores in my—" I hesitate.

"You don't know that, Luke. His semen has to be swimming with the virus right now. A microscopic nick from shaving—"

"He didn't ejaculate on my face."

She blushes, steadies herself. "On your hands, you touch your face . . ."

"Believe me, Mom, he's beaten himself up plenty over that. But I pushed him. I wanted to be close to him. So if you want to blame someone, blame me, not him."

I see her eyes shimmer, but she blinks them clear. "Is that what you two were arguing about in the front yard last night?"

"No." I shake my head.

She doesn't press. She wants to, but she doesn't. For a long while, she just looks at me. I wait while she comes to terms with what she knows she must. Finally she says, "I'm scared for you, Luke."

"I know. You're allowed that."

"Thanks."

"You're welcome."

She smiles weakly at that.

"What's going to happen to Curtis?"

She takes a deep breath and lets it out again. "He's got a long road ahead of him. I won't kid you about that. Studies show that a young man who contracts HIV today and religiously adheres to anti-retroviral drug therapy is more likely to die of something age-related like heart disease than to die of AIDS."

"So, there's really nothing to worry about."

"No, baby. He's still going to have plenty to worry about. The drugs have serious side effects. And he'll have to take them for the rest of his life. And there will always be the risk that he can infect someone else, if he hasn't already. Do you understand what I'm saying to you?"

I understand exactly what she's saying. "Mom, if getting HIV is the worst thing that ever happens to me, I'll consider myself lucky."

"You might not consider yourself so lucky."

"Look, I'm not trying to get sick. I'll be careful. I promise you that. But I'm not going to let that stupid virus decide who I'm going to spend my life with."

"No talking you out of this?"

I shake my head.

She rests her chin in her hand. "When did you get so grown up?" I smile back at her. "We have to get you tested, you know."

"I know."

"I think your dad needs to know too."

I feel all the air go out of the room. "Why?"

"Because, despite everything, you're still his son."

I huff. "You don't need to worry about HIV. Dad'll kill me himself."

"No, Luke, he won't. Him hitting you, that was—"

"It wasn't the first time."

Silence. Confusion.

"What?" she says finally. "What do you mean it wasn't the first time?"

I swore I'd never tell her, but I sense we're in a different place now. It's time to lay everything out on the table. "Last December, when you were at your annual conference. I was feeling pretty low. I came out to him; he lost it."

The shock on her face is profound, and I almost regret telling her.

"You never told me," she says quietly.

I shrug. "I knew what would happen if I did."

"Oh, baby." She reaches across the table and pulls me to her. "You should have told me. If I'd known, we'd never have moved to Odessa."

"Mom. *Mom.*" I push her away, take a deep breath and let it out again. "I'm not afraid of him. I provoked him. And he reacted."

"Don't make excuses for him, Luke. He's an adult. He's responsible for his own actions."

"So am I." I don't know why I'm defending him. But I can't keep blaming him for everything. No matter what's happened, like Mom said, he's still my dad.

"Can I ask you something?" I say. Her eyes rise to meet mine. "Do you miss him?"

She gazes out the window for a long moment. "Did you know I was only in high school when I met your dad?"

No, I didn't know that.

"I was fifteen; he was sixteen. You have his hair." She glances back at me and smiles, sighs, and looks back out the window. "The first time we ever . . . you know . . . we were so scared. It was my sixteenth birthday. He gave me a balloon bouquet. We popped one of the balloons and he, um, tried to use it as a condom."

I've just taken a sip of coffee and about spit it out. She grins back at me. "You wanted to talk adult to adult."

So I did.

"We grew up together," she continues. "I thought I knew him so well. And then I became a doctor, started earning more than him . . . I think he felt threatened. Maybe that's how he feels now. I don't know. But I can't walk around on eggshells anymore. No more secrets. He can accept you, love you, champion you, or he can"—her voice cracks—"he can just go away."

"Is Curtis part of that deal?"

She grips my hand tightly. "Yeah. I guess he is."

Chapter 35

CURTIS

I ease onto a barstool, touch my finger to the bandage on my temple. Corrine eyes me with sympathy.

"Headache?"

"Yeah. How long was I asleep?"

"Not long enough. Four hours, maybe."

I feel groggy, stupid, weird, like I'm not fully present in my body. "Where's Dad?"

"He's out back cleaning the grill. He's making steaks again tonight. He thinks you look too thin."

I look over my shoulder and out the back window. The movement makes my head pound. Dad's standing at the grill, a wire brush in one hand, his cell phone in the other. "Who's he talking to?" His back is to me. I wish I could see his face.

"Vicodin or Tylenol?"

I turn back to Corrine. "They gave me a prescription for Vicodin?"

"No. But there were a few left in the cabinet and you look like you could use one."

I hold out my hand. She unscrews the lid from a pill bottle and takes out one pill and hands it to me. I note that she hasn't answered my question.

I swallow the pill and try to remember what happened before I fell asleep. I cried. It's been a long time since I cried in front of my dad. There was no holding it back anymore. And then he brought pillows from my room and a quilt, lifted my feet to the couch like he used to do when I was a little boy and would fall asleep in front of a movie.

I look out the window again. He's going to want answers. I don't know what to tell him.

"Has Luke been over?"

"No. But I'm sure once Dad gets the steaks started it won't be long."

I laugh a little at her joke.

She smiles back. "He's a good guy, Curtis. You need to hang on to him."

Did she not get the memo? That's absolutely the last thing I need to do.

I prop my cheek on my fist and watch Dad talk outside. My head throbs and my eyes feel heavy. When I feel myself starting to drop off, I get up. "I'm gonna take a shower."

"Don't let your bandage get wet," Corrine reminds me as I grip the banister and drag myself up the stairs.

I angle the showerhead sharply down and step in. I brace one hand against the tile, the other against the glass door, and close my eyes and allow the hot water to pound on my chest, and pound, and pound. For a long while I just stand there.

I need to lie down, but I can't bring myself to leave the steamy confines of the shower. It feels safe in here. No one looking at me with pity or disgust. No questions. No explanations.

When I turn so the spray can hit my back, I feel myself sway and grab for the wall.

"Curtis?"

"Curtis?"

"Holy shit, Curtis."

I feel a blast of cold air and the water shuts off.

"Come on. Put your arms around my neck."

Go away, Luke.

"You gotta hold on to me, okay? Lock your arms around my neck."

"Leave me alone leave me alone leave me alone," I mumble.

"I'll leave you alone after I get you out of this shower. Come on. You've gotta help me out here or I'll have to call your dad."

I scoff. "Haven't you done enough of that?" He drapes my arms over his shoulders and grabs me in a bear hug and lifts. I find my feet under me.

"I think you may have a concussion after all," he says.

"No concussion. No pain. I'm just sleepy."

I feel a towel drying me off, the bed at the back of my legs. Then I'm sitting, then lying on the mattress. Something warm falls over me.

"Your bandage is wet."

His fingers on my face.

"What did you tell them?" My tongue feels lazy, my voice feels choked. "I need to know," I whisper. "What did you tell them?"

"I—nothing. I didn't tell them anything, Curtis."

A towel presses against my bandage.

He's lying. I know he's lying.

"It wasn't yours to tell." I roll over onto my side, away from him.

He kneads the back of my neck. "They're not stupid, Curtis. Talk to them."

"Can you just go?"

"What are you so afraid of? That they'll find out you're human?"

"Please go."

"You're gonna need a new bandage. This one's wet."

"Go, goddammit. Leave me alone."

His hand stills. "I'll check on you later."

Don't bother.

Chapter 36

LUKE

The nurse practitioner drops the swab into a vial. "Okay. Nothing to it. We should have results in about twenty minutes. You and your mom can wait in the waiting room and we'll call you back when we're done."

I nod and follow Mom into the hallway. I didn't think this would be so nerve-racking. I don't think for a minute that I'm positive, but it's still freaking me out a little. I can't imagine how bad this was for Curtis.

"You okay?" Mom asks as we find a couple of seats.

"Why wouldn't I be?"

"No second thoughts?"

Second thoughts, third thoughts, fourth thoughts. But I can't admit this to Mom. I can barely admit it to myself. "No. I'm good."

She reaches into her bag and pulls out her Kindle.

"What are you reading?"

"*One Hundred Years of Solitude.*"

"Interesting choice."

She smiles a little. "Curtis really needs to get into counseling. You know that, don't you?"

"I know." Boy, do I know. But he won't go. I really thought that with his HIV out in the open, we'd be able to talk about it, but he's as closed as ever, maybe more so. I take the Kindle from her and read a few lines. "Maybe when he's feeling a little better," I say, handing it back. "The drugs are kicking his ass."

"It's only been a week. He'll come to tolerate them eventually, or they'll try something different."

I hope so, because right now he's a shell of a person. About the only emotion I see in him is anger now, and I don't even see that very often. But when I do, it always seems to be directed at me.

I check the time on my phone. "You think we can stop by the library on the way home?"

"Sure. Want to do some research?"

I shrug. "Did you tell Dad?"

"About Curtis?" She sighs. "No. Not yet."

"Luke."

I look up at the nurse practitioner standing in the doorway. My heart pounds as we get up and follow her back to the treatment room again. She closes the door behind her.

"You're negative. Everything's good."

I exhale. Mom closes her eyes and presses her lips together.

I'm learning to play Curtis's trombone using YouTube videos.

"Okay, listen to this. C scale." I hack my way through the notes. Up the scale and down again. It's pretty bad. I lower the instrument. "Nice, huh?"

He's lying on his side, a book open on the bed next to him, but he's not reading. He's staring blankly out the window. He blinks, then draws his knees up and pulls the quilt more tightly up under his chin.

"I can play that part of 'The Horse' that goes ba-rum . . . ba-rum. You want to hear it?"

He closes his eyes.

He's been on his antiretrovirals for two weeks. He's nauseated much of the time, and he's been so dizzy that when he drove down on Wednesday to get his stitches out, his dad took his keys. Corrine drove him back up to Huntsville the next morning, missed her own classes, and waited in his dorm room while he attended his. He made it through two before he returned to his room, threw up, and collapsed on the bed.

And he's depressed.

I drove up with his dad this morning to pack up his things and bring them home. He's not going to finish the semester in Huntsville. He can't. His dad is trying to get him into online classes so he won't lose any hours.

Mom warned me this could happen. But I don't think I really believed her. He's listless, he's lost weight. I know it's just the drugs, but it's almost like he's dying right before our eyes.

"I met your roommate today. Jaleel? He seems nice enough. He said to tell you if you didn't want to share a room with him anymore, you should have just said so."

I take the trombone apart and pack it back in its case. Then I climb onto the bed next to him, rub his shoulder through the quilt. "Are you cold?"

He doesn't respond.

"Do you want something to eat or something to drink?"

Nothing.

"Drum major auditions are coming up. I'm expecting you to be there for moral support. I think I might actually have a shot at it. Mr. Gorman says they're taking four drum majors this year. He even patted me on the back and told me he expected a good showing from me."

Silence.

Come on, Curtis. Talk to me.

"I got some more books from the library this morning. Do you know they have two whole shelves of books about..." I stop myself before I say the forbidden acronyms.

He's so still he could be asleep, but his eyes are open. There's stubble on his face and his lips are dry and cracked.

"I brought one to show you." I reach behind me for a small, slim, reinforced paperback and open it. "It's a whole book about condoms. Who knew there was so much to write about?" I laugh a little. He doesn't. "Did you know that latex condoms come in—"

"Can you just go home?" Curtis mumbles.

* * *

I'm frustrated and hurt. Mom tries to console me: "Luke, listen, being close to someone with HIV is not for the thin-skinned or the faint of heart. If you involve yourself, you should expect to get roughed up a bit."

Yeah. No shit.

Chapter 37

CURTIS

All this happy patter is driving me up the fucking wall.

I don't want to hear Luke play the trombone. I don't want to hear about drum major auditions. I don't want to hear about Jaleel. And I damn sure don't want to hear about condoms.

I just want to be left alone.

Why is that so hard for him to understand?

Chapter 38

LUKE

"That bad, huh?" Corrine says when I come into the kitchen a few days later.

"He told me to go home again."

"Don't take it personally. He's beaten us all up pretty good."

"I don't know, Corrine. I think I'm the one who irritates him. I tried to get him to drink some water—his lips are so dry and cracked—but he took the bottle and flung it against the wall."

She smiles at me sympathetically.

"What are you making?"

"Look! Tomatoes from my garden. Pretty, huh?"

She holds up a couple of large yellow-mottled tomatoes. They're bigger than the ones I usually see in the grocery store. One has a hole in it. The other, a rather wide split. I point that out to Corrine.

"Hey! Don't be dissing my tomatoes," she says, clutching them to her chest like she's protecting them from further insult. "You want to stay for dinner? I'm making spaghetti."

"Please tell me you're using Sister Celeste."

"Sister Celeste? No way. I'm making the sauce fresh."

"Are you using those tomatoes?"

"Of course. They're organic."

"There's a worm in that one," I say, pointing to the holey tomato.

She examines the hole. "Hmm. I'm pretty sure he dined and dashed." She grins at me. "Please stay," she says more seriously now. "I know he's being a dick, but it's not his fault. He's just not handling the drugs very well. And he's pretty depressed about not being able to keep up with his classes. Don't give up on him, okay? It'll get better."

"Where are my keys?" Curtis asks from behind us.

We both turn to him. "Hey, baby bro. You're up."

"Where are my keys?"

Corrine gives me a guilty look. "What do you need? I'll go get it for you."

Mr. Cameron enters through the garage door and takes a quick survey of our faces.

Curtis huffs. "I need to get some ChapStick."

"Okay, I'll—"

"I can get it myself," he snaps. He grips the door frame and looks like he's about to pass out.

His dad retrieves the truck keys from a drawer and tosses them to me. "Will you drive him, Luke?"

Curtis slumps in the passenger seat, his head resting against the window. He runs his tongue along his rough bottom lip.

I want to help him. I want to see him smile and laugh again, but I've clearly underestimated how hard this was going to be, for him and for me.

I pull up in front of Walgreens. He makes no move to get out. "I'll be right back," I tell him. "Will you be okay?"

He doesn't respond.

I dash in and purchase a three-pack of something medicated in a variety of fruit flavors.

When I get back to the truck, he looks as if he hasn't moved. I break open the package and fish out the green apple flavor, then uncap it and hold it out to him. He doesn't take it, so I reach across the seat to run it over his bottom lip. His arm flies up and knocks the ChapStick out of my hand.

He snatches the package from me and gets out another.

"I was just trying to help."

"I don't need your help."

Chapter 39

LUKE

It takes a few more weeks, but Curtis is getting better. His doctor suggested taking a magnesium pill along with his medication, and taking them on an empty stomach right before he goes to bed. That seemed to do the trick. He's eating again, getting out more, catching up on course work. The university and his professors agreed to work with him, supplying him notes online, PowerPoint presentations, tests.

Saturday morning, I see him pull the ladder out of their garage and then the blower. I head over.

When I get there, he's shimmying the ladder against the roofline, getting a solid hold. Mr. Cameron frowns as Curtis takes the blower from him and starts the climb.

"Good morning, Luke," Mr. Cameron says.

"A little spring cleaning?"

"Yep." His voice is light, but there's concern in his eyes.

"You want some help, Curtis?"

"I got it," he says flatly without looking down at me.

I look at Mr. Cameron. He nods to the ladder.

Curtis climbs easily. I follow him up, forcing myself not to look down, slipping my left hand beneath the orange electrical cord to grab each rung until Curtis yanks it out of my way. By the time I hoist myself onto the roof, Curtis is already at the peak. He turns on the blower and begins working his way down.

I climb to the ridge and lower myself to the shingles.

From the center of the roof, the height isn't nearly as scary. We're even with the canopies of the larger hardwood trees just throwing off their new leaves, but below the taller pines.

I can see for the first time the way our street hooks and then backs up to the street that is at first perpendicular to it. Because of the layout, our backyard neighbors are not who I thought they were. I count six pools, eight play sets, and a few hurricane-damaged fences that haven't yet been repaired. On the street behind us, some kids are doing serpentines on their Ripstiks, and here and there, neighbors are mowing their yards.

The pine needles are thick in the vertices of the roof, and Curtis has to adjust the blower nozzle so that the air lifts the heavy needles off the shingles before blowing them over the edge to the ground below. Summer, fall, winter, spring, there are always pine needles on the roofs.

I'd offer to take a turn with the blower, but I'm pretty sure he'd refuse. It's warm on the roof, so I content myself with soaking up the sun. It's so pleasant up here; I wish we could enjoy this together.

The blower shuts off and I hear Curtis climb back up to the ridge. He drops down next to me. After a moment, he slides down a little and leans his back against the shingles and closes his eyes.

"Libby's out again," I say absently as the dog bolts from Miss Shelley's front yard.

"Let her have some fun. You can hunt her down in a bit."

You. Not we.

I watch Libby disappear around the dogleg in the street. "It's a good day for a run." I look over at him. "I promise to take it easy on you."

His face remains blank.

"We could run to the lake and back again. Grab Libby while

we're there. Come on." I jiggle his knee. "Let's go run. What do you say?"

"I'll run when I'm goddamned good and ready to run."

Miss Shelley comes out onto her driveway, dressed in a pair of men's cargo shorts (too big) and a sports bra (too tight). I recognize them as her work clothes. I don't know what kind of work she does in her "work" clothes, but I do know that when she wears them, I work hard to avert my eyes. She's calling Libby's name in a completely useless display of authority.

"You need to go get the dog," he says when Miss Shelley calls her name again.

"You get the damn dog." I get up and climb down the ladder.

"So what are you gonna do?" Robert asks later that evening.

We're waiting for our order at the Cold Stone Creamery on Market Street.

I have zero romantic interest in Robert, but we are two hearts waiting to beat, and the companionship fills the time. And besides, he's easy to talk to.

I shouldn't have snapped at Curtis, but I'm a human being too, and sometimes the indifference and the just plain meanness get to me.

"I don't know. Nothing, I guess. Wait it out. Try to be there for him."

"But if he doesn't want you around . . ."

"He's just not himself right now."

"It seems to me like he hasn't been himself for a really long time. That's no reason—I mean—well, he doesn't treat you right. You deserve better than that."

I try not to let his words get under my skin, but they rankle me just the same. It's been almost a month since I had an HIV test. If I've been exposed to the virus, my body may not have had time to build up detectable antibodies. In another eight weeks or so, I'll have to have another. Suddenly I find myself wondering whether it's all worth it.

We take our ice cream and sit on the bulwark surrounding the green. There's a concert this evening—some local country western band. A handful of couples around the fringes are two-stepping to the music.

"Do you dance?" I ask Robert.

"Not to this stuff." He grins at me. "How's the Coffee Lovers Only?"

I shrug. "You want a bite?" I spoon up some ice cream and offer it to him. Instead of taking it, he leans over and kisses me.

"Sorry," he says, looking honestly embarrassed. "I've been wanting to do that for a while."

"Robert—"

"It's okay." He brushes off my reaction and doesn't mention it again.

I see Dad's car in the driveway when I come around the dogleg Monday after school, and for a moment, I consider circling the cul-de-sac and heading right back out again. He's sitting on the porch, his head down, and even from the driveway I can see that his suit is rumpled, like he doesn't care anymore. How long has he been this way? I can't answer that. I usually manage to avoid him when he picks up Matt on weekends.

I make my way to the porch, then step around him to the door.

"Luke, I want to come home."

Don't do this to me.

I grip the doorknob. "Does Mom know you're here?"

"No. I wanted to talk to you."

"About what, Dad? You've already made your feelings abundantly clear."

He shakes his head. "I'm trying to apologize here, Luke. I'm asking for a chance to prove myself."

"To prove what? That you can stuff everything down and pretend to be okay with me? With who I am? With who I sleep with?"

I see his jaw tense.

"Well, I don't want that. I don't want to be tolerated. I want my dad back, but I don't know where he is. And I don't think you do either." I open the door, then pause. "Did Mom tell you yet?"

"Tell me what?" he asks wearily. He looks back at me over his shoulder and I notice his bloodshot eyes, the stubble on his cheeks.

"Nothing."

"I don't know, Luke. He shouldn't have caught you off guard like that." Mom hands me a bag of meatballs. "I know he's having a rough time, but that doesn't change anything."

"He apologized." I don't even know why I'm defending Dad. He just looked so sad sitting there on the front porch, so lost. I dump the meatballs into the sauce and try not to think about that spaghetti dinner I missed with Curtis so long ago. Will I always associate spaghetti with Curtis?

"That's a good first step, Luke. But that's all it is."

"I have an idea," Matt says. "Let's desensitize him. Like that therapy stuff they do for people with OCD—make them touch gross stuff or try to kill somebody with their thoughts."

Mom smiles over his head at me. "Honey, your dad doesn't have OCD."

"But he does have an irrational fear of gay people. We could invite Dad to dinner and invite Curtis too."

"Curtis wouldn't come."

Mom looks at me with sympathy.

I haven't seen Curtis or even talked to him since I left him on the roof a few days ago. He won't answer his phone or respond to my texts. And when I knocked on his door yesterday, Corrine told me he told her to say he was in the shower. Then she stepped out onto the porch with me and closed the door behind her. "He doesn't want to be around people right now, Luke."

"Ask your new boyfriend," Matt says to me.

I stir the sauce. "Robert's not my boyfriend."

"Dad doesn't have to know that."

"Matt," Mom says, "that's an interesting plan, but I don't think—"

"We could try it," I say, stopping her. She looks at me curiously. "I just think, well, he's offering an olive branch. The least we could do is accept it."

"And what's in this for you?"

"I just want everybody to be happy again."

"And what about you?"

I shrug. "I'm willing to try."

She sighs and musses my hair. "Okay. I'll call him, but we are not playing around here. I want you to be one hundred percent you." She smiles. "And maybe a little extra for effect. He can either accept that gracefully, or he can return to whatever hole he's been living in."

I wait until Friday to ask Robert.

"I don't know," he says, tightening the ligature around his reed. He slips the strap of his saxophone over his shoulder and then shoves his backpack deeper into his band locker. "I really don't like the sight of my own blood."

"Come on. My dad's not going to do anything. It's just dinner."

"Can't you make your point without rubbing it in his face?"

"No, I can't. He needs to deal with this head-on. And I can't ask Curtis. He's barely civil to me these days." I regret the words as soon as I say them. For one, that's an understatement and he knows it; and two, I don't need or want another lecture from Robert. "Look, I could ask Spencer or Jackson, but it's not the same thing. It has to be you."

"Just how much is he going to have to deal with head-on?"

I don't answer.

"Great," he says, slamming the locker door. "I don't know why I let you use me like this."

"I'll let you kiss me again."

He looks hurt and turns away. I feel like a jerk as I follow him to his section. He sticks his music on the stand, and it promptly flutters to the floor. I pick it up.

"So am I your boyfriend . . . for Daddy-O, I mean?"

"Yeah."

"And what do I get in return?"

"I'll put in a good word for you with Nic."

"Better be a damn good word."

* * *

I wish it could have been Curtis. I know from all the books I've checked out from the library that his depression is a normal part of the grieving process. But how much longer will this go on? How much longer is he going to isolate and push away the people who love him?

When I round the dogleg home, I get my answer.

Chapter 40

CURTIS

"Currr-tis." Jaleel grabs me in a big hug and slaps my back. "Good to see you, man. But you nothin' but bones, bro." He pushes me away. "Look at you."

I smirk. "Thanks a lot. It's good to see you too."

He takes a deep breath and lets it out. "Really. Are you okay?"

"I'm okay. At least, I think so." I push his car door shut and glance up to see Luke's car drive past. I watch him pull into his driveway and get out. Jaleel follows my gaze.

"Did he give you my message a few weeks ago?"

"Yeah. He gave it to me." The scar on my forehead itches; I scratch it.

I feel Jaleel study me, then he exhales. "Man, why don't you quit fighting it? He wants to be with you; you want to be with him. Figure it out, man. Life is too short for these games."

"This is not a game."

Corrine steps out of the house and squeals when she sees Jaleel.

I glance back at Luke's house one more time, but he's already gone in.

Chapter 41

LUKE

Doesn't want to be around people, my ass.

I watch from my bedroom window as the three of them talk and laugh on the driveway. I haven't seen Curtis smile in months. All this time I've invested in him, worried about him, sacrificed for him, and he's given me nothing in return. And now he's out there giving the best of himself to someone else.

A couple of hours later, Dad's SUV pulls into the driveway.

I've changed my mind. I don't want to do this dinner anymore. It was a stupid idea, but it's too late now.

Matt rushes past me and pulls open the door.

"Hey, buddy," Dad says, faking a couple of punches at him. He grins and musses his hair, then drops his arms to his sides. "Luke. You doing okay?"

"Yeah. Mom's in the kitchen."

He nods. "Well, Matt, let's go see what's cooking."

I move to the window and watch for Robert. I can't help but note that Jaleel's car is still at Curtis's. Within minutes, Robert's Camry pulls into the driveway. He comes up the walk with a green-tissue-wrapped bouquet of flowers clutched in his hand.

"You brought me flowers?"

"For your mom, idiot. But here." He fishes a daisy from the bunch and tucks it behind my ear. I remove it, and tuck the broken stem into the pocket of my jeans.

Deep breath. "Ready?"

"Lead me to the great white whale, Cap'n Ahab."

When we enter the kitchen, the shock on Dad's face makes it clear that he wasn't expecting company.

"Uh, Dad, this is Robert Westfall."

There's a beat where no one says a word. And I just know Dad's going to blow it. It's too much. He can't handle it. But then he surprises me by suddenly reaching out to shake Robert's hand.

"Flowers!" Mom takes the bouquet. "That is so sweet of you, Robert. Let me put these in a vase. You boys want to take the food to the table?"

Mom made a salad with field greens, walnuts, feta cheese, green apples, and grilled chicken with Hidden Valley Ranch Dressing she mixed up herself. Dad likes beef and potatoes. The statement is not lost on me; I suspect it's not lost on him either. He better start liking chicken and lettuce real quick because there's a new world order in this house.

Robert pulls out a chair for me. Dad stops midway to dropping his butt in his usual chair at the end of the table. Mom glares at him and he sits.

"Really?" I mouth at Robert over my shoulder.

"So, Robert, Luke's mom was just telling me you're in the band?"

"Yes, sir. I play baritone sax."

Dad reaches for the rolls.

Matt grins at me and I see trouble coming. "Robert's also in the guard, Dad. He dances. And twirls a flag and a rifle."

I watch Dad's jaw tense, then relax as he takes a roll from the basket and passes it to me.

"And they have a new guard director this year," Matt says in a rush, like he can hardly wait to get to the punch line.

"Is he gay too?" Dad asks, tightly.

"I don't know," Robert says. "He likes pink."

I stifle a grin.

"Robert shaves his legs," Matt pipes in again.

I suck some tea into my windpipe and cough. Robert pats my back.

"Do you use a razor or do you wax?" Matt asks with a cherubic but fake innocence.

Robert's eyes shoot to Dad, who is studying his plate like there might be a hair hiding in his feta cheese somewhere, then he looks back at Matt and blushes a little.

"Um, I wax. It lasts longer."

News to me. But then again, I haven't spent much time studying Robert's legs.

"Luke uses a razor," Matt says.

I do not, you little twit.

Dad gets up abruptly and Mom's head snaps to him. "I'm just going to get everyone some more tea," he mumbles.

When he's out of earshot, Mom snorts. "Robert, you're quite an actor. I hope we're not making this too uncomfortable for you."

"No more uncomfortable than dinner with my own family."

"You never told me that," I say.

He shrugs. "You never asked."

I glance under the edge of the table. "Do you really wax your legs?"

He grins. "Only during marching season. The costumes, you know." He wrinkles his nose and shakes his head. "It can get pretty ugly."

Dad walks back in with a glass pitcher. He makes his way around the table, topping off our still-full glasses. Then he sets the pitcher on the table and takes his seat again. He looks up and smiles at all of us.

I smile back uneasily.

"Well, that wasn't awkward at all," Robert says as I close my bedroom door behind us.

In fact, it was plenty awkward, but at least Matt turned down the flame for the rest of the meal and we got through it without further incident.

"How long do we have to stay up here to drive your point home?" he asks.

I laugh a little. "A while. You did really good. I owe you one."

"You owe me two." He looks out the window. "Which house is Curtis's?"

"Seven down, on the left."

"Hmph. Who's he with?"

I look out the window. It's dark outside, but the Camerons' porch light is on and I can clearly see Curtis and Jaleel on the sidewalk in front. As I watch, they get into Jaleel's car.

Great. A night out.

The last time Curtis spent any time "out" with me was months ago. He was always too sick, too depressed, too whatever.

"That's his roommate," I tell Robert.

"Why is he here? Are they dating now?"

"I don't know why he's here," I snap.

"Well, don't bite my head off. If you're pissed at Curtis, go egg his truck or something."

Oh, wow. I wish he hadn't said that.

I open my closet.

"I was kidding," Robert says as I pull on a dark hoodie and toss him one. "You'll ruin the finish on his truck."

"We're not egging the finish."

"Oh, crap."

He follows me back down to the kitchen. The dishes are still stacked on the counter next to the sink. Mom and Dad are nowhere around. Probably on the back patio talking like they used to do. I open the fridge and find a full carton of eggs under a half empty one and hand it to Robert. Then I grab a bag of flour from the pantry.

"Come on," Robert says, trailing behind me. "Isn't this kind of immature? He's sick, man."

"He's not that sick," I mutter.

We make our way down the dark street like a couple of juvenile delinquents.

"It's probably locked," Robert says.

I quietly release the door handle on the passenger side and smirk back at him. I set the flour on the seat then reach back for the egg carton.

"You're really going to do this?" Robert says.

"I'm really going to do this." *You bet your ass I am.* I climb into the cab and, one by one, smash the eggs on the floorboards, the dashboard, the seats, the windows, backing my way out as I do. *I would have fucking done anything for you, Curtis.* I rip open the bag of flour and fling it by handfuls over the eggs. *Playing games with me. Acting like you cared about me. You don't care about anybody but yourself and your precious little boy-next-door image.* When the bag's empty, I crumple it and fling the bag and the egg carton against the windshield and wipe my hands on my jeans.

"Wow," Robert says, staring at my handiwork. "Remind me never to piss you off."

Chapter 42

CURTIS

Saturday morning we're up early. It was Dad's idea to have Jaleel stay over. The plan is to get back up to school this morning, get settled in, re-acclimate, get a fresh start Sunday reviewing for finals. It feels good to be doing something normal again.

"You want to follow me, or you want me to follow you?" Jaleel asks, hitting the Unlock button on his keypad.

"I'll—what the hell?" I peer in the side window. "God*dammit.*" I open the door and the smell hits me. I brush a few broken eggshells off my seat. "Fucking kids. I don't need this shit today."

Jaleel opens the passenger door. "Whew." He leans back, screws up his face. "Man, that reeks. Don't you people lock your doors around here?"

I grip my forehead. First Robert's Camry in Luke's driveway last night, and now this. Somebody really hates me up there. We'll be lucky if we get back by dark now.

"Oh my God." Corrine looks around the cab.

"You got a putty knife?" Jaleel asks. "Man, you're gonna have to scrape this shit off."

He isn't kidding.

We get most of the junk up with putty knives, but the egg and flour goo is embedded in the fabric. I brush an arm across my sweaty forehead. "You interested in a drive to the car wash?"

I toss a couple of towels on the seat and we get in. Jaleel goes for the window. "You got a kid lock on or something? Roll down the windows. Damn, it stinks in here."

"They don't work. The electrical system's screwed up."

"You're kidding, right?"

"Not kidding. Just hold your nose."

At every stop sign and traffic light on the way, Jaleel throws open the door and makes a big show of sucking in fresh air. I can barely stand the smell myself, but I'm too fucking pissed to do anything about it.

At the car wash, we end up having to take out the seat and the mats. With the high power hot water carpet extractor and a fistful of quarters, we finally get everything clean.

Dad looks around the cab when we get back and shakes his head. "I can still smell it." He exhales. "Let it dry overnight. Jaleel, you okay with another night on the couch?"

In the morning, we try again.

"You want to take the truck and I'll drive your car?" I ask Jaleel.

He slaps me on the back. "Good try, man. Next time, lock your doors."

The seats are clean, but the smell definitely lingers. By the time we get back to Huntsville, the smell of rotten eggs is embedded in my skin.

Chapter 43

LUKE

Okay. It was immature. But Robert's flippant suggestion called to me the way a lightning rod calls to lightning. It offered me an almost irresistible means of discharging all the anger built up inside me.

I regret that now, but it's over and done with. Curtis and Jaleel worked for hours cleaning out the cab yesterday. I watched from my window. But this morning, both their vehicles were gone.

I finish my run and slowly make my way down the street. Up ahead, Corrine is unloading pallets of seedlings from the back of her hatchback. "Need some help?" I call out.

"If you're offering."

I jog up the drive and lift the bags of soil and fertilizer out of the back for her. "Where's Curtis?" I ask, stepping back so she can slam the gate.

"Jaleel came down Friday. He followed Curtis back up to Sam a couple of hours ago." She pauses. "He didn't tell you, did he?"

"No. He didn't tell me."

"He wanted to sit for finals. I'm sorry, Luke."

So am I. I shift the bags to get a better grip. "These bags are kind of heavy, Corrine."

"Come on. You can help me plant these."

I follow her through the gate to the backyard where she keeps a small garden in the sunny middle of the yard. She sets down the pallets next to four or five others. I drop the bags next to them. "What are you planting this time?"

"Um . . ." She looks at the tags. "Summer squash, radishes, okra."

"No more tomatoes?"

She kneels next to the garden and grins up at me. "Too hot."

I sit on the bags and pick up a squash plant, turn the plastic pot over and squeeze until the plant, dirt and all, drops into my hand. "Is he moving back home after finals week?"

"I think so. He was planning to come back for the first day of drum major auditions Wednesday, but someone egged his truck a couple of nights ago and the smell is terrible. The electrical system is acting screwy in his truck, so he can't even roll down the windows. He told me it was so bad he could hardly stand the forty-five-minute drive back to school."

I stifle a grin and get up, toe the bags. "You want me to spread this for you?"

She doesn't answer. I feel her watching me as I reach for a trowel lying on the ground.

"It was you. You egged Curtis's truck."

I don't deny it.

"Oh shit, Luke. He was pissed. I mean, I don't blame you for being mad at him. He's been a real shit. But, holy cow. I'm glad we don't have a rabbit."

"A rabbit?"

"Oh, never mind." She suddenly snorts and falls into a fit of giggling. "God, you should have seen him. He had to use a putty knife to scrape that junk off. He was scraping with one hand and holding his nose with the other"—she demonstrates—"and cussing like a . . . like a . . . I don't know. A lot. He had to sit on a towel just to get the truck to the car wash. It's so bad that he smells like rotten eggs every time he gets out of the truck." She huffs. "He thinks some kids did it."

"You won't tell him, will you?"

"No. I won't tell him. He probably deserved it."

* * *

I don't have the patience or the desire to finesse this. I march right up to Nic in class on Monday. "You should call Robert Westfall and ask him out."

He looks up at me, surprised, then smirks. "I don't ask out boys; boys ask me out."

I don't know what Robert sees in this pompous queen, but figuring out the attraction is not part of the deal.

I swallow my irritation and say in the most diplomatic tone I can puke out, "As Robert Westfall's official delegate, would you like to go out with him Friday night?"

"Where?"

How about the ER for a personality infusion.

I suggest a Mexican restaurant with loud, live music. I figure Whore-Hay will fit right in.

"I don't eat red meat."

"Order the chicken."

He folds his arms, then puts his finger to his chin like he has to think about it. "Okay," he says finally. "He can pick me up at seven."

"This is it," Robert says to me after school Friday.

"Yep. This is it." The final day of drum major auditions, the last day of the three-day process that began on Wednesday.

He tips his chin at Mr. Gorman's office. "Did you know Curtis was gonna be here today?"

I glance over. The door is open and the sound of laughter filters across the band hall. Despite everything, I still feel my pulse rate go up. But I don't want to talk about Curtis. It's over. I give up.

"So you and Nic tonight, huh?" I say.

He flicks his eyebrows. "Sí, señor."

I smile. "I hope you like Mexican food."

"I hope I like Whore-Hay." His eyes shift over my shoulder. "Looks like it's show time."

I look back and see everyone filing out of Mr. Gorman's office. "Wish me luck."

"Good luck, man. Text me later and let me know how it goes."

Months ago, Curtis told me the audition is more ceremony than competition. The directors know us, they know our résumés, they know what we can do. They might get a couple of surprises this week, but beyond that, the roster is probably already set.

That should have loosened the knot in my stomach. It hasn't, and seeing Curtis here compounds my nervousness. It's funny. Months ago, I didn't care whether I made drum major or not. But now, for reasons I can't even explain, I care very much.

The performance days are behind us. Today are the leadership interviews. There's no avoiding Curtis. He's holding the plastic bowl from which we have to draw numbers to determine the order. I get last pick. I pull out a piece of paper and unfold it.

He takes a step closer. "You egged my fucking truck."

I turn the paper and show him. Three.

"Pretty childish. And you ought to know by now that Corrine can't keep a secret."

"You ought to know by now that she doesn't lie very well either. Next time you want to brush me off, do your own dirty work." I turn and walk off.

"Luke . . ."

The encounter with Curtis has me rattled. I have to force myself to focus on what I know the directors are looking for—confidence, a good attitude, integrity, humility, patience.

I sit up straight in the metal chair and listen carefully to the scenarios they lay out. I don't remember half of what I say, but they laugh and joke around with me when I'm done, and I leave the room feeling confident that I didn't completely embarrass myself.

All that's left to do is wait.

Curtis is stretched out on the floor when I return to the band hall, his eyes closed. He still looks frail to me. I imagine this week back at school has been hard on him. I wish I could ask, but we both seem to have crossed into some place I never thought we'd be.

I go out into the hallway to wait for the results.

An hour later, Mr. Gorman posts the list.

Congratulations to our newest drum majors!

Mindy Scarborough
Austin Blake
Annie Trujillo
Luke Chesser

"You done good, kiddo," Mr. Gorman says, patting my back. Then he reaches around to shake my hand.

"Thanks."

"We need to get you signed up for leadership camp soon. Okay?"

"Just tell me when and where."

Curtis slings his arm over Mindy's shoulder and gives her an enthusiastic squeeze, then high fives Austin, then Annie. I don't wait to be ignored; I gather up my duffel bag and head out.

I want to feel good about this. I do feel good about this. But sometimes I think Curtis is hell-bent on sending me a message. He needn't bother anymore.

I got it.

I text Robert the list as I walk. He texts back: Congratulations, man. I bow to your greatness.

"Luke!"

Aw, come on, Curtis. Just let it go.

"Congratulations," he says, falling in step with me. "Gorman was impressed."

"That's 'cause I'm so wonderful." I thumb the Unlock button on my keypad; the lights on my car flash. I reach for the door handle. He reaches too and holds the door shut.

"You're mad. I get that. I even grant you that. I haven't been easy to be around. But you don't have to burn the house down, Luke."

I don't begin to know how to respond to that. So I don't.

"How did your finals go?" I ask.

"Okay, I think. I saw Robert's car in your driveway last weekend. Things working out with you two?"

An awkward silence stretches out between us as I consider how I'm going to answer that question. Finally, I settle on "Yeah. Great."

He looks off at the other kids heading for their cars.

"Was there something else you wanted?" I ask.

He hesitates, then shakes his head. "I just wanted to say congratulations. You earned it."

"Thanks." I reach for the door handle again. This time he steps aside.

Mr. Cameron is working on some project in their driveway when I drive past, and I'm spared having to wave. It's not his fault. But it's hard to be friendly when I'm this hurt.

I find Mom sitting on the brick patio out back, leaning against a column and smoking a cigarette. When I open the door, she starts. "You caught me," she says with a sheepish smile. I sit down beside her. "I'm a doctor. I should know better." She stubs out the cigarette on a brick and tosses the butt into the azalea bed, then puts her arm around me. I lean my head on her shoulder.

"Were drum major tryouts rough?" she asks, rubbing my arm.

"They were okay."

"Who made it?"

"Mindy, Annie, Austin, me."

She holds me away and gives me a long, surprised look. "Congratulations! We should be celebrating . . . or not," she says, taking in my long face. "Was Curtis there?"

I nod and she pulls me back to her. "You want to tell me about it?"

I shake my head, then burrow it under her chin. We sit that way for a good while. "Do you miss Dad?" I ask after a while.

"Yeah. I miss him."

"Why haven't you let him come home? He did pretty good that night."

"Pretty good isn't good enough, Luke. I'm really proud of your dad. I am. But it's not enough. It's not enough for him to tolerate you. He has to accept you, all of you. He has to embrace who you are as a person. He has to respect you. Champion you. Because that's what parents do. And until he does that, it's not enough."

"How does he do that?"

"I don't know. But it's his job to figure it out."

Chapter 44

CURTIS

Even through the closed windows, I can hear the circular saw whine, then settle into a low hum. Dad lifts off his safety goggles and gathers up the pieces of cut wood and drops them on the ground next to a white door lying across two sawhorses. He looks up as I get out of the truck. "Hey, you're home! Wrapped up all your finals?"

"All done. Dorm key turned in. I'm free for the summer." I leave the truck door open so it can air out a bit.

"How did drum major tryouts go? Luke make a good showing?"

"Better than I expected. A star is born."

Dad laughs. "Good for him. Why aren't you two out celebrating?"

"Dad..."

"I'm just saying. You had a part in this. I just thought..."

"What are you building?"

"A spice rack to mount on the inside of the pantry door. It was your sister's idea. I think she's been watching too much TLC."

"I heard that," Corrine says from the doorway. Dad grins over his shoulder at her. She hands him a bottle of water.

"You want to help?" he asks me.

"Ooh," Corrine coos. "Fun with power tools."

I roll my eyes. "Sure. What do you need?"

"You can cut the shelves while I drill some holes and get this frame put together."

"Sure. How many and how long?"

"Use the one by twos. I need six pieces, twenty-one and a half long and . . ." He pauses to consult the plans lying on the door. "Eight pieces, three and a half inches long for supports. Got it?"

"Six, twenty-one and a half, and eight, three and a half. Got it." I reach past him for some boards.

"Whew, Curtis. That smell is bad. We got to get that electrical system fixed and maybe your truck detailed tomorrow. I hope you, uh, weren't too hard on Luke about that."

I scoff. "Just goes to prove how immature he is."

"Oh, I don't know about that. People do crazy things sometimes when they're in love."

"Dad, don't—"

"I'm not. I just think you should cut him some slack. He's been a good friend. Listen, why don't we leave your truck at the garage tomorrow, and I'll drop you at your group meeting."

I lay a one-by-two piece of pine on the table and set the measurement with the miter gauge. From the corner of my eye I see him exchange a glance with Corrine.

I pull on Dad's safety glasses. The saw whines as I push the pieces through.

I can't imagine a better way to spend a Saturday morning than sitting on a hard chair in a kindergarten circle in a stuffy room with a bunch of doomed guys talking about their fucked-up lives. I should have brought doughnuts.

A skinny, older man with no butt and a graying goatee settles into a chair.

"Welcome, everyone. Before we start introductions, I just want to acknowledge that this is a unique group of individuals, but you all have something vital in common—your lives have all been impacted by HIV infection. Our hope is that you'll find in this group a safe place to talk about the issues, concerns, thoughts, and feelings that each of you has about any aspect of your disease and its consequences on your life.

"My name is Albert O'Neal. Bradley and I are the facilitators of this group." He nods across the circle to a younger guy with a shaved head who raises his hand in a small wave. "I'm forty-nine years old," he continues, "and I found out almost fourteen years ago that I have HIV. It was pretty advanced at the time, but I'm doing okay. I'm single"—he laughs like this is funny, then shrugs— "have a mostly supportive family, live a pretty full life." He looks around at each of us. "It's good," he says softly.

"So." He sits up in his chair and consults his clipboard. "Jack, you want to get us started?"

I listen to their stories, the anxiety and despair in their voices, the nervous laughter and lame attempts at jokes. I don't want to be here. I don't want to look at them and see them looking back. I'm sick, I'm going to get sicker, and I'm going to die. Talking about it isn't going to change any of that.

I admit it. I'm doing better, a lot better, relatively speaking. But that's just it. It's all relative now. There will be better days and there will be worse days, until the worse days completely overtake the better. I will never be free of this disease.

In a moment of weakness, I agreed to join this new group. But I didn't agree to it for me; I agreed to it for Dad. He's a problem solver. He fixes things. But his inability to fix me has him increasingly frustrated. He's spending less time at work and more time hovering over me.

One and a half hours of group therapy hell, once a week, for an entire year. But I guess if this makes him feel like he's got some control over the situation, then I can suffer through it.

"Curtis? You want to introduce yourself and tell everyone a little bit about why you're here today?"

I shift in my seat and study the peeling paint on the concrete floor. "I'd just like to observe if that's okay."

Albert darts a quick look at Bradley, then moves on.

Chapter 45

CURTIS

I've gained back almost ten of the twenty or so pounds I lost. Corrine says it's because I'm eating from her garden. I think it's because I've finally quit throwing up.

After the Fourth of July parade today, we're all going to the Red, Hot & Blue Festival next to the Pavilion. I'm actually craving sausage on a stick and funnel cake. It's a good feeling. Almost normal.

All the parade entries are gathered in a church parking lot near the end of Market Street. I follow the pounding rhythm of the drumline until I find the band.

"Hey, man!" Adeeb says when I sidle up to a group of graduated seniors. "Haven't seen you around in a while. Junior now, huh?"

"Yeah. Surprised to see you here. I thought you'd be speeding up Highway Six to Aggieland by now."

"Can't resist one last fling with the band."

I know the feeling. "So, engineering, huh?"

"Yep. Somebody's got to rebuild the infrastructure in this country while you slackers blow your little horns. You gonna try out for drum major next year at Sam?"

"I don't know. Maybe."

I may not even be returning to Sam. What school would ever hire me as a band director anyway? I see no point in finishing. And I see no point in sharing this with Adeeb.

"Can't believe what you did with that bonehead. I sure wouldn't have pegged him for a drum major last fall."

I glance around until I see Luke and the other drum majors talking with Mr. Gorman. He's cut his hair. He looks good—strong, tan, confident in his band T-shirt and khaki cargo shorts. I don't think I've ever seen him wear sunglasses. I find myself smiling a little.

"Turns out he's a lot more than a pretty face."

"Pretty face, huh? I don't know about that. You two still dating?"

"We were never dating."

"Could have fooled me."

I eye my good friend. "He's just a kid."

"Get tuned up!" Mr. Gorman calls out.

Spencer motions the clarinets to him. I saunter over with Adeeb and stand off to the side as Spencer takes command of the section, and Adeeb lets him. A passing of the torch.

The band comes together to play a few warm-up notes, then to run through a couple of songs. I'm surprised when Mr. Gorman places Luke in the center, with Mindy and Annie flanking him on one side, Austin on the other. Luke poises his hands in the air and scans the faces of the band before him. The other drum majors wait for his signal. Then he counts off the beat and the band launches into the medley of patriotic songs I know so well. I watch his hands move, itching to move mine as well. He's so good, so natural, so passionate.

Pride overwhelms me, and I feel my eyes sting when he smiles as the piccolo hits her solo perfectly.

The band moves out. I trail along on the sidelines with the directors and chaperones as the group winds its way around Market Street. I still tire easily, but I fight the urge to bail and sit it out. I pull my cap lower, wipe the sweat from the bridge of my nose, and reseat my sunglasses. I don't plan to miss one second of his big debut.

The band pulls up to a stop as the dance troupe ahead performs to a prerecorded song in front of the viewing stand. A woman steps to the curb and lifts her camera. I take a couple of steps back to get out of her shot. She looks familiar. I look to the band to see who she's taking a photo of.

Robert Westfall beams back at the camera. I can't help note the tanned face, the broad smile, the white teeth, the filled-out frame. He's the picture of health and virility.

The dancers wrap up and the band surges forward. I step up onto the curb and head back to my truck.

"Boy, you're in a bad mood," Corrine says when I slam the truck door. "How was the parade? We're going to the festival later, right?"

I slip past her.

"Um, you want to fire some bottle rockets at someone?" she calls after me. "Nice seeing you too."

I slam the front door behind me, take the stairs two at a time, and change into a pair of athletic shorts and running shoes.

Jack is in tears today. I roll my eyes as I listen to his pathetic tale.

"He just walked out," he says. "He said he couldn't take it anymore. And he just walked out."

Josue leans over and grips his knee. "It's okay, man."

"I don't understand," Jack goes on, hanging his head. "Randy and me, we've been together almost seven years. He didn't even take his things with him. It was like he couldn't even stand to be with me long enough to pack up."

"What did you expect?" I mutter.

"Hey, man," Josue says, shooting me an angry look.

I hear someone else mumble, "He speaks."

Albert looks at me. "What did you mean by that, Curtis?"

I laugh. "Come on. It was just a matter of time. Don't you get that? Look at us. We're walking plagues, man. You think anybody is gonna stick around long for this freak show? You may get a little sympathy for a while, you might even get a sympathy fuck or two in, but it won't last. They're all gonna walk away. The sooner you accept that, the better."

"Hey, man. Speak for yourself," someone says.

I get to my feet. "Why are we even discussing this—boyfriends, partners. We have no right to do to someone else what was done to us. Are you people fucking nuts?"

Jack stares at me like I just shoved a dagger through his heart. I don't give a fuck. He needed to hear it. They all need to hear it.

"How does that make you feel, Jack?" Albert asks.

The truth is, I'm tired of the whole thing. No, I'm bored with the whole thing—the fear, the shame, the doctor visits, the drama. It's over, and I just want to move on. I know what my future holds; I accept that. And I don't want any reminders of what could have been.

But the reminders just keep coming.

On Monday I drive up to Huntsville for a week of Drum Major/Leadership Camp. I agreed to be a student instructor back in January. If it weren't for that, I damn sure wouldn't be going. I imagine if Mr. Martinez knew I wasn't returning in the fall, he'd probably have dropped me. I didn't tell him; I didn't want to have to explain why, make up another lie.

High school drum majors from all across the state are here, so it's easy to avoid bumping into Luke. But Thursday afternoon, I find him in a common room absently moving the puck around an air hockey table.

I know I should keep going, but I can't.

I grab the other mallet. He looks up. "Let's play," I tell him.

I wouldn't exactly call it a game. I slam the puck into his goal over and over again, and easily block his own halfhearted attempts. "You know what your problem is?" I can hear the anger in my voice, but I feel powerless to rein it in.

He makes a good hard hit and sends the puck ricocheting all over the table.

"You're impulsive and reckless and fickle and—"

"I don't need you to chronicle my sins," he says sullenly.

"No. I don't guess you do."

He looks at me across the table.

"I guess you and Robert are getting to know each other pretty well by now. Huh?"

He slams the puck toward my goal. I make no attempt to block it, and it slides smoothly into the slot.

"What do you care what I do or don't do?" He shoves the mallet across the table at me and turns to go.

"I don't, Luke. I don't."

He stops and turns back to me. "Just so you know. I'm not dating Robert. I was never dating Robert. Not that it matters." He drops his eyes and walks off.

Not that it matters.

Chapter 46

LUKE

There are new section T-shirts this year: *Clarinets do it in the woodwinds*. Ha, ha.

When Mr. Gorman calls for a water break, the kids scramble over to get theirs.

It's been almost a year since Curtis pulled on the *Luke Chesser, you are wrong* shirt right here in the back parking lot, over a month since I last spoke to him over the air hockey table.

It's been eight months since Mom threw Dad out of the house.

When Band Camp wraps up for the day I find him leaning against the trunk of my car, staring down at his feet with unfocused eyes. He doesn't move, even when I hit the keypad and the doors unlock. I toss my duffel bag onto the backseat and close the door. A couple of kids call out good-byes, and I return them. And still Dad stands there. Finally I walk to the back of the car and join him against the trunk. We watch the cars leave the parking lot.

"I went to your friend Nathan Schaper's house today," he says, breaking the awkward silence.

"What? No. Please tell me you didn't."

"I wanted to apologize to him, and to his mother and grandmother, for what happened that day."

What happened was a particularly nasty confrontation between my dad and Nate, his mother, his grandmother, and Adam. It was the morning after I came out. The morning after Dad beat the crap out of me. I'd fled to Nate's house. Ms. Schaper called my dad, and Dad came to get me. It got ugly. Insults, threats. But it was a long time ago. Ancient history. And I want it to stay that way.

"Dad—"

"No one was home."

I exhale and slump against the trunk.

"Can I ask you a question?" Dad says, twisting his watch around his wrist. I've never known my dad to be nervous. He looks nervous now. "Was I a bad father? Is that what this is all about?"

I think I know what he's asking, and it pisses me off. I push off the trunk and head for the driver's door.

"Luke, stop," he says, grabbing my arm and then letting go just as quickly. "I'm trying to understand."

"Can I ask you a question?" I snap. "Why not me? You pick up Matt every other weekend for your father/son bonding crap. But you never take me."

"You don't like fishing and camping and ball games."

"You never asked. I would have gone."

That seems to surprise him. It surprises me. But it's true.

"You're my dad. Fathers and sons spend time together. That's what they do. Even if they don't like each other very much. They spend time together." I swipe at my eyes with the collar of my T-shirt. "I would have gone."

"I didn't know."

"It was your *job* to know." I don't want to cry in front of him.

His voice is thick and choked when he speaks again. "I want my family back, Luke. I want my wife back. I want my sons back. *Both* of my sons. I know I haven't been the dad you wanted, the dad I should have been, but you have to know that I love you."

Don't say things you don't mean.

He holds out his hand as if he wants to touch me again, then slips it into his pocket. "I guess all this time away has made me realize what's important. Look, it's not what I would have chosen for you, and it still scares me a little, but I can change. I want to change. Give me a chance. Let me get to know Robert."

"Robert's not my boyfriend, Dad. Curtis is." Or he should be.

That seems to throw him. Maybe it's the memory of finding us in bed together, but whatever it is, it gives him pause. But in a moment, he collects himself. "Okay, Curtis then."

I laugh a little and blink to clear my eyes. "Curtis has HIV, Dad." I know from the look on his face that this is news. "Mom hasn't told you, has she? You still want to get to know him?"

He squeezes his eyes shut and turns away. I yank open the door and get in. Through my rearview mirror I see him walk away.

I really didn't feel like coming to the welcome-back get-together at Northshore Park Saturday. But it's the new normal for me. And I suppose I'd better get used to it. Robert's up on the stage under the gazebo rapping with Spencer, and the kids are eating it up. They're making it up on the fly, trying to best each other with their insults. It's funny and racy and silly.

There are eleven new clarinets this year. Three of them are guys, which is encouraging. One of them has his cell phone camera trained on Robert and Spencer, and I keep catching bits of their comments—*Give it to me, baby.*

Interesting.

The new freshmen all treat me like a celebrity—a little squirmy around me, a little too formal, a little too distant. They make me feel older than I am. And I realize I'm not really a part of them anymore, not in the way I was last year. I'm not just another clarinet now; I'm a drum major.

I grab a soda from the cooler and wander around the fringes where I'm unlikely to be approached by anyone. I haven't run across Curtis again, not since the leadership camp. Corrine tells me he's doing well, attending his therapy sessions.

I'm not a part of his post-diagnosis life anymore, and I'm not going to be. I can't help thinking about how things might have been if he'd never been diagnosed. But he was, and he's cut me off from his life completely.

Chapter 47

CURTIS

Jim, one of the older guys in the group, is talking about his new job. He's a former anchor at a local affiliate, but the HIV has taken a toll on his physical appearance. He lost that job months ago. The new job is at a radio station. He's on air under an alias, a small detail that he finds both empowering and demeaning.

"It's like the real me isn't good enough anymore," he says. "I feel like I'm betraying myself every single time I say, 'This is Dan Walker and you're listening to 102.4 KZHY.' "

The others nod in sympathy. A lull ensues.

I raise my hand.

"Curtis," Albert acknowledges me. "Did you want to respond to what Jim said?"

"No, I, uh, want to say something, if that's okay?" I look to Jim.

"Sure, man. I've whined long enough."

I look around at all their faces. We've been together twelve weeks now. There've been tears, some laughter, anger, despair, fear, a few outright brawls, but mostly there's been a long, steady healing. These are friends, confidantes, little parts of me. It's going to be hard to walk away.

"I've made a decision." I take a deep breath and blow it out again. "I'm going back to school next week."

Everyone starts talking at once. "That's great." "Congratulations, man."

When they quiet down, I give them a small smile. "I've, uh, hooked up with a group in Huntsville, so this is my last time here. I'm really sorry about that, guys."

"It's okay," Albert says. The others murmur the same.

"I'd like to say a few things before I go, though." I swallow past the lump in my throat. "Jack, I need to apologize for what I said to you about Randy. He didn't deserve you, man. You know that, don't you?"

He smiles across the circle at me. "Yeah, I know that now. But thanks for saying it."

"Life goes on, huh?" There's nodding all around.

"Have you thought about what you're going to do about Luke?" Josue asks.

"I think about that all the time," I admit.

"It's okay to be vulnerable," Albert says. "That's what living is all about."

It's not just about being vulnerable though. How can I ask Luke to give up so much for so little?

I scan their faces again. "You guys mean the world to me. I want you to know that. I won't forget what you've done for me."

Someone cries out, "Group hug."

I roll my eyes. And then we're huddled within the circle of chairs. There's a lot of sniffling, a lot of tears, but there's a lot of hope too.

"Good news today, huh?" Dad says, heaving himself onto the tailgate next to me.

"Yeah. Great news." I take a sip of my beer. My T cell count is way up, my viral load way down. It is good news. It means my body is responding well to the antiretrovirals.

I should be elated, but it's an empty kind of achievement.

"What's Corrine doing?" I ask.

"She's using her okra harvest to make you some crab gumbo before you leave. She's quite proud of that okra. Only a few worm holes here and there."

I smile.

He takes the bottle from me, takes a sip with no hesitation whatsoever, then hands it back. I take it, but he doesn't release it. "Just one, okay?" he admonishes.

"Just one." He lets go and I turn the wet bottle in my hands a few times.

"Are you all packed up?"

"Yep. Ready to go."

He pats my back, then leans back on his hands and looks up at the night sky. He sighs. "Pretty moon tonight."

It is pretty—full, bright, hanging at about ten o'clock, framed by two loblolly pines. It's a postcard-worthy sight. It's the kind of view that should be shared.

"I never told you that Dr. Nguyen in the Health Center at Sam knows you. He said you went to UT together."

"Sam Nguyen? No kidding. We go way back." He chuckles. "He used to have such a crush on your mother."

"He didn't tell me that."

"So, Sam finally finished medical school," he says thoughtfully. "Sam Houston, huh? I'll have to look him up."

"Can I ask you something?" I say, turning to study his profile. "Are you happy?"

"I'm very happy. Why do you ask?"

"I just wonder sometimes why you never got married again. Mom's been gone a long time."

"Almost twenty years." He rubs his hand across his face. "I don't know, Curtis. I love my work. I love my family. I guess I don't want to mess that up. And I've had three great loves in my life. That should be enough for anyone." A pause. He nods to the light in the second floor window of the Chesser house. "Is that Luke's room?"

"Yeah."

"You haven't seen him in a while." I acknowledge this with silence. "Can I ask *you* a question?" he continues. "Why?"

I laugh a little. "You sound like the guys in my group. I don't know, Dad. He doesn't need to be involved in this."

"Is that him talking, or you?"

"Dad . . ."

"That's not really yours to decide, Curtis. I may be going out on a limb here, but I think you two had something special going on. And I think you both owe it to yourselves to at least give it a chance."

"I can't." I look away. We haven't had this talk, but the subject has been there. The proverbial elephant in the room. But one thing I've learned from my group is that frank talk is important. And once you get it all out there, all those hard things you thought you couldn't talk about lose their power to intimidate, to keep you silent.

I look at Dad and wait for him to look at me. "He's gonna want to have sex one day, Dad."

"I fully expect that."

"How can I let that happen? What kind of person am I if I do that to Luke?"

He lets out a long breath and rubs the back of my neck. "You know, Curt, there's risk in everything we do. We put on seat belts, but we don't quit driving. We install smoke detectors, but we don't shut off the breaker. We worry about keeping those we love safe, but we don't lock them *in* a safe.

"Can I give you some advice? Do what you need to do to manage the risks, but you've got a long life ahead of you, Curt. Don't be afraid to live it; and don't be afraid to share it. And, um, lock the bedroom door. Your sister is still pretty impressionable."

I smile. He pushes himself back to his feet and stretches. "I hear the first football game is next weekend? That's a big deal for Luke."

I nod.

He stares up at the night sky again. "I never get tired of looking at the moon. Gravitational pull is a funny thing, isn't it? You can fight it; you can even escape it for a while. But eventually, you have to give in to it."

Chapter 48

LUKE

I turn off my light and peek through the blinds. I can just make out
Curtis sitting on the gate of his truck, alone. Two hundred twenty-
one steps. That's all that separates us. It might as well be a billion. I
feel a hand on my shoulder.

"Is Curtis out there?"

"Hey, Dad."

He leans past me to get a look.

"Are you and Mom going out tonight?"

"We're going to take in a movie. You and Matt want to come?"

We're not quite where we need to be yet, but we're paving that
road one brick at a time. The HIV brick was a heavy one though.
But it's been laid and we're moving on.

"No. You two don't need a couple of disrespectful kids hanging
around you."

"Luke . . ."

"I'm kidding, Dad."

"Matt tells me Curtis taught him to play Farkle. I used to be
pretty good in my day. Maybe we could invite him over for a game
or two?"

I smile quietly. "I don't think he'd come."

He pats me on the shoulder as he withdraws from the blinds.

"Well, the invitation stands." He stands there awkwardly for a moment, then clears his throat. "Um, okay."

"Hey, Dad," I say as he's walking out. "Thanks."

The first game of the season. All in all, the performance went pretty well.

We've barely gotten back into the stands after halftime when our team receives the kick and returns it for a touchdown. I step up onto the metal bleacher and poise my hands at the ready. Mindy, Annie, and Austin do the same. Together we count down the beat with our hands and the band blows into the fight song.

When the kicker fails to put the ball between the goalposts for the extra point, Mr. Gorman gives the okay and everyone strips down to their overalls. I pull off my gloves with my teeth and take a long drink from the water bottle a chaperone handed me as I came back up.

Behind me, Mr. Gorman pats my shoulder. "How'd that feel?"

"How did it look?"

"Pretty damn good," he says. I wipe my brow like I'm relieved and he laughs. "I expected nothing less."

I say thanks and he pats me on the shoulder again as he moves on.

I rip the Velcro apart on my gauntlets and shrug out of my jacket and fold everything neatly on the seat. A ripple in the woodwinds barely registers until someone hands me a small square of paper.

It's the prize from a Cracker Jack box. I look back at the flute player—a freshman, Allison?—but she's already chatting with the girl next to her. "Who's this from?" I ask her.

She shrugs. "Beats me. They just told me to pass it to you."

I scan the stands higher up, but all the kids are either watching the game or talking.

I look back at the red and white striped square with the sailor on it and the words "Surprise Inside." The seal has already been broken and the surprise is gone. The only thing left is the instructions on the inside cover for how to assemble the missing pencil topper.

I look back up, higher now, past the percussion section and the brass and the guard until I see him. He's leaning against the rail at the very top of the stands, wearing shorts and a BearKat band T-shirt.

"Hey, Annie, I'll be right back."

"Mr. Gorman wants us to play 'The Horse.' "

Behind her, Gorman is holding up a ring binder with the song title on it. "You lead," I say.

I make my way up the stands as the band starts the number, stopping only to let Mom snap a quick photo of me and give me a thumbs-up. Dad is staring at his new iPhone, and I realize that I'm okay with that. I wave her off and head on up.

Only Spencer senses something is going on. Still playing his clarinet, he glances back at Curtis, then grins into his mouthpiece. He punches my arm as I pass by.

Curtis comes off the rail as I approach and shoves his hands in his pockets. Immediately I notice that his color is better than the last time I saw him, and he's gained most of the weight back. Three steps down I stop and hold up the empty prize packet. "Somebody stole my surprise."

He smiles a little, like he's afraid to, but can't help it. "That would be me. I wanted to give it to you in person."

"You keep it. I don't even have a pencil with me."

He smiles. "You looked great out there." He walks down the few steps to me, and I find myself fighting a sudden twitch in my lower lip.

A few rows below us the tubas dip the bells of their sousaphones to the left and then the right—*ba-rum . . . ba-rum.* They have to be tired with thirty-five pounds of metal resting on their shoulders, not to mention all the twisting, bouncing, and spinning they do. Late in the season it won't be so bad. But the first game has to be tough.

"Were you just here to see the performance?" I ask, turning back to him.

"I'm here to see you."

Don't do this to me, Curtis.

I look down the expanse of the band. "Look, I, uh, need to run to the bathroom, and then I gotta get back. It was really good to see you."

"Luke," he says as I turn to go. But I don't stop. I jog down the long column of steps. I don't even realize he's following me until I head down the ramp and into the area beneath the stands.

"Luke."

He catches up with me, but a band mom intercepts him and grabs him up in a big hug. "I didn't know you were here tonight," she gushes. "We missed you at camp this year."

I leave him behind and head for the men's room. There's no line, but the urinals are all taken, so I head to an open stall and step in. I'm closing the door when Curtis pushes it back in and steps in behind me.

"Curtis, what are you doing?"

He shoots the lock and turns back to me. "I just want to talk."

"I have to take a piss." I turn my back on him.

"I've missed you," he says behind me.

I know that. I think I've known that for a while now. But it doesn't change anything. I focus on breathing as I relieve myself. "I've missed you too."

I expect him to respond to that, but there's silence behind me. On the other side of the partition, a toilet flushes. I can't believe we're standing in a stall in the men's room talking, being honest with each other for the first time in a long time. I finish up and pull the straps of my overalls back over my shoulders. I need to get back. I reach past him to open the door, but he shifts to block the handle.

"What are we doing in here, Curtis? What do you want from me?"

"I want us to be friends again. I miss hanging out with you. I miss . . ." He drops his eyes a moment, blinks, then lifts them to mine again. "I miss cutting down trees, and watching dumb dog movies, and eating skunk spray BeanBoozleds."

I know I should laugh, but I can't muster it.

"I'm glad you're doing well, I really am. But I can't be just your friend. I will always want more than that with you."

Someone raps on the door. "What's going on in there?" Some-one else: "There're a couple of dudes in there."

"Luke—"

"No. Don't say it. Let's just let it go, okay?"

"Not okay. I have to say it. I could never ask you to risk your life for me."

"You never had to ask, Curtis. You just had to let me. I wanted to be there. I wanted to be a part of everything you've been going through. And I wanted to be close to you. I still do. But *you* won't let me."

Another rap on the door, sharper and more insistent. A stadium security guard identifies himself and tells us to come out. Curtis glances at the door behind him, then drops his head. The guard bangs on the door again. I reach past Curtis and open it.

It takes some quick talking from Mr. Gorman before security will release us. Curtis is escorted out of the stadium. I return to the stands with Mr. Gorman, but he makes it clear: My night is over, and very possibly so is my future as a drum major.

My dark mood keeps everyone from approaching me after the game—everyone, that is, but Spencer. As soon as we're released, he herds me toward his car. He doesn't say much until we're out of the parking lot and on our way back to the band hall. "You gonna tell me what happened?"

"What does conventional wisdom say?"

"That you and Curtis were caught in a little mano a mano action in the men's room."

I scoff and watch the businesses slide past us on the feeder road. "What do you think?"

"I think if you'd been spanking the monkey with Curtis you'd look a whole lot happier right now."

That's the damn truth.

At the band hall I turn in my uniform, then help unload the equipment truck. Strictly speaking, it isn't my job, nor is it expected of me, but I figure if I ever want to lead the band again, I better start sucking up now.

When there is nothing left to unload or store or straighten, I stick my head in Gorman's office. "Anything you want me to do?"

"I want you to go home so I can lock up."

I nod and turn to leave, then hesitate. "I just want you to know that I'm really sorry. It wasn't what it looked like."

Gorman leans back in his chair and folds his arms. "Curtis knows better. Whatever it was, he must have thought it was worth the risk."

"Yeah," I say and turn again to leave.

"Luke. You're still suspended for the next two games."

Chapter 49

CURTIS

You never had to ask, Curtis. You just had to let me.

I've thought about his words all week. And now, here I am watching him from the top of the stands again. I've never been worthy of his devotion, and I'll never understand why he's offered it to me. But he never gave up on me. He's sitting alone in the empty section as the band files out onto the field. I roll up the pages of the paperback book I'm holding in my hands, then release them again.

I don't know what I'm going to say to him.

I talked to Albert last night. We talked about the pros, the cons, the what-ifs, the worst-case scenarios. We'd been through all this before in group, but I needed to do it again. I wanted to break Albert; I wanted him to tell me that to let Luke back in was the epitome of selfishness, even narcissism.

But he wouldn't.

He told me there are no easy answers; there never are. He told me not to be a martyr to this disease. He told me I had an obligation to myself, my family, Luke, to everyone who lives with this disease to live my life.

But, of course, he would say those things. He has HIV too.

I pick up my water bottle and head down the steps.

Luke huffs when I slide into the bleachers next to him. He shakes his head. "You're gonna get me in trouble again."

I glance over my shoulder at Mr. Gorman and the other directors under the press box. Their attention is focused on the field. I unscrew the cap from the bottle and offer it to him. He takes it, takes a sip. I cap the bottle and set it on the concrete next to me.

"I should be out there," he says quietly.

"You should be." I look at the book in my hand for a moment, then hold it out to him. "Here, I brought you something. The book you left in my room last spring. You're gonna have a hell of a fine when you turn it back in, you know."

He takes the book and turns it over in his hands, then hands it back. "You keep it. I already paid for it."

I thumb absently through the pages, remembering how irritated I was with him when he showed the book to me. *Condom Sense.* I hated him for reminding me of something I'd never have again.

I don't hate him now.

He just wanted to show me the way, to give me a future I thought was lost forever. He was so naïve; he still is, but I'm inexplicably drawn to him.

"Did you read that they make latex condoms in different flavors?" I ask. "Strawberry, grape, chocolate, mint. They even make them in banana." I laugh a little and wonder at my own question.

Why are you doing this, Curtis?

But I know why. I can't help myself. I can't let him go. I'm as bound to him as the moon is to the earth. He keeps me in orbit; and maybe I do the same for him.

He eyes me, his face a question. From the press box, a booming voice introduces the band, "led by drum majors Mindy Scarborough, Austin Blake, and Annie Trujillo."

The absence of his name shatters the moment. He turns back and watches their salutes, his face pinched with emotion. For me? For the fact that he's not down there with Mindy and Austin and Annie? I don't know.

We watch the performance in silence. I notice that Robert Westfall isn't twirling a flag this year. He's carrying a black sword, playing the devil in the show about good versus evil. I watch him run through the formation, crouch, brandish his sword, then slip behind the trumpet section.

Below us, leaning over the rail, a male cheerleader keeps screaming his name, bouncing on the balls of his feet as he points out Robert to the other cheerleaders. I see Luke glance at him. The show finishes with Robert crumpling to the ground in defeat. The cheerleader whistles with his fingers and claps like a maniac.

"How's the smell in your truck?" Luke asks as the band moves to the sidelines.

"Better now that I can roll my windows down." He smiles, just a little. "How are things with your dad?"

"Better. He and Mom are actually dating again. I think they're talking about him moving back home. He suggested I invite you over for a few games of Farkle."

"He did?"

He looks at me. "I told him you wouldn't come."

Ask me, Luke?

His eyes move over my face, my shoulders, down my arms, back up again. "You look good," he says.

"I feel good. I had a blood draw two weeks ago. My viral load's dropped and my T cell count is up significantly. The doctor thinks I might be undetectable in three more months."

"I'm really glad for you."

I believe him.

On the field, the other band moves into their performance. I fidget as we watch. I feel the moment slipping away, and I don't want it to slip away. I scramble for something to say. Something that will break the ice, make him smile.

"So tell me." I bump his shoulder. "What's your favorite flavor? I bet you like chocolate, right?"

He closes his eyes slowly, opens them again. They remain fixed on the field. "Don't do this to me, Curtis."

I have to do this. Before I can talk myself out of it again. No more joking around.

"You scare me, Luke. You're impulsive and you're naïve and you have no sense of self-preservation."

"If you're trying to win me over, you're doing a pretty sorry job of it."

"I'm scared, okay? I'm scared for you. I'm scared for me. I don't know how this story is going to end. But I do know this—I can't be the only gatekeeper. And I'm not going to take chances with you. Not until I know what's safe and what's not."

He drops his eyes. This isn't what he wanted to hear, but I have to tell him the truth.

"I can't promise you there won't be bad days. In fact, I can pretty much guarantee that there are going to be some really bad days ahead. And I can't promise you that I won't take things out on you sometimes, that I won't withdraw and act like a total dick. Because I probably will. It won't be easy. But I can tell you this." I pause. This is the moment. No going back. "There's no one else I'd rather share my life with. I can't give you back these last months, but I can give you the future. Although, to be honest, I can't for the life of me understand why you'd want that."

The performance ends and the football players and the cheerleaders run back onto the field as the band plays the fight song from the sidelines. "Curtis!" Mr. Gorman barks as he steps into the aisle. "Am-scray."

I look back at Luke. He's closed his eyes. Maybe it is too late for us. I stand, hesitate.

"Go," Mr. Gorman barks.

Luke doesn't look up. Mr. Gorman scowls at me as I slip past him and head down the steps. The band kids jostle past me as they make their way back up. I stop to slap hands, but my heart's not in it. When the steps clear, I continue down. I'm going home. And then I'm going back to school and try to move on. What is there left to do?

On the field the players are lined up for the kickoff. A whistle blows and the kicker sends the ball sailing deep into the other team's territory. And then there's a wild roar from the crowd as one of our own runs it up the sidelines, darting and weaving. I squeeze through a screaming throng at the top of the ramp.

"Curtis! *Curtis!*"

I stop and look back.

"Grape. I like grape," Luke shouts at me.

I take a steadying breath and nod, my eyes swimming. "I'll pick you up after the game."

Mr. Gorman shakes his head.

"He's picking me up a soda," I hear Luke tell him too loudly. *Touchdown!*

"Fight song, people," Gorman calls out over the megaphone.

I watch Luke step up onto the metal bleacher and gaze across the flushed faces of the band. He smiles, lifts his hands, and counts down the beat.

AUTHOR'S NOTE

This book is a work of fiction, and while I strived to be as accurate as I could in my depiction of a young man struggling with the fear and anxiety that comes with such a devastating diagnosis, and the stress it places on the various relationships in his life, the information contained herein should not be construed as informational.

If you are knowledgeable about HIV/AIDS, I applaud you.

But if you're not, I encourage you to become so. I've included some excellent online resources here to get you there. Please note that these sites are not a substitute for professional care. If you suspect you may have contracted HIV, please consult your healthcare provider.

AIDS.gov
HIV/AIDS basics, resources, strategies, and news. Provided by
  the federal government.

AVERT.org
A UK-based HIV/AIDS resource, working to fight HIV/AIDS
  worldwide through education, treatment, and care.

The Body: The Complete HIV/AIDS Resource
www.thebody.com
A site designed to lower barriers between patients and
  clinicians, demystify HIV/AIDS and its treatment, improve
  the quality of life for all people living with HIV/AIDS, and
  foster the community through human connection.

POZ Magazine
www.poz.com
Daily news, treatment updates, personal profiles, investigative
  features, videos, blogs. POZ provides a platform for the
  HIV community to speak to one another and the world at
  large.

Just Between Us

J. H. Trumble

About This Guide

The following discussion questions and playlist
are included to enhance your group's reading
of *Just Between Us*.

Discussion Questions

1. What do you think attracts Curtis to Luke? What do you think attracts Luke to Curtis? How do their past relationships affect how they see each other?

2. Luke's initial response to Curtis's admission that he has HIV is quite negative. Knowing the affection he feels for Curtis, how do you explain that reaction?

3. Curtis says Luke falls in love with guys like a kid falls in love with a new puppy. Considering Curtis has little evidence to make such a claim, why would he say that? Do you believe it's a fair assessment of Luke's character?

4. What keeps Curtis from telling his family about his HIV status? Is there just one reason? More than one?

5. Discuss Curtis's dad as a parent. Do you believe he should have done more to rein Curtis in? Why didn't he? Do you believe the freedom he afforded Curtis is in any way to blame for Curtis's predicament?

6. Jaleel tells Curtis that contracting HIV is no different from getting cancer. Curtis argues that it isn't the same. What do you think? Jaleel also accuses Curtis of being a homophobe. What did he mean by that, and do you agree?

7. Consider some of the negative responses to Curtis's HIV status—those of Jaleel's mother, the guy in the bar, Robert. Are those responses rational? Understandable? How did their reactions affect Curtis or Luke? How would you have reacted had you been each of those characters?

8. Compare those negative reactions to the reactions of those close to Curtis: his father, Corrine, Luke, Luke's mother. If

your son, your brother, your boyfriend told you he was HIV positive, how would you handle the news?

9. Besides the fear of passing on the virus, why else might Curtis have pushed Luke away?

10. Robert suggests that Luke loves lost causes. Do you believe this is true? And if so, is that a valid basis for loving someone? And if not, what is a valid basis for love?

11. Do you believe Luke is just naïve, or do you consider him more of a hero? How so?

12. How does Curtis's therapy group affect his relationship with his father? With Luke? How important do you think groups like this are to HIV-positive individuals? In what ways?

13. Psychologists speak of the five stages of grief—denial, bargaining, anger, depression, and acceptance. How do these stages of grief play out for Curtis? In what way are the stages linear and in what way recursive?

14. Discuss the evolving relationship between Luke and his dad. Do you believe all chasms have been bridged at the end of the novel? If not, what hurdles do you see in the future?

15. A serodiscordant relationship is one in which one partner is HIV positive and the other is not. How do you feel about such relationships? Would you ever consider entering one?

16. Do you believe this novel has affected your understanding of the HIV virus, AIDS, and the struggle of those who are affected? If so, in what ways?

17. Do you know someone with HIV/AIDS? How has the virus affected his or her life? How has it affected your relationship with that person, assuming there is a relationship?

18. We know from *Don't Let Me Go* that Curtis and Luke are still together nine years down the road and planning to be married. Discuss some of the challenges they might have faced in the intervening years.

19. How do you think the love relationship between these two characters will end?

20. Discuss your thoughts and feelings on the responsibilities of someone with HIV to disclose that information to another person. Do you think it's only necessary in a sexual relationship? Whom should Curtis have been more forthcoming with? What about Luke's responsibilities? Do you think he did the right thing by keeping Curtis's secret as long as he did?

THE *JUST BETWEEN US* PLAYLIST

At long last, Luke Chesser gets his own novel. It seems only fitting that he get his own playlist as well. While music does not play as prominent a role in this novel as it did in *Don't Let Me Go* and *Where You Are*, music most definitely played a prominent role in the writing of this novel. I hope you'll listen to the songs below and consider how they reflect on the novel, or just enjoy them.

"Grenade," Bruno Mars
Reflecting on earlier relationships.

"I'm Yours," Jason Mraz
New loves; new possibilities.

"Whataya Want from Me," Adam Lambert
Holding back.

"Animal I Have Become," Three Days Grace
Reeling.

"Somebody That I Used to Know," Gotye
Rejection again.

"This War Is Ours (The Guillotine II)," Escape the Fate
Secrets and repercussions.

"Lost in You," Three Days Grace
Coming together.

"I Do (Wanna Love You)," Hedley
Coming together, Part II.

"Wrapped," George Strait
Two-stepping.

"Jumper," Third Eye Blind
Friends are all they can be.

"Perfect," Hedley
Spiraling and holding on.

"I Won't Give Up," Jason Mraz
Standing by his man.

"One-X," Three Days Grace
Therapy.

"Dying to Live Again," Hedley
The song title says it all.